I0822878

BOUND BY EARTH AND ICE

VOLUMES OF ELEMENTUM
VOLUME II

MEGAN L. ADAMS

Bound by Earth and Ice
Volumes of Elementum
Volume II
by Megan L. Adams

Published by Golden Tome Press

Editing by Katelyn Washington

ISBN: 979-8-9899327-1-9

Volumes of Elementum
Shadows Within the Fire
Bound by Earth and Ice

To my husband and my heart, Paul.

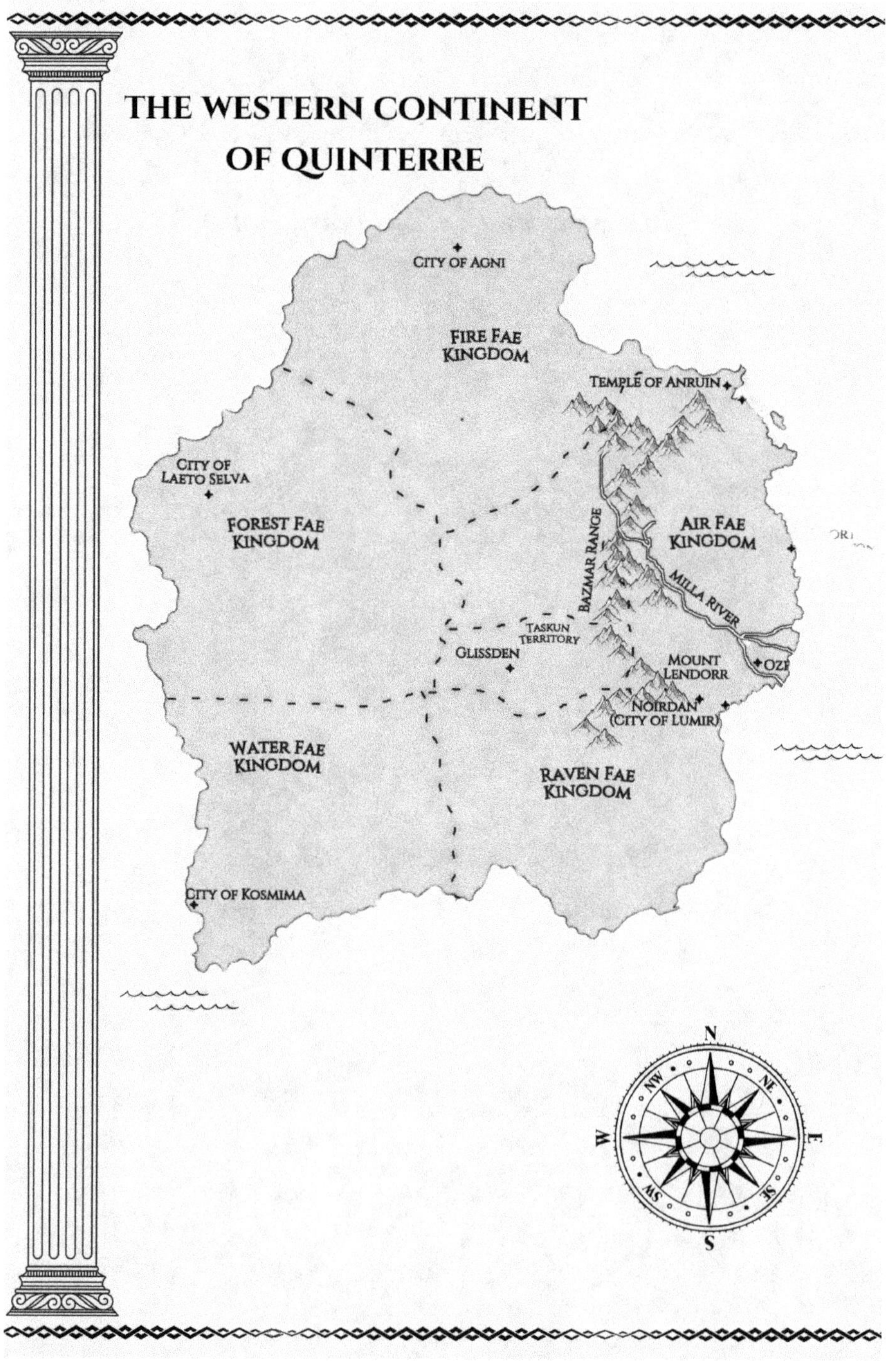
THE WESTERN CONTINENT OF QUINTERRE
CITY OF AGNI
FIRE FAE KINGDOM
TEMPLE OF ANRUIN
CITY OF LAETO SELVA
FOREST FAE KINGDOM
BAZMAR RANGE
AIR FAE KINGDOM
MILLA RIVER
TASKUN TERRITORY
GLISSDEN
MOUNT LENDORR
NOIRDAN (CITY OF LUMIR)
WATER FAE KINGDOM
RAVEN FAE KINGDOM
CITY OF KOSMIMA
N
NW
NE
W
E
SW
SE
S

THE MORTAL REALM OF NASBAR

ILLOTERRA

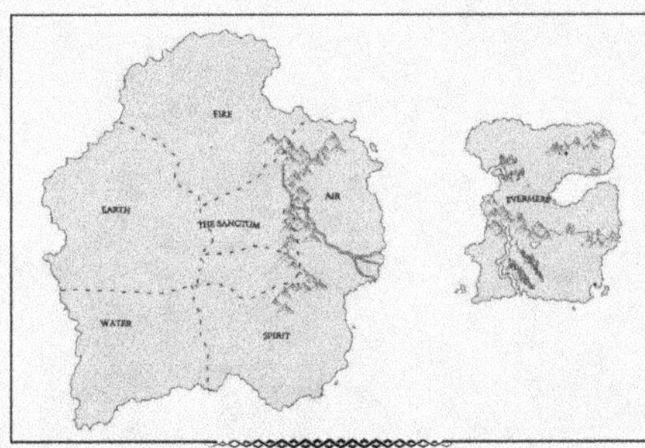

THE GODS REALM OF AESIRA

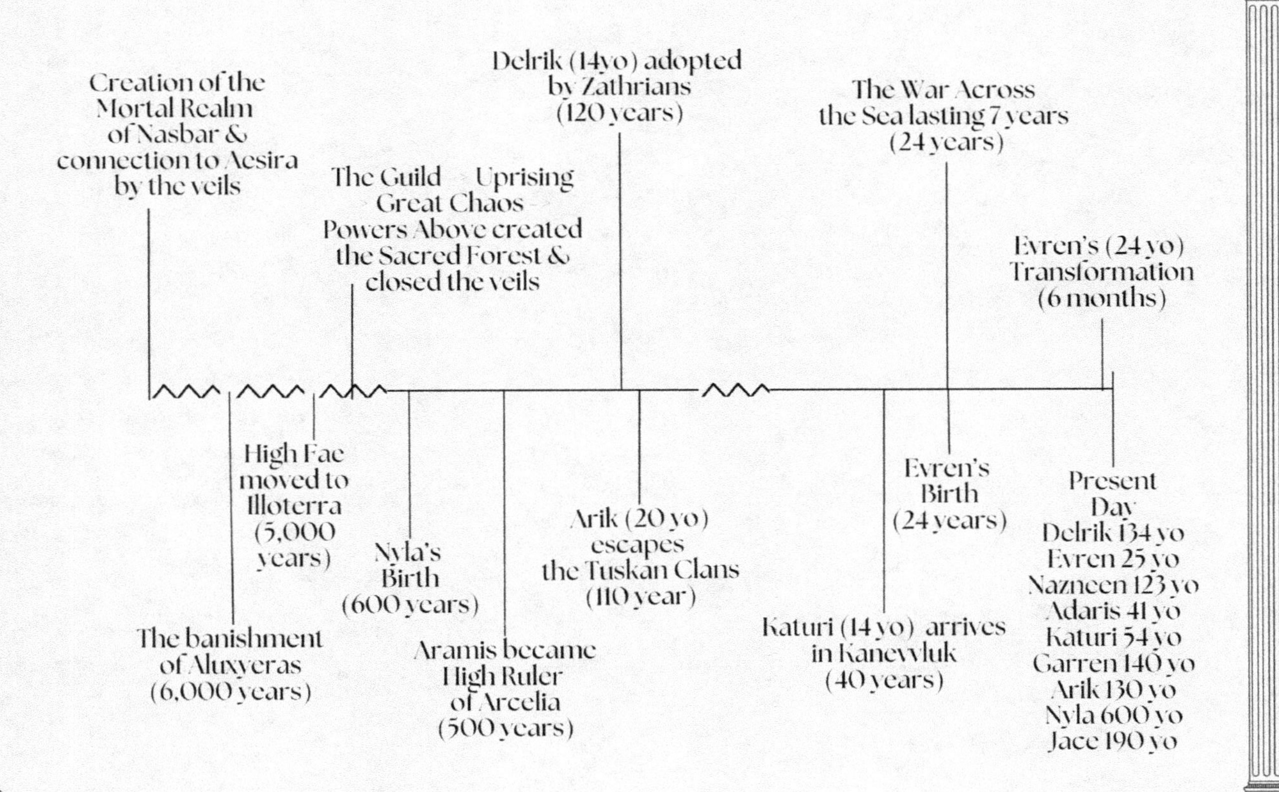
Creation of the
Mortal Realm
of Nasbar &
connection to Aesira
by the veils
The banishment
of Aluxyeras
(6,000 years)
High Fae
moved to
Illoterra
(5,000
years)
The Guild Uprising
Great Chaos
Powers Above created
the Sacred Forest &
closed the veils
Nyla's
Birth
(600 years)
Aramis became
High Ruler
of Arcelia
(500 years)
Delrik (14yo) adopted
by Zathrians
(120 years)
Arik (20 yo)
escapes
the Tuskan Clans
(110 year)
Katuri (14 yo) arrives
in Kanevvluk
(40 years)
The War Across
the Sea lasting 7 years
(24 years)
Evren's
Birth
(24 years)
Evren's (24 yo)
Transformation
(6 months)
Present
Day
Delrik 134 yo
Evren 25 yo
Nazneen 123 yo
Adaris 41 yo
Katuri 54 yo
Garren 140 yo
Arik 130 yo
Nyla 600 yo
Jace 190 yo

CONTENT WARNING

This story contains cursing, violence, sexual content, death, and torture.
For those readers who do not want to read explicit romantic scenes, including dominance and bondage, skip the following chapters. Skipping these chapters will not affect the plot in any way.
Chapter 4
Chapter 41
Chapter 42
Chapter 52

PRONUNCIATION GUDIE

Adaris Byrnes (a-dar-us)
Aluxyeras (Alux) - (al-ux-ee-air-us) (al-ux)
Anders
Aramis Zathrian (air-a-mis zath-ree-an)
Arabelle Halloran Byrnes (ara-bell hal-oh-ran)
Arik Hanover (air-ick)
Aura (aw-ruh)
Cadoc Byrnes (kaa-dahk)
Calia Zathrian (cal-ee-ah zath-ree-an)
Captain Tage Lark (tay-j)
Carpus Musmar (car-pus mus-mar)
Corynne (kuh-rin)
Delrik Valhar (del-rik val-har)
Drake
Dusan (doo-shan), god of earth
Eleni (ee-len-ee)
Elliot Valhar (val-har)
Elenora Allerick (el-a-nora all-er-ick)
Eryx (ee-rix)
Evren Byrnes (Ev-ren)
Garren Eckhardt
Genevieve Hanover Eckhardt
Hadeon Allerick (had-ee-on all-er-ick)
Haizea (hi-zay-uh)
Holden Eckhardt
Jace Eckhardt
Jae
Kairos (kai-rus)
Katuri Harland (kat-or-ee)

Knox
Liam Winfield
Lilliana Hanover (lily-ahna)
Logan Kathmor (kath-mor)
Master Rikard Farren (rik-ard)
Master Endri Salcido (end-ree sal-see-do)
Morgan Valhar (val-har)
Nazneen Zathrian (naz-neen zath-ree-an)
Nyla (nye-la)
Oliver Hanover
Ondine (on-deen)
Renwick Ashewood (ren-wick ash-wood)
Rishley Boldnaire (rish-lee bold-na-air)
Salina (sa-lee-Na)
Tage Lark
Thane Verena (ver-in-a)
Vidarr Fanenos (vee-dar fan-ee-nose)
Wren Fanenos (fan-ee-nose)
Zji'ndar Abril (zen-dar ab-ril)

Cities, Landmarks, and More
Aesira (ee-zi-ra)
Affinity Celebration
Amplifying Stone
Air Fae (ah-ni-mum) (air)
Arcelia (are-sell-ee-a)
Ashlyra (ash-lie-ra)
Basdover Gulf (bas-dover)
Battle of Glissden
Baxmar Range
Bloodthorn
Boreas Sea (bur-ay-us)
Boto Encantado (bow-toe en-can-ta-doe)
Cessan Void (ses-an)
Circle of Dark Hells
City of Agni (ah-g-nee)
City of Kosmima (gee-or-s)
City of Laeto Selva (lay-toe sell-va)
City of Lumir (loom-eer)
City of Proux (pru)

Darkwood

Di-gara (die-gar-a) neve (nee-v) roth (raw-th) var (var). Consors (con-sore-s) par (par) rikni (rik-nye). Kaj-far (ka-j-far) ato (ah-tow) un isla (oon-is-la)

Doloryum (Dolor) (doe-lor-ee-um)

Elementum (el-e-men-tum)

Essence Scrolls

Evermere (ev-er-mirror)

Fiend (fi-nd)

Forest Fae

The Fortress

The Great Chaos

The Great River

The Guild

The Hook

Illoterra (i-lo-terra)

Kanevvluk (kane-vluck)

Kilnard (kil-nard)

Kiscarine Pass (kis-kaa-reen)

Lakeshore

Lilura Steel (lil-er-a)

Magnoch Sea (mag-nock)

Medina (med-ee-na)

Menrath (men-wrath)

Merock (mer-ock)

Milla River (me-la)

Mortal Realm of Naśbar (naz-bar)

Mount Lendorr (len-door)

Mountain Fae

Noirdan (nu-ar-dan)

Ocean of Warwell

Okeanos Sea (oh-kee-on-os)

Osomal (os-oh-mal)

Ozryn (oz-ren)

Port Echnaton (ech-na-ton)

Port Gamcord

Port Kainarr (kay-nar)

Qana Mountains (kaa-nuh)

Quinterre (queen-tare) also known as the Western Continent

Ramshorn

Raven Fae
Ring of Teris (ter-is)
Rivamir (riv-a-mirror)
River of Naraina (na-rain-a)
Rochris Islands (row-kris)
Sacred Forest
Satyr
Snow Sprite
Snowhaven
Snowhaven Fae
Taskun Territory (task-un)
Temples of Anruin (an-ru-in)
Thawvale
The Uprising
Warblade of Silverlight
Wasted Shallows
Water Fae
Whiteband Port
Winterwood
Wood Nymphs
The Wildlands

Bound by Earth and Ice

Volumes of Elementum
Volume II

PROLOGUE
ALUXYERAS

Aesira - 6,000 years ago

My whole existence came down to a pinpoint the moment his lips met mine. He rolled me over to my back and pressed his whole body against me. I smiled against his lips. The long grasses of the field spread beneath us like a plush blanket. He broke our kiss and leaned up on his elbows so that he could stare down at me. I couldn't stop the single tear of joy that rolled down my cheek.

"I love you," he proclaimed.

My heart leapt at the words. Was this what love felt like? I smiled back at the High Fae male with delicate ash brown curls framing his face and kind eyes the shade of a summer sky. The golden light of the twin moons above us illuminated his features in sharp planes and contrasts. Thane Verena had stolen my heart. I hadn't known it was possible. To love. In all my existence, I'd never experienced anything close to the emotion. Love was a thing among mortals. Even the High Fae were considered mortal to the gods.

I, however, was the daughter of gods. In fact, I was the goddess of spirits. Love wasn't something that was customary between the gods. Even my parents didn't show the kind of connection with each other as consorts. Now that I'd tasted the sweet nectar of passion, I'd never return. Who would want to?

"Will you stay with me forever, Aluxyeras?"

My name on his lips was spellbinding. Those seductive, full lips. I traced them with my finger, memorizing them. They were soft and plump beneath my touch. A pang of disappointment tightened my stomach.

"You know I want to," I replied. I cast my eyes down. I didn't want to see our illusion break.

For the gods, having offspring was an obligation between consorts to allow the next generation to take over ruling so that the older gods could go into the eternal resting lands. Procreation was not the product of overflowing, undying, unquenchable affection. My parents gave birth to me as was their duty. I'd been going through the motions over many decades to become what I was created for—a way for my parents to rest when they grew tired of their eternal life.

To keep a balance and a check on powers among the gods, there were five primary gods who sat on the seats of the Sanctum. The seats rotated to the next generation when a god chose to step down or go to the eternal resting place and their offspring took their place. This perfect equilibrium prevented one god from becoming too drunk with power and gave the old gods an opportunity to rest for the remainder of their existence. An island off the eastern coast of Aesira was the home of all mortal spirits and the resting gods—Evermere. My duty was to watch over Evermere and ensure all were at peace.

Another part of my role was to travel between the planes of our universe to ensure the spirits of the mortals traveled unimpeded into the afterlife. I had never thought that when I came to the Mortal Realm of Naśbar that I'd want to give up everything I'd ever known to stay. Aesira, the plane where the gods existed, was my home, but Thane was in Naśbar and he was my other half.

Long ago, the five gods reigned over all. They came together and created another realm with creatures of all manners, including the Fae. The Mortal Realm of Naśbar was a replica of Aesira in every way, except those living there. The mountains, valleys, and rivers were mirrored to our parallel realms. Only a thin plane separated us. Upon witnessing the goodness and bounty that came from the Mortal Realm, the gods wanted to gift their creation and those who dwelled there. They blessed the five High Fae kingdoms with aspects of their divine powers: fire, earth, water, air, and spirit. The gifts brought the creatures of the world joy and helped them to maintain peace amongst themselves. Even some lower beings—sprites, boto encantados, and nymphs—were gifted with small powers. My father, Anders, the god of spirits, was part of the group that gave away the fragment of power. That was well before my birth.

In each of the five High Fae kingdoms, temples were erected to honor the gods. The five Temples of Anruin. They were a place to thank the gods for their precious gifts. However, they weren't only a place of worship, sacrifice, and source of knowledge. Each of these temples were special in that they were connected directly to the gods through portals called veils. From our Sanctum in Aesira, we could travel through the veils to any of the five kingdoms whenever we desired. All it took was a drop of god's blood. As a god, I was expected to travel back and forth between our planes—the one between the Mortal Realm of Naśbar and Aesira—to help maintain order and control. Each god assisted the kings with ruling their kingdoms, preventing conflict and strife, and preserving magical gifts. In return, the mortals gave offerings to the gods.

I had been young when I took over my father's seat. Although I appeared to be only sixteen years old in the eyes of the humans and Fae, I was closer to 800. It wasn't very old for a god. Gods matured at a much slower rate. Since taking over for Father's seat in the Sanctum, I'd grown to know the High Fae and creatures of the Mortal Realm of Naśbar. It had been part of my preparation in ascending into my future role. I'd traveled through the veil between worlds with my father on multiple occasions. Simply observe and nothing more. We weren't supposed to interfere. We only interacted with the leaders of the kingdoms and the highest priestesses of the temples.

Most of the living creatures in the Mortal Realm were frightened of the gods for reasons unknown to me. I was under the impression we only gave them blessings. Maybe it was just the sheer amount of power we possessed or our sporadic presence among them. It was rare that I could walk down their streets without someone noticing that there was something different about me. Even when I used a glamor to make myself appear as a High Fae, they knew I was something ... different. Something potentially dangerous. Something not of their world. A sixteen-year-old female shouldn't have exuded so much power. They avoided eye contact and would avoid crossing my path. Despite all that, I enjoyed being in their world. It wasn't that I didn't like the lands of the gods. Aesira was perfection. Since my ascension, I'd grown to love each of the realms for their individual beauties and spent my time equally between the two planes.

The first time I ran into Thane—and I mean literally ran into him—I was walking through the City of Lumir on my routine trip through the veil. I was scheduled to meet with the King of the Air Fae to discuss the needs of their realm and to collect the annual offering to the Sanctum. Each offering depended on the kingdom where it was being collected. Some had offered up gold and rare gems; others had offered rich spices. The gods didn't need these things, but they represented the time long ago when the gods gave a small piece of their power to create the Mortal Realm. There had been grumblings in the past about these offerings, but they were dealt with quickly and with discretion.

A High Fae male bumped into me while I was deep in thought about my upcoming meeting. I lost my footing on a loose stone (I really shouldn't have been looking up at the sky while walking) on the road, but he caught me by the shoulders. We locked eyes, and he didn't shy away. The sounds of the city around us melted away. He just smiled. Such a simple gesture. He wasn't afraid. He didn't run. He stood, holding my shoulders, and I felt it deep in my spirit. Even among other gods, not many held eye contact with me due to my role in Aesira. But when his hands made contact with me and his eyes met mine, I instantly knew he was someone special. Recognition on a spiritual level. Gods didn't have bondmates, but I knew it was a connection shared between two spirits.

At first, Thane didn't know I was a god. He'd recognized that there was something special about me, but he didn't ask. He was so trusting, and it made me trust him in return. It was refreshing not having to deal with the title and just be me. It had been so long since I had been looked to for one thing or another. When we were together, I could shed my responsibilities for a little while. I'd kept my holiness hidden with a glamor: lengthened my ears to make them like the High Fae, dulled my luminous skin, darkened my eyes to a sapphire instead of their normal iridescent ice blue. I even dressed as the High Fae did—in long, flowing dresses that covered most of my skin. Definitely not my normal attire.

I dropped my glamor a few weeks after meeting Thane. He was stunned to find out I was actually the goddess of spirits. He was confused that I was in his world. He wasn't a part of the royal court in any way. He knew that the gods walked among his world but never expected to actually run into one. It was easier to keep the knowledge of the veils and how the gods moved across the planes a secret, except to the few. Otherwise, there would be mortals trying to cross into our realm at any time.

Thane didn't mind that I was a goddess, and I enjoyed his company. I'd taken to passing through the veil of our realms almost every night, and he'd been waiting for me each time. At first, outside the city walls and then inside the temple itself. Our unlikely friendship morphed into something more.

My mother had tried warning me about leaving Aesira so frequently, but I ignored her caution.

"You've been spending a lot of time in the Mortal Realm lately," my mother had said. She didn't approve. And when she didn't approve of something, she made it known.

"I'm aware of that. I'm doing my duty. And I haven't let any of my responsibilities slip here or in the Mortal Realm."

"I know the other world can be fascinating, but be careful."

"What harm could come to me? I'm a goddess."

She just pursed her lips and narrowed her eyes at me. "Yes, but you are a young god, and you don't want to attract the attention of the other gods."

I had nothing to worry about. I'd been careful. Or so I'd thought.

Thane and I had come to our favorite spot, an open field behind the Temple of Anruin, where you could see the open sky and the ocean beyond. The City of Lumir was surrounded by beautiful grasslands that stretched far and wide. To the west, mountains lined the horizon. To the east, an expanse of water. It was the same as my home in Aesira, but I loved this spot more. Thane's thumb skimmed across my cheek, and he leaned in to brush his mouth against mine. I pressed my hand against his bare, hard chest and felt his heartbeat beneath my hand. My ivory skin shimmered in the moonlight.

"Stay with me," he whispered. His voice was barely audible over the soft wind coming off the sea.

Warmth pulled in my stomach. I longed for nothing more than to stay in his arms for eternity. I opened my mouth to answer his request when the earth fell away beneath me and I tumbled through space and time. I knew what had happened before I landed with a heavy thump on a marble floor. The stone was a shock of cold against my cheek where Thane's hand had just been. I pushed to my hands and knees and looked up to see the five seats of the Sanctum before me and four gods staring back at me with grim expressions. I landed in the center of the Sanctum in Aesira. The circular temple was made of solid darkstone. Roaring flames lit the interior in a circle high above our heads. A pentagram of pure gold was embedded into the floor itself. At the point of each star sat a god's seat.

I tampered down my annoyance, stood, and brushed myself off. The abrupt distribution had been unneeded, but I didn't let it show on my face. It was futile to show my distaste.

"Was that really necessary? You couldn't have just asked me to return?" I said as I leisurely made my way to my seat, the seat meant for the goddess of spirits.

It was more a throne than a chair. It was built of precious alabaster stone and pure light. A design my father had created when he took his position. I didn't see the point of changing it. I sat furthest to the right of the circle, equidistant from the others. The seat thrummed and glowed softly as I approached. I turned to face my fellow gods, and our combined powers, in a unified circle, sent a ripple of magic throughout the Sanctum when I took my seat.

The goddess of air, who sat next to me, winked in my direction, and I smiled in return. Haizea was dressed in a flowing gown of cerulean and cream; silk and layers of translucent fabrics draped her thin frame and gathered at her narrow waist. Her hair was white as snow and her eyes a deep indigo. She was my mentor and closest friend. She sat upon a throne of frosted glass with intricate swirls carved into it. The glass' surface resembled billowing clouds on the wind.

An exhausted exhale came from my left, and my head whipped in the direction of the sound. It was Ondine, the goddess of water who spoke. "Aluxyeras, goddess of spirits, you have wandered yet again. You have been out of Aesira for far too long."

The cool, smooth stone of aquamarine stood out among the others. She lounged comfortably in her seat with her arms draped on the armrests and her legs crossed at the knees. Her dark complexion contrasted the brightness of her throne. She looked as dangerous as a perilous sea on a stormy night. And she was. Only the reckless crossed her path.

"Clearly, I didn't go far enough," I muttered under my breath.

"What was that?" she asked in irritation.

I knew she'd heard me. "I just said, it is my duty to visit Naśbar."

"You aren't needed there on a daily basis. The spirits of the mortals can manage to make it to Evermere without your guidance," Ondine chided.

"How would you know? You're not the one charged with overseeing Evermere," I retorted.

"Maybe you should spend some more time with the spirits in the afterlife than in the mortal realm. We all know you are traveling there for something other than duty," Ondine said.

I rolled my eyes at the goddess of water. She was being dramatic. I'd never neglect my duty to the spirits in Evermere. My temper was on a short fuse, but I again pressed down my displeasure. Ondine wasn't any threat to me, but she wasn't the god I was apprehensive about dealing with.

"So what if I have other intentions in Naśbar than what you know of? It's none of your concern. I am…"

"You are a child and know nothing of responsibility," Dusan, the god of earth stated in a bored voice.

To Ondine's other side sat Dusan, whose seat looked like it had been carved from the side of a mountain. The trunk of a tree wrapped around the stone, and vines extended from it, along with beautiful flowers growing like a halo around him. Though he was the smallest of the five gods, he was not to be messed with. His woody hair was wild and untamed, and his moss green eyes were exotic like the Laeto Selva rainforest.

"I am not a child," I tried to state as calmly as possible. "By traveling back and forth from the Mortal Realm, I am learning how to better suit my responsibilities rather than sitting on my ass all day playing in puddles." I gestured to Ondine. "Or sprouting flowers for the heck of it."

I stared directly into Dusan's eyes in pure challenge. I knew they did more than that. They were the protectors of the land and sea, but I wouldn't let them see me falter. And I wouldn't let them bully me around. Dusan simpy scoffed at my jab. Ondine, on the other hand, erupted like a geyser. A torrent of water shot into the air, then cascaded down. Haizea brushed away the water before it sloshed over her feet.

"Playing in puddles?" Ondine roared. Her voice shook the Sanctum, and lightning crackled across the darkening sky. Was she planning on drowning me in a deluge? "I am the goddess of water. I give and take life, just as you do." A sneer twisted her divine face.

A fist came down on the arm of a seat like thunder. "That's enough!" The earth began to rumble.

"You cannot control me either, Eryx," I challenged.

He curled back his lips in a hiss. "You are not allowed back in the Mortal Realm of Naśbar. Not until you learn more responsibility and respect for your position," Eryx commanded.

The god of fire. The oldest and most powerful (and most selfish) of the gods since my father had stepped down. He'd been in reign longer than any other god before him and wasn't going to secede anytime soon. He was one of the gods that had helped create the Mortal Realm, alongside my father. Eryx's seat sat at the head of the Sanctum. It was made of matte, black stone with veining that glowed shades of oranges and reds. They pulsed with his rage. His eyes, normally the color of ash, blazed red with his anger. They only did that when he was furious. It appeared I'd pissed him off tonight. Wouldn't be the first time. He still fisted his hand tight, and it, too, glowed like embers.

An angelic voice split through the rising tension. "You are a new god. You need to focus on learning your roles for Evermere before focusing on the mortal lands." Haizea was my favorite among the gods, even if she wasn't my best friend. She'd always been kind and gentle. "Sweet child, what has you so drawn to the mortal lands?"

Mortal, as in not eternal like all the gods here in Aesira.

They didn't need to know about Thane. It was pointless trying to explain it to them. And I wasn't a child. I was hundreds of years old. Yes, I was the youngest of the five gods. No, I was not as experienced. But that didn't mean I wasn't capable.

"Can we finish this another time?" Dusan asked. He looked bored as usual. "We can discuss this at our next meeting. Until then, Aluxyeras, stay out of the Mortal Realm."

"But—"

Eyrx interrupted before I could finish. "If you return to the Mortal Realm, there will be grave consequences."

"Who do you think..." I began, resentment thick in my tone.

All but Haizea stood without another word, then disappeared from the temple with the telltale pop sounds made from blinking—one moment they were there, the next they were gone. A clear dismissal. I loathed when they did that. Unfortunately, it wasn't the first time, and I knew it wouldn't be the last.

I slouched back into my seat and released a huff. Even though I was a god, an equal to the other four, I wasn't going to object to Eryx's command. Not yet. I'd only been in my position for a few years. I straightened myself up and rose to return home. Haizea stood as well and began to walk with me. We walked in silence as we exited the Sanctum and stepped into the night. The sky above mirrored the night in the Mortal Realm—two moons and a million stars. I looked up to the sky. Thane would be seeing the same tonight, and that brought me comfort.

"You know he isn't allowed in the land of the gods," Haizea said.

I sighed. Of course she knew about Thane. There wasn't a thing in this realm or the others that she didn't know about.

"I don't know what you're talking about," I fibbed.

"You can't lie to me." She swept her hand through the air. A cool breeze came from nowhere in particular and caressed my skin. Wisps appeared, glittering like tiny threads of spider silk. They floated in front of us for a moment before they were whisked away on the wind. I blushed. Had she known what I'd been doing with Thane this whole time? "The wisps tell me all. Both here in our world and in all the others."

We walked through the streets in comfortable silence until we reached the outskirts of the city. Then we blinked to my home. It was the furthest one could go before you reached the coast overlooking Evermere. I surveyed the land of beauty stretched before me. Rolling hills, a river gently flowing back and forth. Small cottages spotted the hillsides.

"He is High Fae, a mortal compared to you. And it goes against nature to bring him here. Once he comes to Aesira, he'll never be able to return; his magic will be stripped from him, and he won't live longer than a human. Only his spirit will dwell in the afterlife."

I hummed in reply. Could I ask him to sacrifice so much for me? I knew he wouldn't think twice about it.

"And if Eryx has his way, Thane may be prevented from entering Evermere," Haizea continued.

The thought of Eryx interfering in how a spirit passed on into the afterlife infuriated me, but I wouldn't put it past him. He was just spiteful enough to throw a fist if he didn't get his way. Typically, the other gods didn't interfere with the others' roles without a significant reason. However, it wasn't unheard of. Would I have to wait until Thane died naturally? Even though High Fae were considered mortal, they lived extraordinarily long lives compared to all the other beings in their realm. It could be hundreds of years, maybe a thousand, before I saw him in Evermere.

"Then I will go to the Mortal Realm," I said.

"You can't live there either."

I gave her a stern look. "And why not?"

"You know why."

I did. I knew, as a goddess, I belonged in Aesira, and it's where my power was sourced. If I left and didn't return, over time, I would become less and less powerful until I became a mere shell to house my spirit. I would never be able to return to Aesira, even in the afterlife. I'd be trapped between realms.

I sighed and tipped my head back to the sky.

"You'll move past this Aluxyeras. It will just take time."

But wouldn't a short life with my love be better than without him?

Haizea patted my shoulder, and with a pop, she was gone. I was left alone with my thoughts and the melancholy of what my future held.

I waited until the world had grown quiet before I snuck back to the Sanctum. I'd obeyed Eryx's demand for weeks. I hadn't been back in the Mortal Realms, and I hadn't seen Thane, though he was in my every thought. That night was the first opportunity I'd had to get away. The darkstone of the Sanctum gobbled up the light from the stars. It was a new moon, which made the night darker than usual.

Once inside, I followed the stairs downward. It was dark as pitch down in the chamber of the veils, but I knew the way by memory. My heartrate picked up with each step descending into the ancient chamber. I'd learned to associate the stale air with seeing Thane. I didn't need anything to guide me. The slick stone steps spiraled down, down, down into the heart of the temple. At the bottom, a soft, glowing, golden light came into view. I stepped into the chamber of the veils. The same pentagram as above was carved into the darkstone here, too. At the end of each point, instead of the seats of the gods, there was a shining, golden silhouette floating within onyx archways. The veils. Each of the five veils leading to its own temple in the Mortal Realm. The City of Kosmima lined up with the veil of water. The City of Laeto Selva aligned with the veil of earth. The City of Agni with the veil of fire. The City of Proux with the veil of air. And the City of Lumir with the veil of spirit.

I would have to be quick. If I were gone longer than an hour, the other gods would be able to sense my absence. It's how they had known I was gone last time. Each time one of us went through the veil, we could feel the subtle shift in power, a tilt in the balance of power. I pricked my finger, and a drop of silver blood pooled on my fingertip. I brushed it across the darkstone of the archway, and the opaque mass of the veil morphed to a translucent, ever-moving curtain. My reflection stared back at me. My wavy, waist-length blond hair glowed in the gold of the veil's light. While my ears were pointed, they weren't as pronounced as the High Fae. My eyes were bright azul, and my features were delicate.

No wonder no one takes me seriously. I truly appear to be a child.

I brushed away the thought and stepped through the veil. Coolness surrounded me like I was walking through a slippery substance. The Temple of Anruin was an exact replica of the one in Aesira, except it was made of cut stones rather than darkstone. I slipped the hood of my cloak up over my blond hair and made my way through the darkness to the temple's entrance. The night was chilly, and dew dampened the hem of my cloak. When I stepped out into the open, a small gust of wind wrapped around my feet. I recognized the tingle of magic. Haizea already knew I was here. Damn wisps.

I didn't bother glamoring myself. No one was around to see me. The priestesses had all gone to bed and the city was quiet. Thane saw me before I saw him, and he ran, wrapping me in his arms. I'd been gone for weeks, but with his arms now around me, it had felt like years. I melted into his familiar embrace.

"What are you doing here?" I asked him when he pushed back from me. He still held me around the waist.

"I've been here every night since you vanished. I was so worried." He shook his head back and forth. "What happened?" He showered my face with anxious, yet thankful, kisses.

"They summoned me back," I said.

"Who?"

"The other gods."

"What? Why? Can they even do that?" He couldn't hide his look of disgust.

"They have forbidden me from the Mortal Realm."

"They can't do that," he objected. His voice grew louder with each statement. "You are a god. An equal to them."

"Yes. But if they are all in agreement, it's useless to oppose them. They would win. Combined, they are stronger than me."

The knowledge that they could overtake me left me warring with feelings of hate and sorrow. Thane released me and raked his hands through his hair.

"Then I'll come to you," he said.

My heart squeezed. It wasn't a question. Thane would sacrifice his entire mortal life, leaving everything behind, just to be with me in Evermere.

"You can't. If you do, you'll be stripped of your magic. You'll become as mortal as a human."

"I don't care," he interrupted. "You can visit me in Evermere."

"Or worse, Eryx could banish you to the Cessan Void. Being stuck between realms means never entering the afterlife."

The Cessan Void was exactly as it sounded—void of all. The only things there were pain, torment, and a stretching expanse of evil. It was where the Great Chaos was banished and where dark magic thrived.

"It doesn't matter." He shook his head again. "I'll take the risk."

"Thane."

He spun around, his eyes wide. "And I'm assuming the same will happen to you if you stay here."

I nodded my head. "If I stay here, I'll never be allowed in Aesira or Evermere."

He suddenly gripped my shoulders. "I won't say goodbye to you."

Tears began to well in my eyes. My heart was breaking. Each second chipped off another piece. There would be nothing left. Thane pressed his lips to my forehead, just as he'd done a hundred times before. This time, though, it was different. It felt final.

A lump formed in my throat. "I have to return before they sense I've left."

I felt Thane nod in agreement against the top of my head. He knew there was nothing we could do without risking one of our lives. We'd just have to be patient. It would be easier to say a quick goodbye and not drag it out. I wouldn't put it past Eryx to go through with his threat of dooming Thane into an eternity of torment between realms. There wasn't much he could do to me, but I didn't want him to take out his wrath on Thane.

We walked quietly, hand in hand, back to the temple. The night surrounding us was heavy with silence and grief.

"I'll wait for you," he said when we made it to the temple's entrance. He'd followed me in silence to the veils deep beneath the building. Only the priestesses were allowed down here, but I didn't care.

"No." I shook my head. I wouldn't be unfair to him. "I can't let you live your life like that. I don't know how long it will be before I can come back."

He grabbed my face with both hands. "I. Don't. Care."

I was severed in two. And I was about to leave half of myself in the Mortal Realm.

"I will be back as soon as I can." I choked on my words. We both knew it was an empty promise.

I pricked my thumb to open the veil and stepped into golden light. Thane clung to my fingers until the very last moment. My silver blood left a smudge on his palm. And then his touch slipped from mine.

"I'll come back," I whispered into the veil, my chest tight. "I'll come back."

I'd lost track of time; or had I stopped counting? Had it been months? Years? I didn't know. I'd left Thane in the mortal realm so long ago, and my life had been meaningless since. The idea of an endless existence without Thane was crushing. And when he would arrive in Evermere when he passed, I knew he wouldn't be the same. I wouldn't be the same. I'd left half my heart with Thane in Naśbar.

I'd taken to visiting the Sanctum at night and sitting outside the veil just to be close to him again. Tonight was no different. I sat in my regular spot, leaning against the wall and staring into the veil. The gold and white swirls danced like smoke, hanging suspended in the air.

Suddenly, there was a shift in the veil, a light of some kind. And then a shadow appeared. I sat up straight. Had one of the other gods been in the Mortal Realm? I wasn't the only one that traveled back and forth between our worlds. I hadn't felt the shift in powers, but it was possible I hadn't been paying close enough attention.

Shit, I was going to get caught. I quickly wiped the moisture that had gathered on my cheeks. What had started as body-wracking sobs the first several days after I returned to Aesira had transformed into silent tears that stained my face nightly. I wasn't technically going against the other's wishes by being here, but I didn't want to explain myself to them. I scrambled to my feet and sprinted toward the stairwell. Just as I was about to take the first stair, I peered over my shoulder.

The figure that stepped through the veil was no god. It was Thane.

The breath rushed from my lungs, and I threw myself at him before he even realized he wasn't alone. I gripped his neck tight, and tears flowed freely from my eyes. After a second, his strong arms were around me too. We both collapsed to the ground in exhilarated joy.

He gently pushed away from me and held me at arm's length. "Aluxyeras. Powers I've missed you."

"What are you doing here?" I was dumbfounded.

"I had to see you."

I couldn't believe it. Was I dreaming? Thane was here. Here with me. "But how?"

"Don't worry about that now. I couldn't live another day without you. The last three years have been unbearable."

Three years? Has it truly been that long?

Although time in both realms moved at the same pace, I'd been too distraught to count the days. Thane kissed me. Hard. And I welcomed it. I Needed it. I Needed him. There was nothing sweet about his grip on me. It was pure possession and desire.

"Wait." The gravity of his actions came crashing down. I pushed away from him. What had he done? He shouldn't be here. He knew if he came here, he'd become a true mortal and lose all his Fae power.

"How could you?" I smack my hands on his chest. He didn't budge. "Thane. No. What have you done?"

"I had to be with you."

"But Eryx—"

He pressed a finger to my lips to silence me. "I don't care about Eryx. I only care about you. I'll live my short mortal life and then move on to the afterlife. And I'll be able to see you everyday without you passing back and forth through the veil."

He'd really given up everything to be close to me. I pulled him back to me and crushed my face into his chest. I breathed him in like he was life itself.

My eyes snapped open. "We can't stay here," I said.

I took his large hand in mine and pulled him to stand. We made our way back up the winding stairs and out of the Sanctum. I took Thane's hand in mine and blinked us both back to my home.

We lay in bed and talked all night. He told me how he'd waited for the priestesses to go to sleep and then he snuck into the temple and down the chamber of the veils. He wasn't sure how the veils actually worked, but just took the chance anyway.

"I realized that I'd rather live a mortal life lacking magic than never see you again. And then my spirit will remain here in Evermere where I can be close to you forever."

We lay facing each other, heads propped on pillows and fingers intertwined between us. One of my legs was draped across his waist, and he drew idle circles against my skin. Thane rolled over and lifted his pants from where he'd discarded them on the floor. He reached into the pocket and withdrew a square piece of fabric.

"Are you finally telling me how you opened the veil?"

"The night you left, your blood was smeared on my hand when we separated. I cleaned it with a scrap of fabric and saved it." He held the faded fabric between us. It was soft to the touch from age and handling. He placed the cloth in my palm and began to unfold it. "I'd seen you use your blood to open the veil. I figured it was worth a try." He paused for a moment. He almost looked nervous. "I know this is a tradition of the humans, but since we can't have a blood binding like the Fae, and I don't even know what the gods do, I wanted something that would show my unending love."

A small ring rested in the center of my palm. I was speechless. It was a simple woven band. The metal was cool against my skin as he slipped the band onto my finger. He brought my hands to his mouth and kissed each of my knuckles.

The next morning, I woke early. I hadn't slept well the night before. I was anxious about the looming task of speaking to the other gods about my plan. Thane was still sleeping soundly in my bed. The blankets were half on the floor, and a pillow was flung across the room. Loose cotton pants hung off his hips, and his bare back was on full display. The glowing candles danced shadows across his skin. I smiled to myself at the sight. I loved this male.

I left Thane asleep in my bed, much to my dismay, and made my way back to the Sanctum. It was early and the sun had just peeked over the horizon. I needed to talk to the other gods. Haizea had to know that Thane had crossed into Aesira, but with the number of mortal spirits that came each day, I doubted the other gods noticed an extra Fae ... I mean human.

I knew Thane would lose his magic, but I hadn't realized how sudden it would be. It was hard to explain how he'd changed. He looked the same, but more fragile. His skin had lost its glow, and his movements were slower, more like a human. Even the beat of his heart was different. The only things that remained were his pointed Fae ears. And his spirit. I could sense his spirit within hadn't changed. I needed to be sure Eryx wouldn't harm Thane. Maybe if I were upfront about Thane coming here then he'd let it slide. They'd figure it out eventually, so I had no choice but to tell them. I figured if I got ahead of it, I could control their reaction.

"Why did you wake us? This better be important," Dusan grumbled. He looked to still be wearing his night clothes, and his hair was even more of a mess than usual.

I settled onto my seat and faced the other gods. Eryx looked furious at the fact I'd called an early and unplanned meeting. Dusan, as was typical, looked bored. Ondine stared at me with a wary expression. Only Haizea seemed to know why I'd summoned us all here.

I drew in a deep breath.

My words came out in a rush. "I want to step down as goddess of spirits."

"Impossible!"

"What?"

"Why would you want that?"

They all spoke at the same time. All but Eryx, whose eyes were focused on the ring on my hand. He had a knowing glint in his eye.

I raised a hand to silence them. "I know I've only held this position a short time, but I don't want to be here. I'm not happy here."

"You don't have a choice. This is your birthright. The reason you were created. And until you pass it to your own offspring, you are the goddess of spirits."

"No." I was adamant. Nothing would change my mind.

"You don't have a choice." Dusan enunciated the words as he spoke.

"But I do, and you know it."

"Why would you ever want to give up all this?" Dusan said, motioning around the Sanctum. "What could be better? Spending even more time in the Mortal Realm?" He curled up his nose in disgust.

"Maybe there is more to life than controlling beings that don't need to be controlled."

"And what about the spirits in the afterlife? Who would care for them?" Haizea asked gently.

She knew I wouldn't make such a decision so lightly. I had thought through every step of giving up my seat in the Sanctum.

"I have no doubt that the one that takes over my seat will be capable of tending to Evermere," I responded. "I want to become mortal."

Silence. No one spoke. Were they even breathing?

"Why?" Ondine finally asked.

"Love." Yes, it was that simple.

Dusan scoffed at me. "Love is a mortal's emotion. You are a god. You are above love. You are beyond mortals. Don't you see that?"

Eryx shuddered with fury, and his eyes shifted to deep red. He lacked patience on a good day, so it wasn't a surprise he was agitated.

Then, with a snap of his fingers, the pop of someone blinking pierced the silent air. Thane appeared in a crumpled mess at my feet, still in what he had worn to bed the night before. Eryx had summoned him. He looked half asleep. I could see the panic in Thane's eyes as he realized where he was. His gaze shot up to mine, standing above him. His panic matched mine. He was mortal now, a breakable human. And he was in the midst of not one, but five all powerful beings.

"Thane!" I exclaimed. It was a delayed reaction due to my shock.

I knelt and helped Thane to his feet. How had Eryx known Thane was in Aesira? Thankfully, Thane didn't appear to be unharmed.

"All this is because of him, isn't it? Because of a mortal." Eyrx's voice boomed around the temple. It resonated off the columns.

"Is this High Fae the reason you want to be in the mortal world?" Ondine asked.

Eryx turned his attention to Thane. "I should send you back to your world for going against the will of the gods and coming into our lands. Let you live out your now shortened, pathetic life." He propped his chin on his fist as if in deep thought. "Actually, I should banish you to between our realms, to the Cessan Void. You deserve an eternity of torment for going against the will of the gods."

I put myself between Eryx and Thane. "You will do no such thing." My power thrummed in the air throughout the temple. Fire sparked along Eryx's hands and throne. "I will not let you harm him."

Eryx tossed a lazy stream of fire toward me, but with a simple wave of my hand, the fire extinguished. He lifted a brow. Was this a test? If it was, it was a shitty test. He threw a stronger sphere of fire at me. Again, I dispelled the threat with little effort. Eryx stood. I wouldn't let him treat me or my love this way. I stepped forward and shot out a whip of my power. A white tendril that looked like a satin ribbon snapped like a switch, knocking Eryx back a step.

"How dare you go against me." Lines of molten embers spread across Eryx's skin.

Dusan barked out a laugh at Eryx's tantrum. "Come on Eryx..."

"You have gone against everything," Eryx spat with vehemence.

"I want to give up my title! I want to pass it on to the next in line and step down!"

Eryx's voice made the walls of the Sanctum tremble. "And then what?"

"Make me High Fae. Return Thane's magic, and we will both leave. You'll never have to see me again."

"Do you really think you are in the place to bargain?" Eryx burned with rage.

"I know you'd rather be rid of me. And with the combined powers of the gods, Thane and I can return to the Mortal Realm."

The four gods were silent before me. Ondine looked to be in agreement. But Dusan and Eryx appeared to be having an unspoken conversation between themselves.

"No," Eryx said.

Then the unimaginable happened. With another snap of Eryx's fingers, Thane's life was snuffed out like a flame. His body fell in slow motion as his legs buckled. My cry reverberated off the darkstone. The high-pitched sound of pain and loss and despair. Thane's body was a lifeless form on the floor at my feet.

"What did you do?" I threw my body over Thane's and silently sobbed.

Haizea sprang to her feet. "Eryx!"

He waved her away, his cool facade back in place. "The problem has been dealt with."

My heart had been restored to whole, full of love, when Thane emerged from the veil. But with his death, the organ was ripped from my chest, leaving only a hollow cavity behind. Grief consumed me. All the light of the spirits I'd once commanded and looked after fled from the blinding sorrow. Every candle was snuffed, and the fire encircling us from above went out. Only darkness remained, devouring my heart until it was no more. I looked up to Eryx, who was reclined in his seat. He had a look of haughty smugness on his face. He was clouded in a black shroud before coming back into focus. I tipped my head like a curious feline. The cloud over my vision cleared. Interesting. All the hatred I'd ever felt for him was concentrated and potent.

"Aluxyeras, your eyes. What have you done?" Ondine whispered.

Her voice was quiet with fear. True fear. My head swiveled in her direction. I looked her up and down. She may not have killed Thane herself, but she was just as much at fault.

"Thane was the only good thing in my miserable life. And you stole him from me." My voice was not my own. It was crisp and flat. I jerked my head back to Eryx with newfound speed. "So in return, *I* will take every good thing from *you*. I will kill anyone important to you. I will crush everything you've ever held dear. I will bring Aesira to the ground."

A faint rumble grabbed everyone's attention. It grew louder and louder. Bits of darkstone began to fall from above. Suddenly, spirits filled the temple, surrounding the other gods, flocking to me at my command. The bright light emitted by them was blinding. They'd been mine to guide and protect, and now they were mine to control. Slowing, as if they were mirroring my desolation, the effervescent white spirits began to shift into darkness, almost shadows. Embodiments of the void where my heart should have been. They shifted into darkness until there was no light left and we were surrounded by darkness as if it were the dead of night again. The only light was a soft glow coming from Thane's unmoving chest.

I laid my trembling hand flat against his sternum. It was still. So still. Then I reached into his chest and withdrew the light—his spirit. The last one I would ever hold. I held Thane's spirit in my palm like it was the most precious thing in the world.

"I'm sorry," I whispered.

The shadowed spirits around me began to move in a circle, high above, and gaining speed. I hugged Thane's life essence to my chest. I was still kneeling next to him. My sobs and gasping breaths had slowed and were replaced by waves of wrath. With each passing second, it escalated. Like a poison coursing through my body, the fury reached every piece of me. I looked up with pure rage in my eyes. The light in my palms flickered, then dimmed to darkness. I looked down at the swirl of shadow. I sucked in a deep breath and breathed the essence of Thane's spirit into me. When I exhaled, I felt power. His essence gave me strength. It was power, almost overwhelming. The darkened spirits rushed at me and flowed into my body—through my mouth, nose, eyes, and palms. They condensed into a single entity within me. My new source of power. Then shadows exploded out of me, engulfing the entire temple and blocking out all the sun. Dark tendrils poured from me as I released all the rage.

"You will pay for what you've taken from me, Eryx."

I rose on sure feet, stepped over Thane's prone body, and summoned all the darkness back to me. In an instant, the blinding light rushed in. The other gods shielded their eyes from the brightness. They didn't see my attack coming. I lashed out my shadows, wrapping them around Eryx and squeezing. He struggled against my magic, but he wasn't strong enough. Not anymore. Nothing was as strong as my fury. I lifted Eryx from his seat and then slammed him back down, cracking the veined stone into thousands of pieces. The god of fire lay there for a second before he took a deep breath and lifted his heavy body from the ground. Silver blood leaked from the corner of his mouth. His skin glowed like fire, and his eyes were hot embers. The bones I'd broken cracked and snapped as they realigned themselves and he healed.

Dusan, finally no longer looking bored, sent ropes of earth and vines to bind my arms. He bound my arms behind my back. Ondine sent water that froze into ice around those bindings, but I didn't need my hands to command the darkness. Haizea's air tried to blow the shadows from the temple.

I threw my head back with maniacal laughter. "You think you can stop me?" I didn't even recognize my own voice. "You will never be able to stop me."

I dug down deep, reaching into the furthest depth of my power, to the very essence that hummed, and unleashed the darkest pits of shadow onto my world.

Darkstone and marble rained down from above as the temple exploded around me. I snapped the vines and ice restraining me with ease. Shadows twisted and writhed around me like storm clouds about to release a hurricane. More and more and more darkness. I let it overtake me. I gave it everything—every piece of me. The darkness spread from the temple and poured into the streets. Ribbons of umbra slithered like serpents. Each person my shadows reached, their life was sucked into the void. With each life snuffed out, my power strengthened. Screams of panic pierced the morning stillness.

I stepped over the rubble and out into the streets. Bodies scattered the ground where they'd dropped. Buildings shook and began to crumble under the heaviness of the darkness. The land across the water where all those spirits had slept peacefully in the afterlife suddenly filled with noise. Howls filled the air, and Aesira quivered. The sky turned black as spirits abandoned Evermere and came to my call. I'd gone from the goddess of spirits to the goddess of shadows, and I'd never return. This power was bottomless, intoxicating. I wanted more.

Eryx, Dusan, Haizea, and Ondine began to form a circle around me, slowly closing in on me. I laughed in their faces. I was the goddess of shadows. I controlled life and death. And there was only death in their futures. Eryx struck first, a ball of fire surrounding me and the light smothering out my shadows. I countered every blow.

Haizea's voice cut through my fogged mind, but only for a moment. "Aluxyeras!" It was a useless plea.

"Stay out of this, Haizea. I don't want to kill you, but I will."

She'd once been my friend, but now she was fighting against me. She had let Eryx get away with murdering Thane. She should be fighting alongside me.

Traitor.

"Aluxyeras, please."

I turned to my old friend for a split second. Eryx used the distraction to strike. A stream of fire hit me in the back, causing me to stumble forward. Then shackles of stone, thick and strong, wrapped around my entire body again.

"I'm so sorry, Aluxyeras." Haizea lifted me into the air on a ghost wind, and Ondine surrounded me in a sphere of water. "I have failed you."

Her voice was muffled from the wall of water and fire encasing me. I was ripped from my shadows. They dissipated when my connection was broken, and they retreated back to Evermere. Once they cleared, the true level of the destruction of the city was apparent. As far as the eye could see, the city lay in ruins. Buildings leveled to the ground, bodies scattered, people trying to get as far from the epicenter of the blast as possible.

"She must be destroyed," Dusan said.

"There is nothing that can destroy her," Ondine said.

"How dare you go against me!" I bellowed, but they couldn't hear me through the layers of elements.

"So you'd rather her destroy our realm and thus all the realms connected to ours? Do you realize the ramifications of that?" Eryx said.

"This is all *your* fault, Eryx. If you'd just allowed her to leave, this wouldn't have happened," Ondine said.

I tried to fight against their hold, but with all four of them using the full strength of their powers, it was useless. With the shadows gone and my own energy depleted, I was trapped. All I could do was watch and wait for them to determine my fate.

"I agree with Ondine. We should have heard her out. You shouldn't have jumped to conclusions," Haizea said. "Both of you." Her menacing gaze landed on Dusan.

"We will bind her powers and banish her to the Mortal Realm. It's the only thing we can do. She can't stay in Aesira."

The four remaining gods came together, hand in hand, surrounding me, and then we were transported. I felt the tug of crossing between realms. When my vision came back, I looked around to see we'd appeared at a lake in the middle of a beautiful, dense birch forest. I hovered above the lake, still trapped by their elemental powers.

One by one, they released me from their grasp, and I dropped into the water below. I stood, sputtering and gasping for air, my blond hair dripping with water and clinging to my face. I waded my way to the shore.

"Aluxyeras, you are stripped of your title of goddess of spirits and are forever banished to Illoterra." Dusan's voice was calm and commanding.

I looked around and guffawed. "In the Mortal Realm. Are you serious? This is what I wanted in the first place," I hissed.

"And now you will remain here for eternity. Never again to step foot in the land of the gods. Your existence will be wiped from history. The goddess of spirits will no longer be. You've turned the spirits into shadows. You've proven to have too much power. No one should contain that much power."

With that, they all began to chant in the ancient language. Before my eyes, their magic converged, forming a stone of scarlet. From the ruby, magic spread in a sweeping dome that covered the entire lake. It crackled with red streaks of lightning. The silver band around my finger was ripped from my hand, melding with the gemstone.

"No!" My voice was raspy from screaming. That ring was the last piece of Thane I possessed. "You cannot contain me." They ceased their incantations, and the transparent dome disappeared. "I will find a way to escape. And when I do, I will destroy you."

I lashed out the meager shadows I had left, but they reverbated off the protective wards put in place and bounced back to me. I was enraged. Flimsy shadow after shadow. I dumped them all out until the dome was all darkness. My prison's boundaries were made clear. Nothing could escape. When the shadows cleared, the land surrounding the lake had died away, the water had turned murky and the scent of death and rot hung thick in the air. Thane's murder replayed in my head over and over. I felt like my own spirit had died when he did. His face flashed in my mind. I felt his loss again. I collapsed into myself on the shore of the lake. My prison. All because of love.

Haizea stood with the others, unharmed, just out of reach.

"You are never to return to Aesira," Eryx commanded. Then he slipped the ruby ring into his pocket.

"This is only the fault of your own, Aluxyeras. You have doomed yourself to shadows and hatred," Ondine said.

Eryx, Ondine, and Dusan disappeared into nothingness with a blink. Haizea was the only one remaining. My breaths were coming in ragged huffs.

"How could you betray me?" I asked Haizea without meeting her gaze.

"I'm sorry, Alux. I truly am."

And with sadness on her face, she too disappeared, never to be seen again.

PART ONE

ONE
DELRIK

Arcelia - Present Day/Six months after Evren's elemental fire transformation

Evren moaned softly as my hand cupped her ass and pulled her closer. I dragged kisses across the oversensitive skin of her neck and shoulders and she arched into me. I wanted all her soft curves against my body.

"You're distracting me." Her statement was a half-hearted complaint.

"I'm the one distracting you? You were the one who kissed me." My tongue dipped into the hollow space above her collar bone and she moaned. She tasted like the sweetest dessert. I couldn't get enough.

"And you were the one who pulled me down onto the couch," she rebutted.

True. I didn't feel the least bit guilty.

KNOCK! KNOCK! KNOCK!

I sat up quickly from the couch where I had pinned my bondmate down and whipped my head toward the door. Whoever was on the other side of that door had a death wish. Ever since Evren had realized we were bondmates and we'd decided to do the blood binding, I'd been a bit on edge when anyone other than me needed her attention or time. It didn't help that, along with her elemental fire power, she also now held the shadow magic. We knew only one thing about the shadow magic—it was deadly. My innate protectiveness was almost crossing the line. Even though Evren was more powerful than I was, I couldn't help treating her like a priceless and fragile piece of art. I didn't think she truly minded.

The first knock I'd ignored. The second time, a possessive, aggravated growl had come from deep within my chest, but I hadn't stopped trailing wet kisses down her neck. But the third time...

"What?!" I snapped.

"Seriously, you two," Nazneen shouted through the door of my apartment. "Can you go even an hour without jumping each other?"

No. Why would I want to?

Evren didn't bother holding back the belly laugh that barreled through her. The sound was like music. Which made me want to stay locked in our apartment forever. She tightened her grip around my waist, stroking her fingers across my back before wiggling from beneath me.

"We're coming," Evren yelled back to my sister.

"Actually, we're not," I whispered against her bare shoulder.

I stared down at her disheveled clothes and released a groan before straightening her robe where I'd shoved it down to expose her creamy skin. The swell of her breasts were spilling out the top.

Evren had been in the process of gathering everything she needed to get ready for the blood binding ritual when I'd pulled her from her task of laying out her outfit.

"I do *not* want to explain to Father why you are late to your own blood binding," Nazneen shouted through the door again.

Aura swept through the open double doors and perched on the back of the chair near the fireplace. She stretched her wings out before tucking them against her sides. She hiccuped, and a spark came out of her beak. Aura was Evren's little firebird, who closely resembled an owl. Ever since she'd succumbed to the elemental flame, Aura had been with her. She'd been growing over the last months and was now the size of a pigeon. Of course, I'd never let her hear me compare her to a pigeon though. She could be ... fierce? She had the attitude of a teenager and the temper of a tired toddler. I wasn't sure where she'd come from, but her familiar presence had been soothing. Especially as Evren adjusted to her new powers and became a living vessel for the shadow magic.

The Ring of Teris was an ancient object able to harness the powers of anyone who went against the person in possession of it. The stolen power was stored within the ring and could be wielded at the user's desire. After stealing the ring from Evren's father, Evren had been able to use it to free me and steal Alux's shadow magic. A thin band made of lilura steel etched with ancient symbols held the scarlet ruby in the shape of a teardrop. It had remained on Evren's middle finger since that day six months ago. It was cold against the skin of my waist where her hand lingered.

Nazneen banged on the door again. Sisters were the worst.

"Would you just come in already!" I bellowed back.

"Be nice to your sister," Evren said, swatting my arm.

I captured her hand before it made contact and brushed a chaste kiss to her palm before darting to the door, my movements quick as a flash. Although I'd been adopted, Nazneen and I fought like we were siblings. I knew Evren secretly loved it because it reminded her of her relationship with her brother, Adaris. We hadn't seen him since we'd left Rivamir in the River Kingdom, where he was now High Ruler, but that would change today.

I yanked open the door to find Nazneen Zathrian leaning against the doorframe, arms crossed in faux annoyance, but looking stunning nonetheless. She was trying her hardest to suppress a grin. She thoroughly enjoyed poking fun at me now that I was "a lovesick puppy."

"We all know what happened the last time I walked in without knocking," Nazneen said, winking at Evren from under my arm that was propping the door open.

I peeked over my shoulder to see Evren's cheeks flared with heat. Her robe had already slid off her shoulder again, making her look like we'd been up to no good. I didn't need Nazneen to remind me. She'd caught us in quite the compromising position—Evren pressed into the wall, me on my knees, one of Evren's legs slung over my shoulder, with my head buried...

Let's stop that *train of thought now. Otherwise, we'll definitely be late.*

Nazneen ducked under my arm and came into the apartment. I'd never seen her look so feminine. I was used to seeing her wear pants and carrying a bow and sword. Day to day, Nazneen was a commander in the Arcelia Legion and spent her time training the legion forces, but today was a special occasion. A soft green dress hugged her lean body. Her auburn hair, now cropped short, stopped at her chin, and was set in gentle waves. She even had a flower tucked behind an arched ear that made the jade of her eyes stand out. The same ear was pierced with hoops that ran up its length.

Evren had grown close to Nazneen since returning to Arcelia, which made me glad. Once Nazneen realized Evren wouldn't burn the house down with her elemental fire or murder anyone with her shadows, Nazneen had made it a point to visit often. They'd spent time walking through Arcelia and baking cookies in her state-of-the-art kitchen. Nazneen could give our greatest chefs a run for their money. On rainy days, the pair would snuggle up on the couch and drink wine. Nazneen would read while Evren sketched. It was their new normal. And I'd sit with my arms crossed over my chest in the chair across from them, sulking that my sister was nuzzling *my* bondmate.

"We don't have all day. The priestess is already pestering Father about being away from the temple for so long," Nazneen said as she took Evren's hand and guided her to the bedroom.

Evren had made me move to her bedroom when we returned from Arden Valley since it had a better view of the sprawling mountain city and a far superior soaking tub than mine. The doors were swung open, and sunlight poured into the space. The luxurious velvet curtains that had framed the windows when she'd first arrived in Arcelia had been replaced with breezy gauze curtains that floated in the spring air. The Qana Mountains were covered in hues of green and stretched up toward the cloudless sky. She'd transformed our space into a comfortable place of rest and refuge. Finished and unfinished drawings were scattered on the desk. A pair of my boots leaned up against the foot of our bed. A fresh bouquet of jasmine sat on the side table beside the enormous four-post bed. I'd spent so many years running from my past and doing everything I could to not be at home. Now it was the only place I wanted to be.

"I didn't want to do the blood binding in the temple, so she can just deal with it," I said. "She's lucky I'm letting her do it at all."

Unlike my sister, I'd never believed in the fates and didn't bother with the Powers Above. I'd seen too many horrendous things in my life to believe that the gods had any favor with me. So what was the point? The only thing they'd blessed me with was my bondmate ... and my adopted family ... okay, fine. But the priestesses gave me the creeps.

I had followed the pair into my room. As I walked by Naz, I dropped a kiss onto my sister's cheek. "You look..."

"Gorgeous! I know, right?"

She spun in a small circle. I chuckled at her. Always self-confident.

"At least you bathed already," Nazneen said to Evren.

Evren slipped her silk robe off her shoulders, leaving her standing in lace underwear and a bustier. I suppressed a groan at how beautiful she was. I needed to focus on getting through the next few hours, and then she'd be all mine again. Nazneen didn't flinch at Evren's state of undress. Modesty hadn't ever been a concern for Nazneen. Evren, on the other hand, had spent years hiding bruises and bite marks from her betrothed, Renwick Ashewood. It had conditioned her to keep her body covered at all times. But Nazneen was so comfortable with her body, Evren's bashfulness soon went out the window with her after just two months. Granted, she didn't strut around naked like Naz tended to. I'd probably seen more of Nazneen's body than any brother should. Some things would forever scar me. I was just thankful that Nazneen helping make Evren more comfortable with her body meant I reaped the benefits. Evren never hid herself from me. Ever.

Just then, Alux's shadows, well I guess they were Evren's now, danced and writhed across Evren's skin, moving away from the bright light spilling in through the windows. The tendrils shifted over her stomach. My mouth formed a firm line, and my jaw tightened painfully. It took all of my effort not to scowl at the dark magic.

"Stop looking at me like that!" Evren snapped at me as she spun to face me with her hands firmly on her curved hips.

Nazneen dipped her head to avoid our standoff and walked into the closet to retrieve Evren's ritual gown.

"I'm not looking at you like anything."

I forced a smile. It wasn't working. I tried to hide my look of concern, but it was pointless. She knew exactly what I was thinking. Guilt. Fear. Anger. She had those shadows because of me.

"But I know that thing your face does when you see the shadows."

"I don't do a thing with my face."

She pursed her lips at me knowingly. Damn, she could read me like a book.

"Fine. I do a thing with my face. But..." I cut myself off.

The shadows wound up her stomach, up between her breasts, and down an arm like they were protecting her from my stare.

"I'm fine, Delrik. It's been six months, and I haven't had any issues with them." She brushed a finger across the swirl of the shadow on the inside of her arm. "I've grown fond of them."

They moved like a caress against her finger. I didn't know how she could believe that. They would never be a part of her. Ever. Not if I had anything to do about it. The thought of such darkness inside my bondmate made my blood boil. I needed to find a way to pull them from her and end her future suffering. We didn't know if having the shadow magic had any lasting effects, and I wasn't willing to risk it.

My voice turned soft. "Your fire and the shadows are opposing forces, Ev. Aramis suggested you not possess both for too much longer since we didn't know if there would be consequences."

Evren's anger melted from her face. Every time she looked at me like that, she stole another piece of my heart.

"We don't know if that's actually true. We also knew there would be risks when we took them from Alux."

"We thought the ring would contain them, not put them inside you." I felt the ever present regret heavily on my shoulders. If I hadn't needed to be saved from the curse, Evren wouldn't have had to use the ring to begin with. If I'd known the ring wouldn't contain the shadows, I would've found another way to take them on myself.

The blood-red ruby glinted in the sunlight on Evren's middle finger, snagging my attention. It was like it knew we were talking about it. Aramis thought it was best not to take it off in case it was helping her survive both the shadows and the flame. Not that it would come off. When we had first seen the blackness marring Evren's skin, she tried to remove the ring, but it wouldn't budge. We still didn't know if it couldn't be removed. Aramis had a theory that the ring itself was sentient and could choose its wearer and to whom it passed powers to. He believed since Evren was an elemental Fae, that it sensed her strength and held on tight.

"I'm fine, Delrik," Evren said again as she came to me and wrapped her arms around my waist.

"And I'll do everything I can to keep it that way." My forehead creased with worry.

Evren propped her chin on my hard chest. Being close to her made the bond between us hum. My bondmate looked up at me and then pressed a gentle kiss on my mouth. A cool breeze came from the terrace and caressed my skin. I startled at the drastic difference the wind was to the warm spring day. Along with our bond growing stronger by the day, our mental connection was also growing. It was known that bondmates shared a powerful mental connection between each other. Some passed along emotions, while bondmates together for many centuries could even pass on thoughts. So when

Evren's mouth touched my pulse point, a flood of adoration swept through me.

I was already dressed for the afternoon; freshly shaved with my shoulder length hair pulled back into a knot at the nape of my neck. My crisp, white shirt smelled of fresh citrus and wood, a smell Evren loved.

"Even through the layers of clothing, I can still smell your masculine scent. It drives me wild." She pressed another kiss to the underside of my chin. Her fingers trailed along the waist of my pants. My shirt had come untucked during our short makeout session on the couch. "And these pants are fitted in *all* the right places."

My fingers dug into her hips despite my best efforts to hold myself back. My sister was in the room for Powers' sake.

Speaking of my sister...

"I was gone for two minutes!" Nazneen huffed, throwing an arm up in the air in exasperation.

I snorted out a laugh and buried my face in Evren's hair to stifle any more laughter at Nazneen's expense. Evren drew in a deep breath in an attempt to compose herself and spun to face her soon-to-be sister. I reluctantly released her. Nazneen held Evren's ritual gown slung across her arm. Our mother, Calia Zathrian, had insisted on a local Arcelian couturier making the gown for the blood binding. Nazneen draped the gown over Evren's head and did up the zipper along her back. She was the most beautiful creature I'd ever seen. Lilac lace covered a silver silk skirt. Embroidered silver leaves and flowers covered the bodice that clung tightly to her delectable curves. The fabric flowed in waves to the ground and was lighter than air. It was the perfect gown for such a special day.

TWO
DELRIK

I followed behind Naz and Evren as they walked arm-in-arm down the stairs and out into the spring air. Petite, green wood nymphs trailed the pair. They skipped and twirled, singing a merry tune in the ancient language. The creatures stood no taller than a rabbit stretched up on its hind legs. Their wings glittered in the sunlight. They dragged their fingers along the pathway, and colorful blooms erupted from the earth. Their hair was loose and free and wild, and a crown of twigs and greenery perched on their heads. Their ears were long and pointed, and their skin was the color of bright moss. Nymphs weren't always green. Wood nymphs' skin changed with the seasons. More orange and yellow in the fall, brown during the winter, and bright green in spring and summer. Water nymphs typically were blue.

Nymphs were just one of the lower creatures that Aramis Zathrain welcomed in Arcelia. Aramis had been ruling Arcelia and the Mountain Fae for 500 years, following in the footsteps of his father. Arcelia was one of the safest places in Illoterra, protected by wards to make it nearly invisible. Creatures of all kinds were welcome: nymphs, humans, Fae, gnomes. Even the waters of the River of Naraina were full of water sprites and kelpies. Goblins and ogres occupied the mountains, but they remained hidden from those not of their kind. Most villages and cities south of the mountains regulated where and when nymphs could travel. Or at least that was how it had been when Cadoc Byrnes ruled. But things were changing for the better.

Aura floated above Evren's head, squeaking excitedly. Her attitude had grown with her size. She was almost as feisty as Nazneen when she didn't get breakfast. Her sleek black feathers were the exact shade that Evren's had been the night she gave into the elemental magic. To save her brother's life and stop her father from his nefarious plans, she'd given in to the elemental fire. I shivered at the memory of that night. I had thought she was gone that night. I had thought I'd never see her again. I remembered the tang of pure, raw energy that had filled the air. I had watched as her body was torn in half from the force of the firebird. Pure, explosive power.

It had scared Evren too. She refused to use her powers since then. I could sense her hesitation and restraint down our bond. She feared losing control, but if she didn't release the smallest amount of the power, it would overflow. The power was like a river's torrent being held back by a straining dam. If she released it again, she didn't know what would happen. And she hadn't dared touch the shadow magic.

My brave bondmate. She was paces ahead of me and as beautiful and alive as ever. Soon to be mine forever in every way.

Normally, a blood binding ritual was held in one of the Temples of Anruin, conducted by the highest priestess, and attended by all who wanted to witness, but I didn't want that. People knowing about Evren's elemental powers made me nervous. There were few High Fae that were strong enough to handle the drop of power gifted from the gods. Elemental powers were rare. And the fire elemental power hadn't been seen in hundreds of years. Evren's father, Cadoc Byrnes, was willing to kill her just to gain access to that higher level magic, and now she had Alux's shadow magic flowing through her blood too. I was worried someone else might try to take her powers again. Renwick Ashewood was still out there somewhere. Danger seemed to loom around every corner. At least we were safe in Arcelia.

So instead, we chose to hold a private ceremony in my favorite place, away from the heart of Arcelia, near the River of Naraina, just a mile outside the main city. The small clearing had become a sanctuary for Evren and me. The first time Evren stepped into the snowy clearing was the first time she'd come to me of her own will. It was the first time she didn't run from me. It was a turning point in our journey and so was the blood binding. I remember that exact day as if it were yesterday. Nazneen had been with me and told me that Evren was special, and I didn't want to believe her. I didn't want to risk being rejected. But when Evren had turned to look at me and then came to me, I knew our futures would be forever connected.

Aramis and his bondmate, Calia, stood with Evren's older brother, Adaris, near the sapphire river, waiting for us. They were accompanied by a stubby-looking priestess. She did not look happy about being kept waiting. I recognized her from the few trips to the temple. Her hands were clasped tightly in front of her, and her wrinkled mouth was pursed. Her long, light blue robes pooling at her feet were the only things lacking in color as far as the eye could see. Spring in Arcelia was all brilliant shades of the rainbow, and she was a blob of irritation. A long chain hung from her neck with the symbol of the Powers Above: a pentagram surrounded by a ring and a smaller circle nestled in the middle. Small rings sat on top of the pendant—one ring for each level of enlightenment.

Evren ran forward to her brother, and he wrapped her in a hug. I hadn't been sure if he'd make it in time for the ritual or not. Thankfully, one of his trusted guardsmen was able to blink him to the borders of Arcelia. Aramis had greeted Adaris with open arms like he'd known the male his whole life, even though the two of them had never met. Aramis had that way about him. He'd been that way with me when he adopted me. He'd never questioned welcoming me into his family.

Adaris Byrnes had changed drastically in the six months since we'd left Rivamir. He no longer had dark smudges under his eyes, and his clothes didn't hang off his gaunt frame. Last time I'd seen him, his cheeks had been sunken in and his ribs had protruded from his sides. The scars that were now white and faded had been pink and angry slices covering his arms, chest, and abdomen. He'd filled out into a lean, muscular male and stood as tall as me. His chestnut hair was short, and his violet eyes, the same eyes as Evren's, were bright with delight. He was almost unrecognizable. I guessed that was what happened when your father couldn't starve and torture you anymore. The only evidence of his torture under the hand of his father were the pale scars that would always be written into his skin, like the story of his past out in the open. I knew how that felt. The scar across my face made people ask questions.

For the past six months, Adaris Byrnes had been busy reorganizing and purging the River Kingdom of all his father's devoted followers. He was basically building the kingdom from the ground up. I was quite impressed with the young High Ruler. He'd accomplished so much in a short time. I had no doubt he'd be a phenomenal ruler.

The priestess cleared her throat, a not-so-subtle demand that we should begin the ceremony. I huffed a laugh at her impatience. The priestess could just wait. Nothing would happen until Evren was ready. Today was her day.

A circle of red powder glittered on the ground in the middle of the clearing. The priestess gestured with a sweeping of her arm to the circle. The silver bracelets on her wrists chimed together as she invited Evren and me to step inside. Aramis handed the priestess Evren's sheathed dagger and then she joined us inside the circle too.

The dagger held importance to Evren. It had been a gift from her brother. The curved darkstone blade had been passed through generations in the Byrnes family. After Adaris suspected Evren was in danger in her own home, he'd given it to her for protection. And she'd carried it our entire journey from Rivamir to Lakeshore to Arcelia and back.

Naz went to stand next to our mother. Calia wrapped an arm over her shoulders. Aura lightly pecked on Calia's fingers until she made room on Naz's shoulder for her to perch. She nuzzled herself against Naz's cheek, making herself comfortable with a little warble. I looked fondly over at the trio huddled together. Aramis, Calia, and Nazneen were the closest I'd had to a family since my parents died. They'd taken me in as their own and taught me to love again. I'd opened up to them more after watching Evren with her brother, and now they were welcoming Evren into our family too.

I wished my parents were here. The pang of sadness was there. I knew they would've loved Evren. Last night, after she fell asleep, I snuck out into the night to visit their burial sites. It was an unmarked location that only I knew about. Not even Naz knew I visited the spot each time I left and returned home. My mother's body wasn't next to my father's since the guardsmen had taken her away to pay for the crime of being with a half-blooded Fae, but I prayed she was with my father in the afterlife.

I rolled my eyes. "Already tearing up, you two?"

"Stop it," Calia said, waving me off, but she smiled warmly.

"Don't feel special. You know she cries at everything," Nazneen said.

Blood binding ceremonies weren't known for being romantic events. While bondmates were a gift from the Powers Above, two souls as one, the blood binding ritual could be done even between strangers. In the past, they'd simply been ways to combine powers between two Fae and make strong connections between kingdoms, which was one reason we were doing the ritual. By binding ourselves to each other, by becoming consorts, I could help carry the burden of such two strong magical powers. Sometimes, those pairs wanted nothing to do with each other. For example, two powerful families uniting bloodlines. Other times, things were different. Evren and I were lucky in that we were bondmates that loved each other dearly. The same went for Aramis and Calia. Bondmates. Two halves of one soul.

Evren and I stood inside the circle facing the priestess. Evren reached for my fingers and gripped them tightly. I squeezed her fingers back in affirmation. We were both nervous. Not to be bound together in the eyes of the Powers Above, but about her powers—both of them. We were taking a risk. After the blood binding, we'd be able to transfer our powers back and forth as desired. It was something that was a choice between consorts. In our case, we didn't have a choice. We didn't know if, how, or when they could potentially transfer to me. Dark hells, I wasn't sure I was strong enough to keep them under control based on what I'd seen when Evren had taken them on. It was a risk I was willing to take. If we didn't try, the two combined magics could potentially kill Evren. There had never been a High Fae in our written histories that had had two such volatile powers.

The priestess raised Evren's dagger into the air and unsheathed it in a grand, over-the-top motion. I raised my brow at Evren, and she bit her lip to hold back a giggle. The priestess began chanting in the ancient language. I was only able to catch a few words I recognized. I was too distracted with Evren at my side to actually pay attention. The priestess held the dagger in her open palms toward the sky like an offering. The wicked curved blade of darkstone consumed the sunlight. The priestess switched back to the common tongue as she continued with the ritual.

"The threads of the fates have drawn you both together, across time and space."

I side-eyed Naz and she winked at me. She believed strongly in the fates. Always had. She had said Evren was fated to be my bondmate. Fates, wisps, Powers Above ... it's all a bit much for me.

"Your hand." Evren immediately obeyed the priestesses' command, placing her hand in the wrinkled one of the priestess.

Using the tip of the blade, she drew the point across Evren's palm, making a shallow cut. Blood welled from the opening. Evren winced at the pain, but she didn't seem startled with the act and didn't withdraw her hand. The bond in me lurched at the sight of the injury, even though it was slight. Then the priestess turned to me with an unamused look. I didn't hesitate to open my hand to the priestess where she mimicked the action. She then pressed our hands together, threading our fingers together and squeezed. Blood ran between our fingers and dripped onto the ground. My palm tingled at the contact, and I could taste ash and smoke on my tongue. Evren's magic was already reaching out to me.

"May your blood become one, tying your lives together."

A golden cord appeared in the priestess' hands. Its woven threads sparkled like sunlight itself. She wrapped the cord around our interlocked hands and forearms, up to our elbows. I caught Evren staring at me, a smile on her face. She made me so fucking happy. I winked before turning my attention back to the priestess.

"May the goddess of air fill your lungs, intertwining the air you breathe and giving you long life."

A gust of wind swept through the clearing, whipping up strands of Evren's hair and the hem of her dress. The same cool wind I'd noticed earlier this afternoon.

"May the goddess of water cleanse your souls to be fresh for one another." The priestess raised her hand into the air, and a sphere of water appeared. "A sign from the goddess."

It floated to our joined hands. The water dribbled down our arms, and the cord began to warm against my skin as she continued.

"May the god of earth guide you through this life and then welcome you when you return to dust."

The droplets of blood that had dripped from our joined hands were absorbed into the earth. The crimson circle around us pulsed, and the earth trembled slightly at the offering.

"And may the god of fire keep the fire in your hearts burning for only each other in this life and in the next."

For being a ritual that was done between non bondmates as well as consorts, it was very "your soul to take." I'd never been to a blood binding ritual before. Was there something in the words the priestess was saying that had a deeper meaning than what was made to believe?

The cord heated more, almost burning against my skin. I wasn't sure if it was the priestess and her chant, or if it was Evren's fire magic.

The priestess clapped her hands together, and the sound was as loud as thunder echoing off the steep cliffs of the Qana Mountains.

"Di-gara neve roth var. Consors par rikni. Kaj-far ato un isla. Your lives are bound as one. Bound to each other and bound to the gods. A bond not even broken by death."

The gilded cord tightened around our forearms, wrists, and hands and began to melt, embedding itself like metal into our flesh.

"Consorts. The everlasting vow. And bondmates I hear." The old crone gave a closed-mouth smile. "Ashlyra. Of the same soul."

That word. Ashlyra. It was the ancient language for bondmate.

The clearing brightened as if the puffed, white clouds blocking the sky had floated away. The new binding mark on my arm glinted in the sunlight. We were officially bonded in the eyes of the gods.

Ashlyra. A symbol. A title. An honor. My love.

The priestess' eyes crinkled as she smiled at us. I hadn't thought that was possible for her. "A blessing from the gods and proof to all of the sacrifices you've made to each other." And then she disappeared into thin air in a blink.

THREE
DELRIK

I brushed my fingers lightly over the binding mark on Evren's arm. It was warm under my fingertips and had a strange incandescent glow about it. It would take a while to get used to it. My heart swelled. Evren was mine in the eyes of the Powers Above and my consort. Cadoc Byrnes was gone. Renwick ran like a scared dog. *And Evren was mine. Evren. Was. Mine.* The thread of bondmates tying us together hummed, and I could sense Evren's joy, feel it as if it were my own. We'd spent the afternoon celebrating with our family and friends in Arcelia, but now it was just the six of us again having a quiet dinner, catching Adaris up on our lives over the previous six months. We were all curious how things in Rivamir were doing. Our small group had moved to the family's private dining room. It wasn't a large space, but it was cozy, and the fresh evening air was drifting through opened windows. We were all causally seated around the table, and the murmur of conservation filled the air.

"How is the restructuring of Rivamir going?" Aramis addressed Adaris.

Adaris patted his mouth with his napkin before he spoke. "Shockingly smooth. I've removed all the Black Guardsmen who were patrolling villages throughout the kingdom and returned the control to the people. The transition of leadership can be a dangerous time. I kept the borders of the River Kingdom extended as Cadoc had them to offer protection and support. The common Fae and lower creatures in the small towns throughout the kingdom have elected officials to represent them in a summit meeting. We've already had one meeting, and even though it lasted for a few days, it gave me great insight on the state of the kingdom."

Nazneen leaned forward, her elbows pressed onto the table, completely enthralled with the conversation. She'd be taking over as High Ruler in Arcelia eventually, and she'd been studying laws and histories a lot lately. "So each town has someone to speak for them, no matter their rank among the High Fae?"

"That's the plan," Adaris said as he picked up his goblet of wine. "Only a few of the High Fae families have protested the summit."

"That's to be expected," Aramis stated. "They don't want to see their control going to anyone else. Or their level of control diminish."

"Father," Nazneen spoke to Aramis, "I'd like to try implementing some of these ideas here in Arcelia. I know our people are treated equally, but hearing from them could help in the future. I like the idea of an annual meeting or something similar."

Aramis tipped his head in consideration. Calia patted his arm warmly. The pride for their children rivaled many. "I think that is possible. After all, you will be Arcelia's leader after me."

Aramis wasn't like Evren's father or older leaders in Illoterra. He believed in not only passing on his role as High Ruler to his heir before his death, but also that a female could rule as well as a male. He was wise well beyond his years.

A servant came and removed the plates from our finished course from the table. I thanked her with a smile. The dinner of roasted duck and spring salads had filled me to the brim.

"Cadoc made a real mess of Rivamir. I don't know how I'd missed it all these years." Adaris shook his head. "He did everything right under my nose."

"You can't blame yourself, brother. You know he kept you out of the loop on purpose. He was always sending you on random trips just to get you out of the River Kingdom," Evren consoled him. Evren's empathy for her brother's struggles was true.

"I found piles and piles of papers in his desk..."

"How'd you get into his desk?" Evren asked, truly baffled. That thing was a beast of a piece of furniture, with more protective wards than Arcelia.

"I dismantled the damn thing. I guess some of his wards were broken when he died." Adaris let out a hearty laugh. "It brought me so much satisfaction destroying the monstrosity."

"Did any of his notes say what he had planned for the future?" Aramis asked.

"It's much worse than I'd anticipated. He's been working with Hadeon Allerick to prepare for some kind of insurrection," Adaris said.

My whole body stiffened, and the air was sucked from the room. The mention of Hadeon Allerick had killed the celebratory mood. I could feel Evren's confusion down the bond. She placed her hand on my thigh under the table. I'd told her very little about my time during the war. It wasn't something I liked revisiting. Evren was lucky to have been too young to know who Hadeon Allerick and what his role was during the War Across the Sea.

Corrupt and twisted, Hadeon Allerick was the one that first influenced the Raven Fae to trigger the War Across the Sea. He came from a long line of Fae who'd despised the wealthy and proteinous High Fae royalty. His grandfather had participated in the Uprising centuries before. The Uprising had been a group of Fae who grew restless with the distribution of magical powers and unleashed the Great Chaos to wipe out their enemies. It had backfired, and the gods had to step in to save their sorry asses. Hadeon had attempted a similar takeover. He'd led the initial riots and supplied the Raven Fae with weapons. When he realized he couldn't win, he stepped back and let the Raven Fae be destroyed by the Illoterrain fighters. Their entire kingdom had fallen at the end of the war. Hadeon's been in Noirdan, biding his time and pulling strings like a puppet master ever since. And Cadoc had been his favorite puppet. Where Cadoc and his Black Guard wreaked havoc and caused bloodshed, Hadeon sat quietly back and waited. He was a spider waiting for the right prey to ensnare themselves in his web.

I answered Evren's unasked question. "Hadeon Allerick led the Raven Fae riots that triggered the war, and then disappeared when the war turned in our favor."

I pushed back the disturbing images that came to mind of the war. Evren didn't need to feel the burden of my past.

"That's the very one," Adaris replied.

"Shit," I muttered under my breath.

"Wasn't his grandfather a leader in the Guild?" Nazneen said.

"Yes. His father was one of those responsible for releasing the Great Chaos. He has been in hiding since the war. Apparently, he takes after his father." Adaris placed his folded napkin on the table. "That's when Cadoc fell in line with him. When they crossed paths during the war, Cadoc aligned himself with Hadeon in secret. No one knew of their alliance."

Aramis shook his head. I could tell he was deep in thought. "Did you find out what he wants? What's his goal?"

"Not exactly. He's been shipping crates full of iron from the mines in Menrath as well as slaves to Rivamir for the last five years. Renwick Ashewood has been traveling back and forth between the continents as a liaison. Hadeon and Cadoc were also searching for something. He never wrote down exactly what they were looking for, but Hadeon needs it to open something." Adaris shrugged.

"What do they need all that iron for?" Evren asked her brother.

Iron was dangerous for Fae. It depleted our magic. Injuries made with iron didn't heal correctly, and, after long exposure, could kill. The scar on my face was caused by a poisoned iron weapon during the war, leaving my face scarred for eternity. The memory of the burn from the metal made me nauseous. Evren's father had sliced into her with an iron knife when he'd held her captive, the same as he'd done with Adaris. However, when Evren transformed into the firebird and accepted her elemental fire, the flames had somehow healed all the injuries inflicted by her father.

"They've been melting it down and making weapons out of it. He also mentioned some kind of ... monster Hadeon has control over and has been breeding."

Delrik looked thoughtful. "We need to warn Vidarr about the influx of weapons. I don't want him caught off guard, especially if those in the Wildlands somehow get their hands on the imports."

Vidarr Fenanos was the leader of the centaur tribe in the Arden Valley and an ally during the war. His territory bordered the Wildlands, the uncontrolled portion of Illoterra. He had also helped Evren and me find Alux and learn about my powers.

Adaris said, "I've already sent a messenger to him and also invited him to join the summit. He hadn't been able to come to the first meeting. He has a new son."

Dessert was placed in front of me, but I was too engrossed in the conversation to eat. What was Hadeon hiding? And how would it affect Illoterra?

"The only other leader that may have the ability to help us is High Ruler Holden Eckhardt," Aramis said.

"When was the last time you talked with Holden Eckhardt?" I asked Aramis.

Holden Eckhardt had been an invaluable asset during the war. His knowledge of war surpassed everyone, including Aramis. If we hadn't had his skilled and precise tactics, we would have likely lost the war.

"The High Ruler of the Snowhaven Fae?" Adaris asked.

"Yes. He allied with us during the war, too. I haven't spoken with him since we parted ways after we all returned home. Nothing other than a letter every now and then to discuss trade routes."

"We should go see him," I stated matter of factly.

Evren's eyes went wide. Her shock rippled down the bond. Her hand shot under the table again and gripped my knee hard. "You want to go into Snowhaven Territory?"

The sprawling territory north of the Qana Mountains was a savage wasteland of unending winter. Growing up, I'd been told legends of the Fae that inhabited the land there lived a harsh, unforgiving lives full of brutality. However, after visiting during the war and several times afterward, I knew different. Though it was a wasteland of snow and ice and bitter temperatures, it was a beautiful territory. Plus, my best friend lived there. A friend I hadn't seen in more than a decade.

Aramis chuckled in a way only a father could. "You know all those rumors aren't true."

Nazneen let out a laugh. "His son, Garren, and Delrik were thick as thieves during the war. They were always getting into trouble, pulling pranks, swiping extra snacks from the cooks."

Evren had heard about some of the pranks and shenanigans Garren and I had gotten into during the war, but that didn't settle her hesitancy of visiting the territory. She tightened her grip on my knee.

Aramis agreed with this plan of action. "You can blink as far as their borders, but the wards they have protecting their territory are too strong to get through, just like ours here in Arcelia. You'll have to take a ship the rest of the way to Kanevvluk. It's the only way in or out without an escort."

"I can have a ship from the fleet meet you at their border, Whiteband Port," Adaris said. "It can be there in a week's time." The River Kingdom's fleet was the largest in the realm. It was filled with the swiftest ships and most skilled sailors. It was the one thing Cadoc had done right for the kingdom.

"That's an excellent idea." I smiled at my bondmate. "Garren is also a water elemental. I bet he can help you with your powers."

She stared blankly at the table before her.

"Evren?"

I nudged her with my shoulder.

"Sorry. Yes. Let's go. What do we have to lose?"

FOUR
DELRIK

"I can't believe my father was working for Hadeon. I mean I knew he was always a bit twisted, but this?" Evren said to me as we strolled into our apartment. I had her tucked against my side. "I wonder when he switched sides?"

I didn't think Cadoc had ever been on the right side, but that was just my opinion. Evren had been lost in thought since Adaris had mentioned Hadeon. I wasn't sure what exactly she was thinking, but I could feel her conflicting emotions. I closed the door behind her after I let us into the apartment. "Let's not worry about that right now. We have some celebrating of our own to do."

I turned my bondmate by her shoulders to face me. She was still wearing her ritual gown, and her cheeks were a rosy hue from the Fae wine she'd enjoyed at lunch. She lifted her chin a touch.

"We do?" She smiled up at me in a tease. She ran her tongue across her bottom lip before sinking her teeth into it. She traced her hands across the planes of my chest, up to my shoulders. Heat trailed where she touched me.

I wanted to take her right here, right now. But I needed to be patient. Instead, I used my hulking body to walk her backwards to our bedroom. Her violet eyes never left mine. The skirt of her dress swished across the stone floor. Evren kicked off one shoe at a time. I steadied my hands on her waist to prevent her from toppling over. She'd dropped a few inches in height now that she was barefoot.

"You are mine. I can't believe that you are all mine." My voice was rough with lust.

I knew she was mine the moment I saw her all those months ago in Lakeshore sitting in that tree; that first time I touched her arm and there was a zing of energy between us. Now that the bond had snapped into place and the blood binding was complete, it felt so real.

For the first time ever in my life, I felt like I was exactly where I was supposed to be.

Evren lifted her hands to my chest again and gently pushed me away so that I was just out of her reach. Then she reached behind her back and slowly pulled the zipper of her dress down. The top half dropped and settled on the curve of her hips. My breath caught. She was absolutely gorgeous. She shimmied a little to wiggle the rest of the fabric to a heap on the floor. She giggled at the movement, but I thought she was the most breathtaking when she was silly. My bondmate was standing before me—lace underwear, the shadows, and the binding mark the only things on her.

"Can I fuck you now? Please?" I begged.

Evren hummed in response.

Then she let out a startled gasp as I picked her up effortlessly and tossed her onto our bed before pouncing on top of her.

"We were interrupted last time," I said in a deep, sultry voice.

Her mouth parted to respond, but my lips crashed into hers before she could speak. My tongue pushed into her mouth and she tasted so delectable—like honeysuckle and wine. Right before I thought I couldn't take anymore, I broke away and crawled down her body, leaving her panting and flustered. Just the way I liked her.

"Evren..." Her name was a prayer on my lips.

Starting at her ankles, I slowly trailed my fingertips, higher and higher, pressing kisses over her exposed skin. Up to her knee. The inside of her thigh. I paused momentarily at the apex of her thighs, taking in a deep breath of her scent and releasing a growl from the back of my throat before moving on. I was saving the best for last. I shifted so that I was hovering above her now. Her breaths were coming in sharp pants. My fingers feathered across her stomach. Between her breasts. Her skin was soft under my calloused fingers. The shadows moved away from me, giving me the space I demanded. I felt her pleasure down through the bond, and her body heated under my gaze as I moved to sit astride her hips. Evren lifted her hips playfully, bucking into me, and bit her lower lip. The corner of my mouth tipped up at her. She knew exactly what she wanted and wasn't shy about demanding it.

"Greedy female."

I stood and slipped my fingers under the lace of her underwear. I tugged them down her legs. A hum of approval. The intensity of her gaze watching me sparked pleasure all over my body. She didn't break eye contact as I slowly peeled off my layers of clothes. First my shirt. It made a soft sound as it landed on the floor. My broad, bronzed chest lifted with each inhale. I was struggling with the battle of savoring each moment and devouring her immediately. Then my pants were gone and I stood before her in all my masculine glory. A body covered in tattoos and scars, yet she looked at me like I was flawless.

Evren dug her fingers into the blankets at her waist as I bowed before her and trailed my nose up her very center. I looked up to see her head loll to the side and her eyes drifted closed. Her mouth opened in a silent sigh as I traced circles with my tongue over her most sensitive spot. Sweet, teasing circles leaving her begging and wanting more and clawing at the bed sheets.

"Delrik." She was gasping for breath now. This was what she did to me. I was simply returning the favor. She sat perched on the precipice, and I was ready to dive off the edge with her.

"Evren," I spoke against her flesh. So wet and soft.

She plunged her hands into my thick hair and tugged. Not gently.

"Hmm," I growled. "Do you need something, my love?"

She drew me up to her body and guided my mouth to her. I swept my tongue through her mouth, allowing her to taste the sweetness of her arousal on my tongue. Without warning, I drove into her—so hard we slid up the bed and the headboard crashed into the stone wall. I caught her cry of pleasure with my mouth. Over and over, unrelenting, I drove into her, bringing her higher and higher until she could no longer hold back. She shattered around me. She pulsed around my length, and after one thrust, I followed behind with a rush of ecstasy.

"Beauty. Power. Mine." I murmured into her ear.

I dropped my weight onto her, knowing that she loved my closeness and warmth, surrounding her completely. My head rested in the crook of her neck, and she stroked the back of my head and down over my shoulders, tracing my tattoos and scars as she went. I rolled off her and onto my back, dragging her halfway on top of me. I laced my hand with hers, our binding mark glowing softly between us.

"Ashlyra."

FIVE
DELRIK

"Bondmate. Ashlyra." The same words the priestess had used this afternoon.

Evren smiled up at me. "Ashlyra."

Ashlyra. It's so much more than a word. It's more than the bond itself or the physical mark of the blood binding. It's a symbol of my love and dedication to Evren. The endearment was too fitting to not use. Ashlyra was all encompassing.

Evren looked down at our joined hands and sucked in a sharp breath.

"What?" I asked, sitting up and following her gaze.

Shadows danced down Evren's arm and fingers, licking at my fingertips, like they were testing the binding mark. My eyes shot to hers. They were wide and almost fearful. The sudden look of panic made my heart almost stop.

"What's wrong?" I asked.

"Your eyes." She sat up without releasing my hand. "They're black." Her other hand came to her mouth as she spoke. "Just like Alux."

The shadows had crawled up to my wrist but were still firmly woven around Evren's forearm.

"What?" I jumped out of bed and ran into the washroom.

The moment we broke contact, I felt the shadows surge back into Evren like a biting, winter wind. I held my breath as I looked into the mirror.

Normal. Everything looked normal. My eyes were the same as always. Deep brown stared back at me.

"I don't see anything different," I called from the washroom.

I went back into our room to see the shadows settled back to their usual place, wrapped around Evren's torso. I stared down at my empty hand. Only the gilded binding mark was there.

Evren slept deeply next to me, the covers pooling at her waist, exposing her bare back to the warm spring air. The gauze curtains floated on the steady breeze. The hand with Evren's binding mark was tucked under her chin in relaxation. The shadow magic rose and fell smoothly with each breath she took. After the initial shock, we tried to move the shadows again, but nothing happened. When we'd broken contact between our hands the first time, the shadows had returned to Evren, and they weren't budging. Eventually, Evren fell asleep. I couldn't sleep. My mind was too busy. I sat propped up on a pillow watching my bondmate. And the shadows.

That had been odd. I hadn't felt the shadows as they explored my hand. At least not like I had when Alux had cursed me with them. They didn't feel cold or dangerous. In fact, I didn't feel them at all as they tested the new blood bond between Evren and me. The first time the shadows inhabited me, they were cold and painful, sucking the power and strength from me with each passing day. That was the main reason I worried about Evren possessing them. I knew first hand how dangerous they could be. But Evren seemed unaffected by the unknown magic.

I reached a tentative hand out and grazed her warm, creamy skin. She didn't stir. Evren could sleep through almost anything. I trailed my finger down her spine, stopping just before reaching the living darkness resting at the dimples of her lower back. I didn't know what to do next. I sat frozen. I was fascinated by their neverending movement. It was like a breathing, living entity.

Then an inky tendril reached out and touched my finger. Slowly it crept up my finger, wrapping around it gently, and wriggled on the back of my hand. This time I didn't pull away.

Softness. Coolness. And exhilarating power.

The next morning at breakfast, Evren and I met with our family in the dining hall before we began preparations for our trip to Snowhaven Territory. Adaris had left after dinner last night for Rivamir to send a ship for our journey. I knew he wanted to go meet with the High Ruler of the Snowhaven Fae to introduce himself, but he had too much to do in Rivamir, especially if we had another war in the near future.

"So they just came to you?" Naz asked.

She'd joined us at the table only a few minutes after we arrived at the private dining room. Usually Evren and I ate in our apartment, but with so much to discuss, we opted for joining the family.

"I guess. I don't really know what triggered it. We weren't doing anything special."

"Mh hm," Naz said behind a mouthful of omelet.

Aura sat on the back of my chair and nipped at my ear. Thankfully the bird hadn't been around last night. She had the knack of disappearing when I needed privacy with Evren. I waved my hand at her, and she fluttered over to land on Evren's shoulder. Aura chirped an agitated sound at me that sounded a lot like a curse. Evren speared a piece of meat with her fork and offered it to the bird. Aura clicked her beak cheerfully before snatching the food off the utensil and devouring it.

"Shut up, Naz. I meant we weren't trying to transfer powers." I rolled my eyes at my sister.

She was so nosey. And inappropriate. She stuck her tongue out at me, and I tossed a piece of bacon at her.

"Maybe you should try again," Aramis suggested. He ignored our antics.

"Okay..." Evren said. "The shadows seem pretty content to stay with me right now. They haven't moved from my torso since last night. We tried again this morning, too. They only made it as far as Delrik's hand."

"It can't hurt to try." I lifted my shoulder in a shrug. I stood from the table, pulling Evren up with me, and backed up several steps. "But maybe we should try this outside."

After seeing Evren go all exploding fire when she had come into her elemental power, I didn't want to risk any collateral damage if the shadows got out of hand or if I couldn't control them. Everyone pushed their chairs back from the table and joined us out on the terrace. The morning air was warm, and the sun sprinkled through the leaves of the trees above.

I caught Aramis's eyes. We'd discussed my concerns about the shadows when we'd first arrived back home. What if I wasn't strong enough to handle the shadows and they took over? What if they were truly evil just like Alux, but somehow Evren's elemental fire was keeping them at bay? We didn't actually know anything about the shadow magic.

"Aramis, if anything goes wrong..." I started.

"Nothing bad is going to happen." Evren took my hand. I felt a wave of confidence down the bond.

I looked down at our joined hands, the same hands with the binding mark, and waited.

"Nothing's happening," Naz said after several minutes of quiet.

"You don't say," I snarked at her.

She stuck out her tongue at me.

"Aramis, do you and Calia share powers through your binding mark? As consorts, I mean?" I asked.

I'd never asked before. It felt almost like a too personal question. Though their binding mark looked different than mine and Evren's, it was there. Each one was slightly different depending on the couple. They joined hands, and it glowed with the contact.

"Yes, but our powers aren't as strong as Evren's," Calia said. "It may take some time to figure out how to let down your barriers, even between each other, to make it seamless. The first time you use each other's powers is a special moment. Almost more so than the blood binding itself. It's showing true trust and devotion to your partner. You will be at your most vulnerable without your magic, and you're trusting your partner with your life. What was once yours becomes something shared between you both. For bondmates, it's the final step in being completely joined in body, magic, and spirit."

She had a way with words. I knew exactly where Nazneen got her traits. They were so much alike in many ways.

"Try focusing on the origin of your power and then visualize it moving into Delrik," Calia suggested to Evren.

"I don't know the origin of the shadows, but my fire..." Evren placed her hand just under her ribs and took a deep breath.

Evren once told me that she felt the fire was the strongest in her middle. Evren wiggled her fingers in mine, pushing her fire into them. I felt my hand heat, and almost translucent flames encircled our fingers. There was no burn or pain. Her flames never burned me. Then the ground under my feet began to quiver. Above us, ominous clouds crept over the blue sky, darkness covering the sun. The tang of magic filled the air. I recognized that tang of magic. It was the same as the first time the firebird appeared, and for a moment, I grew nervous.

Then the shadows began to leave Evren, like black silk pouring out onto the stones and surrounding her feet. They swirled, tendrils reaching out, seeking a new host, seeking ... me. A tendril drifted to my foot, and it wrapped itself around my leg, moving up my body. I stiffened, remembering the last time the shadows invaded my body like this. Exactly like this. The coldness. The pain. A flashback of them crawling across the ground and invading my senses. The biting cold. Encroaching darkness. Suffocating me as I strained against their hold. The sound of Alux's evil cackle echoed in my head.

But this was different. It didn't feel like it had. The shadows poured into my palm, the one that held Evren's hand, and I felt them sweeping into me in a potent rush. It was a high. The complete power was intoxicating. My blood was brimming with the dark magic. I took a deep breath and welcomed the surge of power the shadows were. Powers Above. Is this what her fire power felt like? As the last tendril of shadow came into me, I felt a shift. Darkness covered my vision as the shadows dug in deep and rooted into my soul. The darkness pulsed under my skin as it filled my bloodstream.

"Powers! Your eyes are solid black, Delrik!" Naz said. She took a step forward but stopped, her face guarded.

Evren didn't release my hand. "Delrik. Are you alright?"

I turned my black eyes toward her voice. That voice I'd loved since first hearing it. So calm. So grounding. The center of my existence. I felt her hand press to the side of my face. She pushed a thread of fire into her palm, and my face warmed with the power. Her thumb stroked the scar that ran down my cheek. I blinked, and the darkness was gone. I could see clearly, but the power was still there, humming just under the surface.

"I think so," I said.

I looked down at my bondmate, and she smiled up at me, squeezing my hand. My arm was covered shoulder to fingertips with the serpentine shadows, but the binding mark stood out gold and bright against the dark. The shadows had fully transferred to me, and I managed to not explode with darkness. I'd call that a win.

"Well, that was ... interesting," Naz said. "*That* was inside you, Evren?"

Evren nodded with a smile. "Yes. I really don't think they mean any harm. If anything, they just seemed protective over me. Like a spirit that is ever watchful."

"And how did your fire like that?" Adaris asked.

"They stayed separate for the most part."

I still gripped Evren's hand tightly. I tested my control over the shadows and encouraged it to move into my hand. The shadows leached from my skin and surrounded our joined hands in an opaque, black cloud. Evren always spoke of her power like it was something living, and now I understood. It responded to me as if it were a part of me, but still separate. If her fire was even a fraction as potent as this darkness... These powers, our powers, were beautiful yet horrific. Shadow and fire.

SIX
DELRIK

"Naz, you're going with us?" Evren was practically bouncing on the morning of our departure.

I, on the other hand, was still drowsy from a night of tossing and turning. I didn't love traveling by water. The anticipation of being seasick had kept me up most of the night.

"I can't let you two have all the fun," my sister said. "Plus, it would be good to create a more permanent relationship with the Snowhaven Fae."

She hadn't planned to make the trip initially, but Aramis had suggested she join us. She was the next in line to become High Ruler of Arcelia and the Mountain Fae. Making lasting connections with other kingdoms in Illoterra would help solidify her transition once Aramis stepped down. She'd already sat down with Adaris while he was here for the blood binding ceremony, and even though Vidarr wasn't a High Ruler, he was the leader of the centaur clans and an old friend from the war. The Snowhaven Territory was the last of the High Fae to form an alliance with her as the upcoming High Ruler. At least in the civilized part of the continent. No one truly controlled the Wildlands.

I knew it wouldn't be easy for Nazneen. Higher Ruler Holden Eckhardt was traditional in his ways. He didn't agree with Aramis in passing down the territory to a female. He'd made it very clear during the war that he was against the idea. He'd refused to speak to Nazneen or listen to her opinions while in meetings. He'd even gone as far as to move her battalion to a lower risk area to 'get her out of the way of the real warriors,' but she'd never let it get under her skin. I commended her for it. She knew her value. She knew fate. And she would be the High Ruler of Arcelia whether he liked it or not. I had no doubt that she'd be brilliant.

I nodded to Liam, the Arcelia guard that would blink us and our travel trunks from Arcelia to the border of Snowhaven Territory, where a River Kingdom ship would be waiting for us, courtesy of Adaris. Liam Winfield was a well-trusted friend and a damned good warrior to have by your side during a battle. Nazneen and I both considered him a good friend. Whiteband Port was the last port before entering the Boreas Sea and the frozen tundra of the north.

With the telltale pop, the world was pulled away and everything in Arcelia disappeared. The push and pull of the magic plummeted us through space. I closed my eyes against the spinning blur.

"You're not going to ruin my shoes again, are you? These are new," Liam joked to Nazneen as we reappeared at our destination.

"You can't blame me. That was the first time I blinked. You caught me off guard. I couldn't help but hurl my breakfast on your shoes."

The warrior laughed.

"You'll never let me live it down, will you?" Nazneen asked.

"Nope. Never," he replied.

Then he disappeared, along with our luggage. He'd taken it to the ship. Five seconds passed, and he popped back up beside Nazneen.

"Everything is taken care of," he said.

"Thank you," I replied and shivered.

The moment my feet hit the ground, I instantly wished I had put on my cloak before leaving Arcelia, instead of storing it in my bag while we traveled. Before my teeth started chattering though, I was engulfed in warmth from Evren's extended hand. My bondmate had been smart and donned her cloak *before* we blinked. I tugged her close and planted a kiss on her temple. She reached a hand out to Nazneen, who took it gratefully. She sighed as Evren's heat warmed her too.

"Thanks. I could get used to your fire magic keeping me warm. It would come in handy on scouting missions," Nazneen said.

"It would make our outings more bearable," Liam said as Evren leaned a warming shoulder into Nazneen's arm.

Most of our legion training took place in the highest peaks of the Qanas, but the dead of the winter in Arcelia couldn't contend with Snowhaven Territory. Even their summers were cold. At least Arcelia had a spring and summer.

We stood on a bluff above a beach. A small schooner drifted in the grayish waters not too far from shore. The cream sails marked with the River Kingdom symbol snapped in the breeze—the head of a fox in front of two crossed swords. A tender was pushed up into the sand,

and a cloaked male shifted back and forth on his feet, trying to stay warm. When the Black Guardsman saw us, he waved us down.

I slung my cloak over my shoulders before taking a step forward. I reached my hand in front of my face into the empty air. I only saw a barren land with dull grasses snapping in the bitter wind. The ripple of a shield pushed back against my hand. The Thawvale. The magic was cold and sharp as knives. The more I pushed against the ward, the more my fingers frosted over. I could feel it all the way to my bones.

"Can you feel that?" I said over my shoulder to Nazneen.

She nodded.

"We're good, Liam. We've got it from here," I said to my fellow warrior.

Liam gave a nod before disappearing again.

"Are we in Snowhaven Territory?" Evren asked.

"No. This is their outer boundary, the Thawvale. They keep the barrier reinforced with wards and magic so that no one can cross it. The Thawvale lines the entire territory all along the coast. Most don't even know it's here. When they come upon it, they find themselves confused. The wards have a way of playing tricks on your mind."

The cold had a way of disorienting you. I'd patrolled along this border many times, walking the barrier back and forth, day in and day out. When I was fresh out of that initial training, I'd gotten thrown off track up along the Thawvale a few times. It was like a right of passage for Arcelia legion members.

"But there is nothing out there. Just empty, dead grass as far as I can see," Evren said.

"That's just what the barrier wants you to see," Nazneen responded. "It works similar to the wards around Arcelia."

"How are we supposed to get in then?" Evren asked.

"There are only two ways in, where the Thawvale has a gap. One port on the eastern side of Illoterra and the one we will go through, the one north of here," Nazneen said.

Just then, an icy breeze whipped up from the water, making the three of us shiver. It swirled around us, then went back toward the open sea behind us.

"Let's get moving," I suggested, "before we freeze out here."

The trip was short, despite fighting the currents and gusts coming down from the north. Four days. It grew colder with each passing day. Soon I preferred to be in my cabin than on deck. A knock came on the way-too-thin wooden door that allowed any and all sound to pass through. It was the only thing that separated our cabin from the rest of the ship. Evren and I had shared it with Nazneen since the ship was small and it was a quick journey. The door opened before I could answer, and Evren's head poked into the room.

"We've arrived! It's beautiful!" Evren's excitement about life was contagious.

Everything was new to her. She'd lived her entire life behind the walls of Cadoc's fortress until fate brought us together. I loved seeing the world through her eyes. I could taste her excitement like sweetness on my tongue. I swiveled my neck around and rubbed a hand across its nape. I was stiff from the uncomfortable mattress, and I'd had a headache for the last two days.

"You alright?" Evren asked.

"I'll be fine, love. Just need to get off this ship."

When she turned away to talk to Nazneen, I pinched the bridge of my nose and squeezed my eyes shut.

Nazneen was sitting at a worn, makeshift desk in the corner, deep in concentration. It was scattered with notes and a potential agreement between Arcelia and the Snowhaven Fae. Nazneen had been working tirelessly in her journal and scribbling notes with various ideas to pull the High Fae kingdoms together.

"What are you working on?" Evren asked.

Nazneen took a deep breath and went to twirl the end of her braid around her fingers but came up empty. She'd chopped off her long hair last week before the blood binding ritual, and it now sat right at her shoulders. Her nervous habit of twisting her braid was no longer an option so she tucked her hands beneath her legs to stop from fidgeting. I didn't see her anxious often.

"While Aramis and Holden are long-time friends who didn't hesitate to assist each other when needed, Holden is traditional in his opinion of females." Her eyes cut to me and then back to Evren. "Due to his traditional opinion of females, I cannot assume the same assistance would be offered to me upon my succession. I want to be prepared for anything he throws my way."

Most High Fae rulers only passed on their responsibilities and kingdoms upon death, but Aramis wanted Nazneen to take over. I didn't blame him after 500 years of ruling and a war.

Nazneen shuffled her papers into a neat stack and slid them into a satchel hung on a nail by the porthole. All I could see was blinding white light. I hadn't bothered unpacking my trunk. I just had a small bag with necessities for the voyage. I pushed my feet into my boots, grabbed my cloak, and followed Evren and Nazneen up to the main deck.

Dark clouds in the distance were rolling in, bringing a deep, low rumble of thunder. I flipped my hood up to cover my face as pellets of ice fell from the sky. Despite the dark clouds above, the water splashing against the sides of the ship was a brilliant teal. My gaze followed the teal waves up to the shore, and my eyes widened at the sight. Sparkling glaciers shot out of the water and up into the air. I let out a breath and it clouded in front of me. The wall of white was blinding as the diminishing sun reflected off the surface of the ice. Well, that wasn't going to help my pounding head. The teal waters were so clear you could see the enormous chunks of ice beneath the water.

The captain came up beside us. "Welcome to The Hook."

"The Hook?" Evren asked.

"It's the only port on the western coast of Snowhaven Territory. Only the most skilled sailors dare to enter its tight spiral that leads to the harbor in Kanevvluk. Everywhere north of here are sheer cliffs into the sea. If you somehow got past the cliffs, the Thawvale would turn you away"

"I've never seen icebergs before. They're huge," Evren said as she craned her neck to look up to their jagged peaks.

"This is just the smallest part. The part under the water"—he gestured downward—"is called a bummock. You can't see it entirely, but most of the iceberg is below the surface."

"You've been here before?" I asked the captain.

He nodded. "A few times during the war."

I felt the deck under my feet, slippery from precipitation, bobbing in the water as the waves crashed into the glacier and then barreled back toward the ship. The bow dipped and so did my stomach. I realized we were moving forward still, but a mountain of ice was directly in front of us. I'd passed through The Hook many times, but it was still nerve wracking each time.

"Are we going to crash into that?" Nazneen asked, pointing in front of us.

The wind howled and whipped across my face. My fingers dug into the wood railing. Suddenly, the ship lurched, the wind catching the sails, and the bow turned away from the ice wall and back toward the water. Evren bumped into my side, and I quickly wrapped an arm around her.

"Nah, we've got a solid crew with us. Just sit back and relax. We'll be at the harbor within the hour." He nodded his fur-lined cap in our direction before returning to his post.

Between the constant pull to the left and the water jostling the vessel, my stomach dipped and rolled like the turquoise waves below. The edges of my vision started to turn black, and an overwhelming feeling of numbness took over. Then another blast of wind shook me from my stupor.

After a while, a sprawling city came into view. A city surrounded by a battlement and a towering citadel standing in the middle. Guards were posted all along the rise. When they saw our ship coming into the harbor, a flurry of activity happened. The battlement ran as far as the eye could see to the north and to the south. Beyond the city, thick evergreen trees stretched. Beyond that, only a blanket of blinding white. The first time I saw the snowy city, I hadn't known what to expect. Kanevvluk was nearly triple that of Arcelia.

Evren squeezed my arm with giddiness. I just focused on not puking. Nazneen came up behind us.

"Four days aboard the ship and your beard has grown. You look like you could belong to the wilderness," Nazneen teased.

"I cannot wait to get off this forsaken pile of rotting wood from the circle of dark hells," I said under my breath, ignoring her statement. I was sure I looked as green as I felt. I'd always hated the water. I couldn't count the number of crossings we'd made during the war. You'd think I'd be used to it, but it got worse with each one.

"You're looking a little queasy, brother." Nazeen jabbed me in the ribs.

I groaned. "You're one to talk."

Suddenly, the blackness came back into my vision and I wavered on unsteady feet. I would need to visit the healer if this fucking headache didn't give in soon.

"Delrik?" Nazneen's voice was distant and hollow.

She waved her hand in front of my face, but I was trying to not pass out.

Evren tapped my arm gently. "Ashlyra?"

I startled and blinked away whatever fog had come over me. "Sorry. I just feel weird. It must be the water."

Nazneen watched me closely for a few moments, only distracted by the sound of a horn announcing our arrival into the port. It was the water. The constant sway of the water was making me woozy, that's all. So why couldn't I shake the feeling of something heavy hanging over me?

PART TWO

SEVEN
KATURI

Kanevvluk, Snowhaven Territory

The narrow spaces between the trees blurred the faster I ran, darting from side to side, leaping over toppled pines. I wanted to shift; I wanted to release the full strength of my power, unleash it on the forest surrounding me. My boots crunched on the snow covered trail I'd created from years of tearing through the evergreens. I skidded to a halt suddenly. Instinct told me to turn around. Something was pulling me back. Well, not something. I knew exactly what was preventing me from going any further. A pang of awareness. I attempted to ignore it. I glared down at my left arm that was covered by my cloak. I rolled my eyes, turned on my heels, and began to trudge back to the citadel. I couldn't see the towering walls this far into the forest, but I knew they were there. The solid stone walls of the battlement were my prison. I was forced into the cage unwillingly. I'd been dumped in the Snowhaven Fae Territory as soon as my powers began to manifest.

I didn't know why the Snowhaven Fae insisted on walling off their cities. No one in their right mind would want to willingly come here. It was always freezing. Literally. The entire time I'd been stuck in Kanevvluk there had been snow on the ground. The summer consisted of sloshing puddles and freezing rain pelting off the windows. Even when the sun was shining, it barely warmed my face.

The trees thinned and the citadel came into view, mighty and imposing. I frowned up at the gates. I stopped just outside them and looked up, the same as I had my first day in Snowhaven Territory forty years ago.

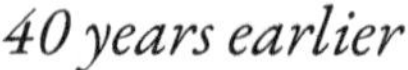

40 years earlier

The large hand of my father shoved me forward, and I stumbled slightly as I went through the towering gates. The thick black of night made it difficult to see past the light of the torches the guards carried. The gate closed with a clang behind me. My father didn't bother joining me. He left me in the hands of four of his guards. He didn't even care enough to see me to my future bonded's side the first time I met him. Instead, he hurried off to a meeting with a trading company to discuss new routes and upcoming shipments.

The citadel rose from thick swirls of frozen mist and reached as tall as the trees that surrounded the wall. I turned to the sky and was met by inky darkness. Nothing but the snow that began falling once we'd reached the Hook. That's what the young sailor had called it. He was also a Forest Fae just like me. He'd chatted with me until his father had called him away.

Fluffy, white flakes were coming down harder now, and a layer of ice from the water's spray made the deck slick. I'd never seen snow before. It didn't snow in Laeto Selva in the Forest Fae Kingdom, my homeland. There was a strange smell in the air that I didn't recognize. Everything about this place was different from home. I'd done everything I could in rebellion to coming to Illoterra. I'd kicked and screamed, but nothing came of it. My parents wouldn't budge. I was being sent to the Snowhaven Fae as prophesied by the royal seer to complete the blood binding ritual, fulfill a political treaty between the two kingdoms, and forever combine our two powerful family bloodlines.

Present Day

I entered the city's eastern gate and wandered down the path that led back to the citadel. The guards didn't even glance my way. It wasn't out of the ordinary to find me coming and going anytime—day or night. I needed to stretch my legs and space to run. I couldn't do that inside the city itself. I was sure the citizens of Kanevvluk wouldn't have appreciated my shifted form. And it was impossible to actually run away, even though I'd thought about it many times.

Once inside the citadel, I stomped up the backstairs, breaking the clumps of ice and snow off my boots. The halls were the same unwelcoming gray as the battlement in this part of the citadel. No one came this far into the residential wing except me so there was no reason to decorate. I wore thick pants, furred boots, and the heaviest wool cloak I had in my closet, and I was still shaking all over. It wasn't even winter. My joints were stiff, and my hair was frozen in clumps against my neck. I threw open the door of my suite and tossed my cloak across the chair before flopping down face-first on the couch with a groan. A medium-sized red wolf was curled up on the chair opposite of me. She opened a green eye at me before she went back to her nap.

"You know, you could've come with me," I said to the creature. She huffed in response. I rolled my eyes at her.

Floor-to-ceiling windows were on two walls, and a view of the city below was barely visible through the freezing spring rain. It was still daytime, but this was Kanevvluk. Even during the day, the dense clouds left everything overcast in gloom. I could taste snow in the air. A storm was coming in and there would be a lot of snow. It would eventually melt since it was summertime, but it didn't stop the north from dumping blizzards on the city on a regular basis.

At least my suite was warm. I kept the fires in both my fireplaces raging strong around the clock. I'd had servants plaster every hole, every crack around the windows, and under the doors to keep as much heat in as possible. Alas, it never failed that I'd find random drifts of snow piled on the ledges around the window panes. I hated Kanevvluk.

I rolled off the couch and onto the floor, sitting up and unlacing my boots. I kicked them off with a grunt, scowling at the puddles of melted snow on the rug before standing. I wiggled my toes in my socks, trying to bring some life back to them. My sitting room was a cozy space. Two plush couches and thick rugs. Beside the window, double doors lead to my bedroom. Both were on the smaller side, but they were bigger than my first suite. When I first moved here, I'd been put in a small room in a random part of the citadel that no one ventured to. For some unknown reason, I'd been moved to this suite shortly after. Not that I was complaining. My new suite had been a huge open space, but I quickly remedied that. I didn't need all that empty space. The one place in this whole Powers-forsaken hellhole where I felt at home was just beyond another set of double doors across from my bedroom. I could feel my magic pressing to the surface, urging me forward, calling to me. It wasn't Laeto Selva, but it would have to do since this was my life for the foreseeable future.

My greenhouse.

I took a deep, controlling breath and stepped forward, allowing the gift given to me from the god of earth to take over. I rose and walked to the glass doors, my reflection looking back at me. My elongated High Fae ears pointed through my thick hair. They were adorned with multiple hooped piercings along the lengths. My septum was also pierced. The small, silver ring reflected light from the fireplace. White tribal marks of my family stood out against my bronze skin and dark hair. I was proud of my heritage, and carrying that small part of me across the realm was comforting. I didn't remember receiving my tribal mark tattoos or piercings. It was so long ago. At home, the tribal marks identified royalty and different tribes within our kingdom. Here in Kanevvluk, I was the only one with tribal marks. At first, I got a lot of looks, but now no one noticed. No one really noticed me. Which is how I liked it. The only part of my reflection that I hated was the golden cord of the blood binding mark peeking out from under my long sleeves and wrapping around my hand and down each finger. I closed my eyes and took a deep breath, tapping into my elemental earth power again.

I pushed open the double glass doors, revealing a flagstone walkway and magicked sunlight pouring through the domed glass ceiling. Moisture and heat brushed my skin in greeting like an old friend. My greenhouse was my refuge. This place was my only escape from the sad reality that was my life. When I was here, I didn't think about anything for blissful hour after hour. Vines from the trees above reached down and caressed my arms as I walked down the path. Lush green spanned from the floors to the ceiling. The ceiling above was made of triangles of glass that had been pieced together, forming a dome so that what little sunlight Kanevvluk saw was able to seep into the space. Wild ivy wrapped around marble columns that stretched toward the dull, gray sky above the glass. The trees of my greenhouse were nothing like the lifeless trees in the Winterwoods that surrounded the citadel. Those evergreens were stiff and dark and empty. The deep green needles were sharp enough to slice through skin if you weren't careful. But my trees, my flowers, my plants, they were full of color and passion and life. I took a deep breath as I walked by the small medicinal herbs, smelling peppermint, calendula, and dolor. I'd brought these very herbal plants from the garden outside my old bedroom in my mother city. My father had said that it was silly, childish, but I hadn't cared what he thought.

I dropped to my knees in front of a small flower bed. I pressed my fingertips into the rich topsoil. Delicate green tendrils appeared from my fingers and rooted into the dirt. My power flowed and a miniature rose bush began to sprout. I withdrew my hand and wiped the excess dirt down my thighs, not caring a bit that my pants were now dirty. I closed my eyes and breathed in the earthy air before rising and moving further into the hothouse. A trickle of sweat dripped down between my breasts. It was almost too warm with my regular clothes on. My earth elemental power buzzed and I stretched out a hand to the trunk of a tree closest to me. An orchid appeared—waxy, emerald leaves emerged from the trunk. Two green stems grew from where they joined, and the soft, lilac petals of the flowers appeared. Vibrant color. Elegant beauty. Finally, a little bit of happiness. The tree's trunk pulsed under my palm as each bloom opened. I focused on the thrum of life surrounding me and tried to let everything else evaporate away.

And then the spell was broken.

The gilded swirls embedded into the skin glowed softly, and the subtle taste of salt coated my tongue. My joy slipped as a frown morphed my features. I felt him approach before I heard him. I felt his power through our binding mark. My body was attuned to whenever he was near, and I hated it. A shiver prickled down my spine. I dropped my hand with the binding mark to my side and tucked it within my long sleeve. I closed my eyes, trying to hold onto the last scraps of bliss from my greenhouse deep inside, but it was useless with *him* nearby. He was like a magnet that I was drawn to against my will.

"You went far today." The deep timbre of his voice made me flinch, even though I knew he was standing behind me. It was a voice that commanded attention and exuded power.

"Did you really just flinch?"

I ignored him. Instead, I used my magic to shift the branches behind me to block his view of me without lifting a finger. He didn't scare me; his voice just pissed me off. It grated on my nerves. It irritated me because it was so hypnotic. And he was in my private suite and greenhouse. I didn't like anyone in my space. I knew he had snuck in when I wasn't around. My maid, Corynne, let me know every time he invaded my privacy. He never touched anything. Other than his fresh, clean scent that lingered, I'd never know he was there.

"I could feel you pushing the boundaries of our binding," he said.

"Don't you have somewhere to be? Or something to do?" My words were cold and flat, emotionless.

I heard him push aside the leaves and step inside the greenhouse. Disgust and a feeling of encroachment burned through me.

"It's disturbing that you watch me so closely, you know. Extremely disturbing," I said.

A soft laugh slipped from him. "Oh, does it bother you?"

"Yes, it fucking bothers me," I whispered through clenched teeth. "You are not welcome here," I said, my voice low.

"Katuri..."

I whipped around to face him. "You. Are. Not. Welcome. Here."

My magic rose to the surface of my skin as my temper flared.

Fuck him.

Icy blue eyes the same color as the glaciers locked on mine, and something inside me sang with elated energy just at the sight of him.

Garren Eckhardt.

The male I was bound to. My consort.

My breath hitched and heat flooded my body. His blond hair that was long enough to fall in front of his eyes was pushed back from his forehead. He habitually raked his hands through the golden waves, giving it a freshly tousled look. His lips were in a pout, but there was a hidden grin under his fake hurt. The heady mix of salt and citrus brushed my senses, and I hated how much I loved the way he smelled.

Garren raised his hands in retreat and took backward steps toward the double doors. His matching blood binding mark caught the light with a glint. Once over the threshold, he leaned on the door jamb and crossed his arms over his broad chest. The muscles of his arms pulled at his shirt with the movement. He was dressed more casual than usual today, in a simple tunic and jacket with fitted pants. He still looked better than most males I'd met. It was one of those things that infuriated me. Typically, he was dressed in pompous finery. He always had to look perfect. No one looked perfect all the time ... except Garren. Even dressed down he was ... nothing. He was nothing. If I thought it enough, I'd be able to convince myself it was true.

He reached out to touch a soft blue orchid the same shade as his eyes that had made its home on the wooden frame just beside the door. Damn. I'd have to change its color now.

"Don't."

His hand froze in midair, then dropped to his side. He drew a circle in the air before him and a soft, green leaf appeared in the air. I could feel him pulling threads of my earth power from me like a siphon.

"Stop," I said with gritted teeth.

I hated when he used my magic. It was almost painful when he used my power. Probably because I was fighting against the blood bond. It seemed wrong to share my powers with someone I hated so much. He gave me a wicked grin, then released my earth magic. I took a fresh breath of air. I drew my magic in close to me as if I could hide it from him. I knew I couldn't.

"Father wants you to join us. We have visitors," Garren said.

I exhaled loudly. I knew I was being difficult, but I didn't care. If I refused to come when summoned by the High Ruler, he'd have one of his guards drag me from my suite. I knew. I'd tested the theory when I was younger. That was before I had the full strength of my powers. Now no one dared touch me. Ever. But there were other ways High Ruler Eckhardt could make my life worse than the circle of dark hells.

I glared at Garren for several moments before muttering, "Fine."

His eyes scanned my body, from the modest neckline of my shirt, down to my dirt-smudged pants and my socked feet. Blood roared and my heart pounded in my ears.

"Are you going to change first?" he asked.

"Why would I? They aren't my guests."

He huffed a laugh. His eyes bored into me and I refused to break eye contact first. He smiled at me and flicked his hand in the air. Out of the corner of my eye, a fountain made entirely of ice gurgled and bubbled like a spring in the center of my greenhouse.

I moved past him, being sure to not make contact with his body. Vines from above came down and pushed the greenhouse doors closed behind me. I heard those same vines smash into the fountain—a crack of ice and the gush of water hitting the floor. With my back to Garren, I smirked at the destruction.

I went back to the couch to gather my muddy boots.

"You couldn't even warn me he was here?" I asked the wolf. Her ears flicked when I spoke, but she ignored me. Of course.

I felt the atmosphere shift as Garren came closer to me, like the way the air charged before lightning struck. I stood quickly and moved to put the couch between the two of us.

"I was just trying to help spruce up the place," he said as he took a calculated step around the couch. He studied my reaction.

Too close. He was too close.

I took a step back, stumbling over a raised edge of the stone floor, and bumped into my writing desk next to the window. I dropped my boots as I attempted to catch the papers that were scattering to the floor. I didn't want to turn my back to him, afraid that he'd use the split second to get even closer. Powers, why did I turn into an idiot when we were within ten feet of each other? Why did he make me so nervous? Not nervous, nervous. More excited nervous.

"I don't need your help. I'm perfectly capable of doing things myself." I stuttered as I straightened myself up again.

Why did my voice sound so strained?

"I'm sure you are," he said, raising his eyebrows at me.

My cheeks, all the way to my pointed ears, flared with heat. "That's *not* what I meant, and you know it."

He laughed with a rakish smirk as he took another step closer to me. "Don't tell me you aren't at least curious."

His scent wrapped around me as he closed in. Delicious, masculine scent filled my nose. The scarlet moved down my neck. His eyes traced the color. I felt my breath hitch at his proximity, but I lifted my chin. I left the papers abandoned on the floor and stood. He stepped over the forgotten pile and came closer, trapping me between him and the desk. My hands clutched the edge of the wood like a lifeline.

"You know I can satisfy any curiosity that you have," he said. His chest was a hair's breadth away from mine. If I inhaled, my breasts would brush against him.

"I'm not curious about anything that has to do with you," I said.

He reached up to brush his fingers across my face, but hesitated before he actually touched me. My skin tingled with the phantom touch. An uncomfortable heat shivered through me at his almost contact. Then, without touching me, he pulled a stray leaf from my hair. The leaf made a whisper as he twirled it between us. This was the closest he'd been. He'd never actually touched me. Ever. Not even a handshake. Not since that first day.

The side of his mouth curled up. "Oh, the things I could show you. The things I could do to you, Little Flower."

Lust burned a pathway throughout my entire body, a warning to move away before I did something I knew I'd regret. I refused to bow down to anyone, even to someone I was bound to. I finally snapped out of whatever trance he'd put me under, and I slid out from between him and the desk. I would never ask him for anything, especially *that*. The distance gave me back my composure. I looked over my shoulder to check he wasn't following me again. He was standing exactly in the same place, but my eyes were caught on my desk. The wood I had gripped was covered in new sprouts of exotic flowers.

"Feel free to blow my mind," I snapped as I slid into my boots and moved toward the door, leaving him standing there with a stupid smirk on his face.

EIGHT
GARREN

I pushed off Katuri's writing desk and followed her out into the hallway. It was so easy to rile her up. The longer she refused to give in to me and accept our blood binding, the harder she fought against it, the stronger my desire to consume her got. My stubborn, defiant consort. She'd been that way since day one. I wasn't happy about the prophecy of the two of us being forced to unite our bloodlines, but I knew it wasn't worth fighting the fates. If the gods desired it, it would come to pass. I was honestly surprised she'd held out this long.

I was used to Katuri wandering the woods around the citadel. She did so practically every day. Only heavy snowstorms kept her within the walls of the stone battlement. Today, though, I was sitting in a council meeting with my brother Jace (the firstborn and the favored son) and my father, High Ruler Holden Eckhardt when I felt a sharp jerk from deep within. It actually made me stop breathing for a moment. I stood and walked over to the window, like if I saw the forest, I'd somehow be closer to her. My father's office was in one of the tallest towers in the citadel and looked out over Kanevvluk. Most of our territory was covered in dense evergreen forests, the Winterwoods, but from this height, I could see open spots where other cities dwelt far off in the distance. Snowhaven Territory was brutal, and most of the cities were located here on the eastern coast. The expanse between the coasts was open snow and ice and mountains. There were remote villages deep within the frigid range though. I'd visited them several times when my father had dragged me out for political reasons. Although my father was a pain in my ass and thought very little of me, he was a good leader. He took care of his people and the various tribes and creatures that inhabited our territory.

The citadel was located in the middle of the city, and, like spokes of a wheel, there were four main streets leading to four outer gates. Each gate represented one of the gods and had intricate carvings dating back to the birth of the city. I stood and faced the east, looking out over the dense evergreen forest. She was out there. I knew she felt the sharp pull too, because what felt like an eternity of tightly stretched connection between us tugged. Then the nagging pull eased. She was coming back. I worried she'd rip my binding mark from my body and make an escape one of these days. I wasn't sure why, but the last few months or so, I'd been drawn to her. It was like my body craved her presence. I was finding it hard to focus on other things.

Luckily, the meeting I'd been ignoring had wrapped up. I slipped from the room. My brother looked up as I left, but our father didn't notice. I doubt he'd even notice if I was at the meetings or not. So I went in search of her. There were only a handful of places she'd be inside the citadel. I'd gotten lucky with my first guess ... her greenhouse.

Katuri Harland was exquisite, standing in the soft light filtering in from above. The deep hues of the greenery surrounding her made her stand out even more. Her dark, windswept hair was streaked with red tones and hung freely landing halfway down her back. Her lean, muscular figure was shown off in the pants she wore instead of her regular dresses. Father preferred her to dress like the princess she was, but when she was traipsing through the forest or spending time in her greenhouse, she always wore pants.

I trailed Katuri, who was several paces ahead of me, toward the greeting hall. Her hips swayed back and forth with each step. The russet wolf trotted alongside her. It had ignored me when I let myself into her suite earlier, and it ignored me now. Her name was Eleni. I had no idea where Katuri got a wolf, but she'd appeared one day and had been here ever since. Kanevvluk had wolves, but none as unique as Eleni. Her coloring didn't match any of the native wolves and she had unique white markings on her face and chest. She also didn't behave like any wolf I'd encountered. It was like she listened in on every conversation and knew exactly what was being said.

Katuri shot me a glare over her shoulder as we walked down the corridor. She knew I was watching her. I smiled sweetly at her, and her bristled glare turned into a scowl. Every line in her face filled with distaste, making the white tribal mark crinkle across the bridge of her nose and between her brows. The white line tattooed down her forehead and down the center of her bottom lip, along with the two parallel lines across the bridge of her nose marked her as Forest Fae royalty. The thin ring of twisted silver in her septum that glinted in the light … I internally groaned. I loved that little ring. It was fucking hot as hell. Her eyes were fierce in their fury—shades of dark green around her pupils, with bursts of light green and silvers radiating out creating a kaleidoscope effect. I'd never seen anyone as captivating as her.

So. Fucking. Gorgeous. Even when she was so angry with me. Which was all the time. I was truly thankful for her beauty since we were forced together by the fates. I couldn't help pushing her boundaries. I blamed it on our binding, but truly, I just liked picking on her because it was the only time she'd talk to me. If she had it her way, she'd live her entire life in her greenhouse and the woods and never speak to me again. But I couldn't allow that now, could I?

Katuri kept her pace brisk to keep a healthy distance ahead of me. We went through the doors of the back entrance to the greeting chamber. We didn't have visitors often. My brother, Jace, and Father were facing away from us. I could hear my father's gruff voice echoing off the marble walls and floors. The room was the first thing you saw when you entered the citadel, and it was ostentatious as hell, but the Snowhaven Fae always put their best foot forward. The white marble floor was so polished that your reflection shined back at you. The Eckhardt Family crest was imprinted into the stone in the dead center of the room—a bear with his maw opened wide with a spear and sword crossed behind it. The walls were bright with gray and navy accents along the massive windows that looked toward the frosted city.

Both Father and Jace wore the Snowhaven Legion gray mantel draped across their shoulders, but there were no weapons to be seen, which meant this was a friendly visit. Father sounded … happy. That was weird. I couldn't remember a time I'd heard him happy that didn't include my mother or my brother achieving something.

Katuri stopped several feet from them and clasped her hands behind her back and lifted her chin. Eleni sat next to her, head raised and chest out. Katuri might appear as a proper princess with all her manners, but I knew she had her rebellious streak. She never let her guard down around anyone in the citadel. The only time I'd seen her relaxed was in her private suite, tucked away by herself. And since I wasn't welcomed there, it was rare to see her without her stoic mask. My father looked over his shoulder, letting his eyes scroll her attire. He stopped at the wolf sitting at her muddy feet, and the canine curled its lips over deadly rows of teeth. Father scowled at Katuri's appearance but didn't say anything. He wasn't willing to start a fight in front of guests. It was a constant battle between them. His son's consort—even his lesser son's—was expected to present herself a certain way. Katuri did everything she could to maintain a semblance of control in her life, including dressing in her own attire rather than what was selected for her.

As I came up to my brother's side, and dragged my attention away from Katuri's pert backside, my mouth dropped open in shock.

"Delrik?" I couldn't believe what I was seeing. My closest friend was standing before me. "The Master of Death and Darkness himself." I squinted like I was examining his full beard. "You get uglier every time I see you. And maybe a touch gray?"

"That's the nicest thing you've ever said to me," Delrik crooned as he stroked his jaw. "You know you're older than me, right?"

In three strides, I crossed the space, and I reached toward the grumpy Fae male to wrap him in a tight hug, but before I got to him, I spotted his sister, Nazneen, over his shoulder. She didn't bother hiding her laughter when I shoved Delrik out of the way and scooped her up in my arms. I clung tightly to her and swung her in a circle.

"And his much smarter, much more beautiful better half," I said.

The siblings had fought alongside me during the war, and we'd been inseparable ever since. Well, as inseparable we could get with hundreds of miles between our homes.

"Nice to see you, too," Delrik said in a flat tone.

I set Nazneen back down on her feet. I pushed back from her and held her by her shoulders. Nazneen was as beautiful as ever. She was wrapped in layers of thick furs, and her cloak's hood draped across her shoulders. Her angelic face was curious about her surroundings, and she scanned the area like she was trained to observe her environment. Her brilliant jade eyes and pink cheeks glowed. Her dark auburn hair brushed the tops of her shoulders, and her pointed ears were dotted with earrings that ran up the arches. She had on well-worn leather boots and held herself in a way of importance as she always did. Her Arcelia Legion tattoo stood out on the side of her neck. The female before me was no ordinary female and had become well-known and respected during the war.

"Well, I don't know if I can be considered his better half anymore," Nazneen said.

That's when I noticed the silver-haired High Fae beside her. I turned to greet the new guest. She had an apprehensive look to her, like I was about to eat her. She was soft and bright. Her violet stare bounced around, taking in the room. I gave her a slight bow in greeting. There was something about her though, something different. She had a hand resting at the base of her throat, and a ruby ring glinted in the light. The reflection drew my attention to the piece of jewelry. A small thrum of magic reached out to me, and my elemental water responded with its own hum. I tipped my head to the side and took a step closer to her. She retreated back a step, and her startled wide eyes shot to Delrik in question. Interesting.

"And who might you be?" I asked the silver beauty.

I advanced another step, and she fell back another step. The teardrop stone on her finger pulsed with light, stopping me in my tracks. It was almost ... mesmerizing in its beauty. Was that what I was sensing about her? It beckoned me like it wanted me to show my power.

"Garren," Delrik said in warning. A low growl emanated from him.

A sharp screech caught my attention. A small, round bird untucked itself from the hood of the silver one's cloak and waddled down her shoulder. It puffed up at my approach. It had the eyes of a vicious predator despite its size. It couldn't have been larger than a merlin falcon. The light in the room seemed to darken like a cloud was passing over the sun, but I didn't take my eyes off the female in front of me.

"I wouldn't get any closer if I were you." Nazneen chuckled.

"You can sense her, can't you?" Delrik asked through gritted teeth. He sounded like he was restraining himself, holding himself back for some reason. Clearly, she was important to Delrik. Tension wafted off him in pulsing waves, and he physically trembled with the effort.

"I can sense her from all the way over here," Katuri said, stepping up to stand next to my brother. I hadn't been expecting her to speak. The soft lilt of her voice stopped me in my tracks and drew all my attention to her. "You're a fire elemental."

The female's eyes turned cautious. She skirted around me to tuck herself beside Delrik. He placed a possessive hand on the small of her back. His shoulders loosened with her in easy reach. Her hand with the ring slipped beneath the edge of his cloak on his chest. The moment it was out of my line of sight, the buzz of energy I'd been feeling disappeared. So it hadn't been her elemental power drawing me to her.

"Evren, this is Garren Eckhardt. Garren, this is my bondmate and consort, Evren." Delrik motioned between the two of us.

"How in the circle of dark hells did you find yourself attached to this monster?" I asked her with a laugh. I jabbed my thumb in Delrik's direction.

Nazneen punched me in the shoulder. "Don't be an ass."

She walked to Jace and wrapped him in a bear hug. We hadn't seen each other since the war ended. We'd grown close during that time. It was a true friendship. War had a way of bringing out the best and worst in people. And these were my people. My family. I wasn't complaining about the reunion, but I wondered what had brought them all this way north. Delrik had been here on occasion, but I hadn't seen Nazneen since returning home after the war.

Nazneen turned to my father. "High Ruler Eckhardt," she said and bowed. He nodded his head in response. He wouldn't bow to Nazneen even though she was the heir to Arcelia. Father turned to my brother to discuss something most likely unimportant. He just wanted an excuse to not converse with Nazneen. For someone who demanded proper etiquette, he was sorely lacking.

A voice from the shadows interrupted our reunion. "Aww, such a warm, friendly greeting amongst friends."

A male was leaning against the wall, lurking. His eyes were focused entirely on Nazneen. I rolled my eyes at my cousin. Arik Hanover. Dark gray eyes and jet black hair, he had the stealth of an arctic fox. Speaking of bringing out the worst ... Arik had an annoying habit of entering a room completely unnoticed, most often when he wasn't even wanted. If I didn't know better, I'd have believed the rumors about him being a spy.

"Why are you here?" I didn't bother turning when I addressed him. He wasn't worth the time. We may be on level terms at the moment, but I didn't like the way he was staring at Nazneen. He looked like he was fucking in love and wanted to devour her whole. Gross.

Arik pushed off the wall and came toward us. "I was the one that greeted them at the docks."

Delrik let out an unimpressed huff. Arik had never met Nazneen before. During the war, her battalion was focused on the western front while Delrik, Arik, and I were positioned along the southern border of the Raven Fae territory. By the time the two battalions had linked up, Arik was on a ship home. She was one of the most decorated commanders in the Arcelia Legion and a skilled spy, and yet my father preferred to lessen his defenses by sending her somewhere she wasn't needed.

"I just happened to be doing my weekly check in with the commander of the fleet."

While he didn't hold an honored, high-ranking role in the Snowhaven Legion like my brother and myself, he took a special interest in the fleet. It was the one branch of the legion neither Jace or I cared to join. Back before the war, when he was new to Kanevvluk, he'd once told me that he loved the open sea. I'd had the strong suspicion, based on what my father had told me about his upbringing, that it was the comfort of having an escape route that truly drew him to the sea. Father had appreciated that he'd volunteered, and I did as well. I preferred to swim, not be stuck aboard a smelly ship.

Nazneen shot me and Delrik a withering glare. "That was rude. I'm sorry for my brother and Garren's manners." Nazneen pulled off her leather glove and reached out a demure hand to Arik. "I'm Nazneen Zathrian of Arcelia." Her voice was sweet as honey.

Arik took a step closer. "Welcome to Kanevvluk."

Pink dusted high on her cheeks. "Thank you."

He took another step closer, bowed low, and took her hand in his. He brushed his lips across her knuckles. Her brows rose a touch, but then the mask of politeness slipped back into place. Uh oh. I knew that look. If I didn't keep these two apart, we were up for some interesting stories.

"And now that I've delivered you into the capable hands of my cousin, I'll depart. It was lovely meeting you. I'm sure I'll be seeing you around."

"Doubtful." Delrik's voice was somber and unbending.

Without addressing anyone else, Arik slipped from the room.

NINE
KATURI

The new male seemed to really like Garren. How could anyone enjoy his company that much? Delrik seemed more fond of Garren than his own brother Jace did. They'd embraced like two long lost brothers. That was after Garren had gotten all his flirting out of the way. He was always flirting—with the maids or visiting families or various females who came for dinner. And all that flirting led to other things. I could only guess how he acted when he was out and about in the city. Not that I was jealous. I didn't care who he flirted with as long as he left me alone.

Delrik was very handsome in that dangerous sort of way you read about in epic hero romance novels. His dark eyes were almost black. He was thick and built like a warrior, which he clearly was based on the legion tattoo on his neck. Garren wasn't a small male either. He was only an inch or so shorter than Delrik and just as built. The pair painted a fearsome picture, even with smiles across their faces. With Delrik's hair swept back into a knot at the top of his head, the vicious scar that stretched across his eye and cheek was on full display. Seeing a Fae with a scar wasn't a common occurrence, between our powers of healing and skilled healers. But when he had looked at his bondmate, the corners of his eyes wrinkled with smile lines and I could see a gentleness there. The female saw him as a protector and watched him with adoration. He couldn't be that bad if he'd taken on a fire elemental as his bondmate and consort and she hadn't burned him alive yet. My eyes scanned Garren again as he watched his friend's happiness. Heat flooded back up my neck.

"Katuri." High Ruler Eckhardt snapped his fingers over his shoulder, completely unaware that I was no longer standing behind him, but rather beside Jace. I rolled my eyes, but turned in response to the rude summons. "Take our new guests to their rooms while we discuss business."

I bit my tongue to cut off the sharp retort that threatened to slip out. I was not a servant and hated being treated like one. Even if the help was treated fairly in Kanevvluk, Higher Ruler Echkardt always spoke with a brash tone. I would've put up more of a fight, but he treated everyone like that, even his own sons. I would rather have the excuse to leave than dig in my heels this time.

The fire elemental looked to her bondmate. He offered her a warm smile and pressed his lips to her forehead. I turned away from their show of affection and made my exit. They weren't being obscene with their affection; I just didn't like being reminded of the intimate ins and outs of bondmates, something I'd never have. I'd resigned myself to being alone the rest of my life a long time ago.

I waited in the corridor for the females to join me. Evren and Nazneen followed behind me shortly. As we made our way to the guest suites in the residential wing of the citadel, I pointed out various rooms and directions to fill the silence. Eleni walked obediently alongside us like she hadn't just let Garren sneak into my suite and ambush me. She was useless when it came to Garren. While she didn't like him close to her, she didn't mind him invading *my* personal space. She bumped her nose against my hand once we'd cleared the greeting hall. An apology? She was lucky she was cute.

"Are you an elemental, too?" Nazneen asked.

She leaned down mid-stride and scratched Eleni's head. To my amazement, she came back with all her fingers intact. Eleni, like me, wasn't a huge fan of strangers or being touched. I twisted my hand in an upward motion, and the dirt from the pot down the hall arrived in my palm in a swirling ball.

"Earth elemental," I answered.

The dirt compacted into a tight ball, and roots grew and entangled themselves around the sphere. Tiny green leaves and tropical flowers sprouted. The ball landed in my upturned palm. I tossed it up into the air once before I rolled it down the hall. Eleni chased after it in graceful leaps before pouncing on it. When her front paws hit it, the ball disappeared into a puff of color. I didn't typically show off my earth power. I didn't like anyone knowing too much about how my elemental power worked. Very few saw me use it. Garren, unfortunately, knew some of its extent with his constant intrusion into my greenhouse. He'd seen the lush trees and flowers I'd created. He also had access to my power through the blood binding. While I refused to give up full control over it, he was able to sample small pieces of it. My power was one of the last remaining things I had control over, and it wouldn't be only mine forever. I couldn't hold him off indefinitely. I had a good feeling about these two females though, so I didn't mind offering them a small gesture of kindness.

Evren raised her eyebrows in surprise. "I can barely control my powers."

"Evren only came into her power last year. It was quite a shock for all of us," Nazneen explained as she looped her arm with Evren's. Nazneen wasn't being unkind. I could see the affection between them. She turned her head to Evren. "You've improved so much in six months. Imagine how powerful you'll be with just a little practice."

"How does Garren know you and your brother?" I asked, changing subjects.

"We all fought together in the war," Nazneen replied. "Although the male that met us at the docks, Arik, I've never seen him before."

I nodded in response. I hadn't been allowed to fight in the war. Mother and Father thought it was dangerous to put an elemental in such danger when I hadn't had a chance to fully train my powers and procreate. I thought they just wanted me bound to a powerful High Fae bloodlines to have an alliance if the war went poorly. Politics always came first with them. Politics and their bloodline.

TEN
GARREN

We received a full update on the southern half of the realm, thanks to Delrik. Father had us move to the council room so we could sit and have a more formal discussion regarding the River Kingdom, the Wildlands, and Hadeon Allerick's desire to create and store iron weapons. It always annoyed Delrik that Father never would include Nazneen in these conversations, sending her away before they could have real conversations. He'd done it during the war, and he clearly hadn't changed his views since then. Looking over the table at Delrik, I could see him reaching his boiling point. He was such a hot head. Which made it all the more fun to poke the bear.

After the war, Father isolated the Snowhaven Fae from the rest of Illoterra. He sensed the unrest with High Ruler Byrnes. Father had fought alongside the Black Guard, the River Kingdoms armies, but that hadn't meant he agreed with Cadoc Byrnes's thoughts on ruling his kingdom and the treatment of lower beings. Aramis Zathrian was the only other High Ruler he kept in contact with. Tensions between the southlands and the north may be eased soon with Adaris Byrnes now controlling the River Kingdom. He wanted to soothe the connections between Snowhaven and the River Kingdom, as well as stop the conflicts in the Wildlands.

As far as the Western Continent, also known as Quinterre for the ones that lived there, from what Adaris could tell from Cadoc's notes, most of the continent was on edge and preparing for another war. The last thing we needed was for the conflict to make it across the Ocean of Warwell and onto our shores. We'd managed to keep the last war away from our home, but just barely. Delrik also informed us of how Cadoc wanted to harness Evren's elemental power and was unsure of the reason. They believed it had something to do with the item they were searching for. Delrik was leaving something out, though. I could tell. He'd shifted the conversation from him and his bondmate as quickly as possible.

"Father, we should send scouts to the Western Continent," I said.

Father ignored me. Not even a brush off, but a blatant rejection.

Delrik spoke up through gritted teeth. "I agree with Garren. We need to send scouts to see the extent of Hadeon's reach. Once they return, we can move forward."

Silence. Father was flipping through papers of correspondence. Jace looked between Father and me. He shrugged his shoulders and was about to speak up in my defense, but I slammed my fist against the table before he could open his mouth.

"High Ruler Eckhardt." My commanding voice echoed off the walls.

My father looked up, a picture of calm and reserve. "There is no need for a tantrum, Garren."

I saw red. We all knew my brother Jace was the favorite son. Father had even said it to my face on multiple occasions, but treating me like that in front of guests, even if it was just Delrik, was inexcusable. Father was jealous of me. He'd had the perfect family until I came along. Jace was already grown and trained to take over as High Ruler of the Snowhaven Fae. And then my mother got pregnant with me. Siblings weren't unheard of for the High Fae. Females could only become pregnant every few years because of our long life spans. And after one child, it became even more difficult to fall pregnant. I didn't remember the specifics of that particular lesson during biology lessons. Needless to say, a second pregnancy was unexpected. And what was more upsetting was for the second born son to have elemental powers. My powers developed at a very young age. Father had worked so hard to mold Jace into the heir he wanted and then I showed up stronger than the two of them combined. Then I went and knocked Father on his ass by accident. I had been only nine and I was mad about it. I didn't even remember now. He yelled at me, and I kind of exploded a violent stream of water at him, knocking him to the ground. He had treated me as a threat ever since with shunning and a cold shoulder. I rebelled against the cold shoulder. I went above and beyond to prove his disappointment by acting out. I slacked off in school. I found all the trouble I could until around the age of thirty when I gave up and accepted my role as "second best."

Delrik's hands fisted on the table as if he was about to lose control. A darkness was cast on his face that I hadn't noticed before. Jace stepped in to prevent the discussion from coming to physical blows. Father had always dismissed my suggestions in council meetings or anything pertaining to how he should run the kingdom. This wasn't a new development. I didn't know why this specifically mattered to me all of a sudden. I just had a gut feeling.

Father waved his hand in the air. "Fine. Scouts will be sent to Quinterre. Jace, have it arranged."

Father took his leave without saying anything more.

"I'll talk to him," Jace offered once Father was out of earshot.

"Don't bother. He won't take me seriously. It isn't worth the time."

Jace studied me but knew me well enough to let it go. I had nothing against my older brother. He would make a wonderful High Ruler when he got his chance, but I was seen as second best to him. Nothing I did was good enough for Father. So what was the point of trying? When you hear your father repeatedly tell you you'll never meet his expectations, never amount to anything, you begin to believe it.

"The elemental power was wasted on you."

Thankfully, Jace never treated me the way our father did. Even with the age gap, we became close friends.

"You are all welcome to stay in Kanevvluk. Once the scouts return with intel from the west, we can decide where to go from there. Maybe being around other elementals will help Evren learn to control her powers better," my brother said.

"She isn't the only one who needs practice with new powers." I nodded my head in Delrik's direction. "You have something to tell us?"

Delrik sat up a little straighter and pulled his hands down into his lap. "It's a long story. Everything is under control."

"Mm hm." I eyed him wearily. Delrik was always one to keep to himself, but I was too curious to give in that easily. I'd have to wait until we were alone to nag him more about it. A side effect from being on his own for so long as a child and having to rely on only himself. He'd been orphaned as a child when his parents were killed by none other than Cadoc Byrnes for producing a non-full blood High Fae. Delrik's mother was High Fae but his father was half human-half Fae.

After Delrik and Jace got caught up on each other's lives, I led Delrik from the council hall and toward the wing of the citadel where all the guests' suites were. We walked in silence for a bit.

"So ... everything is under control?"

Delrik side-eyed me.

"Bullshit."

Delrik grumbled something unintelligible under his breath. Then he said, "The power is new."

"Obviously."

"Evren took them. The power. It's some kind of dark shadow magic. It's kind of hard to explain. And after the blood binding, we transferred the power to me." He lifted his shirt to expose his stomach where a mass of swirling ink was coiled around him. At least I thought it was ink until it slithered up his chest like a snake under his shirt and then reappeared around his neck.

"Interesting."

"We don't know exactly what they can do other than what I experienced when they were used against me," Delrik said.

"Okay, back up. How did you get these shadows again?"

He proceeded to share the entire story of Alux's curse, Evren stealing the powers and being stuck with them, and the transfer of them to him through the binding mark once they'd become consorts.

"That's where the ring came from. I bet that's why I felt drawn to it. It wanted my magic."

"Probably." Delrik shrugged. "I wouldn't worry about it. It's stuck on her finger, and she won't steal your magic."

I knew I was joking before, but the nickname Master of Death and Darkness truly did fit him now. It wasn't a nickname he had given himself, but rather one that was given to him. His particular gift of speed had been invaluable during night raids. Delrik was so fast he could sneak into a camp in the dead of night and slaughter everyone without a sound. When the sun rose, only death remained.

"There's something else." He paused before continuing. "There has been a strange otherness, something oppressive hanging over me since boarding the ship to come here. I can't tell what it is, but I have a feeling it isn't anything good."

"Do you think it's the shadow magic?" I asked.

"I don't know what to think," he said. I could hear the concern in his voice.

We turned a corner to go down another corridor. "What does your bondmate say?"

"I haven't said anything to her yet." He looked down at his feet. "I don't want her to worry."

"She held the magic, right? She knows its strength. I say it's worth asking her."

I was quiet, not sure what else to say. I knew Delrik had battled his own demons in his younger years; and then he'd seen all the death during the war. He was definitely different with Evren as his bondmate. I'd only been in her presence for a few minutes, but I could see that Delrik seemed lighter, happier. But I could see the otherness he was talking about. There was indeed something a little darker about his countenance. I couldn't explain it, but I could feel it.

"I'm surprised to see Arik still lurking around," Delrik said. "Especially after what happened in Glissden."

I rubbed the stubble that had grown throughout the day. "Yeah, Father wasn't happy that Mother wanted him to stay. If he'd had his way, he'd send Arik back to Quinterre, but Mother insisted on giving him another chance."

"He didn't offer those people a second chance."

What was supposed to be a quick in and out, capture the person of interest and leave, ended up being a full blown and bloody battle. Glissden was a small village in the Taskun Territory. One of the male leaders of the village was found passing on our location and movements of our western company. He even knew about our battalion we'd planned to send to Menrath. We needed to dispose of him before any more information was leaked. When our squad showed up, the coward ran. Delrik was faster and the male was brought down before he could take three steps. The others in the village didn't trust us and fought back. They hadn't realized they had a traitor in their midst. There was so much blood. So much screaming. And Arik snapped. He lost it. Even after we'd subdued the villagers and the fighting was over, Airk kept killing. Dismembered the bodies. Burned the huts. Younglings were screaming in fear. Many were running into the desert to get away. It took both Delrik and me to pull Arik back. He'd fought us with everything he had until we'd knocked him out cold. I'd felt bad for knocking him out, but Arik was in a haze of compulsive rage; it was the only thing I could think to do. Father had sent him back to Kanevvluk, and that was that. Until I returned home and found Arik at our dinner table.

"Arik's kept out of everyone's way. Stayed quiet and helped around the city." I shrugged. "I guess I've just gotten used to him being in the background."

Delrik didn't look happy about it, though. As someone who'd lost his entire family, I understood why. His parents had been unjustly murdered. While some of the people in Glissden weren't innocent, the deaths were unnecessary.

"So what did you do to piss off the grumpy female?" he asked, changing the subject.

I barked out a laugh. "That, my friend, is my bonded, Princess Katuri Harland of Laeto Selva." I lifted my right hand and wiggled my fingers at him to show off the binding mark.

"The Forest Fae from the Western Continent?" I nodded in confirmation. "Since when do you have a consort? You never mentioned her before. And aren't you supposed to at least *like* each other?"

"She arrived before we left for the Quinterre. And apparently liking your consort isn't a requirement."

Delrik stopped walking and grabbed my arm. "And I'm just now hearing about this?"

I looked down at the hand he had on my arm. The gold winked in the lights that lined the corridor. "Father forced me to keep it a secret."

"Have you tested each other's powers yet?"

"She's refused. She won't let me get within five feet of her." At least not until recently. I smirked to myself. "Father didn't want anyone to know about the alliance between our kingdoms during the war. So I had it glamored. If you ask her, she's being held against her will."

"Against her will?" he asked, cocking a brow.

"Yes. She is from one of the few remaining High Fae families on Quinterre. Their bloodline has records going back to when the gods gifted the High Fae with their magic. Her family's royal seer foresaw our bloodlines being united soon after she was born. She was promised to me within weeks of her birth. Father didn't object to the union. It was too good an opportunity to pass on having connections on Quinterre. Her parents shipped her here when her powers began to develop and forced the blood binding on her."

40 years ago

I was slouched in my seat in the throne room, bored out of my mind. I'd been sitting here for over an hour, waiting for the princess to arrive.

"Sit up straight," my mother hissed under her breath.

I rolled my eyes, but straightened a little. She'd pinched me into the most uncomfortable tunic and overcoat possible. Apparently, my normal clothes weren't fine enough to greet the female I'd be bonded to.

Fourteen years ago, Father received a letter from the King of Laeto Selva of the Forest Fae, an old city deep in the lush rainforests of Quinterre. Quinterre. I needed to remember that name. My tutors had always referred to it as the Western Continent. The royal seer to the Forest Fae saw that their daughter was to be the consort to the youngest Eckhardt son.

Me.

After months and many hours confirming the vision with the Snowhaven seers, it was determined the King was correct, and plans were set in place to bring the princess to Kanevvluk once her powers began to develop, much to my father's dismay. He would've preferred the princess to be consort to the heir of the Snowhaven Fae, but nope, the unlucky girl got me instead. Maybe I'd be the lucky one and be able to use her to escape Kanevvluk and the scrutiny of my father's watchful, yet ashamed, eyes.

I was about to stand to leave when the doors burst open and four sentinels in burnished bronze surrounding two figures walked up to the throne. A short female bowed her head low. I didn't recognize the kind of creature she was, but I knew she wasn't Fae or human. Her soft pink skin and brightly streaked hair gave her away. A taller figure, yet clearly one of a young female, stood beside her. Her whole body was hidden beneath the heavy folds of a travel cloak. Her hood shadowed her downcast face. Her shoulders were damp from melted snow, and mud lined the cloak's hem. She didn't look like a princess to me.

One of the sentinels stepped forward and handed Father a rolled parchment. "May I present to you the Princess Katuri Harland of Laeto Selva of the Forest Fae."

The princess didn't budge to remove her hood. She stood still as an ice statue.

The sentinel snapped at her in a harsh foreign language, making her jump. Her gloved hands darted up and quickly dropped her hood. I bristled at his harsh tone, but I couldn't drag my eyes from her. Her sudden movement stirred the air, and her scent crashed into me with the force of hurricane winds of the Boreas Sea. There was something about her. Her dark hair was smoothed back away from her face which still was looking at the floor. The princess was young. Much younger than my 100 years. This couldn't be right. I knew age didn't truly matter among the High Fae, but she was a child. Our fathers couldn't expect us to go through with this. Not until she was older. Great. Now I'd be stuck babysitting for the next twenty or so years.

Father, who'd been ignoring both his consort and me up to this point, stood and walked toward the princess. He lifted her chin in a jerky movement. I wanted to spring from my chair and shove him to the floor for using anything except the gentlest touch with her. He towered over her petite form. When she finally pulled her eyes from her feet, I expected to see a timid, soft girl. Instead, anger and defiance stormed in her emerald eyes. She stared right back at my father and didn't waver. I quirked a smile. She may give my father a run for his money with that attitude.

"Your father has sent you to me under the conditions of you becoming my son's consort. You are now under the protection of the Snowhaven Fae."

He released her chin and stepped back. She pulled her head away but didn't break eye contact. She was headstrong for sure.

"Garren." Father reached out toward me and snapped his fingers to get my attention. I rolled my eyes behind his back. "She is your responsibility now."

Then he stomped from the throne room, followed by the four sentinels. My mother scampered after him. The heavy door slammed, and the small female creature beside the princess startled. Now it was just the three of us alone in the throne room. I stood and smoothed my hands down my coat. I drew in a deep breath and then released my frustration with the exhale. I might as well pretend to make the best out of the situation we found ourselves in. There was still time to find my way out of this predicament. Hells, maybe we'd become friends in a few years when she was older and cause mischief together. That was wishful thinking. When she was older, we could complete the ritual. I had time. I stepped down from the raised platform where my family's thrones sat.

I gave Princess Katuri a bow in greeting. "Welcome to Kanevvluk. I know the circumstances are ... odd, but I hope you will like it here."

Did that sound genuine? I wasn't sure because the white tattooed tribal marks on her face were pinched between her brows when she scowled at me. I opened my mouth to continue when she interrupted me.

"I will never be yours."

Um. Excuse me.

"I will never do the blood binding. I will never be your consort. And you will never touch my power."

Then the vicious creature turned her back to me and walked away. The pink-skinned female dipped in a small curtsy before taking off after the princess.

Alright then. That hadn't gone well. Who did she think she was? Did she think I wanted this? I wanted to be bound to a mere child? I scoffed at her obstinance and stormed from the throne room.

Little did I know that the arrangements for the blood binding ritual had already taken place. That night, before dinner, Mother had dragged me to the temple. Katuri was already standing before the priestess inside a circle that'd been drawn on the floor with red, shimmering powder. An older male stood just outside the circle and had a hand on her thin shoulder. Father stood to the male's left. The princess wore a plain gray dress with panels that wrapped up her body and around her neck and down her back, exposing her thin frame and delicate arms. Her hair was twisted into an intricate braid. Perched on the top of her head was an elegant crown made with gems not native to our lands.

When Father saw me approach, he introduced me. "King Harland, this is my son, Garren Eckhardt."

The king glanced at me briefly before turning his attention back to his daughter. He was tall, standing several inches taller than my father. He had dark skin and dark eyes. Jet black hair was elaborately twisted and braided down the center of his head and was closely shaved on the sides. White tribal marks spread across his cheeks and forehead, similar, I noticed, to the ones the princess carried. Though his were bold and looked more like war paint than anything.

My father gestured for me to join Katuri inside the circle.

"I didn't realize—" I began.

My father cut me off. "We are doing this now. There is no need to waste time."

"Father," I whispered, hoping to not insult the Forest Fae king. "She's just a child."

He couldn't really expect me to bind myself to a child. He didn't respond, but grabbed my shoulder and pulled me forward. It was useless fighting against him. I'd heard what the seers had seen. I'd read the letters from the king. The princess and I were to be bonded, merging our bloodlines, and nothing would change that. Anger rose inside me that I was being forced into this now. I wanted to push back, like I did with every other part of my life, but I didn't. I would use this to my advantage one day. I just needed to bide my time. I'd make my father regret this day.

Katuri didn't seem to be putting up a fight despite what she'd said to me in the throne room. When I stepped into the circle, out of the corner of my eye, I saw Katuri jerk forward like she was trying to move away from me. Her father's hand tightened on her shoulder. I eyed them with suspicion. Whatever. I didn't need to concern myself with whatever family drama they had going on.

The priestess hurriedly proceeded with the ritual in the ancient language of the High Fae. "The threads of the fates have drawn you both together, across time and across space." Her words were rushed.

King Harland handed a small throwing knife to the priestess. It was no longer than my hand, with a thin bronze blade and rounded handle. At the sight of the knife, Katuri jerked again, this time clearly away from her father. That harsh foreign language punctuated with a sneer had me stiffen in anger. It reminded me of the way my father spoke to me when I was that age. I pushed the memories aside and focused back on the priestess. Hopefully, this wouldn't take too long.

I rolled my eyes. Was she afraid of the blade? Of a little blood? If my bonded was easy to scare, that would make our lives interesting. I didn't want to be bound to a coward.

"Your hand?" the priestess asked. Katuri didn't move. She stood frozen. The priestess shifted nervously on her feet. "Princess. Your hand, please."

Her hand rose slowly in front of her, but she was trembling—like she was fighting against an unseen force. I looked at her father. His face was blank with focus. Was he ... forcing her?

I opened my mouth to ask, but my father's hand made contact with the back of my head. "It's not your concern."

The priestess took Katuri's hand and drew the blade across her palm. Blood welled from the shallow slice. Katuri's whole body was shaking now, and silent tears poured down her cheeks. Then the priestess gestured for my hand. I looked at the female beside me. My future. Something was off about all this, but I had an urge deep within me telling me to protect her. And I couldn't do that if she left Kanevvluk, if she went home with her father. So I lifted my hand to the priestess, where she inflicted the same wound. She pressed our palms together, mixing our blood. The princess' hand was so small in mine. So fragile. When our blood touched, my body buzzed with recognition. The taste of earth and smell of roses overtook my senses for a brief moment.

"May your blood become one, tying your lives together."

I tuned out the rest of the priestess' rambling as she wrapped a gilded cord around our bloodied, joined hands. Dark scarlet seeped from between our fingers and dripped onto the stone floor of the temple. I couldn't take my eyes off Katuri. The cord heated against my skin and embedded itself into my flesh, forming the blood binding mark. I could feel the sadness and betrayal and pain Katuri felt through our new bond. Her father was indeed using compulsion to force the blood binding on her.

"Di-gara neve roth var. Consors par rikni. Kaj-far ato un isla. Your lives are bound as one. Bound to each other and bound to the gods. A bond not even broken by death. Consorts. The everlasting vow."

We were bound now. Bound forever.

The moment the priestess uttered those final words, the king of the Forest Fae released his daughter from his grip and she caved in on herself. Her knees cracked on the stone floor and her shoulders slumped over. Our joined blood soaked into the gray fabric of her dress and spread upward in bloody trails. I didn't release her hand as she went down, and she didn't pull away. She was crying freely now. Her body shook with sobs.

"What did you do to her?" I asked King Harland angrily. I wasn't sure where this anger was coming from, but it was rare and heavy.

"It doesn't matter now. What's done is done." He bowed to my father and left the temple.

Katuri and my fingers were smeared with our combined blood and dripped down her arm, leaving stains like tears on the temple floor.

Present Day

I guided Delrik down a long corridor past the family suites to the guest ones. "She was fourteen when she arrived. She had been forced into the blood binding. Her father had used compulsion on her to comply with his wishes. It was sickening. And no, my father isn't happy we haven't fully exchanged powers yet."

"Wow. Fourteen. Her parents couldn't have loved her too much if they sent her to this frozen hell and gave her to you."

"Nope." I popped the p. "Even though we are indeed consorts as foreseen, she was basically a pawn in their political scheme. The war started the year she turned twenty-five. We never went through with exchanging powers completely. I can tap into the barest amount, and I've tried pushing mine to her, just for kicks and giggles, but she rejects it. Since I returned home from the war, she's refused to even be in the same room as me except when forced. I've held Father off for years about using each other's powers, but he's finally given us a deadline. She has until the end of next summer to comply or he has threatened to force it on the both of us."

I wasn't sure how Father planned to force Katuri to share her power with me, but I didn't put it past him to try. I was an ass, but even I wouldn't force her into something so intimate as sharing her power if she didn't want to.

"Damn. And here I thought you were never turned down by females."

All the jokes. Although Delrik was making light of the situation, I knew he understood its weight. I'd been rejected by my father, and now my consort.

"Well, she has held her ground this long. And I have no idea how to deal with that. At first, I tried to be friends with her, but I gave that up quickly. She wanted absolutely nothing to do with me." Just like everyone else in my life. Well, except Delrik, Jace, and Nazneen. I mean, I couldn't blame her. In her eyes, I was the male who stole her future.

I remembered knocking on her door on multiple occasions to either escort her to dinner or give her a tour of the citadel. Her maid had politely declined each time. The same maid that Father wanted to ship back to the Western Continent. I somehow convinced him not to. The maid was the only person in Illoterra she knew and who spoke her native language. She was already isolated. I couldn't bear her being completely alone. I knew how lonely life could be. I'd experienced the solitude and abandonment when Father rejected me.

I didn't see her for the first few weeks after she arrived. Then I spotted her one afternoon sitting on a bench in the snow covered garden. I didn't know why we called it a garden. Nothing ever grew there. She hadn't heard me approach. When she saw my feet as I came to stand in front of her, she looked up at me with the saddest expression. Her eyes were puffy and red rimmed. She'd been crying. I couldn't imagine how she must have been feeling being shipped off to a foreign continent and bound to a stranger.

That instance in the garden was the one and only time she'd ever shown me anything other than her mask of indifferent irritation. I sat in the garden with her while she silently cried. We didn't talk, and I didn't try to comfort her. There was nothing I could do or say to make her feel better. Dark hells, I couldn't even express my own emotions. When she'd finally wiped the moisture from her face, she rose without speaking and left me sitting alone in the snow. I went straight to my father's head of household and had Katuri moved to the largest suite available, one that was large enough to house a hothouse. Her homeland was in the middle of an enormous rainforest. I thought the greenhouse would not only give her a task to focus on, but a place she could find comfort. A small piece of home. I planted the idea in her maid's head with a quick side comment. And I had been right.

It was an added bonus that her new suite was only around the corner from mine. I walked by her door every day but never knocked again. It wasn't until I ran into her maid in the hallway several months later that I knew she had filled the greenhouse with all different species of herbs, exotic plants, and trees. She'd placed her tiny pink hand on my arm and thanked me for treating the princess with kindness.

I didn't feel kind. I'd never told anyone what I'd done for the princess. It was the least I could do. I was as much of a captor as my father.

Soon, Katuri's door was surrounded by richly deep green vines peppered with fragrant blossoms. Over the years, the vines transformed as her mood did. At first, the joy the greenhouse brought resulted in gorgeous orchids of all species and colors. I'd had to look up their names in our library. I had even had several tomes sent from Laeto Selva so I could study the more exotic varieties. After a year in Kanevvluk, the flowers wilted and died, never to return. Now the thick vines were covered in vicious black thorns that bit into the wall. Cracks radiated from where they pierced the stone.

When the War Across the Sea began and I'd had to leave Kanevvluk, Katuri didn't bat an eye at the news. She hadn't joined the rest of the family at the docks when we departed. She'd insisted on staying behind. The connection between us through the blood binding was a dull buzz in the background by then. It hadn't completely diminished, but it was faint. I'd stayed in Quinterre for the entirety of the war and focused all my energy on proving myself as a valuable warrior. I was surprised at how easy it was to be separated from her for so long. I'd found myself forgetting about Katuri completely for days on end.

Upon my homecoming, I was shocked when I laid eyes on Katuri again. It was like the first time all over again. Except the female standing before me had completely transformed. Before, she was a willowy thing, long limbs that were soft and juvenile. After seven years, she'd blossomed into someone new. She held herself with confidence, not sorrow. Her body was all feminine with lean muscles like she'd been exercising regularly. She wasn't mellow or shy any longer. She had a sharp tongue and a sharper wit. And the power of her elemental magic had grown immensely. I could sense it when I walked in the room. My eyes had snapped to her standing tucked aside against the wall. Her chin was lifted high and her hands primly clasped in front of her. That strange feeling I'd had the first time I'd seen her so many years prior flared to life all over again with such intensity. She still had no interest in me in the slightest, but I wanted to be near her. I was drawn to her, stronger than before.

Since the first day I'd laid eyes on her, I'd been attracted to her. It wasn't lust back then. I couldn't pinpoint exactly what it was, more like a protector. As she matured, the attraction shifted to a physical attraction. It simmered under the surface. However, a few months ago, something transformed within me. There was nothing else I wanted more than to be near her. I didn't know why and, honestly, I didn't really care. I wanted her attention, needed her attention, even if it was negative. It felt like I couldn't breathe if we weren't in the same room and she was ignoring me. The pull was so strong. I found myself walking to her, moving to her, searching for her, without even knowing it. I had to be near her. She had turned a blind eye to all my gestures of kindness, so, instead, I found ways to make her off balance and rile her up. I was going to blame the fates on this one. Who was I to fight the fates? Nothing had been able to crack her hard exterior thus far.

Katuri kept everyone except her maid at a healthy distance. No one dared to enter her personal bubble of space or dared to touch her in any way. The only maid she allowed in her suite was her maid,

Corynne. Most servants skirted around her when passing in the halls or serving her food at meals. It was as if she had an invisible bubble around her no one was allowed to cross. Until I'd stepped inside that invisible circle.

Delrik and I walked into the suite set aside for him and his bondmate. The sight before me brought me back from my wandering thoughts. A smile was on Katuri's face and she was laughing. A warm, full laugh that made her glow. Her head was tossed back and the slender column of her throat was exposed. I'd never heard her laugh before. For the second time today, I felt pulled so strongly I was almost brought to my knees. I stopped at the threshold, surprised to see all three females sitting in the middle of the bed. Katuri's wolf was curled against her legs, and the sleek black bird was propped on Evren's shoulder. They were talking in hushed tones like they were old friends being reunited after years apart.

"So y'all are friends? Just like that?" Three pairs of eyes turned toward me. When Katuri caught sight of me hoovering at the threshold, her mood took a nosedive. She cleared her throat and looked down at her hands in her lap. She tucked her left hand under her right. Was she even aware of it, or was hiding the binding mark an unconscious action?

I stepped a foot further into the room. "Is that how it works? You just meet and become instant best friends?"

Nazneen shrugged her shoulder. "Who knows? But it works for us."

"I wouldn't know. I've spent the last four decades surrounded by heartless ice soldiers."

Did Kat actually just talk to me? On purpose?

A smile spread across Evren's face and her eyes bounced between my consort and me. Evren was stunning. I could see why Delrik was attracted to her. "Well, now you have Nazneen and me to keep you company."

Evren reached over and squeezed Katuri's hand. Katuri allowed the touch. The only person I'd seen ever touch her was Corynne. Sour jealousy rolled through me. The gesture made *me* want to reach for Katuri's hand, but I knew better. The wolf would remove my fingers before I got within five feet of her.

"That's so sweet," I said.

Katuri's eyes cut to mine. "Fuck off, Garren."

There it is.

My corners of my mouth curled into a satisfied smirk. I couldn't help it. I loved her defiant side.

Delrik brushed past me with his speed.

I will have to get used to that again.

He leaned down and wrapped Evren in his arms from behind and nuzzled against her neck, making her giggle and swat him away. "What are you three up to? Plotting to overthrow the citadel?"

"Oh, most definitely," Evren quipped.

"Don't give them any ideas," I said as I closed the door behind me. Katuri went on high alert, stiffening her spine like a trapped animal as the door's latch snapped closed. She'd become skilled at avoiding being in closed rooms with me since I started testing that invisible radius around her. It was only in the last few months that her defenses had been easier to break down. So much time refusing me had put a strain on her resolve. She'd discovered that distance was the only thing that kept the binding mark from pulling at her magic, the only thing that made it easier to ignore my existence. I grinned a wicked grin at her. I could feel the earth power just outside my reach. I brushed a mental hand down it, and it recoiled from me with such abhorrence I almost laughed out loud.

"Katuri was just telling us what to expect during our stay," Nazneen said, snapping me back to the conversation. "Basically, all you males bossing us around and no fun to be had."

"And lots of snow," Evren said.

"Sounds about right," I said. "Once you all get settled, I can show you our hot springs. I know you have bathing chambers, but nothing beats the hot springs after spending so many days on a ship."

And maybe, just maybe, if Evren and Nazneen invited her, Katuri would come along.

ELEVEN
GARREN

With a hiss, I slipped my naked body into the water. Suddenly, my body was stiff and aching. I rested the back of my head on the marble tiles and let my eyes drift closed. I hadn't realized how exhausted I was from today's training. I was leaning against the edge of the hot spring's main pool when Delrik swam from the private changing room. He waded toward me, the water lapping at his torso. One arm was covered in inked ancient language. The other arm was golden to the elbow with the binding mark. Waving black swirls wrapped around his shoulder and over his neck, hiding his Arcelia Legion tattoo. While I was curious about this new magic, it was also something I'd never seen before. Not even the dark magic used during the war gave me this feeling. The hot springs were located in a chamber deep beneath the citadel. The ceiling reached far above us. A waterfall poured over a nearby wall. The rushing sound gave a calming effect. The chamber was dim with soft glowing coming from the walls and ceiling. It looked like spelled icicles and orbs of snow had been enchanted to give off light. The air was heavy with pleasant smelling moisture. The waters were as teal and clear as the waters in the harbor beneath the surface, but steam from the heated water floated on the surface, concealing my naked body below.

"Do you still spend an absurd amount of time down here?" Delrik asked. I'd left him standing in the hall making out with his bondmate, but he'd caught up with me.

"The water in the hook is freezing this time of year with all the melting snow," I answered.

"Does it ever actually melt here?" Delrik quipped back.

I rolled my eyes at my friend.

The females weren't far behind us. Evren and Nazneen appeared from the other private changing rooms. Katuri had *not* come with Evren and Nazneen, but it wasn't the end of the world. I hadn't really expected her to give any thought to their invitation. I'd gotten lucky enough to interact with her today. That was more than most of the time. And she'd spoken to me. Twice. Even if it was all snark and cursing. Normally, I wouldn't care about having a conversation with her, but hearing her voice made my body hum with pleasure. Her laugh gave me a visceral reaction.

They didn't see us at first, and I couldn't help the mischievous grin that came to my face.

"Want to freak them out?" I asked Delrik.

"Of course," he whispered, sinking further down into the water so that it covered his shoulders.

Him and Nazneen were always playing pranks on each other. I might have instigated the pranks a time or two.

Nazneen's voice echoed off the cavernous ceiling. "So is this where we're going to spend the next few weeks?" She was talking to Evren. "If not, someone is going to have to drag me from this pool."

Evren laughed, but I heard her sigh with contentment. Nazneen dunked her head below the steaming surface of the water and came back up with a big breath. Water traveled in rivulets down her face.

"Do you think Katuri is going to join us?" Evren asked Nazneen as they swam closer to the center of the chamber.

"No. She mentioned she had a few things to do before dinner," Nazneen said.

"She's missing out," I whispered to Delrik as I gestured to my naked torso before I settled deeper into the water.

"Are you sure she's just not avoiding you?" he replied.

I shot him a death glare.

Evren abruptly let out an ear piercing squeal. "Something brushed against my leg." Her voice resonated off the cathedral high ceiling and walls.

"What?" Nazneen's face paled.

"There's something in the water," Evren said as she scrambled toward the edge of the pool.

"Fuck no!" Nazneen cursed.

She was faster than Evren. She'd made it to the side and had pushed up with her arms until the top of her curved ass was just above the water's surface.

"You should probably stop her unless you want the full show." Delrik laughed.

I raised my voice so that they could hear me over their screaming and splashing. "Don't worry. He won't bite."

Nazneen looked over her bare shoulder at me with deadly eyes.

Shit, I might have just started a war.

Evren was clutching her arms across her chest and breathing heavily. Just then, a sea dragon the size of a dolphin lifted its head from the surface. Its large wide eyes studied Evren and Nazneen curiously. His iridescent cyan scales were smooth and shining with droplets of water. He opened his mouth and chirped at them playfully.

"That's Drake. Don't mind him. He's just nosey," Garren said.

Nazneen had met Drake briefly, but he was much larger that time and hadn't been lurking in the water where she was swimming. The sea dragon chuffed and then dove back beneath the water.

Nazneen swam over and swept her arm through the water and sent a wall of liquid right at my face. With a flick of my wrist, I redirected the water right back at her.

Evren made her way to her bondmate's side. "This place is incredible." Her neck craned back to get a full view of the ceiling high away. "How deep are we underground?"

"I don't know exactly, but pretty far. The first High Fae that arrived in Kanevvluk built the citadel above this chamber when they discovered the natural hot springs."

"He was smart to keep this to himself and build the citadel above it," Evren said.

Arik had followed us here and had already made himself comfortable across the pool maybe thirty feet away. I wondered how he'd known we were coming to the hot springs and how he'd gotten here without us seeing him. His deep brown chest was proudly on display. He was more puffed than a peacock. The water rippled away from him as he shifted to a comfortable position. He leaned against the wall, sitting on an underwater ledge, arms spread out to the side in a powerful stance. It was hard to see the family resemblance between him and my family. Where Jace and I both had white blond hair and teal eyes, Arik's raven black hair was mussed from running his wet hands through the short waves on the top of his head. The sides were shaved close to his scalp. He was a cousin on my mother's side. His mother was my mom's sister. She'd been kidnapped and sold into slavery a long time ago. Arik had found his way back when he was younger after his mother had been killed.

Despite Delrik's hostility, Arik was a picture of casual calm.

Nazneen noticed Arik and gave his body an undisguised look over. "You again," she said to him.

"Me again."

"You know it's rude to not introduce yourself, especially this being our third interaction."

I rolled my eyes at Nanzeen's lame flirtatiousness. She already knew his name.

"You've been counting?" He smiled, one side of his mouth tipping up more than the other. "I'm Arik Hanover."

"Arik. It suits you," she said, batting her lashing.

Wow. Really Nazneen.

Arik shifted against the rock wall, standing to his full height, then moved closer to us. The water came dangerously close to revealing all of his manhood. He wasn't tall, only a few inches taller than Nazneen actually. The look on Delrik's face could have killed. His head swiveled back and forth between Arik and his sister as darkness pooled around him.

"Don't even think about touching my sister," he growled as he swam past Arik, slamming his shoulder into Arik's chest on the way. He was putting space between my cousin and himself.

Evren followed and pulled herself close to Delrik and placed a reassuring hand on his chest, like she was trying to calm him. She was whispering something into his chest, but I couldn't hear what she was saying. The binding mark on her hand was glowing softly, and the shadows had moved to the center of Delrik's chest, and her fingers were tipped in umbra. Evren slowly pushed Delrik away from our intimate group, back toward the private changing areas.

Nazneen leaned over to me and whispered, "What was that all about?"

"I'm not on the best of terms with your brother," Arik said with a wry grin.

She tipped the corner of her mouth and leaned a touch closer to me. "He isn't quite the type I usually spend my time with, but Powers Above." She fanned herself with her hand and shot a wink at Arik. "I'm having indecent thoughts over here."

She was not trying to hide her comment from anyone. Evren laughed, and Delrik, who'd recovered from whatever was going on, groaned. "Naz, don't be gross. No one wants to hear about your adventures."

"There is nothing wrong with appreciating the male body. I've been so busy recently, I haven't had time for ... well, you know."

Arik's steel gray eyes were concentrated on Nazneen. There was something intelligent and perceptive in those eyes. He arched a dark eyebrow in a challenge. Drake reemerged from the depths and brushed by Nazneen, bumping his tail against her shin. She jumped, and Arik's mouth quirked into that crooked smile.

Delrik huffed. "Stop making eyes at my sister."

I laughed at his brotherly remark. Arik didn't tear his gaze from Nazneen. Not in the slightest. Then, with great intention, his eyes dipped to the swell of her breasts.

"Oooo. He wants to play. Game on, Arik," she said more to herself. Then, more loudly so that Evren could hear her clearly, "I know how I was going to keep myself entertained while we're in Kanevvluk, and *that* gorgeous specimen of a male is named Arik Hanover." She gave Arik a wink and then turned her attention back to us.

Delrik reached for a bar of soap and handed it to Evren. I found one for myself, and soon suds from the soap surrounded us and the delicious scents of lavender and vanilla filled the air. I scrubbed myself clean and let the decadent waters of the hot springs soak into my cold body and tired muscles. Delrik rinsed the soap from Evren's hair, untangling the long locks of silver.

I leaned over to Nazneen and wrinkled my nose up. "Are they always this way?"

"This is tame. Just wait."

TWELVE
KATURI

I hadn't joined the others in the hot springs. Instead, I'd opted for a cold dunk in my bathtub to snap myself out of the fog Garren had put me in earlier. He'd gotten under my skin—again. It had been happening more and more lately, and I didn't know why. Six months ago, he'd wanted nothing to do with me, and now he was everywhere. Every Meal. Around every corner. And today, he'd shown up in my suite uninvited.

I looked at myself in the floor-length mirror with a sigh. Corynne twisted my hair to keep it off my neck, and she'd picked a simple, yet elegant gown. She had an eye for finding gowns that fit High Ruler Eckhardt's unreasonable restrictions, but were understated just the way I preferred. I wasn't ashamed of my body or the way I looked; I just didn't like drawing attention to myself. I preferred to stay hidden in the background. It kept people from asking too many questions. Tonight, Corynne had picked a soft beige gown that flowed loosely and had a modest fit. Exactly how I liked it.

High Ruler Holden Eckhardt was one of those males that had formal dinners every night. Even my family in Laeto Selva and all their royal flourishes didn't have formal dinners every night. My only reprieve had been during the war when I was left behind. What a gloriously free seven years.

I took a deep breath and smoothed my hands down the front of my gown. I could get out of affairs every now and then, but with our new guests here, I couldn't escape tonight.

"You look lovely," Corynne said in our native tongue. She rarely spoke the common language. She squeezed my shoulders and then left me standing and staring at my appearance. I was still feeling flustered from my multiple encounters with Garren today. This was as prepared as I could be.

I exited my suite and walked down the empty corridor to the dining hall. The click, click, click of my footsteps was the only sound. That and the pounding of heart in my chest.

I was the first to arrive at the formal dining hall. Good. I had time to calm my rapidly beating heart. Garren had caught me off guard and knocked me off kilter. Ugh. Why was I still thinking of him?

I sat in my regular seat—as far from Garren as I was allowed—and downed a full glass of water. A servant promptly refilled my glass before he discreetly returned to his spot against the wall. Shit. I needed to relax. Why was I so jittery? I shook out my hands under the table, flexing my fingers, and blew out a breath between my lips.

I reached for my glass of Fae wine instead of the water and took a significant sip. The sound of voices in the hall caused me to freeze and hold my breath. When I saw my hand trembling, I quickly set my wine glass down. Delrik, Evren, and Nazneen strolled in. Thank the Powers Above it wasn't Garren. I'd had enough one-on-one time with him today. Nazneen took a seat across from me. Her and Evren were each dressed in floor-length dresses appropriate for the elegant dinner High Ruler Eckhardt no doubt had planned.

"Katuri," Evren greeted me cheerfully, "we missed you earlier."

I offered her a smile as she pulled the chair out next to me and sat down. "I prefer to go to the hot springs later in the evening when no one is there," I said.

Delrik took the seat next to Evren, pulling his chair closer to hers and placing her napkin in her lap. "That's understandable. I can see how being at the hot springs alone could be relaxing and rejuvenating."

"Garren is a bit loud if you're looking to relax," he said. "But I'd give him a chance."

My temper flashed in me, but I stared at him blankly. I didn't show him any weakness. Of course, Garren would tell his best friend about me. Had he also told him how I was being forced into this ... relationship? I was sure Garren had filled him in on all the things I'd been doing over the last decades. Or rather, things I *hadn't* been doing.

"Did you get everything done you needed to?" Evren asked.

"What?" I asked, confused.

"You said you had a few..."

"Oh. Yes. All taken care of," I lied. I really just didn't want to be with Garren. "I got a chance to relax a little, too." I shifted my attention to Nazneen so as not to be caught in my deceit. "How are you settling in?"

"Quite well. It's so beautiful here. We have snow in Arcelia, but not like this," she answered.

I rolled my eyes at her. "I hate the snow." It's cold and wet and depressing.

"Then why are you in Kanevvluk?" Evren asked with curiosity.

Hm. Interesting. Apparently her bondmate had not shared my oh-so-joyous news of being Garren's consort with her yet. Had Garren asked him not to, or was Delrik more understanding to my situation than I gave him credit for? Maybe I'd been too quick in my judgment. I pressed my hand to my stomach. I was going to take advantage of telling my new friends myself rather than letting Garren get his word in first.

"If it were my choice, I wouldn't be here at all. My parents sent me here when I was young to fulfill a prophecy."

I twisted my napkin in my lap, hiding my hands and the binding mark. I didn't know why I was suddenly spilling details of my pathetic captivity. I must have been lonelier than I had thought all these years. I mean, I could go days only speaking to Corynne and no one else. I knew I'd just met these three, but I was quickly becoming friends with them. I hadn't had anyone I could talk to, be close to, since moving here. I hadn't realized how isolated I truly was until this moment.

"Ah. I know all about that," Evren said. Her eyes softened with understanding. "My father tried to force the blood binding on me. None of them stuck, thank the Powers."

"Is that how you two met?" I gestured to Delrik and her.

Evren let out an unexpected laugh, followed by a snort that I couldn't help but smile at. "Powers, no." She pointed over her shoulder at Delrik. "He kidnapped me and held me hostage until I gave in to his woes."

Evren could definitely relate to what I was going through. I couldn't help my surprise at what she had just said. "He kidnapped you?"

"Yup."

"And held you hostage?"

"Uh huh." Her eyes were bright, and I noticed the binding mark on her arm flared to life brightly.

"Ignore those two love birds. It's sickening how much in love they are with each other," Nazneen said as she stuffed a piece of bread into her mouth.

"Sisters are so irritating," Delrik said under his breath.

A roll flew into the air and nailed Delrik square in the face. Nazneen stuck out her tongue at her brother.

"So, you are bound to someone here in Kanevvluk?" Nazneen asked.

I avoided Delrik's eyes, but he cleared his throat and lifted his water glass to his mouth. Nazneen didn't miss any of it. She was too observant.

"What about you?" I asked Nazneen, instead of answering her question.

She must have sensed my discomfort because she answered without skipping a beat. "The fates haven't blessed me with a bondmate yet. That's okay. I have faith they will. And in the meantime, I'm having a lot of fun." She winked at me. "Maybe one day I'll settle down with a consort if I get bored."

"Don't get her started with the fates and the future," Delrik said as he draped his arm over the back of Evren's chair. "She'll talk your ear off about it for the next month if you do."

Garren's voice came from behind me. "How in the Powers did you get her to smile? And twice in the same day."

And just like that, the smile on my face disappeared. Garren had that effect on me. A chunk of half-eaten bread flew across the room and hit Garren square in the face. Nazneen had impressive aim.

"Be nice to my friend," Nazneen snapped at Garren.

The pure shock on his face from being pelted with bread was priceless. That put the smile back on my face. My heart thundered in my ears as Garren watched me carefully.

"Stop wasting all the bread," Delrik complained.

"Powers, Naz! I was just kidding around." Garren pouted.

Nazneen stood from her spot, walked around the table, and plopped down in the chair next to me. "I'm claiming her as mine. And I'll kick your ass if you mess with her."

I couldn't help straightening my shoulders and facing Garren with a smug smile on my face. He sat in Nazneen's old seat across from me and lounged back in the chair with his legs spread wide. He raised a goblet of Fae wine into the air in a toast. Garren's eyes surveyed the closeness of Nazneen and me. His indecent smile made my insides curl in embarrassment. I could feel every inch of my skin heat.

"I'm not usually one to share, but I can make an exception this once."

Disgusting, self-centered bastard.

"You look beautiful tonight," Garren said after he took a sip of wine from his glass.

I swallowed thickly. Awkward silence hung over the table. Arik slipped into the room as silent as a snow fox and took the seat next to Garren. I'd never been as happy to see him as I was at this moment. I noticed his gaze flick to Nazneen before he settled himself into his chair. My eyes darted to her in interest. This must be what she had meant by keeping herself entertained.

"It's good of you to join us, Arik," I said, still peering back and forth between the pair. I noticed Nazneen shift next to me and then she pinched my leg under the table.

"Everyone has to eat," Arik said.

"Where have you been? You disappeared rather suddenly from the hot springs," Garren said.

"Nowhere in particular. I had an errand in the city," Arik responded.

I didn't know Arik well. He was High Ruler Eckhardt's nephew and, according to rumors, had unexpectedly showed up in Kanevvluk some time before I arrived. There were more rumors, but I knew better than most that the majority of rumors weren't true. I didn't see Arik around the citadel often. He kept to himself as much as I did.

The doors smacked against the walls as High Ruler Eckhardt rushed into the room, Jace trailing along behind him. A servant ran forward to pull his chair from the table. The High Ruler brushed the servant away with an irritable wave of his hand.

"Where is Mother?" Garren asked.

Jace cleared his throat and sat beside Nazneen. "She's having dinner with friends." Nazneen smiled warmly at Jace.

High Ruler Eckhardt grunted in confirmation.

"Katuri. Nazneen. Evren." Jace nodded at each of us in greeting.

I liked Jace. He was probably the only other person in the citadel that I didn't immediately run from. We hadn't had much interaction, but he was polite and spoke kindly to me. He and Garren shared the family features of blond hair and blue eyes. They could almost pass as twins in many ways.

A round of servers appeared and placed the first course before us. They were all snow sprites. They flitted around the room without a care in the world, trays balanced precariously in their tiny hands. Their skin twinkled and was as white as snow, and their hair and eyes were a soft silver. They were only about four feet tall, but with their glittering translucent wings, they showed no sign of struggle when reaching over the table to place plates of food.

Dinner had been growing more awkward with each creeping minute. High Ruler Eckhardt shoved food down his gullet and the rest of us kept our eyes down for the entire meal. We ate in silence for each course until the High Ruler wiped his face and tossed his napkin onto this plate. He mumbled a goodnight under his breath and left the dining room. If his consort wasn't at the table, dinner was a tense, yet thankfully, short affair. He'd left the room with a barely there goodbye, and the servants had cleared the last of the dishes from the final course. High Rulers Holden Eckhardt wasn't my favorite person in the realm. He wasn't cruel. He ruled the Snowhaven Fae wisely, but he was ... brash. He never filtered what he said and spoke in harsh, commanding tones, even to his bonded. The whole room let out a sigh of relief at Holden's departure. The rigid manners and postures relaxed.

"Asshole," Arik mumbled under his breath.

"Agreed." Garren lifted his glass to Arik and took a swig.

"Go fall into the dark circles of hell," he retorted, but then lifted his glass in return.

After years of back and forth, Garren and Arik had finally come to somewhat of a truce. They didn't go out of their way to hang out as cousins or become friends, but they were no longer at each other's throats. I never knew what had gone down between them.

"Anything you ask," Garren sniped back.

Delrik rolled his eyes with an exaggerated groan.

"Well, that was tense." Nazneen laughed.

"Drink?" Jace asked, and a resounding yes went around the table.

"I'll be off," Arik said. He stood and folded his napkin on his plate.

The males ignored me, continuing their discussion.

Evren gave him a polite smile before saying, "Have a good evening, Arik."

He nodded his thanks and then bowed toward Nazneen and me. "I hope you have a pleasant evening, too." The smile Nazneen gave him lit up the room.

"You too, Arik," she said and wiggled her eyebrows at him playful-ly.

Delrik, Nazneen, and Jace had moved to the other end of the table and were in a heated debate about ... something. I wasn't quite sure what. I wasn't paying attention to them. I was focused on finishing my dinner. My mind had wandered off, trying to ignore the rising level of noise. I wasn't used to the energy of so many people, and it was starting to overwhelm me. My plate was removed the moment I took my last bite and my wine glass topped off. Damn.

I had been planning to escape, but I didn't want to be rude. I traced my fingers along the bottom of the crystal stem. It was ice cold against my skin which was a stark comparison to the warm flush I was feeling from the alcohol. I could feel Garren watching me. His eyes were leaving hot trails as they raked over my body, stopping on my face. I dared to glance in his direction and watched his fingers tap quietly against the table. Those deep azul eyes held me fixed. The corner of his eyes crinkled. I wanted to know what he was thinking. The firm line I'd drawn in the sand was washing away like he was the tide getting closer and closer. Damn it. Garren slipped his hand inside the breast pocket of his coat and pulled out a leaf. Was that the leaf he'd taken from my hair earlier? My hand floated up to touch my hair, and he smiled and gave a single nod in confirmation.

"Don't worry. I won't pester you. I'm just going to sit here as a proper host should. I promise not to bother you with excessive conversation."

I took a sip from my glass. Okay. Well, that was different. Usually, he didn't shut up. He loved to hear himself talk. Was he really just going to sit there in silence? I studied his handsome face. His cheeks were rosy from the wine and his too blue eyes were bright.

"What makes you assume I don't want a conversation?"

What was I saying? Of course I didn't want to have a conversation with him. Though I would be curious to hear what was going on in his head. He raised his tumbler of amber whiskey to his lips to hide his smile. Then he leaned forward and propped his elbows on the table. He watched me in silence for a few beats.

"Well, usually you tell me to fuck off when I walk into a room."

I sputtered on my sip of wine, earning me a soft laugh from Garren. I quickly grabbed my napkin and covered my face, hiding my embarrassment and wiping my mouth of the spilled wine. I mean, he wasn't wrong, so why did I care now? I must have had more wine than usual tonight, because I was feeling bold. Usually, I kept firm control on what I said to him. It almost felt good to release a little bit of that control.

"Your presence usually pisses me off."

"Ha!" He barked out a laugh. "True, but you didn't seem to mind my presence earlier. Maybe we're finally coming ... to an understanding."

I bit down on the inside of my cheek. The silence buzzed between the tension. He held my gaze and I struggled to not squirm at this drawn out attention. Thank the Powers for the table separating us. He arched a well-groomed blond brow at me. He was always well-groomed, put together, dressed to impress. It was truly frustrating how handsome he looked all the time. All the males in the citadel were handsome, but Garren was different. I realized with sheer shock that he was flirting with me. I held his gaze and for a split second. I felt a flash down my arm and the binding mark—something raw and wanting. Then it was gone a second later.

Out of all the moments Garren and I had shared over the last forty or so years, I'd never seen him so vulnerable, so fragile, as in that second. That raw wanting wasn't lust; it was something much deeper. Butterflies filled my stomach and I had to look away. My reaction to his vulnerability made me uneasy. I shouldn't care about what or how he was feeling.

"I'd be willing to remind you if you've been forgotten." He shifted in his chair and leaned his elbows on the table.

And he was back to his normal self. I leaned back on instinct. Goosebumps covered my arms as a chill raced across my skin. The tips of my pointed ears burned. I didn't need to be reminded of how his presence made me feel, and he knew it. He taunted me with his pure male smugness often enough. And it clearly was having an impact on me.

I hastily stood. My chair scraped loudly on the floor, drawing everyone's attention. "I'm tired. I'll see you all tomorrow."

Garren snickered into his crystal tumbler as I rushed from the room.

THIRTEEN
KATURI

The new group had been in Kanevvluk for a week now, and I had spent almost every day in the library with Evren and Nazneen. I'd shown Evren the library the day after our arrival when she began peppering me with questions about the elemental powers. I wasn't bothered by all the questions, but I knew I didn't have all the answers she was looking for. In fact, I really enjoyed the conversation. Evren had told me that the library and historical texts in Arcelia were located in the nearby Temple of Anruin. They were closely monitored by the priestesses. They saw all her questions as a nuisance and had no problem telling her so. I wished I'd had had someone I trusted that I could have asked questions when I was coming into my power. As soon as my earth elemental began to develop, my father had me shipped here. I was completely alone, figuring everything else out on my own.

Yesterday, she'd discovered that High Fae with elemental magic were shifters. While there were other Fae who had characteristics of specific animals, they carried the characteristics all the time. Shifters were able to move back and forth between the animal form and High Fae form at will. Evren had told me she could transform into a firebird, but she hadn't been able to shift since that first time in Rivamir.

"You should really try to shift again," Nazneen said.

"Even just testing the basic parts of my power is tiring, and I can't shake the lingering thoughts of being consumed by my fires. Alux planted that seed in my head."

"I'm a wolf when I'm in my shifted form," I told them. It took me years, and lots of failed attempts, before I could shift without thought. And even longer to figure out how to shift without destroying all my clothes."

"What do you mean clothes?" she asked me.

"Well, my wolf is much larger than my High Fae form, so when I shifted, my clothes were torn to shreds."

"So, when you shifted back, you were just naked?" she asked. "Actually, thinking back on it, the first time my powers showed, my evening gown had been burned in places. And when I exploded into the firebird, I'd been clothed in flames, so yeah, my clothes were definitely destroyed. I'll have to remember that in the future. That could get awkward real fast."

"How often do you shift?" Nazneen asked.

"Every day." I stroked the fur of Eleni. "Mostly at night though."

Nazneen looked impressed. Nazneen and I had followed Evren into the library today. We had made our nest for the day in the main area of the library that was full of plush couches and fireplaces evenly spaced along the walls. Sturdy tables and chairs sat off to one side. Evren had piled books on the one closest to us. And bookshelves. The two story room was lined floor to ceiling with bookshelves. Tall ladders reached the highest volumes, and no matter how far I walked through the rows, I never found the last row.

We had claimed one of the large couches. Naz sat with her feet tucked underneath her with a throw blanket across her lap. I was lying on my back with my feet up in the air, resting on the back of the couch with a pillow tucked under my head. The skirts on my dress were pooled at my thighs. My legs were covered in thick leggings, and I'd kicked off my shoes. I wiggled my socked toes as we chatted. A maid brought a platter of hot tea and snacks, which was perfect for the gloomy day. A heavy fog had settled over the citadel and cast long shadows across the library. Eleni was sprawled in front of the roaring fire, and Aura was snuggled up under her chin.

The Snowhaven library, although smaller than the one at home in Laeto Selva, had so much more to offer. The wealth of knowledge the Snowhaven Fae possessed blew my mind—and we had unrestricted access to it all. It wasn't long before Evren had pulled several tomes from their shelves and had a circle of open faced books all around her on the floor. She couldn't get enough of the High Fae history and elemental gifts.

The large windows looking over the city showed a white, glittering landscape, houses peppering the blanket of snow, tendrils of smoke curling from their chimneys. The wind whipped around, sending swirls of snowflakes through the air. Heavy clouds hung low in the sky.

"I love the contrast of the bright white and the cold gray," Nazneen said from the couch. A plate was propped on one knee. "What kind of jelly is on these scones?"

"Guava. It's my favorite from home," I said. Guava was one of my favorite fruits. I even had a tree in my greenhouse, but there was always a jar of guava jam in the kitchens whenever I had a craving for it. Fuck, I missed the rainforest. I missed the smells, the tastes, all of it. I slung an arm across my eyes with a groan. "It's so dreary here. I miss home."

Nazneen reached over and lifted my arm from my face. I tipped my head back to peer upside down at my new friend. The look of empathy on her face struck my heart. I'd never had someone show me empathy.

"That's right. You aren't from here."

I shook my head. "No. I'm from Laeto Selva. It's in the Forest Fae Territory on Quinterre. I think you all call it the Western Continent. There are such funny names for things here."

Nazneen peered down at me. "Tell me about your home."

I leaned forward to one of the books opened beside Evren and pointed to a city on a map. "The City of Laeto Selva. It's hidden deep within a lush rainforest. But our palace breached the canopy, and there was a deck I'd spent a lot of time on. Even though it rained every day, there was nothing more beautiful than the forest." I smiled as I gazed off into nothingness in memory. "The ground was always covered in soft moss and ferns. Thick vines with large flowers of all colors stretched from tree to tree. The animals were always singing, and I never wore shoes. My earth power thrived there. Not like here." Then my mood shifted into sorrow. "Nothing is like the harsh snow here."

"I'm sure being so far from home must be hard," Evren said with understanding.

"Yes and no. I don't really miss my family. We weren't close like you all, but I do miss the sun and running through the forest. Eleni and I used to race through the rainforest from the palace to the river. Eleni never wants to run with me now in this cold place."

"Do you have any brothers or sisters?"

"I have a younger brother, Logan Kathmor, but I don't really remember him. I'd probably not recognize him now. He was three when I left."

"What about your parents?" High Rulers here in Illoterra were the same as kings on the Quinterre.

"King Kairos and Queen Nefali Harland." My stomach churned when I spoke my father's name.

"So, that makes you a princess," Nazneen said.

No one called me princess anymore. Garren used to at first, but not anymore.

"The same as you, right? Aren't High Rulers here in Illoterra the same as kings in Quinterre?" I asked.

"I suppose so," Evren said thoughtfully, not looking up from the book in her lap.

I loved that Evren wasn't high and mighty about her heritage or status within the realm. It was so different from other royalty and powerful High Fae bloodlines I'd interacted with.

"I wasn't close to my father." I shifted uncomfortably. "I do miss my mother some. I've just resigned myself that I won't see her again. It's easier that way."

Evren was sitting on the rug beside the couch, using it to rest her back on, and a book was propped on her knees. She brushed her toes across Eleni's snout with affection.

"Her fur is so soft. I noticed that she has similar markings as your tribal mark," Evren pointed out.

She did in fact have a white line of fur down her forehead and two across her snout. Even the line down her chest was the same as mine. My tribal mark went all the way down my torso.

The fire crackled in the enormous fireplace. A bitter draft came through a crack in the windowsill, creating a high-pitched whistle. I shivered at the chill and Eleni's ears twitched. When you came from a kingdom that had never seen snow, being in a place that never saw the warmth of summer was depressing.

"I swear, no matter how large the fire or how many I have in my suite, I am always shivering," I said as I rested a mug of hot, steaming liquid on my stomach.

"Evren!" Nazneen clapped excitedly, poking me in the shoulder. "Do the trick."

"The trick?" I asked, craning my head back so I could see Nazneen again.

Without looking up from my book, Evren reached behind her and touched my arm. She pushed a thread of her fire into her fingers, warming my skin with a simple touch.

Powers Above! Now that's a fancy trick.

"Powers Above! That's amazing," I said in surprise. "How did you do that?"

Evren snapped her fingers, and a flame sprang between them, violets and oranges dancing together. "Small shows of power are much easier since the blood binding. With the shadow magic dwelling in Delrik, my fire power was growing stronger. I still hadn't summoned my wings again or done anything more than small flames, but I could feel the strength, and summoning small threads was becoming second nature."

A knock on the door had all three of us turning to look who was interrupting our girl time. For the most part, the guys had been off to themselves catching up on their lives. Delrik didn't wait for a response before he entered the library. He strode to Evren. She reached out her hand, and he took it. He brushed his thumb on the inside of her wrist, along the binding mark and then bent to kiss her palm. My heart tugged at their obvious devotion to each other.

He was dressed down, a simple tunic and pants. His sleeves were rolled to the elbow. One arm was covered in ebony artwork, the other in the binding mark. The shadows, as Evren called them, had moved to cover a collarbone peeking from the V of his tunic and the side of his neck, masking the Arcelia Legion tattoo. Their location varied, sometimes remaining completely hidden, other times on full display. Evren had told us that the shadows had a personality of their own.

"Did you ladies forget about training? It's our first lesson, and we can't be late," Delrik said as he stood again.

Nazneen and I both jumped up, excited at the prospect of getting in some practice. We'd been comparing our combative skills all morning in preparation for our first training session. I hadn't fought in the war, but I'd had a private trainer that taught me hand-to-hand sparring as well as how to use a variety of weapons. Evren, on the other hand, was not looking forward to these training lessons as much as everyone else.

"I'm going to go grab my bow. I'll see you there, Ev," Nazneen said. Then Nazneen and I bounced from the room, followed by Aura and Eleni.

FOURTEEN
DELRIK

I walked to the door and closed it behind Katuri and Nazneen. "Those two are becoming close."

"Mh hm," Evren mumbled, not looking up from her book.

Her lips moved slightly as she read through the page. I loved that little habit of hers. She twisted one of Aura's sleek black feathers between her forefinger and thumb, then tapped it against her lips. Every day I was with her, I found one more thing that I loved about her, even after almost a year together. The click of the lock, as I turned it, echoed off the bookshelves. That got her attention. Evren's head popped up. She pulled the book up to her chest, rested her chin on its spine, and drummed her fingers on the cover.

"You're interrupting my research," she scolded me, but there was a hint of playfulness in her voice.

"Were you able to find anything on Alux's shadow magic? Maybe where it came from?" I asked hopefully.

"No, nothing." Her silky, silver hair was draped over her shoulder. The curled ends pooled near her waist.

I tried to hide my disappointment, but I knew she could sense it. The strange feeling that started on the voyage here was still looming in the background of my mind. I couldn't seem to shake it. I'd been trained on how to guard my mind during legion training. I needed to implement that with Evren. I hated to hide parts of myself from her, but she didn't need to have anything else weighing her down while she learned to control her new power. She patted the floor beside her for me to sit.

I smiled at her. "So beautiful."

I walked over and sat behind her on the couch instead of on the floor. I plucked the book from her lap and snapped it closed, examining the cover.

"The Great Wars blah blah blah. Well, that sounds boring as hell."

"You know, it's impolite to read over someone's shoulder." She snatched the book from my grasp. "It's actually more interesting than you'd think. I've been trying to organize how the High Fae kingdoms came to be. I knew that the Powers Above gifted the High Fae with magic and that the elemental powers are a special gift given to only a few. Did you know there are five main bloodlines where the elemental magic has appeared, but only four kingdoms on the map? Why would there be five bloodlines but only four kingdoms?"

She pivoted, moving to kneel in front of me, her hands on my knees. The skirt she was wearing had slits up the sides and she was wearing leggings underneath. The skirt pooled in layers around her in shades of blues. Her shirt was shaped to her curves and she had the sleeves rolled to her elbows. She was kneeling before me and looking up with those piercing violet eyes.

"Fascinating. I'm sorry I interrupted you," I said sarcastically.

I knew out of the two siblings, Adaris was the avid reader. However, Evren had taken to spending more time with her nose buried in dusty books than with charcoal staining her fingers. I could care less about how the Fae kingdoms came to be. I just wanted answers about the shadow magic. I needed to know if my bondmate was in danger from me. I didn't trust that the shadow magic wouldn't turn on me and, thus, turn on my bondmate.

"I know how you can make it up to me," she said, pulling me from my negative thoughts.

She looked wonderful today—all soft and feminine. Her lips were pink and plump, and her skin had a glow from sitting in front of the fire all morning.

I leaned forward and sifted my fingers through her unbound silver hair and massaged her scalp before tipping her head back. "How can I make it up to you, Ashlyra?"

"I want you closer."

I leaned forward a few inches. Evren's hands came up to encircle my wrists. She traced her fingers along my arms, over my shoulders, to my face.

"Am I close enough?" I asked.

She shook her head back and forth. Her eyes were all hunger. Her hands slid down to my chest and beneath the fabric of my shirt to touch the shadows. I felt them shift on my skin to greet her. At least they still recognized her as home. She swallowed thickly. "No. Closer."

The corner of my mouth tipped, and the space between us was now just a hairsbreadth. My lips barely brushed hers. A helpless, impatient sound came from her.

"How about now?"

"Nope. Closer."

I tangled my fingers deeper into her hair and ran my tongue along her bottom lip. I felt the thread of our bond thrum, and our powers reached out for each other. The swirling darkness traveled to my fingers, making them dark as night. Her skin glowed under my touch. The shadows and fire met where our skin touched. I felt the binding mark warm. Her violet eyes flashed like dancing flames. The contact sent ripples of pleasure all throughout my body. She fisted her hands in my shirt and tugged. I allowed her to pull me off the couch and onto the floor, on top of her.

"You would really do anything to avoid training today, wouldn't you?" I asked without pulling away from her.

"I don't know what you're talking about."

Then her mouth was on mine.

FIFTEEN
KATURI

"We need to start with the basics," Master Endri Salcido, the head weapons master of the citadel, said in a raised voice to the group.

Well, somewhat of a group. Evren and Delrik were still missing. Nazneen and I'd left them alone in the library, so it was a fair assumption that we wouldn't see them for a while.

"The weaknesses of one will be the weakness of the entire group." He was pacing back and forth with his hands clasped behind his back, assessing each of us.

I'd never worked with him before, but I'd seen him around the citadel. Master Endri Salcido stood tall and proud as he addressed us. Garren and Arik were well acquainted with the male from the City of Kosmima on Quinterre, or the Western Continent as everyone in Illoterra referred to it. I'd visited the City of Kosmima several times as a child. It was located in the Water Fae Kingdom. The kingdom itself took up the southwestern half of Quinterre. It's northern border aligned with the Forest Fae Kingdom. The Taskun Territory and rugged mountains separated it from the Raven Fae Kingdom to the east. Wild forests and lakes covered most of the land, but its coast was its true beauty. Hundreds of islands dotted the coastline. The Okeanos Sea was known for its crystal clear, royal blue waters. The sea was home to many creatures. It was the first place I'd ever seen a sea dragon. There were also major cities throughout the kingdom for creatures of all kinds.

Master Salcido was a brute of a male, with strong arms he tended to cross over his barrel chest. He was known for his skills with a spear and shield, but could expertly handle any weapon handed to him. He'd led the training for all Snowhaven Legion before the war and stayed behind when everyone crossed to Quinterre to train the next round of trainees. Kanevvluk had been left under his protection with High Ruler Eckhardt gone.

Nazneen stood next to me while Garren, Jace, and Arik stood across from us. We were in one of the main training areas in the citadel. It was too cold to train outside, except for specific lessons. So today we were in the sand-filled arena. Praise be the Powers for that. I'd only been here a few times. I preferred to keep my skills and training to myself. Elemental powers were not common among High Fae. It was to my advantage to keep my abilities hidden. If someone didn't know how dangerous I was, I had a better chance of surviving if I was attacked. I'd also be seen as less of a threat. At least that's what my private trainer, Master Farren, had told me. So we kept my sessions under lock and key.

"Higher Ruler Eckhardt has updated me on the situation in the River Kingdom and with Hadeon Allelrick."

It made sense he'd update his weapons master, but I saw Garren stiffen at the mention of his father's name.

"Today we will break into—"

Master Salcido was interrupted by unstifled laughter coming from the hall outside the arena. Evren and Delrik stumbled into the arena, a tangle of limbs. When they saw us all staring, they straightened and ceased their giggling. Evren's hair had a fresh tousled look, and her lips were pink and swollen. I bit back my smile. At first, their closeness had made me uncomfortable, but they were basically two teenagers new in their love and goofy as hell. I couldn't help but love them too.

"We all know why you two are late," Nazneen said to them, inspecting her nails.

"Better late than never," Master Salcido said in the same curt tone he'd been using to instruct us. "As I was saying, we will break into groups so I can assess where you are with the basics, and we will go from there."

I knew he meant to assess me and the newcomers. He could've easily spoken to Master Farren. Master Farren had worked under the weapons master for many years. Though I was not sure he would've given his superior many details. Master Farren had always taken my request for privacy seriously. My guess was he wanted to see me with his own eyes. I didn't like the idea of being watched and judged by a stranger. This was way out of my comfort zone. The only reason I was here was to help Evren.

"What about using our powers?" Evren asked, clearing her throat of the giddy laughter.

"We will focus on that after you've mastered the basics of handling your weapon of choice and hand-to-hand combat." Master Salcido clapped his hands together. "Your powers will only get you so far in battle. Once your energy has run dry, you must rely on other skills. Alright, ladies over here. Gentlemen, feel free to warm up and get started with your drills."

Nazneen, Evren, and I followed Master Salcido across the arena where weapons was laid out on a table. Delrik, Garren, Jace, and Arik went about their drills. I inspected the table, but I had my own weapon I'd brought from Laeto Selva. I held my sheathed short sword in my hand. Nazneen brought her own bow as well.

"These are several weapons that I'd like to train you with. Being comfortable with a variety of tools can save your life."

Evren looked a little lost and uneasy.

"I have a dagger, but other than that, I've never used a weapon," Evren said. "I am not fond of using them."

Evren lifted the hem of her dress where the slits ran up the side of her legs and slipped a sheathed dagger from a hidden holster. She showed Master Salcido the dagger she had brought with her. Salcido raised a brow in question, and Evren nodded. He took the dagger from her and unsheathed it. It was a beautiful, curved Darkstone blade.

He returned the blade to its sheath and handed it back to Evren. "This is a vicious world, Evren, especially for females. Males are faster, stronger. You have to be prepared to fight. Otherwise, they will silence you."

Master Salcido led us to the center of the arena.

"I don't think I could take someone's life," Evren said.

"You don't need to make a killing blow. A simple nick in the right place will disable your opponent," Master Salcido explained.

"I don't understand." Evren's confusion was written all over her face.

"For example, by slicing across the back of the leg at a tendon, you incapacitate your opponent so they can't run after you." He pointed to a spot behind his knee and then the back of his ankle. "You can also use the butt of your hilt and strike here. It will knock your opponent unconscious." He pointed to a spot along his neck.

"And my personal favorite," Nazneen cut in, "is the groin. Even if someone is wearing armor, there is a joint here where a blade can easily slip through. Bleeds like hell."

Nazneen was unlike Evren in her fondness of a good brawl. Being a top commander in the Arcelia Legion, she'd have to be used to violence. I knew she had knowledge of fighting and war, and I looked forward to learning as much as I could from her while she was here. Evren nodded her head as she took in all the advice being thrown at her.

"Alright, let's try with these." Master Salcido lifted wooden sticks and handed one to Evren.

"You want me to attack you? With a stick?" Evren asked.

"By practicing in an environment where hitting is encouraged, you risk being struck." He swung the wooden practice sword in a sweeping motion and hit Evren against the leg ... hard.

"Ow! What in the dark hells," she cried.

Oh shit. Delrik would not be happy.

Master Salcido took a step forward and swung again, the exact same as last time, but Evren took a quick step back and brought her wooden sword down and blocked him. He held the position and raised his eyebrows at her.

"Remembered pain makes the lesson stick and you're less likely to make the same mistake over and over," he said.

Evren nodded, then readied herself for another attack. Nazneen stood next to her and showed her how to stand. I watched on and took mental notes. Master Fallen had the same teaching tactics as Master Salcido, though he'd never hit me as hard. I guessed hitting a princess was frowned upon. However, Master Salcido didn't hold back. He struck hard; the crack of the wooden sword rang out through the arena each time it hit its mark. He did let her get in a few strikes so that she could feel what it was like to attack. I really enjoyed his teaching style.

"Each time you attack, you open yourself up for a counterattack. So keep a close eye on your surroundings. With each attack, you need to have a defense at the ready." Nazneen lunged forward, her empty hand thrust forward. Evren copied her. Master Salcido moved with exaggerated slowness to show his next move so Evren could go on the defense.

After about two hours of Master Salcido teaching Evren different stances for blocking attacks and the variations of weapons available to her, we came back together as a group. She'd catch on; it was only the first day after all. She'd gain more confidence once she was able to combine her new skills with her magic.

"For the last half of our training, I want you to break into pairs for some light sparring," Master Salcido announced. "Nothing fancy. Let's keep powers to a minimum. Focus on your physical strengths."

In a flash, like a literal blur of movement, Delrik was standing behind Evren. Such incredible speed made my head spin.

"Dude, enough with the speed," Arik complained. "No one is going to touch your precious female."

Delrik bared his teeth, growling at Arik, while possessively pulling Evren's back against his chest, his hand splayed across her stomach. Even Evren released a small snarl, guarding her bondmate from the verbal attack. She looked so small in his arms. Ugh, Nazneen was right. They were stupidly adorable.

"Why are you even here?" Delrik snarled.

Arik just ignored Delrik. "Nazneen, it'd be an honor to work with you."

And I swore Delrik released another low rumble.

"Don't you dare harm a hair on her head," Delrik said through clenched teeth.

"Don't worry brother, I won't take it easy on him. He'll be begging me to stop before you know it," Nazneen said.

"You know he won't pry her off you when she starts to claw your eyes out," Garren laughed.

Arik walked over to where Nazneen and I stood. From the corner of my eye, I saw him lean in close and heard him whisper, "I would never beg you to stop."

"Gross, you two." I wrinkled my nose and took a step away.

Nazneen laughed and swatted Arik in the chest with the back of her hand. She must have had some force behind the smack because Arik grunted on impact. Between Evren and Nazneen, I'd never get a break from the sexual tension. I couldn't get away from the flirting. It was everywhere.

Meanwhile, Master Salido followed Evren and Delrik away to continue to give Evren pointers. In my opinion, with Evren's fire power, she didn't need to be skilled with weapons. She was a weapon herself. Or so I'd been told by Nazneen. I'd yet to see the full strength of her flames, but if her elemental was as strong as mine, she'd be a fierce opponent.

"I guess that means you're stuck with me," Garren said without approaching me.

I whipped my head in his direction. Damn it. Garren made a show of rolling his neck and rotating his shoulders to loosen up. He was just showing off. He'd been running drills with Delrik for the last two hours. He was plenty warmed up. I looked around for Jace to take pity on me, but he was nowhere to be seen.

"A council meeting," Garren answered without turning around. He bounced on the balls of his feet.

"Joy," I said, deadpan. "I guess I don't have a choice."

I hadn't seen Jace slip out. For years, I'd managed to keep my distance from Garren, but within the last few weeks, I'd been alone with him more than I could count. The proximity was messing with my mind. He went from basically ignoring me to pestering me any chance he got. And now we were being forced to train together? I was not amused.

Garren moved over to the wall where he'd stashed a canister of water and a towel when he'd first arrived. He bent to pick up his water and lifted it to his mouth. His shirt showed off his shapely form and shifted across his biceps as he lifted the bottle to his lips. Then, with his back still to me, he reached over his shoulder and yanked his shirt up and over his head in one smooth movement.

My eyes went wide, and my jaw hit the floor as I took him in. Muscles. Muscles upon muscles upon muscles. His back was defined and rigid like it had been carved from ice. The bands of his muscles stretched as his arms moved when he bunched up his shirt and dropped it on the floor. It was impossible not to stare. I'd seen shirtless and naked males before. I studied art, and I'd watched the legion train on occasion, but damn. My eyes followed the length of his spine down to where a scaled beast was tattooed into his fair skin. The ink wrapped around his side and disappeared below the waistband of his pants on the opposite side. His pants clung tightly to his ass and his thick thighs. Thick, powerful thighs. He clasped his hands behind his back and extended them in a stretch. Dangerously strong hands. Fuck. I blew out a shaky breath. Why was he affecting me so much?

Garren turned and my eyes took in all the scales as they ran across his torso. A sea dragon's head, its mouth opened wide in a fierce, toothy snarl, was tattooed into his smooth chest. My gaze drifted downward, following the angular ridges of the deep V and sea dragon tail that plummeted below his belt.

My mouth went completely dry. He was a Powers-damned gift to every High Fae that walked the realm.

A sword swept in a graceful arc in front of Garren's waist, bringing me back to reality. A flash of heat swept through me. I turned away from him as quickly as I could. I stalked toward the middle of the arena. I needed to put as much distance between us as possible. I heard Garren laugh as he followed behind me. He knew exactly what I'd been staring at and how it affected me.

Focus Katuri! Pull it together. He is not delicious. He is not available. Remember how horrible he is? Remember all the times you've seen him with others. All his questionable nighttime activities. Really any time of day for Garren. That body carved from stone that he is flaunting is the kind of body any Fae, really any creature, would fall to pieces over. Male and female alike. How many females I've seen coming and going from his rooms. Physical attraction. This is just a natural physical attraction. Just keep remembering that.

I forced the memory of a random Fae female standing between his legs into my mind. I'd endured many social gatherings and parties over the years where females threw themselves at Garren ... rubbing their palms over his shoulders and digging their nails in like a cat. Trailing kisses across his throat. Drifting hands. I didn't care. He wasn't getting any sexual satisfaction from me. A lot of consorts didn't have sex with each other except to reproduce. He might as well get it from someone, but something seared in my chest each time I saw him with someone else. A creeping pang of disgust hit me ... or was that jealousy? No. It definitely was *not* jealousy.

You are a strong, independent female. Powerful. No male can match you.

"What was that?" he asked me.

Shit, I must have said that last bit out loud. I ignored him and tried to clear my mind.

The rising tension between us was another reason to leave Kanevvluk and Garren as soon as I could. I hadn't thought about leaving Kanevvluk before now. I didn't think it was an option. But the more High Ruler Eckhardt pushed Garren and me to use each other's powers and begin thinking about heirs, the more I realized I needed to get out of this city as soon as I could.

"Why have we never trained together before?" Garren said. He was approaching me at a quick pace, his sword hanging low down by his side. His binding mark started at his fingers, which were gripping the hilt, and twisted up to his elbow in gilded ropes. I'd never seen it before, at least not like this. I avoided looking at his hand as much as I hid my own. The mark drew my eye and I could feel my own mark heat at his proximity. Fucking blood binding mark. The physical proof of my father's betrayal and my imprisonment. The sudden rage made the haze of lust evaporate faster than steam. My father had ripped my freedom from me and Garren had been a willing participant.

"Because I do everything in my power to stay as far from you as possible." I hurled my words at him.

They didn't slow him one bit. He crowded my space. "You are being a touch temperamental."

I turned away from him, clenching the handle of my weapon tightly. I couldn't even look at his smug face.

Great. Now I'm breaking the most basic rule just to get away from Garren.

Master Farren's number one rule: don't turn your back on your enemy.

Garren made my mind mush.

"Am I? Maybe you should go find someone else to spar with," I snapped, spinning to face him again. This time I raised my short sword between us.

Garren stopped his advance just far enough away that the tip of my blade touched the sleek, inked scales just above his heart. Oh, how I was tempted to drag the blade across his pristine skin and draw blood. Make him feel just a fraction of the pain I had felt when the priestess sliced into my palm. A scrap of the agony for resisting the compulsion. It had taken me days to physically recover from the blood ritual. I hadn't been strong enough then to fight against my father's compulsion, but I'd been practicing. I was stronger than I'd ever been. No one would ever use me against my will again.

Garren looked down to where I could easily land a deadly blow and then back up at me. Delight danced across his features and that stupid rakish grin appeared. How could he be smiling when I was being torn apart on the inside?

"Maybe I like the threat of being stabbed by you." He swung his sword, casually knocking mine out of the way.

"You're lucky that you're still breathing after the stunt you pulled last week."

Shit. Why had I said that?

His eyes, the color of crushed teal gemstones, glittered with the reminder of cornering me in my greenhouse. With my own words, the memory of him invading my personal space, his mouth so close to mine, the way his warm breath made goosebumps cover my skin, crashed into me. All the anger and pain dissipated. Had that only been a week ago? I took another step back. Why did he insist on being so close to me? Garren stepped to the left, and I countered. We continued to circle each other.

His body was truly a masterpiece. His movements were precise and calculated. Why did he have to look so damned good?

Garren said something in response, but of course, I'd missed it. His bare chest was a distraction. My blade dropped, just an inch, but it was enough of a window of opportunity for him.

And he took it.

Garren lunged. I couldn't bring the sword up fast enough. I winced at the burst of pain that lanced through my shoulder.

"Dark hells, Garren!" I cursed at him.

He'd struck me with the flat of his blade. I scowled at him, and his eyes turned liquid, a storm of whirling water and ice.

"I wouldn't actually hurt you. I turned my blade at the last minute." He chuckled.

The ass actually laughed at me. Outrage rumbled through me like an earthquake. I launched myself at him, dipping under his arm and coming up behind him. He twisted and swung his blade, but I wasn't there. I'd dropped to the ground and swung out my leg in a kick. He was quick and jumped before my leg made contact. I pivoted again, making it to my feet several feet away and had my blade poised for another attack. My breaths were coming hard and fast. I was having trouble focusing on my breathing. My mind was befuddled and it was slowing me down. Garren, on the other hand, looked completely relaxed and at ease.

I swallowed and forced myself to take in a deep breath. For the first time, I realized how much of a threat he really was to me. Not only physically, but mentally and emotionally. Garren was dangerous. Maybe I should've been taking my training more seriously.

Garren took a swaggering step forward, and a sharp pull in my chest sucked the breath from my lungs. I wanted to lunge at him again, but I was frozen in place. I couldn't do it. Something was holding me back. I lost all my senses. All my instincts of self-preservation went out the window. An ethereal awareness of the male in front of me made me want to surrender to him.

I reached for my power—something, anything to free me—but it was quiet. It was there, but it refused to surface.

What the fuck is going on? Is he doing this? Is he somehow preventing me from using my power against him? Did he take it from me without me realizing?

Garren kept coming at me, backing me up, step by step. My back met something solid. I couldn't breathe. How had we gotten so far from the middle of the arena? Surely, someone was watching and would save me from him. Right? Where was Nazneen when I needed her?

Without warning, his hand shot out and grabbed my wrist, squeezing tight until I dropped my sword. It hardly made a noise as it landed in the soft sand at my feet. Garren had never touched me before. Not even a kiss on the hand. He'd gotten close, but never flesh to flesh. Not since the day of the ceremony.

With that single touch, my entire world condensed and expanded all at the same time. The awareness I'd been feeling on and off the last six months grew tenfold. I felt as if I was unraveling. I knew he felt it too, because his eyes went wide. A spark of energy passed between the two of us and his breath caught.

"Stop." My voice was almost inaudible. His calloused hand was warm against my skin. "I don't want your hands on me."

I was lying. I *did* want his hands on me. I wanted them all over me.

A moment of concern flashed across Garren's face as if he wouldn't push me with my denial. Then his features changed. Suddenly, like I could feel what he was feeling, a moment of pause came to my mind. Was I sensing his emotion somehow through the binding mark? Then, with a swift switch, I came to the realization that Garren *knew* I was lying. I could taste the lie on my tongue. Wild exhilaration coursed through me at the anticipation of what would happen next—his wild exhilaration.

I half heartedly reached for a knife I had at my waist, but he was faster. He grabbed it from my belt with his free hand and tossed it to the side. Garren rested his sword against the wall, took my other wrist, and then pressed both of them to the small of my back with a single large hand. With little effort, he urged me forward so I was pressed against his chest. My pounding heart ratcheted higher. I didn't dare lift my chin to look at his face. I wouldn't be able to resist if I looked into his deep, azul eyes. I kept my gaze firmly on the hollow of his throat where his collarbones met.

"Interesting," he said.

"What?" Fuck my stupid breathlessness. "What's interesting?"

"You can't feel that? You can't feel me?"

"All I feel is you," I snapped and tried to wriggle from his grip.

"You know what I mean," he said.

I knew exactly what he meant. Soul recognition.

He lifted his free hand and tipped my chin so I was forced to look him in the eye. His thumb pressed into my bottom lip where part of my tribal mark was. Then, as if he was whispering in my ear, I felt a surge of lust rush through me. It wasn't my lust. It was his. I was sensing him. And then it clicked. The only way I could be feeling his feelings was if we were...

No. No, that couldn't be true. We couldn't be... I shook my head back and forth.

"Hello, Ashlyra."

I tried to pull away from him again. "Let go."

He leaned in and whispered against my forehead. "I think you *do* want my hands on you. You just don't like giving up control."

His words hung over me like a knife. I shivered like a Powers damned damsel. He was taunting me, and Powers Above, I ... I loved it.

"I belong to no one."

I felt his lips against my forehead as he smiled.

"I can feel your heart, Little Flower. I can feel your desire, whether you accept it or not. You are enjoying this."

The connection between us surged to life. I gasped at its strength. My whole body came alive with it. I tried to pull away, but Garren squeezed my wrists tighter, holding me against him. My heart almost stopped at the pleasure that swept through me. I wanted him, but I also wanted nothing to do with him at the same time. I felt his magic and his mind caress me.

Fuck.

His chin dropped, and for a moment, his lips hovered over mine. Instead of pressing his lips to mine, he kissed me gently on the side of my neck right below my ear, and then breathed me in deeply. "Until later, Little Flower." He released me and left the arena, shirtless and all, taking the other half of my soul with him.

SIXTEEN
KATURI

Today had been disaster. Not only was I Garren's consort through the blood binding, but we were actually bondmates? How was that even possible? Wouldn't we have known by now? It had been forty years? Surely, the bondmate thing would've kicked in by now. This was some cruel joke from the fates for sure.

I had shifted into my wolf as soon as I knew Garren was gone and ran from the citadel. I ran as far south as I could through the Winterwoods until I felt a sharp tug deep in my gut. I nearly tripped at its suddenness. I pushed past it for a few miles and then couldn't go another step. So I circled back east along the edge of the forest before turning back to the citadel. The sun had set long ago, and my muscles were finally tired, even if my mind wasn't.

I was prowling along the edge of the battlement, still in my wolf form, when I saw Nazneen lean her head out the door leading to the back stairs of the residential wing. I sat right along the edge of the forest and watched her from the gate. A line of thick evergreens stretched as far as I could see to the left and the right. The Winterwood. They were heavy with snow. There was a winding staircase that no one ever used except me. Nazneen looked left, then right. Then she stepped out into the frozen night. Her breath clouded in front of her face in the numbing air. I saw her pat her side, checking for her favorite dagger I assumed.

Snow had fallen this afternoon, and still more flakes drifted from the sky above. The courtyard was blanketed in fresh whiteness ... except for the footprints. Soft footprints led away from the citadel, toward the towering wall of stone. My footprints. I guessed the snow hadn't covered them yet. I knew Nazneen was a curious soul. There was no way she'd see footprints and not follow them. There was no reason someone would be out this late, unless they were sneaking out. Two guards dressed in the legion navy and gray nodded as

Nazneen came closer to the gate. They didn't mind her going outside the wall, so she just kept walking like she did this every day. I knew they wouldn't give me away, even if she asked. I may remain hidden a majority of the time, but I was still Garren's consort and watched closely by the guards.

A well worn path was visible on the ground beneath the trees where the thick, waxy canopy above hardly let any snow accumulate on the ground here. The branches and pine needles were crushed into the earth and muffled Nazneen's footsteps, but with my increased hearing in my shifted form, I heard them loud and clear. A frosty wind cut through the trees and stung my eyes. Nazneen pulled the hood of her cloak up and tucked it closer to her body. She hid her hands in the thick wool to keep as much warmth in as possible. She wasn't dressed to be traipsing through the snow. There was nothing like the cold of Kanevvluk. I knew she was trained to withstand the cold, to survive no matter the elements, but this land of ice and snow ... I couldn't imagine being out here for any length of time with my thick fur coat. The cold was too severe to survive.

As she walked further into the woods, I followed her on padded feet. Interlaced branches let in only pale streaks of light from the double moons. The light cast an eerie glow into the thick forest. I wandered through the dark trunks, weaving in and out. She was sure to leave a trail as she went so that she could follow back to the citadel. The forest was shrouded in a white fog that hung close to the ground. She followed my footprints until they suddenly stopped. There weren't any signs of anyone nearby. They had just ended. That is where I'd shifted earlier this afternoon. Nazneen spun in a circle, examining the ground and then the surrounding trees.

I'd had enough fun; I needed to show myself and make sure she didn't get lost out here. I lifted a paw and stepped on a branch just to my left. The snap was as loud as thunder in the quiet forest. Nazneen whipped around, her dagger drawn, and an invisible threat masked by the night and shadows.

I was the something dangerous was lurking in these woods. Instinct had her freezing, assessing her surroundings, primed to defend herself. She didn't appear afraid. She'd been trained to ward off multiple attackers. But there was no way she knew a large wolf was lurking. I could see her listening closely for another sound, but there was nothing. Not a chirp, not a rustle of leaves, or a flutter of wings. Nothing.

Nazneen scanned the dimness around her again, back and forth until she spotted my luminous emerald eyes through the darkness. I exhaled twin puffs of air from my snout as I stepped onto the path, blocking her route back to the citadel. There would be no way she could outrun me. I was easily the size of a horse. The deep brown of my fur was a stark contrast to the white backdrop of snow. I prowled forward a step. My massive paws made no noise as I approached. I tipped my head curiously. I wondered if she thought I'd eat her. I was hungry. I could use a snack. Running always gave me back my appetite. Red streaks in my fur glinted in the faint light as I slid a paw closer. Nazneen held her ground. She didn't want to appear to be easy prey. Smart. Another step forward. I was close enough now to reach out and touch, but she didn't dare. She squinted into the dim light. I chuffed out a puff of air, making the hood of her cloak fall off her head and her hair blow back.

"Powers Above, what kind of forest is this?" she said into the night.

The ground began to shake underneath me, and snow and dried pine needles began to swirl on a gust, surrounding Nazneen and me. With a small burst of light, my wolf was gone. I stood in my High Fae form before my friend. The look on her face was priceless. I wore only a thin chemise, and my feet were bare. The cold would soon freeze me to death without my fur. Eleni bounced in circles around us yipping with excitement. She loved Nazneen.

"I thought you were going to wet yourself there for a moment." I grinned.

"Not gonna lie, me too." She let out an exaggerated breath.

"I know you said you shifted into a wolf. I just pictured a wolf more along the size of Eleni, not the beast that had just been standing before me," Nazneen said. She placed her dagger back in its sheath at her waist and bent to pet Eleni.

"What are you doing out here?" I asked.

I walked over to a folded pile of clothes tucked in the trunk of a tree. I slipped into each piece and my boots, and I threw a cloak around my shoulders.

"I saw a door leading to the eastern gate open and footprints in the snow. I was curious," she said with a casual shrug. "And I was growing antsy being stuck inside day in and day out. What are *you* doing out here?"

"Running."

She arched a brow at me. She'd caught me in my half truth. I was running to get away from Garren. To get away from the binding mark and the Ashlyra and my future that was even more planned out without my knowledge. When she didn't say anything, I continued.

"I needed to get away from ... the citadel."

She could tell I wasn't telling her something. Damn spy skills. I twisted my fingers, and my gaze darted away from her. I couldn't deceive her. She knew me too well, even after such a short time.

"What did you need to get away from, Katuri?" she pressed, taking a step closer to me and crossing her arms.

"It's Garren," I said, exasperated, dropping my hands. My shoulders drooped.

"Well, that was a lot easier to get out of you than I was expecting. You know, I sensed the tension between the two of you since day one."

"Did you see him during training today?"

"He did seem quite ... invested in your sparring match," she said, smiling.

I groaned and then turned back toward the citadel. Nazneen rushed to catch up with me. When she reached my side, she took my hand and looped my arm through hers. The canopy of the trees seemed to bow as we passed, blocking out any snow and wind that were able to make it through the trees. It was like the forest knew my inner turmoil. Eleni yipped and then bounced ahead of us down the path, chomping at the snowflakes as she went.

"He is your consort," she said and pointedly looked down and the hand I had resting on her arm.

The gilded binding mark was visible, even in the dim light. Of course, she'd figured it out. I didn't know why I had thought I could hide it from her and Evren.

"Ugh. Yes, but I can't stand him. I've been trapped in the damn frozen hell for forty years and he's always ignored me. He lives his life, and I live mine. But recently, he's been taunting me." I stopped walking and turned to face her. "It's like he's gotten bored with his life and sees me as easy amusement."

"How?"

"At first, it was little things. Showing up at my lunch hour in the kitchen. Or sitting next to me at dinner when he previously sat across from me. And he'd ask me endless questions." I was so frustrated with everything. "He cornered me in my room, the day that you all arrived actually. That's why we were late. He has never come into my suite. Well, except when he'd sneak in when I wasn't around. He just barged in. I can't think straight when he's near me." I thrust my hands through my long, tangled strands, wind-whipped from running through the forest. Flecks of dirt speckled my hands. "And today at training ... he's never touched me. The moment he made contact with my skin, it took everything I had not to surrender. My powers and self-preservation were just gone. I couldn't push him away."

Nazneen reached up and plucked a twig from my hair.

"Nazneen, Garren is my bondmate. For some reason, it clicked into place this afternoon. And I have no idea what to do about it."

"So, I take it you don't believe in the fates and bondmates?"

I swallowed a lump in my throat.

"I know bondmates exist. I've seen it before; I just didn't think it was something I'd ever experience. But I can feel it, that connection between us. But I've hated him for as long as I've known I was bound to him. Even before we actually met. I'd been told my entire life I was destined to be his through the blood binding. The idea of belonging to anyone is revolting. Then, like a switch, everything changed, and now I can't keep him out of my mind. And the more I'm around him, the more I'm drawn to him. I don't need anyone to take care of me. And I refuse to surrender my elemental power." I let out a deep sigh. "My body and brain just aren't on the same page."

"Well, that makes complete sense."

"Yeah, but I don't think he feels the same. He's always treated me like an annoying little sister that he's forced to play nice with. He's been against being with me all this time. So why now? It can't just be that easy to change."

"Are you sure? Maybe he's changed his mind. Bondmates are a powerful thing."

I just shrugged my shoulders. "It's just a game to him. He can't seriously change just because we are fated bondmates now."

"You know you can't actually run away from a bondmate."

"I know." My shoulders drooped in defeat.

"But we can have a little fun in the meantime. We can make him jealous."

"Now that seems childish."

"Of course, it is! But we have to find some sort of fun while we're stuck here. We might as well pick on the boys. Plus, I don't think

Garren would want you to pass your time the same way I prefer," Nazneen said, winking at me.

"Poor Delrik. He had to grow up with you."

"Oh yeah, he's gotten the brunt of my pranks for years." She pulled me toward the wall again. "Come on. Let's go find Evren. We're going to need her help."

SEVENTEEN
KATURI

Nazneen didn't release my hand as we sprinted past my suite. She slammed her fist hard three times against the room where Delrik and Evren were sleeping. She didn't wait for a response before she flung the door open wide and yanked me inside.

Evren was snuggled in bed with Delrik—naked and sated.

"Do you ever *not* barge in?" Delrik bellowed as he flung himself across his bondmate to cover her naked body from view.

"Do you two ever stop..."

"*Don't* say it," Delrik threatened, pointing a finger at his sister.

"We need your bondmate. And I've seen her naked, so you can stop attempting to cover her."

I was red from head to toe at the sight of the bonded pair naked in bed. Nazneen threw back the covers on Evren's side of the bed, ignoring the fact that she was completely naked, and crawled in to snuggle with her.

"You two look so cozy," Evren said as she ran her hand along the fluffy sweater Nazneen was wearing. She didn't seem concerned about her modesty in the slightest. "Where did you get this?"

"Oh, Katuri showed me this cute little boutique in the city..." Naz started.

"Argh!" Delrik flew from the bed with his speed, but not fast enough to prevent me from getting a glimpse of his finely toned ass. I quickly covered my reddened face, but it was too late. Evren was a lucky female indeed.

"Just remember you love me!" Nazneen called after him.

"Do you do this often?" I asked.

"Do what? Kick my brother out of his own blissful bed? Yes."

"Usually, she waits until we're finished," Evren said distractedly as she looked around the room. I wasn't sure what she was looking for.

"You were finished. It's past your bedtime. You're usually passed out by now," Nazneen said.

Evren climbed from the bed. "Do you see my nightgown?"

Nazneen pointed to a random chair behind me. "It's over the back of the chair."

It was haphazardly thrown into the sitting area. Nazneen's lack of modesty had clearly rubbed off on Evren as she strutted across the room as naked as the day she was born to fetch the flimsy fabric.

"I don't know how you sleep in those things," Nazneen commented.

"Well, if someone didn't barge into our room whenever she wanted, maybe I'd sleep naked."

"I'm with Nazneen on this one. I hate wearing anything while sleeping. Ugh, and don't even get me started on bras and underwear. So uncomfortable. They are overrated."

Evren just shook her head at us and slipped her nightgown over her head.

"Is there a reason you're preventing me from getting my beauty sleep?" Evren asked incredulously.

"Kat is in a predicament and needs our help," Nazneen said.

"Is this about Garren practically drooling on you today while you were supposed to be sparring?"

I groaned and covered my face with a pillow. How did she know? Was it that obvious? "Ugh. I don't know what to do. He's never acted like that before." I pulled the pillow from my face and flopped down onto the mattress.

"I love how dramatic you are," Nazneen said, laughing at me.

"One moment, the thought of him near me makes my stomach churn, and then the next, it feels impossible to ignore him."

Nazneen not so quietly whispered, "The bond snapped into place."

Evren's face lit with delight. "I *knew* it!"

"And now being separated from him is almost painful. When I was running today, this damn connection literally prevented me from going too far. It's like I've been tossed around on violent waves and I can't seem to find my way back to land, and Garren is the one dragging me back."

"Why don't you start with how you felt about him kissing you?" Evren said.

"It wasn't a kiss!"

"Um, his mouth was on you. It may not have been your lips, but it still counts," Nazneen pointed out.

Evren joined us back on the bed. "Agreed," she said.

"I had made up my mind. After meeting you both, I'd decided to leave Kanevvluk with you guys when you went home. But now? Now I don't know what to do. I'm feeling so many things all at once. It's so confusing."

Nazneen spoke over my head to Evren. "She's feeling the bond hardcore after that "show of affection," but she thinks he's just messing with her."

I pulled at the wrist of my long sleeve sweater to cover my hand with the binding mark. I never wore anything that went higher than my wrists outside of my bedroom and the hot springs. Even today at training, my arms had been completely covered. I hated for anyone to see the binding mark. I hated to see it. And now this bondmate thing was happening.

I felt the blood drain from my face. "I can't do this."

"I don't think that's how bondmates work," Nazneen said.

"What if I don't want a bondmate?"

"It's kind of late for that." Evren spoke gently.

She placed her hand on my arm. She knew Garren wasn't an easy topic. I'd told them how the blood binding was forced on me.

"I've been controlled and told what to do my entire life. Garren is a stranger. And I'm just supposed to submit to the bond? Submit my power and my life to him?"

Evren stroked my tangled hair off my forehead. "He isn't a stranger."

"But he is. He is a cocky, arrogant male who thinks he is a gift to all females around him. We've lived under the same roof for decades and I know nothing about him. And he knows nothing about me. He wouldn't even notice if I went missing." I took a shaky breath. "What I know for sure is I have never had friends and you two saved me from a miserable existence. And I'm not willing to give that up."

At the same moment, Evren and Nazneen buried me up in a hug. I couldn't help but laugh at my friends. Tears of laughter were coming now. This wasn't the darkest moment in my life, but it was pretty close. However, having these two support me allowed me to see light through the darkness.

"Of course you are welcome in Arcelia. Always. But I think we should find out first how Garren really feels about you."

"How are we going to do that? I can't just walk up to him and ask," I said. I sat up again and attempted to finger-comb the tangles from my hair. Evren reached over to her nightstand, picked up her brush, and began brushing the ends of my hair.

"I mean, you could," Nazneen said.

Evren smacked her arm. "You know it isn't that easy."

All of a sudden, Nazneen's face turned positively feral. A wicked smile formed on her lips.

Evren's hand froze in the air. "Uh oh. That's her face when she has a bad idea."

"Oh, it's definitely a bad idea."

EIGHTEEN
GARREN

"Learn to fight. Know how to defend yourself. Then no one will be able to control you," Master Salcido said as he paced back and forth before us just as he had last week.

Unless your father was the ass that ruled the kingdom.

I leaned over to whisper to Delrik. "Where did this guy even come from?"

"You tell me. He is *your* weapons master."

Delrik was still brooding from last night. I'd caught him more pissed than a wet cat, stomping from his room and slamming the door behind him. He'd been mumbling something angry under his breath. He'd been struggling to pull his pants over his bare ass in jerky movements, his shirt hanging in his teeth. It was quite a sight to see.

The Previous Night

"Whoa! What happened? Did Evren finally come to her senses and kick you out?"

"My sister and your new bondmate just kicked me out of my own bed!"

I curled over in laughter. "What? No fucking way!"

Fury. And those shadows.

"And you just let it happen?" I couldn't catch my breath.

"Well, they climbed into bed with my naked bondmate. What else was I supposed to do? Sit and have a chat?"

And then he'd stomped off down the corridor. When he'd rounded the corner, I took a step to follow after him. Then I heard a round of laughter come from the other side of Delrik's door. Katuri's laughter.

"Do you do this often?"

Her voice. Katuri. I'd recognize her voice anywhere. Was she actually in his bed?

"Do what? Kick my brother out of his blissful bed? Yes."

"Usually she waits until we're finished," Evren chuckled.

"You were finished. It's past your bedtime. You're usually passed out by now."

"Do you see my nightgown?"

"It's over the back of the chair."

I pressed closer to the door to eavesdrop.

"I don't know how you sleep in those things."

"Well, if someone didn't barge into our room whenever she wanted, maybe I'd sleep naked."

"I'm with Nazneen on this one. I hate wearing anything while sleeping. Ugh and don't even get me started on bras and underwear. So uncomfortable. They are overrated."

My whole body tensed. Did I seriously just hear those words? That was definitely Katuri speaking. I needed to go back to my suite before I broke down the Powers damned door and carried her off like a hormonal savage.

Delrik shoved my shoulder. I gave him a silent shrug. Evren, who was leaning against his chest, looked over at me in confusion. I'd let my mind wander to Katuri. In her bed. Sleeping naked. I cleared my throat. Katuri had always been beautiful. It was impossible to not be attracted to her. I'd just never seen it so clearly as I did now. The moment my hand touched her, a wild sensation crashed into me like waves off the sea. My entire body tingled. I was brought internally to my knees. My whole perspective on life shifted and refocused on the powerful female standing before me. A tether grabbed hold of me and affixed itself deep within. It was a bridge between our two souls. I knew she felt it too. When she finally met my eyes, something primal awoke. I would never be the same. I didn't want to be. This beautiful creature, full of tenacity and courage, altered my very being. Walking away from her yesterday was the hardest thing I'd ever done. But I didn't want to ravish her right there in the arena. So I took a deep breath and left.

"Today we will start with using our powers, learning to control them," Master Salcido said.

"And for those of us that have no issues wielding our powers?" I said with a flick of my wrist.

Water appeared from thin air and danced in a circle around Katuri's feet. She was standing with Nazneen and Arik. As it moved and swirled, ice crystals formed like diamonds. The look Kat pierced me with was sharp enough to cut glass. Flecks of power shimmered in her mossy eyes. I winked at her, and her scowl deepened, squishing the tribal mark in that adorable way I loved. I loved her sassy looks and sharp words.

Her mane of dark hair was pulled back into a sleek ponytail this morning. Her elegant neck and arced ears were on full display. Her skin-tight leggings were cropped and stopped mid-calf. Her feet were bare, and her flowing tunic was cropped at the sleeves. I hadn't seen her binding mark since the day the priestess performed the blood binding. She kept it covered at all times. Even the length of her sleeves went all the way to her fingertips most of the time. The gold was beautiful against her warm brown skin. The neckline of her shirt was unbuttoned at the neck and dipped down her chest. I could see the top of what appeared to be another white tribal mark plunging down between her breasts. I'd never seen her in such revealing clothes. Not that they would be considered revealing for a normal High Fae, but for Katuri, she was practically nude compared to her normal attire. I wanted to peel her clothes off and search every inch of her skin to see how much of her body was covered in the white tribal ink. I wanted to hold her down and make my own marks on her perfect skin. The thought sent raw desire through me.

I raked my hands through my hair.

"You all right?" Delrik whispered to me.

"Yeah." I swallowed. "Fine."

I'd never had such thoughts before, but I couldn't stop coming up with scenarios on how to claim her as mine. My gorgeous, defiant bondmate.

She took a step forward, breaking through my ring of water and ice. "I think everyone could benefit from practice." She shot me a look over her shoulder. "It may also be useful for Evren to see how we control our powers and help to focus hers."

"That's true," Master Salcido said before I could open my mouth to retort. "Have you fully shifted into your elemental form?" he asked Evren.

"I think so? Only once. But I shifted back into my High Fae form almost immediately."

The weapons master nodded. "It takes time and focus to learn to maintain your shifted form. Katuri, would you like to demonstrate?"

Oh, this would be interesting. I'd never seen Katuri in her shifted form. Hell, I'd only seen her use her powers for the smallest of things. I knew she was powerful. I could feel it through the blood binding. I'd tapped into them a few times, but she was so resistant I could barely do anything with the fragment of earth magic I was able to test. I'd seen her greenhouse, but she'd always kept her powers hushed. They'd just begun to develop when she arrived in Kanevvluk, so no one knew what she was truly capable of.

"I'm not so sure...." she began, but I cut her off.

"Come on, Kat. Don't be shy," I goaded her. "For someone who claims to have so much control on her power, I've never seen you use it. Actually, I've never seen your elemental form either."

Nazneen stepped up beside Katuri. "Well, I have."

She had? I straightened. How? When? I didn't like that.

Nazneen ran her finger up Katuri's arm almost ... seductively.

She better get her hands off my bondmate.

"She's quite beautiful in her shifted form."

Nazneen's finger curled around a stray piece of hair at the end of Katuri's ponytail and wrapped it around her finger, keeping her eyes locked with Katuri. Katuri blushed at the compliment, or was it the soft way Nazneen was looking at her? Then Nazneen leaned in, turning into Katuri, and whispered something inaudible in her ear. Katuri laughed in response, quickly covering her mouth and nodding her head.

I loved the way her tribal mark crinkled across her nose. Her laugh was musical and soft. It was the purest sound I'd ever heard. I should be the one making her happy, making her laugh. What was going on between those two? Since Nazneen and Evren came, Kat's been glowing with radiant joy. I'd never heard her laugh so much. Even the ever-present vines surrounding her door had new orchid blossoms in every color.

"Alright. Evren, I'll show you," Katuri said, her confidence anew.

Katuri gave Nazneen's hand a tight squeeze before walking toward the center of the training arena. Her bare feet were noiseless on the sand. With her back to us, she rolled her shoulders and shook out her neck, making her ponytail cascade like a wine and brunette waterfall down her back. The tips swished against the sweet curve of her ass. The ground vibrated beneath my feet, and the scent of her magic wafted into the room as it grew in power. Her scent. The one I'd committed to memory—fresh air, sandalwood, and rose. My water elemental power flickered awake in response, making me take a step closer to her. It surged inside me, reaching for her, and for once, I didn't resist it. I summoned it to the surface and latched on.

The taut muscles of her thighs flexed like a predator about to pounce.

And then Katuri shifted.

It was so fast, so powerful. Her back arched, snapping her head back before collapsing forward onto her hands and knees. No, not her hands and knees. Her hands had transformed into massive paws, as did her feet with a flash of light. The dark copper locks of hair turned to thick fur that covered her whole body—a body that had tripled in size. Off somewhere in the distance I could hear Eleni howl. The wolf typically stuck close to Katuri's side, but I hadn't seen her today. Katuri answered in a low howl that made my heart skip a beat.

I sucked in a breath as she flicked a long, feathered tail, and, just as she had done in her Fae form, she peered over her shoulder directly at me. The same white tribal mark ran across her snout and forehead. There was also a trail of white fur that went all the way down her chest and stomach. Did Kat's tribal marks go that low too?

I recognized this wolf. I'd seen her before. The day I'd come home from the war, to be exact. I'd been walking the perimeter of the citadel because I couldn't sleep. Nightmares of death and violence had plagued my dreams. It had been snowing outside, but I had an urge, a draw, to go outside. I'd thought at the time, the cold would do me some good—it would remind my mind and body that I was home and not back on the Western Continent. I'd been near the eastern gate when I felt like I was being watched. The back of my neck prickled. A massive wolf had been sitting in the treeline just outside the battlement. It'd been absolutely stunning, just as she was now. I hadn't known it was Katuri. Maybe if I would've gone to her sooner. I'd wasted so much time not seeing Katuri for who she really was.

The same luminous, green eyes from that night, with streaks of silver, met mine, and she winked.

The fucking wolf just winked at me.

Everything else in the arena melted away until it was just the two of us. I was so turned on it wasn't even funny. I shifted on my feet in a failed attempt to gain my composure again and found myself moving closer. Just the two of us. I forgot everything. Who I was. Where I was. All I knew was the bond. And my bondmate was only paces away.

"Well damn, Kat," I said.

The massive body of the wolf turned and stalked toward me. I froze, still as death. She towered above me. She lowered her head and came nose to nose with me, glaring down at me.

"Incredible," I said in reverence.

I reached a hand up to touch her. A flash of annoyance. Her eyes sharpened, promising death for my blunt comment. For a moment, I thought she was going to eat me. I would have let her. I would've let her do anything to me. She huffed out a hot breath of air from her snout and stomped a massive paw into the ground. A flash of sparkling white. She'd snapped at my fingers in warning. Beautiful savage. I jumped, yanking my hand back. Nazneen laughed so hard I thought she was going to fall on the floor. Even Evren let out a laugh.

"Sorry," Evren said as she choked back her laugh. "It wasn't funny. Promise." But I could see her struggling to compose herself.

Katuri had changed so much. She'd been shattered into pieces when she'd first come to Kanevvluk. She'd been broken by her father and by the blood binding. I'd assumed she was still broken after all this time, still picking up the pieces of her life. That was a dangerous assumption. The proof was standing in front of me now.

Nazneen walked over to Katuri, unfazed by the fierce wolf, and tucked herself against Katuri's front leg, weaving her fingers through the russet colored fur. Katuri turned her attention to Nazneen and nuzzled her snout against Nazneen's head.

"Alright Ev, your turn," Nazneen said, breaking my attention from Katuri and the Arcelia warrior standing in front of me, *touching* my bondmate.

"You made it look so easy," Evren said nervously, shaking out her hands. Tiny sparks flew from her fingers and extinguished into the sand. She took a tentative step forward. Delrik stepped closer to her. She narrowed her brows in determination.

Katuri's voice to my left made me jump. Again. Dammit, why was I so jumpy today?

"Your element obeys you, Evren." Katuri's voice was smooth and relaxing.

When the fuck had she shifted back? And how the hell had she managed to not shred her clothes to scraps? If I was meticulous with my shift, I could sometimes spare my pants. Her shift had been so sudden. So violent. She clearly had more grace than me. She was standing next to Nazneen again, hip popped out to the side and arms crossed over her chest. Her silky ponytail was swirled into a coil that draped over her shoulder, showing the smooth column of her neck. Eleni now stood at her feet. The wolf had appeared from nowhere. I could see now that the wolf was an exact match to Kat's shifted form. Her familiar. I should've known that, though I hadn't known her shifted form was a wolf.

"Trust yourself and trust your power." She spoke again.

Evren's little bird, Aura, flew to prop itself up on her shoulder. The thing looked like it had grown since they arrived. Must be all the mice from the stables. She was the size of a small falcon now.

Evren held her hand extended in front of her, her palm open faced. The ring with that strange ruby caught my attention. I'd forgotten about it from our first meeting. That time in the greeting hall, the light could have easily been mistaken for light reflecting off its surface. Not this time. Suddenly, a small flame sprang to life in her hand. Through the flames, the red gemstone pulsed with power. It glowed brightly like embers of the flame. It was no ordinary piece of jewelry. Delrik stood close to Evren's side, head bent low, offering encouragement. Her veins began to glow as the elemental fire spread throughout her body. It started in her middle and radiated outward. The small flames grew, writhing as they engulfed her hand. They licked up her arm closer and closer to that little bird, but the bird didn't seem too concerned with them. It snapped its beak playfully at flames, making Evren smile. Then, with a swift movement, she unleashed her power, and the orange and violet flames consumed Evren and her bird in entirety.

My eyebrows nearly touched my hairline. Um, was no one concerned that Evren had just been engulfed in flames? Was that normal? The inferno was so hot I could feel the heat on my face all the way over here. It was so bright I was squinting, trying not to look away in case I missed anything.

Then, massive wings exploded from the ball of fire in a kaleidoscope of color, stretching wide. A massive firebird flew toward the ceiling with a powerful downbeat, wings beating effortlessly as it swept across the arena. Sharp violet eyes of a predator scanned the arena, looking for her bondmate. She found Delrik and careened back toward us.

When she touched back down, her dark, sharp talons dug into the sand. The firebird stretched her wings wide and then drew them close to her body. And as if the flames were smothering out, the silver-haired High Fae appeared in the heart of the flames. She took a step forward, and with that, the flames were gone. Her clothes were gone but were replaced by a dress of glowing, red embers. Her bird sat on her shoulder completely unharmed. Tiny tendrils of smoke curled around her, and Delrik waved them away.

"Alright then," I said, dumbstruck.

"Good thing I've got extra clothes in my bag," Katuri said.

At least I wasn't the only one that shredded my clothes when I shifted. I guess she more likely incinerated them. I'd seen fire magic before, but never to that magnitude. Obviously, she was a supreme fire elemental, but I was still impressed. Most High Fae that possessed any form of fire magic were limited to small balls of flames or creating small explosions in battle. If we'd had Evren during the war, it would've been over in a matter of months, not years.

Nazneen clapped her hands together and ran over to Evren, squeezing her tight in a hug. "I knew you could do it."

Evren dipped her chin and blushed. She wavered a little on her feet, but Delrik was right there, gripping her elbow with gentleness and pulling her close.

"I haven't ever used that much power at once. It takes so much from me."

"Your power will ebb as you use it, and you'll need to refuel yourself. The more you practice, though, the longer you will be able to sustain it," Master Salcido said. "And you never want to drain your power completely. You'd be at your most vulnerable then."

"The first time I saw her use her power, she literally lit herself on fire," Delrik said, smiling at some memory. "And the second time, she was defending her brother. I think she was in too much shock to be drained. She'd had the power suppressed for so long."

Master Salcido nodded as if he knew what Delrik was talking about. He may be a weapons master, but he knew more about magic and the various powers among the Fae than anyone I'd ever met. Though he knew nothing of the shadow magic.

"The bird makes sense now," Arik said, stepping up to Nazneen's side again. He'd been quietly observing this whole time.

"Aura?" Evren asked. She turned her head to look at the bird.

"She's your familiar," Arik said. "She is an embodiment of your power."

"I thought she was just a little bonus gift from the River Kingdom when we visited. I thought she'd just attached herself to Evren," Delrik said, poking the bird in the belly, making her hiccup a flame. She puffed up her body and made a tutting noise at Delrik.

Katuri stepped forward, and with a swirl of her hand, the wolf disappeared and reappeared on the other side of the area. "Our familiars can come in handy. They are manifestations of our elemental power. They can be any form your power chooses. They can be used as spies or ways to send messages to people. And as you grow stronger, she will too." She nudged her head toward the bird. "She'll be able to go further from you, grow larger, and support you if needed." Eleni began to trot back to us. With each step she took, she grew in size before our very eyes to the size. When she reached us, she was almost as big as Kat had been in her shifted form. Her tail thudded on the floor twice before curling around her body. "Eleni is my familiar."

"She is the most precious," Nazneen cooed at the canine. Eleni shrunk back to her normal size. Then she jumped up, pushed her ears back to her head, planted her paws on Nazneen's chest, and covered her face with kisses, her tail wagging furiously.

I rolled my eyes at Katuri's back. The wolf's head swung around at me and snarled its lips.

Fuck.

"You've got a fancy carrier pigeon basically," I said. The fiery bird rushed me, pecking at my head angrily. I waved my hands around, trying to bat it away, but when my hand made contact with what should have been a feathery body, it became smoke and my hand passed right through it. "Okay, okay! I'm sorry. You're not a carrier pigeon! You're a mighty fire beast!"

I'd just been bested by a damn fledging.

NINETEEN
DELRIK

Summer was almost at an end, which meant the Affinity Celebration was well underway. When the War Across the Sea ended after seven years, everyone rejoiced across Illoterra. The day we arrived home was designated a holiday and the Snowhaven Fae had been celebrating with a week-long festival ever since. Fae and many more took advantage of the warmer weather and lack of snow to travel to Kanevvluk for the occasion. Booths of food, textiles from across the territory, and crafts lined the streets of the city. Actors and singers reenacted the arrival to Illoterra and construction of the citadel. And dancing. Music filled the air, and wine flowed freely every hour of the day and night.

Bright laughter pierced the air, and my head turned in its direction. Nazneen was hand in hand with Katuri. They were spinning in circles with their heads tossed back. The further into the night it got, the more the music shifted to a more upbeat cadence. I brought the ladies goblets of wine and our group was all smiles and happiness. It wasn't until they started heading back to the citadel that Nazneen spotted Arik. She quickly abandoned the group and skipped toward him. I didn't like her friendship with him, but I held my tongue. Her face was painted with the same sparkling mask as many of the children that were running around, and she wore a crown of twisted ice crystals on top of her head, tipped at a precarious angle.

"Where have you been all night?" she asked Arik.

"Around."

"Katuri made me taste literally everything, and I've had so much wine, I don't think I could dance another song, even if I wanted to."

"You make it sound like I'm forced to eat everything. She—" Katuri pointed at her friend and then looped her arm with Arik's on the opposite side from Nazneen"insisted I show her all my favorites."

The trio strolled like that, the females bracketing Arik, back to the citadel. They chattered about their afternoon and evening, not leaving out a single detail. I didn't think Arik could even understand what they were saying. They were talking so fast and over each other it just sounded like a garbled mess to me. I almost felt bad for Arik. Almost. It had been a long day, but a much needed one. It was late into the night, and I was feeling the Fae wine I'd indulged in as much as Nazneen was. Evren was by my side as always with a big smile painted on her face, along with glitter swirls. Today was the first time I hadn't felt the heaviness hanging over me in weeks. I contributed the reprieve to Evren not leaving my side all day. I didn't think her hand had left my arm at all. She kept her fire burning to keep us both warm while we enjoyed the festival. Summer was still cold in Kanevvluk, and while the rain and snow held off today, the sun refused to make an appearance.

"Sir Arik."

Someone was calling after us as we came into the entrance hall. I turned to find Arik's private servant running toward us.

"Sir, you've had a letter arrive," he said with a quick bow.

Arik took the letter from him and went to stuff it in his chest pocket.

"What's that?" Nazneen asked playfully. "A letter from a secret admirer?" Her cheeks were flushed and her smile was full.

"It's nothing," he said sweetly to her.

I stopped dead in his tracks. Something felt off. Letters were common, but not in the dead of night, on a holiday much less. "Who would be sending you a letter in the middle of the night?"

I couldn't help but be skeptical. I didn't trust him. Not after I'd seen what he did during the war. I didn't trust that he had good intentions.

"It doesn't concern you." He brushed me off.

My speed came in handy at times just like this. Suddenly, the letter was gone from his hand. I was so fast, even in my inebriated state, that no one saw me move. I clenched the envelope in my hand.

"That isn't for you," Arik snarled and lunged for the letter, but, of course, I was faster.

I ripped it open and began scrolling through the words. There was no telling what the letter contained, but if he was going through so much trouble to hide it, then it couldn't be good.

"It seems our friend here has received a letter from someone in Port Gamcord in the Wildlands." I elevated my voice so that Garren could hear clearly over the traitors whining. "Why would someone be writing to you about ships leaving Quinterre?"

"It's a private matter," Arik snapped.

"It is? Interesting how secret messages are arriving in the middle of the night about ships leaving Quinterre and we are tracking the movements of weapons coming into Illoterra."

"This has nothing to do with..."

"You're a lying bastard." Dark umbra flashed before my vision, or maybe I had just imagined it. The shadows moved down my arms to my fingertips.

Arik took a deep breath and pinched the bridge of his nose. "It has nothing to do with weapons coming into Illoterra. I'm simply looking for someone, and an old friend spotted them on the western coast of Quinterre."

Before I knew it, pain pierced my fist. I lashed out and landed a punch faster than my own eyes could see. I hadn't realized I wanted to hit Arik until I already had. I felt blood trickling from my still clenched fist. The smell of the blood in the air made the shadows sing with power. I reared back for another blow, but Arik was expecting it this time. He quickly put a shield in place. My fist crashed into the invisible force field and I howled in pain. It was like punching a wall. I curled over, cradling my fist against my chest. When I lifted my head, shadows hovered in my periphery.

"Delrik," Nazneen shrieked as she stepped between the two of us.

I darted around my sister and tackled Arik to the ground. His head cracked off the marble floor, but he managed to swing his elbow up. The strike split my cheek. I landed a swift punch in his ribs, the letter still clamped in my fist, and then Garren was pulling me off him.

The shadows and blackness disappeared as swiftly as they'd come, quickly followed by rational thinking. Arik may have deserved a good beating, but I wasn't sure what had set me off so easily. I pressed my hand to my now throbbing head. Maybe I'd had too much Fae wine. I wobbled on my feet for a moment.

"What in the dark hells is wrong with you?" Nazneen said, turning her back on me and focusing on Arik.

Nazneen reached out her hand and pulled Arik to his feet. I shook my head back and forth to clear the darkness from my head. What *had* I been thinking?

Evren was at my side in an instant and gripped my face between her hands. "We should go." I could feel her summoning the shadows to the surface. I didn't fight it when they flowed into her waiting hands. Her eyes melted into pools of black before returning to violet. "You're tired and can't focus on control. Nazneen, take Arik and go, please. Garren, can you come with us?"

My bondmate only released me when Garren was by my side. Was she afraid of me? My whole body deflated at the thought.

"I'll help Nazneen get Arik back to his suite," Katuri said.

Evren took the letter from my grasp and handed it over her shoulder to Nazneen. I tried to pull it away, but she nailed me with a glare colder than death itself. Garren slung his arm over me and turned me around, leaving Arik alone with Nazneen and Katuri. I looked over my shoulder as I was being led down the hall to see Nazneen gingerly addressing the gash on Arik's temple.

"Let's find a healer," she said.

Darkness swept across my vision again and I had the urge to end that bastard's life. And that wasn't the shadows talking.

TWENTY
KATURI

That strange tattoo had shifted to cover Delrik's neck and along his hands, and black, inky veins crept across his face. Even the temperature plummeted in the hall right before he attacked. What was he? I'd overheard the conversations of a strange shadow magic, but this was beyond what I'd thought. This had to be dark magic.

"No, it's fine. I've had worse," Arik said, trying to brush Nazneen's hand away from his face. "It will be healed in a day or two."

I was sprawled across Arik's couch. They had been having this argument for the last fifteen minutes. The moment Delrik landed the first blow, my sobriety returned in full force, along with a subsequent headache. "You know if you don't let her help you, we will be here all night."

"At least let me clean you up," Nazneen said, reaching for his face again.

Arik winked at her. "I'd prefer if we'd get a little dirty."

Nazneen stared at him with annoyance. "Really, Arik? That was lame and you know it."

"Yeah, I'm not at my best right now," he said with a cringe.

I rolled my eyes. "Also, I'm sitting right here."

I could see Nazneen trying not to smile. She'd always found talking to Arik easy. She could have a conversation with the grumpiest guard and have him laughing by the end. Arik finally gave in to Nazneen's demands and plopped down on the couch. Nazneen headed straight for the washroom like she'd been here before. I wondered if she had.

Arik looked woozy, but I wasn't sure if it was from Delrik's fist or the wine. Nazneen returned with a towel and bowl of steaming water. She knelt on the floor between Arik's knees and began to dab the blood that had dripped down the side of his face. The ease and laughter had died away and was replaced by a solemn mood.

"Arik," Nazneen started, but he stopped her.

"Don't Nazneen. It's nothing to worry about." His eyes bounced back and forth between Nazneen's eyes, searching for something. Then he took a deep breath. "It's from a ... friend I have in the Wildlands. At least that is where he is at the moment. He tells me about the comings and goings from the port there."

"Why would you be interested in that?" Nazneen asked.

I think they'd forgotten I was here. Nazneen had leaned in close to examine the cut. Arik's eyes closed with a flutter and he leaned into her hand.

"For my own reasons," he said.

Nazneen didn't say anything, just focused on the gash on his face. When she looked satisfied that the wound was clean, she lifted the hem of Arik's shirt and began to pull it over his head. He lifted his arms to help but winced at the sharp pain in his side. I'd give Delrik credit where it was due; he had a vicious fist. By the dark shades already blooming on Arik's skin, I thought he had a broken rib or two. Nazneen urged him to lean back and she tenderly lifted his arm to assess the damage. The spot was already turning black and blue.

"It's about my family," he finally said into the quiet. His eyes were fixed on the ceiling. They shone with unshed tears.

Nazneen's hands stilled for a brief moment before she resumed examining his side. I saw her take a deep, calming breath. I'd never heard him speak about his family. Ever. He didn't say much at all about anything. His family and where he came from had always been a question. I assumed his family was all dead. Otherwise, why would he be here?

Nazneen pushed to stand up. There wasn't pity or sadness on her face. I could also see the questions wanting to burst free, but she didn't ask anything. She was good about that. Waiting for you to come to her and not pestering you with questions.

"If you ever want to talk about your family, I'd love to hear about them." She laid her hand on his shoulder. She studied his face for a few moments before she said, "Good night, Arik."

I followed Nazneen out of Arik's suite, and we walked quietly down the hall side by side. We didn't speak until we reached my suite. Arik and I were similar in that we were both missing our families. Mine had abandoned me all the way across the realm, but Arik's past was clearly more haunting than anyone knew about.

"Want to come inside?" I asked Nazneen when we reached my suite.

"Sure." She smiled at me, but it didn't reach her eyes. Whatever Arik was going through was taking a toll on her as well.

We were both too exhausted and tipsy to talk, so we just snuggled into the soft bed with Eleni between us and dozed to sleep.

"Let's resume our lesson. Katuri and Evren, I want you to work on basic control of your magic. Katuri, you can guide Evren," Salcido said. "There are two levels of magic—passive and active. Evren and Katuri, you both have active powers. Your powers have a bigger bang. They can physically change your surroundings and yourself. Passive powers have just as much umph without physically affecting others. For example, mind control is passive; you can mess with people's minds to harm them, but it's not like impaling someone with a sword of ice."

We'd taken a break for lunch and then reconvened after a long morning of drills and conditioning. We were all dragging from the late night before, and the atmosphere was tense. My head throbbed with every movement.

Master Salcido turned to Nazneen and Arik. "Nazneen, what are you working with?"

Her hands were planted firmly on her hips. A sword was strapped to her back now. She must have retrieved it from her suite during our break. The pommel peaked out above her shoulder. She'd watched her kick Arik's ass in hand-to-hand combat on multiple occasions. If she was as talented with that weapon as she was with her hands, I didn't doubt her ability to kill.

"Besides being the best spy in the Arcelia Legion and a badass swordswoman?" Nazneen asked.

From working with Master Salcido for only a short time, I could already tell he didn't normally have a sense of humor with anyone. He'd taken a liking to Nazneen and her sass though.

"I'm just kidding with you. Aberration. Basically, I can distort the sound around me to my advantage. It comes in handy when I'm spying on my brother. Actually, now that he has a bondmate"—she winked at Evren, who was next to me—"it's more useful in drowning the two of them out."

With a flick of her wrist, the sounds around us distorted and then silenced completely.

"No wonder you excel as a spy. Does it work both ways? Can you disguise your own sound as well?" Master Salcido asked.

Another flick of her wrist and Nazneen was standing on the other side of an invisible sound barrier with Delrik. She turned and punched him hard in the arm. I saw his mouth form an "ouch" but heard nothing. Not even the contact of her fist with his body. He swung out at her, but she dodged him easily. A dismissive wave of her hand and her voice filtered back to me.

"It varies with how much background noise there is. It's harder to hold when there is complete silence already," she said.

"Arik, your magic compliments Nazneen's quite well," Master Salcido pointed out.

"Oh?" Nazneen said.

"I'm a shield wielder. I can't block out sound, but I can protect myself from physical attacks." His eyes darted across the arena where Delrik and Garren had returned to their volume. Arik lowered his voice. "It was perfect for me growing up since I wasn't as strong as other fighters when it came to physical confrontations."

I wasn't sure if he was opening up about himself for Nazneen's benefit or Evren's.

Without warning, Garren shot a stream of water at me. Arik didn't even need to move to block the water. It hit the invisible wall and sprayed everyone. In fact, he never broke eye contact with Nazneen.

"Shield Wielder," Garren confirmed like he'd been part of the conversation the whole time. He was so nosey. "During the war, Arik protected the frontlines during battle."

At the mention of the war, I saw Arik tense. He didn't like talking about the war. Whenever it came up in conversation, he'd discreetly disappear. I'd heard rumors of an incident he was involved in but didn't know anything beyond that.

Nazneen's brows lifted. "You can spread your shield that far? That's impressive."

Arik's spine straightened with pride.

"It protects against elemental water. What about fire?" Delrik motioned Evren to his side. "Care to test a theory?" There was an evil glint in his eyes. Those eyes that had turned as dark as pitch last night.

For a moment, I doubted Arik's ability to protect himself against Evren's fire. I'd seen how she shifted. It was violent and explosive. I didn't want to be on the wrong end of her scorching inferno, but I knew Arik wouldn't back down. Nazneen made eye contact with me. She looked a touch worried as well.

"Throw a fireball at Arik." Delrik's face was sinister.

"What? I'll kill him!" Evren exclaimed.

"There are healers somewhere around here. He'll be fine."

Evren looked at Arik in question. At least she asked permission first. He gave her a nod of approval and prepared himself for an attack.

Her palm glowed with a ball of fire. "I don't know if I have enough of an aim to do this without hurting everyone."

"Here." Nazneen stepped up with her bow and lit the tip of an arrow in the elemental fire.

Fuck. This just got intense real fast.

"Ready?" Nazneen asked as she drew back on the bow.

"Don't warn him. He wouldn't have any warning during a fight," Delrik said.

Nazneen's eyes flashed with irritation at her brother. "Don't be an ass. It doesn't look good on you."

Did she just stand up for Arik against her brother? Wow.

Nazneen took a deep, steadying breath and released the fiery arrow, aiming for just above Arik's shoulder. The shield shuddered under the impact of the arrow, but it held. Thank the Powers. With the fire pressed against it, the shield was visible to everyone. The convex of the sphere vibrated under the strength of the flames. I could feel the heat from them as they writhed against the barrier.

"Very nice, Arik," Master Salcido said.

Arik threw his shield to the side, and the fire arrow landed a few feet from him in the sand, still alight.

"What about mind shielding? Can you do that too?" I asked.

Arik nodded. "It's been essential over the decades in guarding my thoughts from potential enemies as well as keeping things to myself I didn't want others to know about." He turned to Evren for further explanation, knowing she was newer to understanding how Fae magic worked. "Mind shielding isn't a power limited to the High Fae. Just like alchemy and spells, it can be learned. Anyone can do it with practice. Would you like me to show you?"

"Please," Evren said.

Delrik pressed his lips into a firm line in disapproval.

"You know shielding my mind is a useful skill, Ashlyra," she said to Delrik.

He scowled. He must've been sending his emotions down their bond.

"Alright. The rest of you, off to sword practice. Let's keep up the stamina. When our magic runs low after using it for an extended time, you have to rely on our physical strengths again. So practice while your magic levels are low." Master Salcido guided Katuri, Evren, and me off to the side.

"We may need Jace for this. His power is mind projection. He can't change your thoughts, but he can plant ideas from his own mind into another's. For example, by picturing a cupcake in his mind and projecting into yours, you'd suddenly find yourself craving a sugary dessert," I explained.

"I'll get him," I said. Eleni popped up next to me out of thin air. "Could you find Jace please?"

I scratched Eleni under the chin. Eleni playfully chomped at my fingers. Then she bound away like a rabbit with a happy yip.

Evren looked confused.

"Familiars can be used as messengers. It's something you'll be able to do eventually with Aura," Katuri explained.

We sat down in the sand to wait. Sure enough, ten minutes later, Jace arrived with Eleni nipping at his heels, like she was herding him to us.

"You summoned me?" Jace said.

I gave him a sweet smile and batted my lashes. "We were hoping you'd help us with mind shielding practice."

He settled on the ground next to us.

Arik began. "Think of your mind as a home, a greenhouse, a refuge; someplace you feel safe. You'll need to build a wall around that safe place. The wall will block unwanted mental intrusions and keep your thoughts safe from others."

"Let me show you first. Clear your mind completely. I'm going to put a suggestion in your head. Tell me what you see," Jace said.

An idea came to mind. I watched as Evren smiled too.

"I see a bird flying through the trees," Evren said.

"Me too," I confirmed.

"Perfect. Now I want you to build that wall, and Jace will try again. Evren first."

Evren focused, but I could see the moment Jace projected into her mind. Her brows furrowed and she frowned.

"A flower in a field," she said dejectedly.

"It takes practice," Arik reminded her.

"It goes both ways. Someone who is telepathic can see your thoughts if you don't have your mind guarded against them. We can use your bondmates for now as an example. Since you're bonded, you can sense each other through that bond. Evren, think of something and then safeguard it with your walls." Arik motioned to Delrik. To my surprise, Delrik followed Arik's instructions without complaint. "Delrik, see if you can sense Evren through the bond."

Delrik looked at his bondmate and smiled. They held eye contact for several long moments.

"I can see something, feel something, but it's fuzzy. Like I'm looking through mist."

"Good. That's excellent." Arik turned to me. "Would you like to try?" His eyes cut to Garren, then back to me

I just glared at him. Was he serious? He raised his hands in supplication. "Moving on."

We practiced with Jace over and over until I couldn't tell which thoughts were mine and which were planted by Jace. My head was throbbing. Jace excused himself to continue with his work.

Steel on steel pierced the air. The sound rang out and echoed with the high ceiling. I watched Nazneen wield her sword with practiced elegance. She moved with lethal grace. The Warblade of Silverlight. The sword was pure Lilura Steel, impregnated with wisdom from the Powers Above. Mountain Fae believed it brought guidance to the one that wielded it. It gleamed in the arena lights as bright as the day it was forged. The solitaire sapphire encircled with diamonds of the pommel glinted with each smooth movement as she went through steps of a routine she'd memorized to keep her skills sharp. Sweat soaked her shirt, making it cling tightly to her torso. Garren and Delrik had discarded their shirts, and sweat slicked their chests with the exertion of their sword practice. Nazneen was taking on both Garren and Delrik with ease. The way she moved was as graceful as a dancer. Sweeping arcs, fluid attacks and retreats, and quick footwork. I didn't know how long they'd been at it, but I could tell Nazneen had the upper hand, even with two against one.

"I don't think I could ever be as good as Nazneen," Evren said. She was leaning back on her hands and had her ankles crossed out in front of her. Aura was perched on the toe of her boot. I was lounging next to her, tossing a ball for Eleni to chase.

"She has years of experience. I'm sure if you trained as hard and as long as Nazneen, you'd be able to master any weapon you picked up," Arik said.

I offered her a warm smile.

When they'd finished, Nazneen sheathed the Warblade of Silverlight into its scabbard. The aged wood was engraved with ancient symbols of the old language. She wiped her face with the edge of her shirt, exposing her toned stomach.

Arik approached her. "I see why you are a legion leader."

"I know I make it look effortless, but it wasn't earned easily. I've worked hard every day of my life and will continue to do so until my last breath."

"I heard about you during the war. It isn't common for a female to lead a battalion, much less a territory. I wish we'd had a chance to meet during the war. I would've loved to fight alongside you."

Nazneen gave Arik a wink and took my arm. "Maybe, one day. If you're lucky."

TWENTY-ONE
GARREN

Delrik and I had moved off to the side to catch our breaths and rehydrate. Nazneen's sword skills had improved so much over the years. She didn't give me a break the entire hour.

"Your sister almost had me there," I said to him.

Delrik wasn't paying attention to me. He observed his Ashlyra closely as she chatted with Nazneen and Katuri. He watched her like a hawk. Now that the bond had become a real thing in my life, I understood why he was so focused on Evren. I felt it too with Katuri, but she was still avoiding me.

"What about you? Are you just going to avoid it, or are you going to show us what you've got?" I asked him.

"I don't know what you're talking about," Delrik said lazily.

He was such a liar. He knew exactly what I meant.

"I saw it. I saw the shadows last night. Your eyes shifted when you first arrived too." I pushed. "You went all protector when I approached Evren that first day."

"It doesn't concern you."

"It does when you keep telling me about all the dark thoughts you've been having."

Delrik had mentioned that he'd felt off when he arrived. He'd said it was like dark thoughts and dreams were starting to come every day. They seemed to put him in a trance or fog at times. Things as simple as wanting to trip Arik on the stairs to the urge to test his shadows on an unexpecting legion guard during training. He never acted on those thoughts. I knew he wouldn't. He was strong-willed enough not to. But he needed to face the problem head on rather than ignoring it.

"You can't not explore this power. It's strong. I can sense it. If you don't learn to control it, it will take control of you. And then?"

His face was a hard mask of indifference. He knew I was right. Even Evren agreed with me. There was only so much reading she could do on similar magic. He had to push past his fear and use the shadows. Delrik had always been one to keep secrets. I'd known him for more than a century and still had only brushed the surface of his life. And I considered him my best friend. So I did what I do best—I pushed him.

I took a step toward Evren, my sword drawn and ready. Ice formed around my other hand. "You won't show off your new power, even to protect your bondmate?"

Without taking my eyes off him, I threw my hand out, and a shard of ice flew toward Evren. The bastard didn't even blink. She screamed and threw her arms up in front of her with a wall of fire, melting the ice before it even got close to her. I knew her power would protect her. She was never in any real danger, but it was enough of a threat to trick Delrik into action.

In a split second, Delrik moved faster than an arrow shot from its bow. His hand was wrapped around my throat and lifting me into the air. The force of his impact would've taken me to the ground if he didn't have a death grip on me. My toes brushed the sand. Darkness swirled around his knuckles, and the blackness of his eyes swallowed up his pupils, leaving behind only a void of darkness. A veil of shadows. The veins of his neck and across his forehead were swollen black, making the lethal scar stand out even more. I felt my water power flare in response to his predatory attack, but I pushed it back down.

"Now your nickname really fits," I choked out, his crushing hand cutting my words off a bit, making the sound come out hoarse. "Master of Death and Darkness."

"Don't call me that," Delrik said between clenched teeth. His voice was deeper and echoed through the arena. Not his own. A voice ancient and dangerous. What was this magic?

"But it's more fitting now with those shadows flowing under your skin."

Delrik's eyes shifted to solid black as onyx shadows crawled over his shoulders and up his arms. The black veins crept across his face. Serpent-like black tendrils floated around him, threatening to strike at any second. His hand squeezed my throat, cutting off all the air now. I tried to suck in a breath, but it was useless. My best friend had gone all death demon killer on me.

Evren appeared by his side. She stepped through the floating mass of shadows and placed her hand on his forearm. "Delrik." She spoke so softly I almost didn't hear her. Delrik's head slowly swiveled to face her. The shadows pulsed when his eyes locked onto her. Blackness started to appear in the corners of my vision as I fought to remain conscious. After a beat, he closed his eyes and obeyed her unspoken demand to release me. He slowly lowered me to the floor and released me. Air rushed into my lungs as I heaved in a breath.

"Shit, man," I said, rubbing at my throat, gasping "That was dark." I took a sharp breath in. "Get it. Dark. Like the shadows."

He just glared at me. Thankfully, his eyes had returned to normal. The shadows remained, floating around Delrik.

"You should've seen when Evren passed the shadows to Delrik the first time. It was freaky," Nazneen said. She kept her distance from her brother, even with her light-hearted tone.

Evren brushed her fingers on the back of Delrik's hand, the hand with the binding mark. Her flames arched between her fingers. As if the shadows were responding to her, they moved closer, coming off Delrik's arm and into the flames themselves. The binding mark stood out, bright and ethereal, under the flames and shadows. The two powers seemed to flow back and forth between the bondmates, feeding each other. Shadow and fire, smoke and light.

Katuri moved closer. I made to grab her arm to hold her back, but she shoved me off with a withering glare. "Have you tried to swap powers again since the blood binding ritual?"

"No," Delrik answered, but he was still focused only on Evren.

"If you're willing, I'm intrigued. I'd like to see how it works," Katuri said.

Interesting. Was Katuri curious because of their powers, or was she curious for other reasons? We'd never discussed power swapping. Well, other than her telling me she'd never let me near her earth elemental.

"We have only transferred the shadows, not the elemental power."

Katuri had refused to exchange powers with me. We'd completed the blood binding, but swapping our magic was the last part of our bond she'd refused. Well, that and everything else that normal consort had. I didn't want her for her powers, but I didn't know how to even begin that conversation when she wouldn't even let me touch her.

It didn't take Delrik much effort to shift the shadows to Evren. They weren't even touching each other. After the initial exchange, physical contact between consorts wasn't needed to swap powers, only the desire to do so. As if they were summoned, the shadows pooled like silk at Delrik's feet and slithered to Evren. Swirling tendrils wrapped up her legs and body. She dropped her head back, and the darkness poured into her mouth and nose. When she looked back at us, her eyes were solid black. Her veins danced and swirled with black and burning gold. The mark of the shadows snaked up her arm, around her neck and around her torso.

"Your bondmate is a tad unhinged, don't you think?" I asked Delrik. I could feel my powers healing the bruises already. Evren just smiled a wickedly sweet smile, and it was the first time since we met that I was truly terrified of her.

"I know. She's absolute perfection," he said without missing a beat.

"Well fuck, you two are a dangerous pair," Katuri said.

TWENTY-TWO
KATURI

"You can also do a partial shift," I said.

It was the next day, and since the fun we'd had yesterday, I was looking forward to training with Master Salcido. We returned to the arena for another round of training after another morning in the library. I didn't mind the daily drills anymore. It felt good to move. I'd felt antsy for so long. Even with my nightly runs in the forest, I still felt caged. And with Garren's sudden interest in pestering me, I was on edge. So exercising my powers helped relieve the pent up energy.

"A partial shift?" Evren asked.

I smiled at Evren, and sharp fangs appeared as my canines grew. I knew my eyes had changed shape. They were the same as my wolf form. Eleni yipped at my feet. A large stick appeared in my hand, and I tossed it across the arena with the strength of my wolf. Eleni sprinted after it and then brought it back, nudging my legs with it. I didn't do a partial shift often. There wasn't a real need for it. I used to do it, though, when I was a youngling, to scare my cousins.

Nazneen was sitting on a bench, swinging her legs back and forth, watching us while munching on a snack. "Like when you had just your wings, Ev."

"Yes, just like that," Katuri said.

Evren focused, closing her eyes. I could feel her power responding to her summons and pushing out to the surface—slow and controlled. She'd learned so much in a short few weeks. Then a miniature version of her elemental form's wings appeared behind her. Evren opened her eyes, and I could see the fire power dance in their violet depths. The smile she had on her face made them even brighter. The tips of Evren's wings stood a foot taller than her. Wings of pure fire. They were brilliant. The light coming from them was so intense I had to squint. The wings swept outward and formed a wall of fire behind her. The force of the movement dragged her back, and she had to take a step to stay on her feet.

Evren concentrated, closing her eyes and taking deep breaths. Then her face scrunched. "Well, that didn't work."

"What were you trying to do?" I asked, giggling at her reaction.

I remembered learning to control my powers. Corynne was my guiding force. It wouldn't have been so easy without her, so I was glad to be here for Evren.

"I was trying to make the flames go away." She cleared her throat. "It's harder than you'd think."

Delrik approached his bondmate despite the inferno around her. He brushed his hand first along her cheek and then trailed it up the arc of a wing with adoration. Evren's frustration melted away. With his touch, the blaze vanished like embers into the air. What remained were wings covered in sleek, onyx feathers, dark as the shadows the two of them shared. The white-flamed tips brushed along the sandy ground as the heavy appendages drooped with their weight. When she moved the wings on their back, they caught the light and glimmered like polished darkstone. Delrik's hand was still on her wing. His fingers caressed the feathers. Aura flitted around the pair before she landed on his shoulder.

"It doesn't burn you?" I asked. "The flames, I mean."

"No, her flames have never burned me. Even back when she still thought I was a pain in the ass," Delrik laughed.

"She still thinks you're a pain in the ass. Just a bonded pain in the ass," Nazneen quipped.

I ignored the siblings. "Do you think you could fly?"

Evren stretched out her wings behind her again to their full span. They stretched more than double her height.

"I don't know if I'm brave enough to try flying with them yet. It's taking a lot of effort to keep them out." Evren folded them into her body. "They are so heavy."

"Your muscles will grow stronger the more you practice with them," Master Salcido said. "Whenever you can have them out, practice summoning them."

"How was I able to shift so easily last time, in Rivamir?" She was breathing hard now with the effort.

"Our powers can be triggered by extreme emotion," I said.

"Well that makes sense then," Delrik said as he pressed his forehead to hers. "The first time your fire appeared, you'd been scared by that breaking glass at dinner and you were overwhelmed by your emotions. And the second time, you were protecting your brother. It was also the first time you'd shifted. Your powers had been suppressed for years. When you finally tapped into that power, it was..."

"Explosive," Nazneen supplied.

"Suppressed?" I asked.

Evren looked almost shy, but Delrik rolled his eyes and answered. "Her mother poisoned her."

Shock stretched across my face.

Evren swatted at him. "You make it sound like she was trying to slowly kill me..."

"She could have," he said under his breath.

"My mother knew my father wanted to steal my powers somehow and use them for some perversion. So when she noticed my powers beginning to develop, she dosed me daily with Bloodthorn to keep them from growing, thus"—she gave Delrik a stern look—"keeping me safe from my father."

"And I thought my parents were bad," I said.

Would I have chosen poisoning over compulsion? Evren looked pensive and focused on extending and retracting her wings again.

Nazneen broke the awkward silence. "So about this extreme emotion triggering a shift..." Her face tilted in thought. "*Any* extreme emotion?"

"Yup," I said.

Then I caught the devious grin on Nazneen's face. "Want to test that theory?" she asked.

My head snapped in her direction. "Nazneen, I don't think that's a good idea."

Evren studied me briefly.

"You said my other idea was too difficult," Nazneen said to Evren.

"I did but..." Evren started.

"And this plan will definitely give us answers," Nazneen responded.

Evren rolled her eyes and ruffled her wings. "Fine."

"What? No. I did not agree to this," I said, shaking my head and backing up a step.

Delrik looked between the three of us, but his gaze landed on his sister. "What are you three up to?"

Nazneen scolded her brother. "Why do you always assume I'm up to something?"

"Because you usually are."

Nazneen hopped up off the bench and strolled toward Katuri. Evren covered her grin and her cheeks turned rosy.

"What's going on?" I heard him whisper.

She waved her hand at him dismissively. "Just wait and see."

"Whatever is happening, it won't end well, will it?"

"SHH!"

Shit. She was really doing this. I mean, I did want to know what Garren thought about me, and I wasn't going to walk up and ask him to his face. I pressed my hand to my stomach. The thought of that conversation made me woozy. I guessed it was too late to turn back now. I took a deep breath and turned on the charm.

"Hey, Garren," I called over to where Master Salcido and he were near the weapons chest.

"Yes, Little Flower?" he said, turning a devilish smile on me.

Ugh, I hated when he called me that. I was about to make a smartass comment back when I felt Nazneen's fingers on my chin, turning me gently with slight pressure to face her. She was close, almost nose to nose with me. Her eyes darted down to my lips. She gave me a quick wink no one else could see before she closed the distance between our mouths.

Her first kiss was a simple press of her lips. She was making sure I was okay with this. I smiled at her, knowing her plan. I closed my eyes, leaned in, and sank into the moment. I deepened the kiss, parting my lips and allowing Nazneen in. She took the lead. Her body moved in closer so it was flush with mine, her hands digging into my hair. She was a damned good kisser, I'd give her that. I'd never been kissed before, but I was wholly for it if Garren kissed anything like this.

"Circle of dark hells," I heard Delrik say.

Nazneen pulled away, nudging her nose against mine before stepping back. I turned back to Garren with a wicked smile on my flushed, just kissed lips. Nazneen let out a hum of appreciation.

"See, Evren?" Nazneen said, gesturing to Garren. "Extreme emotion can trigger your power, even for someone that has so much control."

His jaw was on the floor in shock. His hands were balled into fists at his side. Sure enough, Garren's forearms were covered in sleek scales in shades of blue, cyan, and teal. His hands were balled into fists at his sides, and tiny spikes pierced from his knuckles. Two horns had sprouted from his head, twisting up. His aqua blue eyes had turned to icy vertical slits, and mist curled around him. Danger flickered behind his eyes as he tried to rein in his emotions. A menacing glare full of desire and heat pressed into me. Well, I gave Nazneen credit. She may have come up with a childish prank, but it was clear that Garren definitely felt *something* for me. Otherwise, he wouldn't have looked so jealous. Now, I just needed to figure out what, exactly, he felt.

I flicked my ponytail over my shoulder and bumped my hip into Nazneen. "Garren, your sea dragon is showing."

TWENTY-THREE
GARREN

Master Salcido was showing me a new sword that I'd asked him to have the blacksmith make for me. Something lean and lighter than my current longsword. I was examining the three options when Katuri's voice filtered my way. The bond in my chest buzzed with hearing my name on her lips. Typically, when she said my name it was dripping with disdain.

"Yes, Little Flower?" I couldn't help myself. I knew the nickname got under her skin.

Anger flashed on her face but just for a second. Her face softened as Nazneen's fingers brushed against her chin. Nazneen was standing so close to Katuri, there was barely any space between them. And then their mouths ... were on each other. The moment their lips touched, it was like lightning struck my heart. The bond seized my heart from inside in a painful vice and almost knocked me to my knees.

What the actual fuck!

My body froze, my power burning within wanting to rip Nazneen away from my bondmate. Katuri pressed her body fully into Nazneen and deepened the kiss. Jealousy formed a knot in my stomach and I saw red. That was my consort. My bondmate. Mine. She was mine and that cocky warrior had her hands all over what was fated to be mine. A dull roar filled my head. I felt my water power slipping, my sea dragon growling to be released. The arena was large enough. If I shifted into my sea dragon, I wouldn't be able to control myself. I would tear Nazneen to ribbons easily.

Finally, after what felt like a soul crushing eternity, they moved apart. My jaw cramped from grinding my teeth together.

"Circle of dark hells," Delrik said.

This had Nazneen written all over it. I'd kill her. I'd make her pay for her fucking pranks.

Katuri turned to face me. A smile teasing and wicked spread across her face. My eyes went directly to her mouth. The mouth I desperately wanted to kiss. The mouth I'd been dreaming of claiming for the last month. The mouth Nazneen had now claimed before me. Between my water power and the bond, I was losing control of myself. Blood pounded in my ears, matching my rapidly beating heart. All other sounds were blocked out.

Betrayal. Fury. Jealousy.

"Garren, your sea dragon is showing," Katuri taunted, with a flick of her ponytail. I wanted to wrap that ponytail around my fist. I wanted her to be mine, belong to me. But that wouldn't happen, would it? I'd always be second best. Why would she want the second best? Was it possible to change her mind? I drew in a breath. I had to try. The fates wouldn't be wrong about us as bondmates. I somehow needed to change her mind.

Me.

My chest was heaving like I'd just swam for miles. I'd always seen Katuri as a chore, as something my father wanted for me and a way to defy him by not doing the power exchange. I'd felt the bond, but it had been easy to ignore. But seeing her grow, close with another and then seeing her submit herself to Nazneen, pushed me over the edge. There was no denying the bond now. It was pulling me like the moons pulled the tides. Damn it. I would die if I didn't get my hands on Katuri.

Evren strode past me to the exit with Nazneen and Katuri linked arm in arm. Nazneen smiled as she walked past me and patted my cheek like the competitive ass she was. "You're welcome."

I stood, frozen to the spot, and watched Katuri's back as she walked away from me. Again.

I sucked in a deep breath through my nose and forced my sea dragon back into the deep recesses of myself. I unclenched my fists and splayed my fingers. I didn't make eye contact with anyone. I didn't say a word. I didn't want to see the looks on their faces. As calmly as I could, which took considerable effort, I left the training arena and didn't stop until the frigid evening air stung my lungs.

Katuri would be mine. No matter how, I would make her mine.

TWENTY-FOUR
KATURI

I sat with my legs curled under me while I brushed the tangles from my wet hair. Then I snuggled deeper into the blankets of my bed with a smile on my face. I was finally toasty and warm. Evren had made the fire in my fireplace burn bright on our way back from the training arena and the heat was still filling my room. After a hard afternoon of training, I'd run straight to my suite and submerged my soon-to-be sore muscles. Okay, that was a lie. I didn't want to admit how seeing Garren jealous made me feel. Excited? Needy? Bonded? Conflicted more than anything. Nazneen had joined me in my suite for dinner while Evren had chosen to dine with the guys. I couldn't face Garren. Not yet. I may have been bold enough to go along with Nazneen's joke, but all my bravado disappeared as soon as I'd stepped out of the arena.

For the first time since arriving in Kanevvluk, I was truly content. I would say I was even happy. Having Evren and Nazneen here gave me a future to look forward to. Wherever they went next, I wanted to go with them. At first, it was a joke, but the more I thought about it, the more freedom called to me. No more abiding by the rules of the High Ruler. No more hiding in my suite. No more snow. I could ignore the bond. It would be easy once Garren wasn't within easy reach. And maybe Nazneen was right. In the meantime, giving Garren a taste of his own medicine would make the time worthwhile. I knew he would never take me seriously, so I wouldn't waste my time.

The sky outside my window was surprisingly cloudless. Twin golden moons filled the night sky, accented by a blanket of stars. Moonlight drenched the snow covered landscape, making Kanevvluk look ghostly. It was a perfect night for a run through the Winterwood, but I was too cozy to move.

The sound of heavy, hurried footsteps in the hall grabbed my attention. They grew closer and closer. Then someone pounded on my door.

"Come in," I called across my room. I was used to nightly visits from either Nazneen or Evren. Sometimes both. Usually, they didn't bother knocking though.

Nothing.

"Nazneen, come in. It's too cold for me to get out of bed," I called again.

Another knock sounded, this time louder, angrier.

BANG! BANG! BANG!

That was *not* Nazneen.

I unfurled myself from the nest of blankets, flinging my covers off myself and swinging my legs over the side of the bed. My skin pebbled at the loss of heat as I quickly made my way to the door. My blush silk nightgown was sheer in the moonlight. The door handle began to turn right as my hand made contact with its cold surface. I swung the door wide, ready to tell off the person on the other side, but I came up short. My mouth closed with a snap.

Garren towered over me in the doorway. His blue eyes were swallowed up by the black of his pupils as he glared down at me. Endless aqua eyes raked down my body, over my scarcely concealed breasts and stomach, all the way down to my bare feet thanks to the moonbeam flowing in through the windows. My legs were exposed since my nightgown stopped just past my butt. A shiver rippled down my spine that had nothing to do with the cold. I quickly wrapped one arm across my chest and hid my binding mark behind my back. I felt completely exposed. I should've closed the door in his face, but I was rooted in place. He lifted both arms and gripped the top of the doorframe.

His voice snapped me from my initial shock.

"So, you welcome Nazneen into your bed, too?" Garren said, his voice as smooth as silk and as sultry as sin. A look crossed his features. The same look I'd seen when I turned to him after Nazneen had kissed me this evening. Jealousy, maybe?

Why did he care who was in my bed?

"I don't have the energy for this," I said and went to slam the door in his face.

"Neither do I," he snapped, and his hand made contact with the door before it closed, pushing it back so forcefully it bounced off the wall with a loud crack.

I swallowed thickly. "What are you doing?"

Garren took a step into my suite. "I'm not going to stand in the hall and argue with you."

I took a good look at the male standing before me. He was a mess. His hair stood on end, I assumed from raking his hands through it. His shirt was disheveled and his clothes ... they weren't the same ones he'd been wearing earlier, but he looked unkempt. He was a male possessed.

"Evren said you and Nazneen had dinner here tonight?"

The black edges of the sea dragon tattooed into his skin poked out the top of his shirt. His strong forearms were covered in thick veins. His binding mark glowed gold with his nearness. My heart skipped a beat.

I took a step back, giving me the space I wanted, needed. He must have taken that as an invitation, because he moved further into the room. "Don't come in."

"I can come in if I damn well please."

I retreated from him, walking backward into the room. I willed my earth power forward, but it wasn't responding. Instead, the bond of mates was flaring to life, tugging me to him. The bond wanted the distance between us gone. It was like I was stuck on an undercurrent pulling me to him. I was a wave crashing against a sheer, rocky cliff. This wasn't just desire. This was a cosmic shift in my world, refocusing entirely on him.

"I don't want you in here. I want to be alone," I said, my voice shaking.

That wasn't very convincing, and he knows it.

Garren closed the door with a loud thud instead, ignoring my weak demand.

"You don't truly mean that," he said as he prowled even closer to me, his lips curling up. His gaze had turned feral. "I can feel that me walking out that door is the last thing you want. Your true feelings are coming through our bond loud and clear."

He was right. I hated how my knees trembled with the realization. I begged them to stop. And I mentally begged him *not* to stop.

As Garren invaded my space, I tried to move around the furniture to get away from him, but the room was growing smaller with each step he took. I didn't know why I bothered. I didn't want to get away from him. It was all just a show, but it sent exhilaration through me. I looked at Eleni sprawled out on the couch on her back, legs sticking into the air. She rolled over when Garren approached, and Eleni looked up at him. She was drunk on sleep, and her lip was stuck on one of her canines.

Very fierce, Eleni.

He smiled down at my familiar and then reached down and patted her belly. More proof that Garren was indeed my bondmate. Eleni was an extension of me, despite how independent she acted. If she accepted him, my mind and body had too.

"Traitor," I said to the wolf. She chuffed and then rolled away from our standoff to sleep.

Garren chuckled to himself. He caught me by the arm as I turned to run from him. His grasp was firm yet gentle. My binding mark glowed at his touch. Just as it had during training today, his touch was shocking in its intensity.

In a panic, I lashed out. My hand flew up and slapped him across the face. The moment my hand made contact, I pulled it back to my chest with a gasp, stunned I'd actually hit him. His arrogant, handsome face. I'd actually just slapped him. Hard. His cheek was already turning red with an imprint of my palm. I felt shock and then humor flashed down through the bond.

"I'm sorry," I whispered, but he didn't respond. "Let go of me."

I tried to pull away, twisting my arm, but the friction burned my skin. He loosened his grip slightly and took a step closer, pressing his body against mine, curling his body to fit mine like a glove. His free hand reached up and brushed a strand of wet hair from my eyes. As his gaze traced over my features, my traitorous body filled with yearning. Need coiled in tight ribbons through my body. He was lulling me into a false sense of safety. Or was it true safety? I tried to resist, but I was falling. The fucking bond was making it impossible. I was falling into an oblivion of emotions.

As if he could sense the change, he smiled. He took a deep breath, drawing my scent into him.

"Your scent is intoxicating. Rose, sandalwood, and fresh air."

His hand slid from my arm down to my waist. His roughened palm was scorching hot through the thin fabric of my nightgown. It was huge on my narrow waist. He flexed his fingers and then dug them into me, bunching the fabric in his strong hands. His other hand came up and wound my hair into a thick rope in his fist. The thick hardness of him pressed against my stomach. Powers Above, I could feel him everywhere.

He gave my hair a quick yank, lifting my chin so I was staring directly at him. "I've wanted to do this since you flicked that tight ponytail at me earlier." A muscle ticked in his jaw.

"Get off."

I almost laughed at how fake the words sounded to my own ears. I didn't want him to get off me. *I want more of him*, the bond sang in my heart. *More, more, more.*

He tugged my head back further, and I sucked in a sharp breath.

"Hm," he hummed, "I'm planning on it." His mouth hovered over the pulse point in my neck.

He lowered his head with a groan, his teeth nipping at my chin. Pain and pleasure—the perfect amount of both. I'd never known that was something I wanted before. He kissed the corner of my mouth with what was almost reverence. Then he angled his lips over mine and claimed my mouth. Hot and heavy and full of need. I stiffened at his invasion, but my body quickly relaxed, giving into the yearning that burned a path inside me. As my body molded to his, he growled his approval and pushed his merciless tongue into my mouth, parting my lips, and drinking me in like his life depended on it. This was nothing like Nazneen's kiss. I could feel this kiss in my soul. My chest hummed, the bond pulsing even stronger now that his mouth was touching me. I couldn't shut it down or pull away from it. The draw was too strong. And it made me feel ... weightless.

Garren broke our kiss. Both of us just stared at each other, struggling to fill our lungs. His bright aqua eyes were all but swallowed with passion. Too brief. His kiss was too brief. The panic began to seep back in. What was I doing? I tried to push away from him, but his grip on me was unrelenting.

"You like it," he said with confidence. His expression was devilish.

I pulled my lower lip between my teeth and bit down. Did I like it? I shook my head no, or tried to. His unforgiving grip on my hair made it almost impossible to move.

"Liar," he whispered against my mouth. "You are mine, Princess Katuri Harland of Laeto Selva. You are going to give in to me. You will submit to the bond and submit to me whether you like it or not. The fates do not make mistakes."

Pure High Fae male arrogance. And my Powers damned knees quivered.

I finally found my voice. "You will have to drag me kicking and screaming. I'll never give myself or my power to you."

"It would be my pleasure." His heavily lidded eyes blinked down at me. "I like it when you put up a fight."

My heart was beating wildly in my chest, giving away how much his words affected me. I tried to shrug out of his grip with no success. He groaned when I shifted against him. "Katuri," he said through gritted teeth. His hand skated over my hip and squeezed my barely covered ass. "You will be mine."

This was a game now. How many times could I tell him no and make it sound convincing? "No."

"You will."

My bravado was slipping. How was he so confident? "How can you be so certain?"

"I always get what I want."

"Spoiled brat." I licked my dry lips and then regretted it instantly as his gaze flashed with heat.

He chuckled darkly. With that, he gave my hair a final rough tug and then he was gone. I felt weak and off balance without his arms holding me up. I stood exactly where he'd left me, letting the cold air cool the heat roaring through my veins.

Momentary weakness. That's all that was. A momentary weakness. Even if I did like his mouth on mine, and the roughness of his hands, it had to end. I wasn't going to think about the way he'd tasted. Or how he'd held me so possessively. Or the way he'd demanded I submit to him, taking pleasure from me. One kiss and I was irrevocably changed for life. Shit. I was screwed. Or, at least, I would be. And yet, as I climbed back into bed, I couldn't help but press my fingers to my swollen lips. They were swollen and thrummed. Powers Above, I wanted more.

TWENTY-FIVE
GARREN

When Evren showed up to dinner without Nazneen, I almost lost it. The water in my glass turned to ice and shattered, sending deadly shards skittering across the table.

After I'd left the training arena in a thundering fury, I ran to the Hook to release all my frustration and built-up power. I ran up the glacier overlooking the fjord and dove straight off the edge. My sea dragon exploded from me, shredding my clothes to pieces, just before I hit the frigid water. Icy water enveloped me, shocking me to the core. I welcomed the burning cold as it washed over my scales to numb the chaos that was overwhelming my mind. I swam at a punishing pace until the bond snapped taut in my chest, forcing me to turn around. It had never been this strong before.

"You know they were fucking with you, right?" Delrik said.

"What?" My fork froze mid-bite. I was gripping the damned thing so hard it was beginning to bend. I'd thought it could be a game Nazneen was playing, but as I replayed the kiss in my head over and over, when I remembered Katuri giving over to Nazneen, I doubted it was pretend. Hearing Delrik confirm that it was all a show brought back the jealousy and anger.

"Come on. Naz is the queen of pranks."

I knew that. She had pranked us without mercy during our time together during the war.

I turned to Evren. "Did you know?"

She refused to answer me, but she had a look of guilt on her face that gave her away. They'd planned it all. Just to push me over the edge. And fuck, it had worked. I fell into the trap like a helpless animal. I dropped my fork with a clatter onto the table and sprinted to Katuri's room. Whether Nazneen was messing with me or not, I wouldn't let Katuri get away with that kiss. I was going to show her exactly what I thought about her kissing anyone who wasn't me. I was going to show her that I was serious about the bond. I wanted Katuri with my everything. *I* was not a game to her.

The look on her face when I barged into her suite was priceless. When I'd finally gotten my hands on her, her wide, emerald and sage eyes gave away exactly what she was feeling. I knew she could feel the bond the same as me. The feel of her body against me, how she fit against my body, I couldn't get enough of it. Her heartbeat was rapid against my lips on her neck. I smelled her desire. And then she gave in, just a little. She melted into me. She'd stopped fighting against her stubbornness. It gave me renewed hope.

How I was able to leave Katuri just standing there in that scrap of sheer fabric she claimed was a nightgown was beyond me. The flickering firelight danced golden hues over her beautifully exposed skin. The light glinted off the silver septum ring in her nose. Holding her in my arms was surreal. I raked my hands through my hair for the hundredth time that night. I was right; her tribal tattoos did go all the way down her chest. I'd seen a peak of the ink this afternoon. The silk did nothing to conceal it. I wanted to start at her navel and run my tongue up, following the intricate curls and loops of that sexy as fuck tattoo. And I couldn't help digging my fingers into her soft ass. Her breathy words that slipped from her full lips were all lies. Powers, and her scent! She smelled so good. I wanted to touch every part of her body, every part of her soul. The taste of her mouth, the weight of her in my arms, the sound she made in the back of her throat—she overwhelmed my senses.

I'd had many females throw themselves at me since I came of age, offering me everything. But none of them compared to Katuri.

"You will have to drag me kicking and screaming. I'll never give myself or my power to you."

I didn't think it would take much convincing. She was already mine.

TWENTY-SIX
KATURI

I didn't sleep well last night. I woke restless and exhausted. Thank the Powers we didn't have training today since Master Salcido had a new group of younglings to mentor. Which meant I had today off and I could lie in bed all day. Hazy morning light tried to break through the gray clouds, but it was useless. It looked like there was another snowstorm coming in. Wonderful. So much for the clear sky last night.

I exhaled loudly, puffing my cheeks out. I didn't want to move from the comfort of my bed, but I needed to pee and brush my teeth. I looked in the mirror above my dressing table and touched my lips. Garren had kissed these lips just hours ago. His scent was still on my skin. Masculine and something luxurious. He'd left me in a haze.

A light tap at the door signaled my maid had arrived. How she knew the minute I woke each morning was beyond me.

She poked her head into my room. "Would you like me to bring you breakfast?"

And apparently, she could read my moods, too.

Corynne had been with me since I arrived in Kanevvluk. She was a boto encantado, a river dolphin shifter native to my homeland. I wasn't sure why she volunteered to travel with me. Her kind preferred to stay near warm waters. Thankfully, she was allowed to visit the hot springs as often as she wanted. I'd asked her once why she came all the way to Snowhaven Territory with me. She'd simply shrugged and said, "I wanted to offer the princess protection."

Encantado were known for protecting those that were kind to them. Though they could be vicious when provoked. Not much was known about how their magic worked. I'd heard stories of how those that double-crossed an encantado wound up being led to the water and were found drowned at the bottom of the river bed. They typically stayed close to the rivers that ran through the Forest Fae Territory, but several of them worked at the palace.

By some miracle, Corynne had been allowed to stay with me. I asked my mother to allow me to bring my nanny, whom I'd grown up with, with me when she shipped me to Snowhaven, but she'd refused. She'd said I was too old for a nanny and needed to learn to do things for myself. Corynne had been a complete stranger to me, but we'd grown close over the years.

At first, I'd felt so lost without my nanny. Corynne had held me while I cried myself to sleep every night on the voyage from Laeto Selva. By the time we'd landed in this frozen city, I had no more tears to cry. Corynne was my bright spot during the endless days. She loved music and dancing. I'd often find her singing in our native language while she went about her tasks. Her voice was soft and hypnotic. It was easy to get lost in the ups and downs of her melodic songs. That's probably how the encantados tricked their enemies to their watery deaths. Entrancing them with ethereal voices.

"Thank you, Corynne, that would be wonderful."

Corynne was beautiful. Her skin was a soft pink in color. Her hair almost matched her skin but was streaked with coral and orange highlights. Her eyes were bright and clever. Nothing slipped past her.

With all the training we'd been doing, plus my forest runs at night, I had been eating twice as much as usual.

"Want me to start a bath for you?" She started toward the washroom, but I stopped her.

"Maybe later. I just want to curl up in bed for now."

She smiled softly, gave me a pat on the hand, and left the room with a click of the door.

I headed to the washroom to take care of my morning routine. I didn't bother to close the door.

Just as I was about to brush my teeth, the door to my suite burst open and Nazneen and Evren came in in a giggling whirlwind. Aura swooped in with a soft, shrieking hello and landed on Eleni's head.

"Morning, Sunshine!" Nazneen's voice was way too loud this early.

I just grunted a greeting.

"You really are *not* a morning person, are you?" she asked as she poked her head into the washroom.

"Nope," I deadpanned. I was not a morning person, especially after tossing and turning all night. "But I brought you a present,"

Nazneen said. She kissed my cheek and danced back into the sitting room to deposit the cake on the table.

"Is Corynne bringing up breakfast?" she asked.

"Yes. She should be back soon."

"Powers, Kat, I've never met anyone who sleeps with as many pillows as you," Evren called from the bedroom.

I bent over the sink to splash water on my face. Nazneen tossed me a clean towel before turning to jump into my bed, snuggling up with Evren who'd already made herself comfortable amongst the many layers of blankets. I smiled at my friends and then climbed back into bed with them. This morning routine was becoming familiar to our little group, and I loved it. I loved having friends for the first time in ... well, I don't even know how long. I guessed I'd never really had friends at home. There weren't many who wanted to befriend a princess.

"How did you sleep, Evren?" I asked

"Like a rock! I knew using my powers would drain my energy, but I ate an obscene amount of food for dinner and fell asleep almost immediately after."

"Aw, poor Delrik. Guess he didn't get lucky last night," I said, laughing.

"No, but someone else did," Evren said, elbowing Nazneen in the ribs.

My eyes went wide. "Do tell!"

"I caught her and Arik in the kitchens making cake," Evren said, making air quotations with her fingers.

"Oh, we definitely made a cake." Her high cheekbones flushed. "Among other things."

I reached across Evren and swatted at her. "Nazneen! Arik?! Again?"

"I'm used to having my fill of fun. It's been dreadfully dull since we left Arcelia." She flung her arm across her face dramatically. "And Arik isn't all that bad. He's actually very sweet ... and talented."

"He and Garren are in a constant competition to see who has the biggest cock," I said. "And it's tripled now with Delrik here."

"Well, Arik can't be on the losing side of *that* competition," Nazneen said with a smirk while wiggling her eyebrows at the two of us.

"Naz!" Evren said, tossing a pillow at her sister. "Seriously?"

"I don't know why you're so shocked. I'm a sexual being. But no, we haven't had sex yet."

"Yet?" I asked her.

"We keep getting interrupted. But I've felt it." She raised her hands and gestured to a size right as Corynne came into the room.

Nazneen quickly pulled her hands to her lap, and we all erupted into a fit of giggles.

"I figured you two would be here so I went ahead and brought enough food for ten," Corynne said. She placed a tray overflowing with food and a steaming pot of water on the table in front of the fireplace. Evren waved her hand, and a fire roared to life, instantly heating the space.

"You're the best, Corynne," Nazneen praised.

"Enjoy ladies. And don't think for a second I don't know what you were talking about." She winked. "Let me know if you need any advice. My kind are known for their enchanting pleasure." And then she disappeared.

We burst into another fit of laughter as we tried to untangle ourselves from the sheets and each other's limbs to eat.

I moved over to the couch and started to make myself a cup of strong tea. "Ugh, I need all the caffeine I can get this morning. I didn't sleep at all."

"Why?" Evren asked as she plopped down next to me. She eyed me up and down. "No wonder you're always freezing, Kat. Does that nightgown cover anything?"

I looked down at myself, the light, almost transparent silk clinging to me. "What? You're lucky I wasn't naked when you came in this morning."

Evren and Nazneen were actually the reasons I'd had Corynne order me nightgowns. They'd seen plenty of me during their first few visits. The first time Nazneen ran and jumped in my bed, she'd gotten an eye full, which she didn't seem bothered by in the slightest. She was the most open, immodest female I'd ever met. And she'd slowly converted Evren to the dark side.

"I bet Garren wouldn't mind finding out you sleep in the nude," Nazneen teased.

I choked on my tea. "What?" I said, coughing up the liquid. "Why would you say that?" I could feel heat flushing my skin and down my chest. I suddenly wished I was wearing more clothes.

"Kat. Chill. I was just kidding, but now I need to know why you reacted like that."

I put my cup down on the table too hard, causing a loud clunk that rattled the tea tray. I stood and rushed to my closet, pulling on a pair of leggings and a thick sweater, like if I didn't cover myself, they'd be able to see all the places on my body Garren had touched.

"Don't think you can ignore me Kat!" Naz shouted.

I came out of the closet slowly, guilt written all over my face. "He was here last night," I whispered shamefully.

Nazneen actually dropped the sweet roll she'd been holding, and it rolled across the floor. "Excuse me?" Eleni was quick to snatch it up.

"He was here? Last night?" Evren chirped in. There was way too much glee in her voice.

"How long? All night?" Nazneen looked overly eager about the potential of that.

"No!" I practically yelled.

"Did he see you in that nightgown?" Nazneen said, pointing at me up and down even though none of my skin was showing now.

Was it possible to turn more red? Damn. Just remembering how he'd walked into my room with his list of demands? Of me being his bondmate in *all* the ways—I twisted my fingers together.

"So, I guess our little stunt yesterday pushed him over the edge," Nazneen said, bouncing up and down, clapping. She was seriously the most expressive person I'd ever met. All I could do was nod.

"I mean, I was a little turned on by our kiss too, Kat," she said with a wink.

"Me too," Evren piped in.

I rejoined them on the couch and recapped how Garren had come in, grabbed me, demanded me to do the power swap and submit completely to the bond, and kissed me. By the time I'd finished, Nazneen fanned herself with a napkin.

"Powers, Kat! Someone likes to be told what to do?" Nazneen said.

"I do not."

Nazneen's mouth formed a knowing smile. Hell, before yesterday, I'd never been kissed. How would I know what I liked? I mean, I'd read plenty of romance novels, but they weren't real life.

Do I? I mean, maybe? I'd never been with anyone. I'd never been turned on before. I'd never felt the bond like that. There was only so much exploring you could do by yourself. No one within the citadel walls would think about touching me. Maybe I liked the idea of

Garren telling me what to do. Which was funny because I hated being told what to do in every other part of my life—not with me being consort to Garren. Though it didn't stop females from hanging all over him. Such a double standard. But last night when he was here, I didn't worry about anything. I only saw him, only thought about him. It was freeing. I could see how potentially giving up control in that aspect of my life, letting Garren have control, could be *very* freeing. I shivered at the memory of the exhilaration I had felt when Garren was so demanding. It felt dirty and I loved it.

"How would I know? I've been locked in this stupid citadel forever."

"Yeah, it's pretty shitty that you've been deprived for your entire life. Sex is a beautiful, beautiful thing," Nazneen said, practically rolling her eyes into the back of her head.

"Agreed," Evren said. "You've had it even worse than I did."

This was all new territory for me, and I had no idea what to think.

"All Garren and I have ever shared was awkward silence and snarky words. Dark hells, he'd never even touched me until yesterday.

"Well, there is nothing wrong with a little playful bantering in the bedroom," Evren said. "I mean, I thoroughly enjoy when Delrik is controlling."

Nazneen slammed her hands against her ears. "Gross, Evren. That's my brother!"

"Oh, deal with it. I've heard and seen all your antics. You'll survive."

"I don't see him as someone who'd want to spend his life making love with the same female for the rest of his life. I've seen all the females coming and going."

"Do you think he's been trying to distract himself? Maybe he hasn't felt the bond until now either."

"But he wants more than just the blood binding. He wants my power."

"And the problem is?"

"I ... I don't know." I was lying. I knew exactly what the problem was. I didn't want to let him have that much control over me. If he did, he'd be able to hurt me, break me. I didn't think I could put myself back together if I ever shattered again.

"Aren't you fated to be consorts?"

"There is a difference between bondmates and a couple who simply do the blood binding. I know in my heart that my parents were not bondmates. They were together to bridge powerful High Fae families and magic. But bondmates, that's something special. It's a gift from the gods. The two halves of one soul brought together."

Nazneen smiled at Evren. "I knew you'd eventually see my side on the fates."

"Yeah, yeah. But what I'm saying is it was prophesied that you two would do the blood binding and share powers. It wasn't prophesied that you were bondmates."

I remembered back to when the royal seer first told my father about Garren. She was right.

I sighed. "But I can't be happy here. I can't make Garren happy. He hates me."

"It didn't seem like he hated you yesterday during training. He seemed quite jealous with my tongue in your mouth," Naz argued.

She was trying to bring some lightness back into the conversation.

"And if he hated you, he wouldn't have shown up here last night," Evren said.

"I bet Garren would bend you over if you begged him to."

Evren scolded Nazneen. "Can you be serious for one minute?"

Nazneen held her hands in surrender. "All I know is that it's pointless worrying about something that has already been foreseen." She turned to me. "I know your life has been hard and lonely. I know your father betrayed you. But Garren is not your father. You need to take a leap of faith, Katuri."

I hung my head. "I just don't want to disappoint anyone."

I felt fingers under my chin. Evren lifted my head. "You could never disappoint anyone that truly matters."

We had been stuck inside all day with the heavy snow and winds that came in quick from the north. The storm came down so hard and fast that I hadn't been able to get out for a run before it was too snowy. I was antsy and twitchy and was pacing back and forth in front of the fireplace. My mind was still processing everything my two friends had said. I knew deep down they were right.

"Katuri, you're making me dizzy," Nazneen complained.

"I can't help it. I hate being trapped in this suite."

And I did feel trapped. The walls were closing in. My heart was pounding. I needed to get out of here.

"Well, then let's go find some trouble to get into," Nazneen said, jumping up from the couch.

When we left to go out, Nazneen, Evren, and I ran into Garren in the hallway. He was coming around the corner as we closed the door behind us. He stopped, eyes bouncing back and forth between the three of us. He looked much different than the feral male I'd encountered last night. His hair was wet from a shower and his clothes had been freshly pressed. Even his boots were shining. He was calm and collected. How the fuck was he able to be so calm.

"Good morning," he said. Cool manners and countenance.

"I take it you had a satisfying night." Nazneen spoke to Garren, but she was looking at me.

Powers! Leave it to Nazneen to immediately make it awkward. I pinched the back of her arm discreetly.

A muscle in Garren's jaw ticked. His gaze dropped to my chest where my tribal mark was hidden by the bodice of my dress. His lips parted on an inhale. Then his eyes flicked to Nazneen.

"It was, thank you."

It wasn't until he looked away from me and spoke that I realized I'd been holding my breath since he appeared.

Okay ... something was off. He was too amiable. I half expected him to start a verbal sparring match with Nazneen right in the corridor. He was livid with her after her kissing me last night. He may have appeared mellow, but I knew based on the look in his eyes and the pulsing jealousy through the bond he was one breath away from pinning me to the wall and stealing another heated kiss to prove who I belonged to.

"Excellent," Nazneen said with a stupidly wide grin on her face.

She was seriously the worst, and I'd make her pay for this later.

Thankfully, Evren stepped between Nazneen and Garren to come to my rescue. "We were just on the way to the library. Have a good day."

Then she pulled me against her side so we could escape.

Garren gave us a bow. "Ladies."

I walked past him without lifting my gaze from the floor. His body turned toward me. Garren's fingers brushed the back of my hand. The lightest of touches. My breath caught at the zing of energy that passed between us. My eyes flashed to his face, and for a moment, our eyes locked. All I saw was adoration and hope.

TWENTY-SEVEN
DELRIK

It had been three days, and the snowstorm was still going strong. It had started a week after Nazneen's little prank, which meant we were all feeling the rising tension and had no way of escape. I'd passed the time testing the extent of my powers and doing target practice with Garren and Arik. I was basically showing up Garren who, after losing several bets, had put his own foot in his mouth.

A guard came into the practice arena just as I drew back my bow. "The High Ruler has requested your presence."

Garren let out an exaggerated groan. "Tell his Highness we'll be there momentarily."

The guard gave a short bow and then left.

"I guess that is the end of this session," I grumbled.

We began to pack up and made our way to the council room. We ran into Arik in the hall outside the doors. I looked him up and down, then placed my hulking frame in the center of the corridor and crossed my arms over my chest. He no longer had the evidence of my attack on his face. I figured he'd refused a healer since he showed up to breakfast the next morning sporting a black eye and busted lip.

"What are you doing?" I asked the scumbag.

"Going to the council room for the meeting." The bastard didn't even look intimidated by me, even though I'd beat his ass. I knew for sure I'd broken at least one rib thanks to the tongue lashing Nazneen had given me the following morning.

Arik stared blankly at me. When I continued to stare and block his way through the hall, he said, "And?"

"You haven't been summoned."

I didn't want him playing a role in finding answers about Hadeon. I didn't trust him. He rolled his eyes at me but didn't argue. He turned on his heel and went the opposite direction.

Garren and I made our way into the council room. A long table surrounded by chairs sat in the center, covered with remnants of papers and scrolls from previous meetings. The other areas of the citadel were elaborate compared to the private wings. The private rooms were more comfortable and understated—smaller in size, with fires that kept everything glowing warm. This room was no exception. While it was used by others than the family, it was welcoming and cozy. I walked to a set of chairs near the roaring fire and dropped into the soft leather.

"Do you know what this is all about?" Nazneen asked as she settled into the chair next to me.

"Not a clue," I responded.

Jace sat across from us. "The scouts have returned," he offered.

Evren and Katuri were already sitting around the table. Aura was propped on the back of a chair next to the window. When I entered the room, she swiveled her head toward me, then lifted into flight—a long swooping arch had her landing on my shoulder. I grunted at her weight and her talons digging into my skin. Just over the last few days with Evren's mastery of her elemental fire growing, the familiar had grown to the size of a hawk and was no longer the light pocket-sized bird we'd met in Rivamir. Her talons weren't small either. Aura bent her head close to my face and her violet eye met mine. There was so much of Evren in those eyes. I scratched her head, and she gave me a low, nasally whistle in hello. Then she pushed off my shoulder and returned to her perch.

Garren had been the last to join us. He'd stopped just outside the door to speak to a guard. Well, except for Holden, who did things at his own pace and at his own convenience. Garren rounded the table, pulled his chair noticeably closer to Katuri, and plopped down beside her. Katuri wrung her fingers on the table and leaned away. The barest of movements. She'd been ignoring him for a week.

"Good morning, everyone." He reached for the carafe of water in the center of the table and poured himself and Katuri a glass. Using a single finger, he slid the glass to her.

"I don't need you to take care of me," she said quietly, her face turned down. "I don't need a big bad water beast to provide me with something to drink. I'm perfectly capable of pouring my own water."

I saw Garren shift closer to her, and he not so quietly whispered, "Technically, I'm a sea dragon."

He traced his pinky finger across the side of her hand before sliding even closer and pressing his thigh against hers beneath the table. It wasn't hard to miss the gesture, and he wasn't doing anything to disguise it from the rest of us. I rolled my eyes at his show of possession and test of boundaries.

I cleared my throat. Evren had also updated me on the Garren-Katuri situation the night Katuri and Naz had infiltrated our bed. Katuri was digging in her heels, and Garren was being feisty about it. He hadn't gone into detail, but he'd told me he'd confronted Katuri last night after dinner. Eleni trotted through the door and made her way to Katuri. Before the familiar lay at Katuri's feet, she nudged Garren's hand with her nose.

"Also, I can safely say that after the other night, I've found a few new ways to keep that snarky mouth occupied." His eyes dropped to Katuri's mouth. Her teeth sunk into her plump lower lip. I thought Garren was going to combust on the spot. The sudden tang of magic pulsed around the two. "And I'm not afraid to use them."

Katuri flared scarlet.

I choked on my own water, sputtering with a laugh. Evren cut me a disapproving look.

Holden appeared and made his way to the head of the table, killing the mood immediately. The moment he sat, a Legion guard stepped forward.

"High Ruler, your scouts have returned." His shoulders were covered with the formal gray mantle of the Snowhaven Legion.

Seeing the warrior reminded me of the war. They hadn't worn the thick cloaks on the Western Continent. It was too hot for them. But here in Kanevvluk, I'd seen them in their traditional dual-sided cloak—grayish white on one side to match the snow and dark green on the other to blend into the evergreen forest. It was a necessity in this climate. The Snowhaven Fae had joined forces with Arcelia early on. We'd even voyaged across the Ocean of Warwell as a unified fleet along with the River Kingdom's Black Guard. The Snowhaven Legion fighters were vicious in their fighting skills. They had skills on horseback as well as on foot. Their weapons of choice were bows with arrows made of unmelting ice, but they were quick with swords and axes too. They had spies almost as talented as Nazneen. Although the Snowhaven Fae secluded themselves in this tundra, they had scouts all across Illoterra and throughout the Western Continent.

The head scout who Holden had sent to find Hadeon Allerick stood at the door, waiting for permission to enter. Holden waved him in, and the male bowed to him. When he came into the room, Arik slipped in behind him and pressed back into the shadows. I caught Garren's attention and nodded at Arik. Garren gave the slightest of head shakes. I couldn't tell if he meant it was okay for him to be present or not.

"We found a city in the southern part of the western continent near Menrath," the scout began.

Menrath was a city that was used for trading, even before the war. It was a very poor city. It had been decimated by the Raven Fae after they'd lost the war. Most of the city was pillaged and then burned. So many were displaced. I hadn't been back since the end of the war.

"Hadeon and his consort, Elenora, the powerful seer. Renwick Ashewood was also there."

I instinctively leaned in toward Evren. When she stiffened at my side, I placed a protective hand on her back. Evren shivered at the sound of Renwick Ashewood's name. Each day, the connection between us had grown stronger. While we hadn't mastered conversing through the bond, deep emotions flowed easily back and forth between us. I was stunned. I could feel her fear and outrage, but the terror of hearing his name overwhelmed me. It crushed me. My bondmate, my Ashlyra, had suffered so much at the hands of Renwick. I'd seen the bruises, the marks he'd left on her, when we first met in Lakeshore, but it wasn't until this moment, when I felt it through the bond, did I understand the full gravity of it. I felt every blow, every bite, every sinister thing he ever did all at the same time. My natural instinct told me to protect myself from the pain and slip a mental shield between us. Evren had had to live with that monster day after day and suffer his violence first hand. The least I could do was to offer empathy. She'd never told me the full depth of his depravity. But now I felt it. But if Evren had to live through the torture, I would too. One of these days, I'd hunt him down and pull him apart, piece by piece. There was no punishment severe enough for what he'd done.

Evren straightened and turned to Holden. "My brother mentioned that our father had been working with someone from the Western Continent. He'd accept unmarked shipments often coming from Menrath."

"We already knew that," Holden said dismissively.

Evren sank back in her chair. And I wanted to throw my water glass at Holden's face. Holden wasn't a sadistic prick like Renwick, but he could be cruel in other ways.

"Yes." The scout nodded at Evren in acknowledgment. "The shipments he's been taking are smuggling iron into Illoterra. Blocks of it mainly, but also shackles, nails, weapons. There were also whispers of Bloodthorn as well, but I didn't see any with my own eyes, so that's just speculation."

"Why would he need to bring weapons to Illoterra?" I asked.

I looked around the table, but no one spoke up.

"What about the city itself?" Holden pushed on.

"The city in question, Noirdan, is where Hadeon Allerick has centralized. It's about a day's ride on horseback west of Menrath and nestled against Baxmar Peak. There isn't much there. It looks like it's Fae and other mortals that were displaced from the war. It's all blackened and desolate. I'm not sure anything could thrive there except Hadeon. There are a few structures, nothing too large. Only Hadeon's private home and the remnants of a crumbled temple. No reinforcement or guards. There seemed nothing amiss. Which means we need to take a closer look. It was too quiet, too normal."

Evren spoke up again. "The Lendorr mines are under Mount Lendorr, one of the highest peaks of the Baxmar Range."

That time, Holden didn't brush her off. He readjusted himself. "And your brother..." he prompted.

Evren didn't hesitate to supply her brother's name. "High Ruler Adaris Byrnes."

"Yes. Byrnes. He has information about the mines?"

Evren nodded.

Holden snapped his fingers, and the guard appeared next to him. "I want to see High Ruler Byrnes."

The guard bowed and was gone with a pop.

Was he really expecting Adaris to just drop everything and come when called? Actually, Adaris would be smart to accept the summons. Kanevvluk was nearly impossible to get into, and Holden never met with other leaders outside the Snowhaven Territory. Even Aramis had come to Kanevvluk in the past. This could potentially be common ground between the two territories. That could open up communication and trade.

"Let's move on. What else?" Holden said.

The scout continued with his briefing. "The port in Menrath is easily accessible. There are guard towers along the coast. Most of those in the city and the surrounding smaller villages have fled because of Hadeon's control. The only remaining are Fae and directly related to the trade ships. I believe some of them are the remaining Raven Fae from after the war."

"How many are working with Hadeon?" Jace asked.

"Several hundred. Not anything to be concerned about at this point. The Raven Fae clans have aligned themselves with him. The only potential problem was the fiends. Hadeon wasn't bothering to hide them from view. He'd built a whole training and breeding facility." The scout didn't seem fazed by this information. Just presented the facts.

"What are fiends?" Katuri asked.

When it seemed like Holden wasn't going to respond, too deep in his own thoughts, Jace answered Katuri.

"They are beasts that were originally created with dark magic, long ago during the rebellion. Hadeon's bondmate Elenora is a powerful seer. She also wields dark magic that she used to transform Fae desperate enough to fall into Hadeon's lie into hideous beasts. Not many Fae survived the transformation. Many of them died. But those that did survive destroyed peace everywhere they went. Some even have wings. They have incredible strength and are as blood thirsty as a hoard of osomals. And they are completely expendable to Hadeon."

"But that was during the war. Now, they've been breeding," the scout said.

"If he released them, they'd easily devour the whole continent," I said.

"Were you able to figure out what he has planned? What is his goal?" Holden was growing impatient and turning redder by the minute.

"You mean besides just being an ass?" I quipped.

My comment was not appreciated by Holden. He shot me a look. Nazneen covered her goofy grin with her hand.

This meeting had already taken twice as long as any I'd taken part in before. Holden liked his information to be delivered quickly so he could move on the next phase of his plan of attack. His efficiency in the middle of chaos was the reason Aramis had stepped down and let Holden lead the Illoterran armies.

Once she'd composed herself, Nazneen leaned forward. "I've had word from my contacts in Arcelia, Rivamir, and the Western Continent..."

"You sent out your own scouts?" His words were laced with distrust and anger. "You don't trust that mine can do their jobs correctly?" Holden clenched his jaw tight.

I saw Arik take a small step forward from the shadows. How the fuck had he snuck in here? His jaw was clenched tight. I didn't like how fond he'd grown of Nazneen. She didn't need a loser like him to protect her. Nazneen held Holden's gaze, refusing to back down to his authority. She had a look of determined annoyance written all over her face.

"I trust they are capable. I don't trust that the information will make it back to me. I have to protect my kingdom. Just as you have to protect yours." Nazneen lifted her chin. I was so proud of my sister. "Anyways, the Arcelia scouts have tracked another elemental High Fae to one of the original Temple of Anruin in the City of Proux."

"Why would we need to know about another elemental? There are three sitting in this room," Holden said.

Evren spoke this time. "If my father wanted me for my elemental power and he was working under Hadeon Allerick, that means that I'm probably still of interest to him. My elemental flame is still of interest. If he can't get to me, what is preventing him from finding another elemental Fae instead? Elementals are rare, but not impossible to find. Wouldn't it be smart to get a step ahead of Hadeon?"

She was right. Whatever Hadeon planned for Evren, he would search elsewhere until he found her. And if Nazneen's scouts found the elemental, it was only a matter of time before Hadeon did, too.

"Where is the City of Proux?" Evren asked.

"It's in the northern part of the Western Continent in the Air Fae Kingdom," Nazneen said. She pulled a map from her pocket and unfolded it. "This is the map my scouts sent to me with the location of the temple and other points of interest." She pointed to a region on the northern part of the continent.

"Is that close to where you are from, Katuri?"

"No, my homeland is far from the coast." She leaned across the table to reach the map and pointed to another spot off in the west.

"We won't be able to blink to the Western Continent. It's too far for so many people. A ship is the only option," Garren said, finally speaking up.

He'd been absorbing the information quietly.

"I won't be able to go with you. I have too many tasks here that I can't leave," Jace stated. "I can work on this end though, depending on your needs."

"Perfect. We can find the elemental and send back the information we gather," Garren said. "I'll also look for coastal ports and cities where we can dock if it comes to that."

Holden pulled his attention back to the conversation. "No. That's unacceptable. I will send a group of legion warriors to handle it."

Suddenly, Garren was on his feet. He slammed his fist into the table. The salty taste of magic pierced the air, and a ripple flowed like a shock wave. Ice and frost scattered like a star where his fist met wood. "No." It was more of a growl than a word.

"What do you mean, no?" Holden said. He'd jumped at the resounding thunk of Garren's fist but only for a moment before he slipped his facade back in place.

"I've had enough of your shit. I am capable of going on a scouting mission. I am capable of finding the elemental. I am capable of sending back information. Or are you doubting my loyalties to the Snowhaven Fae?"

Holden glared daggers at Garren's outburst. "That is enough."

"I *will* lead this mission."

Holden was on his feet so fast that his chair toppled backward. "I am High Ruler."

Holden Eckhardt wasn't a small male. He stood several inches taller than Garren, and with his muscular build, he looked like a mountain staring down the valley below. The room grew cold as Garren's ice prowled along the edge of the table toward his father.

"Are you challenging me, son?"

"Oh, now I'm your son."

"Ha!" Holden guffawed. "The lesser of the two."

Garren's face turned dangerous. Scales crept down from his hairline, and his eyes turned into sharp slits. Fingers turned to talons. "Am I, Father? Am I the lesser of the two?" Garren's supreme elemental power was showing its dominance and strength. "Just because I knocked you on your ass when I was a child does not give you a reason to treat me like trash."

Holden's power was the same as Jace's; mind projection. He was no match for Garren.

"You may see me as lesser than, but you know that if I chose to challenge you, there would be nothing you could do to stop me." His words hissed through his teeth, which were now needle-sharp points.

Then I saw Katuri's hand move. She softly placed her hand on his hip. It wasn't a gesture to calm him but rather one of support. Her stare at Holden was as fearsome as Garren's. She was standing with her bondmate, whether she noticed or not. He must have sensed her alliance because the ice stopped growing in size but held strong. Holden's eyes slipped to Katuri. He was outnumbered and outpowered.

"Fine," Holden said through clenched teeth. Then he stomped from the council room. Tension was thick, and all waited with bated breaths to see what the sea dragon would do next.

"We will have to wait until the blizzard is over," Garren continued. The ice disappeared, but Garren's fierce appearance remained. He made eye contact with Jace, who nodded in brotherly approval.

"Once the storm has passed, we will use one of the Snowhaven trade ships as a disguise. Delrik and I will lead a group across to the City of Proux and find this elemental. When we find the elemental and determine how far Hadeon's influence has spread, we will make a decision on how to proceed from there."

Garren took a breath and turned to his brother. "Jace, you'll remain here with your obligations and reinforce our borders. Reconnect with our allies in Arcelia. High Ruler Byrnes is hopefully on his way so you can discuss things in person with him."

Jace had always wanted Garren to stand up to their father from the very beginning, and I could see the pride he now held for his younger brother.

TWENTY-EIGHT
DELRIK

"There is nothing in this whole damn library about the shadow magic." Evren slammed the book closed in frustration. "Not even in the books about dark magic."

With the sound of the slam, Garren jerked awake and nearly toppled his chair backward. He'd fallen asleep with his feet propped on the table, a book still open across his lap, over an hour ago. He was leaning precariously balanced on the back two legs of the chair. Eleni was stretched on the rug beneath his legs. She was often seen with Garren rather than Katuri these days.

We'd all relocated to the library after listening to the news from the scout. Well, almost all of us. Jace went off to console the High Ruler and his bruised ego, and Arik had disappeared into the shadows again, which was perfectly fine with me.

"What did I miss?" Garren yawned and raked his hand through his hair.

His eyes immediately searched for his bondmate. The fact she was sitting in the same room and within ten feet of him was a statement. Actually, seeing her stand alongside him while he'd faced off with Holden was proof their bond was strengthening. Nazneen and Katuri pressed their heads together, laughing and whispering from their spot on the couch across the room. We'd been searching (well, Evren had been searching) all the books in the library for weeks, and we'd come up empty handed. If Evren wasn't in the training arena, she was in the library.

She looked up at me. "I can't find anything."

My bondmate. My Ashlyra. She was my whole heart. She'd spent countless hours searching for answers to the dark shadow magic. Garren had been right; even though we didn't know exactly what they were and the full extent of the power, I still needed to try to learn control over them. Evren and I had gotten good at passing the mysterious shadows back and forth, but we still didn't know the extent of what they could do. Alux had used them for pain and death, but there wasn't a safe way to practice that. Not that I wanted to. I had no desire to be a killer again. I'd been able to summon the shadows and form them as a barrier or to block out light, but there was a lingering sense of otherness that I couldn't pinpoint. I didn't think it was necessarily stemming from the shadows themselves. It started right after I'd taken in the shadows for the first time. I'd been plagued with nightmares again, worse than any from the war. Flashes of dark thoughts would come randomly. They'd only grown worse in the passing weeks. Now, I woke Evren most nights with tossing and turning. The other day during training, when Garren and I had teamed up against Naz, the thought of using my shadows against Garren was an urge that took me by complete surprise. Garren was my best friend and like a brother to me, and I'd wanted him to feel the pan of the shadows. We'd asked the priestess in the nearby temple, but none of them could point us in the right direction. Although they'd heard of Alux, they didn't know where the magic originated from. They had suggested we find one of the priestesses in the original temple to talk to while we were on the Western Continent. Maybe they knew more since they were older.

Illoterra was new compared to Quinterre. When the gods created our realm, they fashioned Quinterre as an exact replica of Aesira. (I'd learned so much from Evren's studies.). Eventually, the Fae began exploring past the borders of Quinterre and found Illoterra. That's when the Snowhaven Fae, Mountain Fae, and River Fae expanded to the new continent. The Temples of Anruin in Quinterre were far older than those here. Their histories of the Fae and magic were more extensive.

It felt like there was something sitting on my shoulder, whispering sinister thoughts in my ear and pushing me to act on the dark thoughts that crept into my mind. Even when Evren took the shadows at night, I'd still have a heaviness over me when waking. I didn't want to burden her with two strong powers since she was still learning. Her fire had grown stronger without the shadows. Without the shadows, she had the clarity to focus on mastering her fire power.

The only time the lingering otherness was gone was when Evren shared her elemental fire with me. I could only hold the flames for a few minutes and only a fraction of the power. Then they'd begin to flare out of control. My Ashlyra was so strong to be able to withstand both powers for such a long time. I had almost lit an entire bookshelf of novels on fire the other afternoon. And it made Aura pissy when I had them.

It had been a long day, and I felt drained. I really just wanted to fall into bed and sleep, but I could already feel the nightmares waiting for me on the other side of consciousness. I heard Evren hiss from the bathroom as she lowered her sore body into the hot, steaming water. I'd never been more proud of my Ashlyra than the last few months. She'd come so far, worked so hard, and hadn't once balked at the responsibility thrust upon her shoulders. I joined her in the bathroom and slipped out of my clothes before stepping into the tub behind her. Thank the Powers this thing was made for two people. Evren hummed and leaned back against my chest. The shadows and her fire reached for each other where our skin met.

"Thank you for trying so hard to find an answer," I said against her hair.

She lifted my hand and kissed the shimmering binding mark on my palm.

"I'd do anything for you." She tipped her chin up to look at me. Her beautiful violet eyes showed through long silver lashes.

I leaned in closer. "I don't deserve you."

And I didn't. This female was all goodness. And I was all darkness and destruction. I lifted a cup and dumped water along Evren's hair. Then, I reached for soap and began to wash her hair. My calloused fingertips massaged the suds into her scalp. This was one of my favorite things to do. I rinsed the soap with fresh water and then moved the silky curtain to the side to expose her creamy skin. My thumb idly stroked her shoulder. Evren melted into the touch.

I sighed. "I'm worried about the nightmares. And the otherness."

"I know you are," she replied.

"I feel like it's changing, becoming stronger. It's almost like voices in my head now."

Evren shifted so she could see me face to face. "Hearing voices is more concerning than the nightmares."

I nodded and scrubbed my hands over my tired face.

"Do you hear them all the time?"

"It's not actual voices. More like thoughts that aren't quite mine. They come and go."

Evren turned to sit on her knees, and water sloshed over the edge of the tub and onto the floor. She leaned and pressed her hands flat on my chest. "When we get to the Quinterre, the first thing we will do is find someone who has answers."

I hated that whatever this otherness was, it was becoming a burden to my Ashlyra. I'd never wanted her to hear the horror of my past, and now she was having to pick up the slack because I couldn't figure out how to manage the shadow magic.

"I've got you," she said and pressed her forehead to mine. "I've got you."

TWENTY-NINE
GARREN

High Ruler Adaris Byrnes arrived several days later and right on time for dinner. A Snowhaven Legion guard had blinked him and one of his Black Guardsman from the Hook to the citadel since the storm hadn't let up any. I was shocked that the captain of his ship had been able to navigate his ship through the rough waters stirred up by the blizzard. The harbor had been particularly choppy with the incoming storms. I knew the Black Guard were excellent sailors, but not many in their right minds would've taken on that challenge.

As I was making my way through the citadel to meet the new High Ruler in the greeting hall, I overheard Arik. He was whispering to someone hidden in the shadows. If I hadn't already been running late to meet Adaris, I would've stopped to eavesdrop more. I was able to catch a snippet of the conversation. However, I wasn't able to see who Arik was talking to.

"I sent my contact on the Quinterre notice that I'd be arriving next month. I didn't know how yet, but I'd find a way onto the ship, even if I had to sneak on board."

I needed to remember to follow up with Arik on this. I hadn't planned on Arik joining us in Quinterre, but I also wasn't completely opposed to the idea. Although I didn't fully trust him, he still had experience with the terrain and the group of Fae we would be dealing with. I knew Delrik wouldn't be happy, but he'd deal. Right now, I needed to focus on High Ruler Byrnes and welcoming him.

I didn't know what I was expecting when I saw Adaris Byrnes, but the male that appeared in the greeting hall was not that. He stood tall and wore the garnet and black of the Black Guard. One of his guardsmen stood at his side. When I approached him, Adaris gave me a small bow before he offered a generous smile.

"You must be Garren. Evren has told me so much about you." Adaris reached out a hand to me. Almost his entire hand was covered in narrow scars an inch or two long. I paused for a split second before gripping his hand tightly.

"Hopefully only the good things," I said in return. "Come. Your sister is anxiously waiting for you in the dining room. And dinner will be served shortly."

Adaris gave me a nod and then introduced the other male. "This is Garret Sorrell. He is my head guard."

He gave me a swift bow but didn't say anything.

Adaris and I walked and chatted about the weather and his journey, Garret trailing behind us. It was clear he had bred and trained to be a High Ruler. He was young, Evren had told us, only forty years old. He was much younger than any other leader I'd met. He hadn't fought in the war, but he had the air of someone who had been through the circle of dark hells and back. He'd seen defeat and loss but had survived. I saw a lot of myself in that part of him.

"Thank you for your assistance," he said to me before I pushed the doors to the dining room open. He was assaulted by a squealing Evren.

"You actually came!" Evren was practically shrieking when she jumped into his arms.

The siblings looked nothing alike, opposites in every way. His dark hair and towering height to her silver and slight frame. Except their eyes. Their violet eyes were identical. He lifted his sister off the floor in a sweeping embrace before setting her back on her feet. Aura chirped and hovered around his head with steady beats of her wings.

"Sweet Aura. You have grown so much," he cooed to the firebird.

She puffed out her chest, preening, and pushed fire to her wings. Adaris conjured a piece of meat and tossed it into the air for her to catch. Delrik gripped his forearm in greeting before hugging him. Nazneen shoved her brother out of the way, and Adaris bent to hug her.

"Beautiful as always, Nazneen," he said before kissing her on the cheek.

Nazneen looked at Evren's brother, like they were well acquainted and comfortable in each other's company. I was thankful that Delrik had another friend he could rely on.

She dusted invisible lint from his shoulders. "High Ruler looks good on you."

"I was High Ruler last time you saw me."

"Yes, but it was still fresh. Now you look all regal and in charge."

Evren took Adaris's hand and pulled him to us. "Everyone, this is my big brother and High Ruler of the River Kingdom, Adaris Byrnes."

He greeted each of us in turn.

"You made it in perfect time. Dinner is ready," Nazneen said. She spotted Garrett and smiled. "I was hoping you'd tag along." She reached up and kissed him on the cheek. "How's Liam?"

"He's doing great. Ready for you lot to get home."

Father and Jace were seated at the head of the table. Once Adaris had greeted everyone, he stepped forward to address my father.

"High Ruler Eckhardt, thank you for the generous invitation." Adaris bowed low and humble.

To everyone's shock, Father stood. "Congratulations on your ascent, High Ruler Byrnes." He bowed and shook Adaris's hand before gesturing for him to sit next to him. "This is my son and heir, Jace Eckhardt. Welcome to our home."

Either he'd recovered quickly from our argument or he was putting on a mask of indifference. My guess was the latter.

"I hope we can build a powerful alliance. I know my father in the past was against it, but I am making changes in the River Kingdom."

"I'm sorry for your loss."

Adaris looked uncomfortable, but he gave a nod.

Father snapped his fingers, and servers appeared with our meal. A show of power, but I saw how Adaris looked from his hand to the servants. He then looked to their wrists to see if any were slaves. I liked him even more now.

"What can you tell me about your father's moves?" Father asked with a mouth full of salad.

Father didn't waste time. He got straight to the point of the visit.

"I've allowed the shipments from Hadeon to continue since my father passed. I've planted spies within their crews. I knew there was something going on. I didn't want to cut off the flow of information. My spies have provided me with detailed cargo documents and crew manifests. Cadoc was storing iron and Bloodthorn at the Black Guard camps across the River Kingdom. I don't have a specific time frame for his plans, but Hadeon wants weapons and supplies ready for a movement to Illoterra.

"Renwick and Cadoc were his point people on this continent. Renwick hasn't stepped foot back in the River Kingdom since

Cadoc's death. I can only assume he's on Quinterre since none of my spies have mentioned him aboard their ships."

Everyone around the table listened intently to Adaris's update. Evren smiled at her brother, and he winked back at her. The movement of iron and weapons sounded right up Hadeon's alley. And the fact that he was using others to do his grunt work and stay hidden in the shadows aligned too. Renwick Ashewood was slimy enough to participate.

"Since taking over as High Ruler, the ships we believe carry contraband have bypassed Rivamir's ports and are making their way to a port in Ramshorn. Vidarr Fenanos of the centaur clan in the Arden Valley has been helping with making sure none of the weapons get into the hands of those in the Wildlands, but something is stirring there. I think we should be prepared for an attack from both sides—the Wildlands and Quinterre in the west."

"Nazneen's spies found an air elemental. I'm sure she's updated you on that," Adaris continued.

Father nearly choked on his wine. He sent a withering glare to Nazneen. "Spies?"

Adaris motioned to Nazneen. "The Arcelian spies spotted Reniwck hiding out in Noirdan not too long ago. He was on the trail of an air elemental. They were the ones who informed your scouts and pointed them in the right direction. Cadoc wanted to use Evren's elemental powers for something and did everything he could to take them from her. We never found out why. I believe that Hadeon looking for another elemental is something we should look into."

Father's face had turned the same crimson color as Adaris's jacket. He knew Nazneen had informants but hadn't realized they were the ones who'd beat his own scouts to the punch.

Evren had mentioned earlier that day that her father wanted to use her powers, but I hadn't known what she meant.

"What do you mean by 'he did everything he could to take them from her'?" I asked.

Adaris looked at me. His demeanor immediately shifted from a friendly ally to a dangerous opponent, but his face remained unreadable. I didn't know what had made him change so quickly. I recognized Cadoc Byrnes in him at that moment, and that made me nervous. I didn't think Delrik would be friendly with him if he were anything like his father, but you never knew what people could hide, especially if they were protecting someone they loved.

Adaris returned his attention to his sister. She nodded to him with permission to continue before he spoke again.

"As you know, once the blood binding has occurred between two Fae, the bonded can pass their powers back and forth. Cadoc had planned to blood bind Evren to Renwick Ashewood in an attempt to gain access to her power. When that plan fell through, he was going to provoke Evren, through either torturing her or using her relationship with Delrik to attack him, and use the Ring of Teris to steal her powers."

"The ruby." I pointed to Evren. "I've seen it glowing, reacting to power. That's why, isn't it? It can sense our magic." I was more intrigued than fearful.

I looked to Evren who not so subtly covered the ruby that rested on her finger. Evren had turned pale and audibly swallowed. All eyes turned to the band that rested on her middle finger. As if it recognized the attention, the ruby glowed, the light shining bright between her fingers. A thrum of energy pulsed through the room. Once. Twice.

"Yes," Evren squeaked. "I can feel all your powers. It's more ... intense ... drawn to your power when you're using it. It's how I received the shadow magic."

"Evren was able to take the ring before Cadoc was able to use it on her," Delrik said. He rested a protective arm across the back of Evren's chair.

"That is why I believe finding another elemental could help us. Plus, one of the four original Temples of Anruin may have information on elemental powers and how Hadeon could potentially use them."

"You've spoken of these shadows before," Father said. "What is the significance of them? Where did they come from?"

I'd purposely left my father in the dark regarding the true nature of Delrik's shadows. Father didn't take kindly to being challenged in any way, especially when it came to magical strength. Delrik stiffened at the question, but I answered.

"It's nothing of concern. Just a small amount of dark magic from Alux that we need a priestess to remove. That's why we will be heading to the temple as soon as we arrive on Quinterre."

THIRTY
GARREN

I groaned as I heaved a trunk onto the cart, readying it to be lifted up to the decks of the ship. We were hitching a ride on a trading ship to the western continent to disguise our arrival from anyone tracking movement for Hadeon along the coast. I hadn't seen my father since he left our meeting about the scouts, except for the dinner with Adaris. I preferred him ignoring me than the constant put downs. Jace had come here to send us off in Father's place. I was thankful that my brother was supportive of my decision. I never wanted to take the role of High Ruler and he knew that. I was no threat to Jace's future.

I stood and wiped the sweat from my forehead, squinting into the bright sun reflecting off the chilly water across the bay. The storm had moved on after four brutal days. It took another day to dig ourselves out of the drifts. A chorus of laughter made me turn. Evren, Nazneen, and Katuri were striding up the dockplank, each with a pack slung over their shoulders. They were laughing at something Adaris had said.

The other night was the first time I'd met the new High Ruler of the River Kingdom. After just an hour with him and seeing how he handled my father's crass attitude, he'd gained my respect. Plus, Delrik spoke highly of him. He'd told me about how Adaris had protected Evren and his mother during the years after Cadoc returned from the war. He was the one that had helped Evren escape from the fortress too. Adaris was a male of loyalty and honor.

Katuri was the last one up, with Eleni snapping playfully at her heels. Even Corynne was traveling with us. I couldn't help watching the sway of her hips. The leather pants she wore were molded to her. I wanted to feel that ass under my hands again. I'd been dreaming of her since that night in her room, but she'd kept her distance. Each time we passed each other or were in a group, I brushed her hand or whispered sweet words into her ear, making sure no one could see or hear. I wasn't doing it for show. I wanted to show her how much I cared for her. I'd do anything to be near her. Each time, thrilling chills raced through my body—coming from both her and myself. Powers, I'd even sat in the library to watch her read. A sliver of her time was better than nothing.

Katuri and Nazneen leaned over the taffrail, and jealousy stirred deep within me. I knew their kiss had been a prank, but my primal side still saw Nazneen as competition. I was pretty sure Katuri had been sleeping in Nazneen's room at night since our kiss. I'd walked by several times, pacing back and forth in the hallway like a deranged stalker listening for movement. Every time I pressed my ear to the door I heard only silence. And no one ever replied when I knocked. Not even Corynne. The few times I'd followed the bond to find her, she'd been in Nazneen's room. She couldn't hide from me forever though.

Delrik broke me from my lust-filled thoughts with a groan. "I am not looking forward to this trip."

"You've always hated traveling by water," I said distractedly.

"I don't mind the water. I hate being trapped with a hundred other smelly men." He looked me up and down. "Reign it in, Garren. You're drooling."

Katuri briefly looked over her shoulder to me. Her eyes met mine for a split second. That thin thread tugged at my insides.

"If Naz has anything to do with it, she'll be begging for you to ravage her by the time we reach land. She loves to play matchmaker. And you two have made her job easier with being bondmates."

He clapped me on the back and then followed them to the ship. One could hope.

I braced myself against the taffrail while the ship careened to the left as it took the sharp turn leading out of the Hook. I closed my eyes as the briney air whipped at my face. The smell of the glaciers and the open water made my elemental power shiver with a thrill. I stood at the front of the ship where I saw nothing but ice and water and open sky. I hadn't been out to open sea since before the snowstorm. Nothing beats the sea. It was calling to me, almost as strong as the bond.

When we exited the Hook, bright, teal waters spread out before me and the water smoothed, no longer breaking against the sharp edges of the glaciers. Adaris was onboard with us so he could spend a little more time with his sister. Our ship bobbed up and down in the water while we waited for Adaris's ship following behind us.

I was joined on deck by Delrik and Evren. Delrik looked queasy, but Evren seemed to be enjoying the open air as much as I was.

"I can't wait until I learn to fly," she said. She closed her eyes and tipped her face upward. "To feel that freedom."

I agreed. Well, not the flying part, but being able to feel free, to stretch my powers and not feel constrained. I had the ability to fly, but I preferred to swim when in my shifted form. There was just something about the water. Nothing matched my speed and power beneath the surface of the waves.

"You should test out your wings while we travel. We're surrounded by water. What's the worst that could happen?"

"Um ... I could light the ship on fire," Evren pointed out.

"Nah." I waved her off. "You've got this. Plus, water elemental, remember?" I wiggled my fingers at her.

"Try, Ev. I haven't seen you use your power since you left Rivamir months ago," Adaris encouraged.

Adaris had finished speaking with the ship's captain about the new trade routes proposed in the meeting between him and my father. They'd secluded themselves in his office for hours in deep discussion. I did not envy him.

Evren looked to Delrik, and he nodded with an encouraging smile.

"Okay," she said and shook her hands out nervously. Aura flitted around her. Her glossy, black wings shifted into flame-tipped beauties.

Tiny embers hit the desk near my feet, and I stomped them out before she could notice. She placed her palms on her stomach and drew in a deep breath. The tang of powerful magic filled the air, and wings burst forth from Evren's back. Only this time, they weren't entirely made of fire. They matched Aura's down to the last texture. The sleek black feathers curved upward and ended in white hot flames. The rush of the air from the ship's movement caught her spread wings. Evren was forced back a few steps, but she quickly regained her footing. Her stretched wingspan cast a long shadow across the deck.

Her face alighted with wonderment. "Powers! The air, it feels divine. I want to fly!"

"Woah now, Ashlyra," Delrik said with a hearty laugh. "One step at a time."

Evren extinguished her flames and folded her wings into her sides. Adaris looked on with fascination and pride. Then he moved forward and wrapped her in his arms, wings and all. I envied their closeness. Jace and I were close, but our relationship was nowhere the same as theirs. Or Nazneen and Delrik.

Nazneen and Katuri had appeared with Garret in tow. It was hard to not judge the male based on his attire. I was used to the ruthless ways of Cadoc's Black Guard. Adaris had assured me that the males in his guard now were to be trusted. Garret had remained quiet during his short visit to Kanevvluk. He only spoke with Nazneen, Delrik, and Evren.

"Are you guys having fun without us?" Garret quipped.

"I just wanted to see Evren's wings again," Adaris said over Evren's head.

"Unfortunately, I have to break up this party if we want to catch the current," Garrett said.

"That's okay, Garrett. Thank you for bringing my brother to see me," Evren said. She released Adaris and hugged the guardsman.

Evren hugged her brother one last time. "I'll miss you," she said into his chest.

"I'll be back soon. Whether it's here or Arcelia, I'll see you soon. Keep practicing. I want to see you soaring through the sky next time." He ruffled her hair and stepped back.

Adaris said farewell to everyone and then he was gone with a pop. With another pop, Adaris and Garrett appeared on the deck of the River Kingdom's ship. The High Ruler waved before turning to his crew for departure.

Evren sighed heavily.

"So how long is this crossing supposed to take?" Leave it to Nazneen to break the silence. "I don't know if I brought enough cupcakes to last the whole trip."

"Did you bring enough to share?" Katuri and Evren asked in unison.

I needed to try these cupcakes everyone raved about.

"Of course." Nazneen looped one arm with Katuri's and the other with Evren's.

Wild possession flashed within me. I swallowed down the possessiveness that threatened to burst free. Katuri held my stare, and her mouth formed a tight line. She must have sensed the surge of envy. The words from our first meeting ran loudly in my head. *"I will never be yours."*

I shook off the painful memory. "It isn't that far. Maybe two weeks if the winds and gods are in our favor."

Kat scrunched her nose. "I hate ships."

Of course she did. She was an earth elemental surrounded by water with no land in sight. And the last time she was on one, she'd been stripped of her freedom.

"You're afraid to spend two weeks trapped on a ship with me, Little Flower?"

Anger contorted her beautiful face.

"Go jump off a ship, Garren."

I lifted my eyebrows at her challenge. I kicked off my boots and pulled my shirt over my head and dropped it at my feet. I tossed it in her direction, and she caught it on instinct. I stood there, bare chested, letting the glacial air shock my skin. Then, with a wink, I did just as she'd asked. I dove overboard into the fjord.

My power thrummed at my fingertips. The water was coming at me fast. The last thing I saw as I threw myself overboard was Katuri's startled face.

The wind whipped past me with a hollow howl. Saltiness coated my tongue as my sea dragon took over. Bones lengthening, scales covering my skin in rippling waves, starting at my head and working their way down. All my senses heightened in my shifted form. I ran my tongue across my razor sharp teeth.

Katuri's startled voice rang out as I fell through the air. "Garren!"

I took a deep breath and tucked my chin right before I made contact with the water.

THIRTY-ONE
DELRIK

"Show off," I hollered after Garren.

Katuri leaned over the railing, searching the waters in desperation.

Garren would just dive overboard to make a point. I'd seen him shift into his elemental form a few times, mainly on the trips to and from the western continent during the war. He preferred to swim back and forth rather than be tossed around on the ship. I didn't blame him. He wasn't around deep, open water as often as he'd like. It was a chance for him to stretch to his full size without restriction. His shifted form was almost as large as the biggest warship in the Snowhaven Legion.

I thought back on the time he'd once shifted on the deck of the enemy's ship to scare the shit out of the sailors during the war. He'd shot ice-like spears from his mouth, piercing the sailors and shredding the sails.

Suddenly, a colossal scaled body covered in sleek cyan scales lept from the water and over the bow of the ship. The water glimmered like prisms in the sunlight. Leather-like wings were spread wide, blocking out the sun for a moment and dripping freezing cold water on us from above. Battlescars could be spotted on those powerful wings. Leftover reminders from our time in the war. With a heavy splash, the sea dragon dove back into the water and disappeared into the depth of the Boreas Sea. Seconds later, an identical, yet much smaller, sea dragon lept from the water following Garren.

"That's his familiar, Drake," I said.

The sea dragon flapped its damp wings as it flew over Katuri's feet and dropped with a wet plop onto the deck. Eleni snarled at the beast, but didn't get any closer.

"I knew he had a familiar, but I've never seen it in person," Katuri said next to me, more to herself than anyone else.

The sea dragon shook itself out like a wet dog. He swung his head back and forth, looking at his audience, then waddled and wiggled his elongated body as he walked in a circle, looking for something. His talons clicked on the deck. He lifted his head to look up at Katuri. He was roughly the same size as Eleni.

A burly male came up to us, his heavy boots making his footsteps shake the deck as he approached.

"He's always scaring the new recruits with that trick. Shifting right on deck. Other captains didn't find it funny, but I laughed so hard the first time I almost wet myself at their scared faces.," he said with a throaty laugh. "Get on out of here, Drake."

The familiar did not obey the order. With a chirp, he scooted himself so that he was touching Katuri's leg. Apparently, he was guarding his master's bondmate.

The captain shook his head but carried on. "I'm Captain Tage Lark. Come. I can show you to your cabins whenever you're ready."

We all followed Captain Lark across the deck and toward his stateroom. The captain was a Fae, clear from his pointed ears, but he didn't possess any powers. That didn't stop him from being a skilled sailor and fighter. His long, blond hair hung in knotted waves past his shoulders, and he had a full beard covering the lower half of his face. His baby blue eyes sparkled with life. He wore a thick, wool overcoat, a belt straining against his protruding belly, and scuffed boots. Another male was standing nearby, his thumbs tucked into the loop of his belt, and a pocket watch tucked into his breast pocket. He had golden-bronzed skin similar to Katuri and striking green eyes. Dark, long wavy hair was up in a half knot, and he wore tight leather pants and a white shirt that was opened down his chest. Tattoos of all colors covered his chest and neck. He cut his sharp eyes to his captain protectively and then pinned us with a glare. His features shifted so fast. He clearly didn't like newcomers on his ship.

"Let me introduce you to my first mate." Captain Lark gestured to a male standing to his right. "This is Zji'ndar Abril. If you need anything, he'll be able to assist you. He will show you to your rooms. And if you have any questions or concerns and can't find me, he'd be happy to help."

The male looked anything but happy that his captain was offering the sentiment.

I extended my hand to him in greeting. "I'm Delrik. And this is Evren, my bondmate, my sister Nazneen, and I'm not sure if you know Katuri Harland."

"Zji'ndar was on the ship that brought me over from Laeto Selva." She smiled warmly at the male. "He's actually from there as well."

"I haven't been home in a long time, Princess," he said in a thick accent to Katuri.

Then he gave her a gracious bow and spoke in their native tongue. I wasn't sure what he'd said, but Katuri's cheeks turned pink.

Zji'ndar nodded toward Nazneen and Evren. When he turned to me, he just stared blankly, leaving my hand suspended in the air. His mouth was in a firm line. He assessed me with keen eyes like I was a threat.

"Um. . ." I looked back and forth between the male and Captain Lark.

Zji'ndar finally spoke. "Delrik Valhar?"

"Yes," I said warily.

His jaw clenched tighter, if that were even possible. "Delrik Valhar? The same Master of Death and Darkness from the war?"

My stomach bottomed out. "I don't respond to that name," I said sternly, dropping my hand back to my side and standing a little straighter.

Who the fuck was this guy? I didn't recognize him from the war. I knew I had a reputation, but no one had ever been so blatantly upfront with it in my face.

"Have we met before?"

"No, we haven't. But you killed my father."

It was like a punch in the gut. The air completely left my body. It took everything in me not to fall to my knees right there. I had wounded many during the battles, killed even more. Countless lives were forever changed by my hands. I'd spent numerous years over the last century trying to repay the Powers Above for the harm I'd done, and it still wasn't enough. I thought I'd escaped from all the memories of the war.

Down, down, down I spiraled. Everything around me was spinning, and I was out of control. I pressed my hands to the sides of my head. The pressure was too much. It felt as if something was squeezing my head. I pinched my eyes closed, but my world was tipping on its side. The otherness slammed itself against my mind. Talons raked down the inside of my skull and down my spine, splitting me open. It rushed in in a fury. Blinding pain. Stolen breath. The otherness raced in and latched itself to my very essence. It pulled me down, down, down.

"You could end him easily," a beautiful voice whispered in my ear. "What's one more?"

My head snapped up. What was that? I looked around but only saw everyone staring questioningly at me like I'd gone insane. I heard Evren suck in a sharp breath at my sudden imbalance.

"It would be so easy to snap him in half. Like breaking a twig. I bet he'd scream."

The voice laughed, soft and melodic. I wavered on my feet and heard Evren call out to me, but it sounded like I was underwater.

"Delrik?"

I shook the voice from my head and tried to focus on what was happening around me. I couldn't focus. All I could do was cling to Evren's presence and the firm grip she had on my arm.

"I'm sorry for my first mate's behavior." The captain's voice was muted. "I'm sure there is some misunderstanding."

There wasn't a misunderstanding. It was very likely I'd murdered his father.

"It must be the water. He doesn't handle ships well," Evren said to the captain. "I should probably get him to a place he can rest. If I have any questions, I'll be sure to find you."

"Go down two levels and the first few doors on the left."

"Thank you," Evren said and nudged me forward.

"There is nothing wrong with a little death."

I squeezed my eyes shut. Evren pulled me along as Captain Lark finished giving us a tour of the ship and showing us to our staterooms.

When we stepped below deck, the moist air and tight hallway were crushing me. I couldn't control my breathing. I was gasping for air that wouldn't fill my lungs. Then Evren was standing before me and gently pushing my shoulders so that I would sit. Suddenly, the brackish smell of the sea coming in from the port window and the tilt of the ship made my stomach churn. I leaned my hands against the wall to balance myself. Flashes of murder and blood and screaming crossed my mind. I squeezed my eyes shut and tried desperately to come back to the present, but a voice was tugging at my mind to succumb to the dark memories.

"You are a true monster."

It was like a shroud over me. Suffocating.

"Death will always surround you. It's your fate."

Evren's hand landed on my arm, and the warmth of her palm lifted the shroud, and everything came back into focus. Our room was small—a bed pushed against the wall and nailed into the floor. A small table and wash basin sat opposite the bed. Our trunks were placed under the window but sat ignored. I dropped down onto the bed. Ashamed of my past and whatever had come over me, I stared at the floor instead of looking at Evren.

"Maybe I am the Master of Death and Darkness," I said as I dipped my head into my hands again. I'd been thinking about this for a while, but I'd never voiced it. Since the nightmares started again—since the otherness and the voices.

"What are you talking about?" The bed dipped as Evren sat next to me. I could feel her worry through the bond, and I knew she could feel my fear. I was causing her pain by just being bonded to her. I did my best to raise a shield around my mind to stop my emotions from overwhelming her.

I was the reason my parents were murdered, being a mixed blood child. I was a killer in the war. I was a killer as a bounty hunter. And now I was cursed with shadow magic that can torture. It wouldn't be long until the shadows took control and I killed someone else. I'd already shown signs of losing control.

"You are not the Master of Death and Darkness. You were not called to be a killer," Evren said. Her voice was stern. She gave my arm, the one dancing with shadows and binding mark, a hard squeeze to bring my attention back to her, but it wasn't enough to pull me from my mood.

"The fates seemed to have made it clear to me. I am a bringer of death, a weapon released onto this world."

"You don't even know how to use this magic. You're not strong enough for it," the sweet voice purred into my ear.

That voice. I dug my fingers into my head. It was like a crackling pain along my mental shield. It flooded me and drowned out everything else. The thoughts I'd had for years had turned into this voice that I couldn't drown out no matter how loud my surroundings were. I had so much to lose, but I couldn't press the voice away. It had its claws in deep.

Evren's attitude shifted when she realized I was blocking her from the bond. She knelt before me. I knew she couldn't hear the voices, but she could feel my anguish no matter how much I tried to shield my mind from her.

"Do not ever speak that way again. You are not evil. You are not a bad person or a curse on the world. You were not at fault for your parents' death; my father was." It was like she was reading my mind despite my shields. She grabbed my hands and removed them from my head. Our binding mark glowed. Her elemental flame caressed my cheeks. "The war was out of your control. You fought in a war to save innocent people from danger. You may have killed, but it was a lesser evil than what was spreading in the realm. You saved so many, Delrik. This realm wouldn't be free if you hadn't risked your life to help restore peace and balance. And these shadows, you will learn to control them. They can be used for good. Alux just chose to use them for bad."

I leaned my head onto her shoulder and breathed her in. The familiar smell of honeysuckle and jasmine centered me. My Ashlyra centered me. I would never get tired of hearing her perspective on me—reminding me who I really am. Up to this point in my life, I'd only had Naz, Aramis, and Calia to remind me, and I'd spent so much time away from Arcelia, hiding from my feelings, it was difficult for them to remind me. But I couldn't run from Evren. I never would run from her. She was my Ashlyra. That time after the war, before I found her, was my darkest period. Battling with my inner demons and thoughts. Now it felt like I was moving backward to that place in time again.

"Come on. Let's get some sleep," she said.

I laid back onto the small, lumpy mattress and pulled Evren down next to me. I tucked her into my side and buried my face in her silver hair, her scent relaxing me. Evren was my balancing force. I didn't deserve her, but at least the fates were good to me when it came to her.

She traced her finger along the Ashlyra. "You're not alone in this. I'm here."

EVREN

Delrik woke with a start, sitting straight up in bed, breathing heavily and covered in a sheen of sweat. He'd had nightmares before, but they had grown in their intensity since we arrived in Kanevvluk. His eyes were wide-open, and he was mumbling words I couldn't understand. As hard as I tried, there was nothing I could do to settle him. All I could do was lie next to him and speak comforting words as he thrashed around fitfully. Then hold him until he woke up.

I'd never been able to wake him during one of his nightmares. Tonight was no different. But something was fuzzy between us. A haze hung over the bond. When he'd been awake, I could tell he was shielding, but when he'd finally drifted into sleep, the shield fell, and I understood the depth of his turmoil. This haze though, this was not a shield. This was something completely different. I called the shadows to me, and they willingly came, pouring from Delrik in inky tendrils and into me. I had hoped it would help, but he still thrashed and called out unintelligible words. I'd never once thought the shadows were the cause of this new otherness he said was hanging over him, but it was the only thing I could think of. Until...

I pressed my hands to my chest and pushed flames into him. Not just a nugget of my power, but the full strength of my elemental fire. I gave him all of it. Fire engulfed us. Delrik screamed and tried to pull away from me. I gripped his shirt with my fist and pressed my forehead to his. I knew I wasn't hurting him. My flames had never hurt him before, and I knew in my heart they weren't now.

Suddenly, a weight was lifted. I could feel his relief through the bond. Delrik was welcoming the fire. And then, like a mask had been removed, the bond was clear and Delrik fell back onto the mattress. I settled back down next to him, but I kept my head on his chest, over his heart. The flames and shadows danced around us as a sphere of protection. Delrik's sleep that night was peaceful with my elemental flame guarding him from the darkness. I, however, couldn't rest. I just lay next to him, stroking his hair and wondering how I was supposed to protect him from something I couldn't even see or hear.

THIRTY-TWO
KATURI

I was sitting on my bunk, looking out the circular window at the rain beating against the glass that poured in a deluge. A wave tossed the ship, and I had to grip the bed frame so I wouldn't fall off the bed. I huffed out a breath and lay on my side, facing the wall.

Garren.

The bond fluttered inside my chest. Powers, even thinking his name made the bond pulse. I bit down on my lip and tried to suppress the need to be near him. I'd been skirting around Garren for the better part of a week. Each time I was in his presence, the bond grew stronger, which only made the confusion worse. I didn't have the uncontrollable rage toward Garren that I once did. Evren and Nazneen had talked me down from that ledge. They were right about all of it. But it still didn't change my fear of being only wanted for my elemental power and being controlled.

I let out an audible groan and rolled over to face the door. I squeezed my eyes shut, willing Nazneen to return and catch me in what I was about to do. Knowing her, she felt my desires through the fates and was purposely staying away so I'd go see Garren. I rolled my eyes. She was supposed to be on my side, not his.

Reckless. This was a reckless idea. Powers Above, why was I being so rash? I sat up quickly and hung my legs off the top bunk, then jumped to the floor. I walked to the door and put my hand on the doorknob.

"No," I said out loud to myself.

I couldn't do this. I'd fought against this for so long. I couldn't give in just because he was a good kisser and made me feel like I was floating and someone worth worshiping. The bond was drawing me to him against my will, like a compulsion. And my father's compulsion was how I wound up in this mess. But at the same time, it was completely different. All this wasn't Garren's fault. Yet, I couldn't resist the urge to just be in the same room as him. Deep down, I really didn't want to stay away.

I paced back and forth in the box of a room, trying and failing to resist the nagging pull. Before my mind knew what I was doing, my body strode to the door and flung it open. I walked down the narrow hall, my fingers pressed to the wall for balance, given the crashing waves. I found his door and didn't bother knocking. I knew it wouldn't be locked. So I pushed the door open, slipped inside, and closed it behind me.

I pressed my back into the cool, damp wood. Garren was sitting with his back propped against the wall. He tossed a small knife up into the air and caught it again. He didn't seem surprised to see me in the slightest. He'd felt me coming. How could he not with how much my brain was going back and forth?

His striking blue eyes sparkled with humor. "It took you long enough. I was about to get up and come find you," he said.

Ugh. I hated his arrogance. Was it arrogance if he was right? I knew I shouldn't be here, but it was like my brain had no control of my body anymore. I didn't know what I was doing.

"You ... you would've come looking for me?"

"I'll always look for you."

"Garren ... I..."

"Just come here, Katuri," he said.

He reached out a hand toward me. An offer. A request.

I took a deep breath and slowly crossed the short distance to his bed. I hesitated only a moment before I climbed onto his lap, planting my knees on either side of his hips and settling onto his thighs. My hands rested on his strong shoulders. It was like my body was moving of its own volition. Why was he so beautiful?

I should just leave.

His hands gripped my butt, digging his fingers into the fabric of my pants. A low rumble in the back of his throat called to the bond. It urged me to keep going, to keep closing the distance between our bodies and our lives.

I took a shaky breath. "Garren. I don't..."

"Stop thinking, Katuri. Just feel."

Then our mouths came together in a tender kiss. It was nothing like our first kiss. It was soft and brief.

"You are the definition of temptation, you know that?" he said, his voice low and seductive.

Before I could even think, I whimpered in approval. I couldn't help myself. His sea dragon growled in response, and I felt the vibrations to my very core. He pulled me closer, gathering me to his chest. Our torsos were pressed flat together. He leaned forward and pressed his mouth into the hollow of my throat. My head tipped back as I closed my eyes, relishing in his touch. His mouth was like a breath of fresh morning air. This is what I'd wanted. This is what I'd been craving.

His broad hands traveled up my waist. I rolled my hips against him, and his hands bunched the fabric of my shirt. They glided over my oversensitive skin until they rested against my ribs, his thumbs grazing the underside of my breasts. In my haste to get to him, I'd forgotten my bra, so he could clearly see my peaked nipples through my shirt.

He pulled back and said, "Do you ever wear underwear, or are you always bare under your clothes?"

"It's such a waste of time."

His thumbs grazed over my nipples lightly, and I couldn't suppress the gasp that escaped me.

"I couldn't agree more."

My back arched on its own accord with a surge of need, pushing my breast into his waiting hands. My fingers dove into his silky blond hair, digging into his scalp. I couldn't get enough of the feeling of him.

He leaned in close. "I've been waiting to taste you again."

I was shaking with anticipation. He ran his tongue across my collarbone, and his teeth bit into my shoulder. I only felt pleasure as his teeth sank into my flesh. I didn't even care if he drew blood if he kept making me feel this way.

"Finally," he said. "I knew you'd come around. It only gets better from here. For the rest of our lives..." He stopped short when he saw my panicked expression.

I was frozen. Fresh dread surged in me. What had I done? I'd just thrown myself at him. I was in his room. In his bed. On top of him. Dark hells. I pushed away from him and stared a moment before scampering off his lap like a scared pup and backing away.

Hurt flashed across his features and down our bond. I'd hurt him.

"Kat." His voice was pained. He stood and came to me. "The night I first saw you, you looked so scared. Your big emerald eyes. Even with your bold words, I could see the fear you held back." He brushed his thumb across my bottom lip, across the tribal mark there. My lip bounced back when he released it. "I left for the war, and when I came home, something had shifted. You'd changed. You wore this unforgiving mask of anger. You'd walled yourself off from everyone, but I'd never been more drawn to you."

"Garren." I backed away from him, wanting desperately to run, but feeling stuck standing in front of him. My blood was pounding in my ears. "I don't know how to feel this way."

All this was so easy for him. The bond. The attraction. The intimacy. I had no idea how to do this. I couldn't force myself to calm down. Calm was the last thing I felt. My whole body was trembling. I didn't know how to voice what was going on in my head. The bond wrapped a thin string around me, and my heart lurched and dragged me forward a step. Did I want more? Did I want to give in and become Garren's bondmate in every sense of the word? Ashlyra. Did I want to give him my body, my soul, my power? I raked my hands through my hair, shaking my head back and forth. Why was this so difficult?

He took a step closer to me. "I'm not trying to control you. I—,"

"I know," I said, cutting him off. He had never tried to control me. He may have pushed my boundaries. Okay, let's face it—he'd blasted through my boundaries, but I had never felt like I was in danger like I did with my father's compulsion.

"Then what is it?" he asked.

Although he was calm on the outside, I could see the frustration roaring to life on the inside. I didn't blame him for being so frustrated with me. I was frustrated with myself.

"You scare me," I blurted out. "This scares me. It's so strong."

His face morphed into understanding. "There is nothing to be afraid of. I've got you." He reached for me, but stopped. "I would never hurt you, Katuri."

A hot trail of tears spread down my cheek. I tried to wipe it away with the back of my hand before he saw. "Don't you see I am already hurting?"

All these years I'd been suffering being stuck in Kanevvluk and a future forced upon me. I was never given a choice in any of it. He'd never shown me any interest. He'd been blind, too focused on ignoring me, to see my true pain. So why now? Was he just going along with it because it was what he thought he had to due to the bond? He didn't seem to want my power. Why would he? He had his own elemental magic. Was it a search for physical intimacy? His father hadn't been quiet about his desire for us to procreate sooner rather than later. No. I didn't believe he would just willingly go along with his father. I couldn't deny the physical attraction between the two of us. Every time he touched me, my body went berserk. I wanted to know what else it was about me that he liked, not just the bond.

"I'll never force you into anything, but our lives are tied together, whether we like it or not, in all the ways the fates have intended. It's inevitable."

Why was I desperate for his touch? Why did I want to submit to him fully? My pulse was wild in my chest.

He took my hand and placed it on his chest, right above his heart. "You can trust me. Share your life with me. Be mine."

I watched my hand rise and fall with his breaths. There was so much about this male that I didn't know.

"Katuri, please."

The sound of my name on his lips again made me suck in a sharp breath, breathing in him. He was becoming my weakness. It was too much.

I turned and ran from his room before I could do something I truly regretted.

Just before the door slammed behind me, Garden called out, "Powers Above, Kat! You can't run from me forever."

THIRTY-THREE
GAREEN

I found myself staring off into the blue of the early morning sky. I was leaning against a set of stairs leading down to the back deck. The girls hadn't seen me when they'd started their training. I was impressed they wanted to keep it up, even though we were traveling. I didn't want to interrupt them. I just wanted to watch Katuri without her guard up.

"Ugh. It's too early for this, Naz. And it's so bright," Katuri complained.

"We literally have nothing else to do. We may as well get some practice under our belts," Nazneen said. She had one arm crossed over her chest, stretching her shoulder.

I watched the two bicker back and forth. Evren was nearby, too, working on her partial shift. Wings out. Wings hidden. Over and over. All around us was water, as far as I could see. The further we got from Kanevvluk, the warmer the weather. Don't get me wrong, it was still freezing, but there was sunlight and I could be on the deck without my thick, wool cloak.

Katuri grunted when Nazneen landed a punch in her stomach. Her surprise and discomfort shot down the bond. I had to hold myself back from coming to her rescue.

"I didn't hit you that hard," Katuri said, dropping her hands to her sides.

Nazneen smiled, then reached out and smacked her open-handed on the arm. "Yeah, but it made you drop your guard. You have to strike hard and strike fast. It's your life or theirs."

"You've been spending way too much time with Master Salcido." Katuri grunted as she kicked and missed Nazneen by a mile.

Nazneen laughed. "I grew fond of him. I like his style."

No offense to Master Salcido, but Nazneen was a better teacher. I'd seen Nazneen teach more to Evren and Katuri over the last few days than weeks with the weapons master. There was just something about getting a female's point of view that made all the difference.

Nazneen threw a punch, and Katuri ducked out of the way. "I saw Arik last night."

I listened closely. I knew Nazneen and Arik had become friends. Maybe she knew what he'd been up to.

Katuri stopped and dropped her hands to her side. "Nazneen, I don't want to hear about all your exploits today."

Nazneen gave a wicked smile. "Would you rather tell me about yours? You weren't in bed last night when I got back to our room." She lifted her brows. "Were you with Garren?"

Kat scowled and threw a lazy punch toward Nazneen.

"Ah. So you were with Garren? I bet he is quite a talented lover."

I covered my mouth to stifle my giggle.

"Stop being nosey," Katuri said.

They continued to circle each other, striking out at each other and retreating. I watched Katuri move with grace and agility. I could see the wolf in her. I didn't know how I'd missed it for so long.

"I have this nagging feeling Arik's hiding something." She bounced on her feet and held her arms ready in front of her. "Yes, just like that," she encouraged Katuri, who was taking note of her movements. "You need to keep your body ready. Keep your feet moving. It will make you generate more power behind your kicks."

Katuri nodded and then threw another punch. "He's always been closed off. Maybe he's just not a trusting person."

Or maybe he isn't a person to be trusted, I thought to myself. Arik had been on good behavior since we all returned to the war, but that letter had the hackles raised.

"Your form has improved tremendously," I said as I came into view from my hiding spot.

Katuri faltered for just a moment, before she saw Nazneen's next move and lept out of the way of her kick.

"I didn't mean to cause a distraction," I said. "I was actually coming out here to offer help."

Katuri was breathing heavily now. "We don't ... need ... your help."

"I actually meant for Evren." I turned toward her and nodded at her relaxed wings.

"Are you sure? I'd hate for you to waste your time," she said a bit bashfully.

My pupils shifted into vertical slits, and scales appeared around his hairline. Then leathery wings sprouted from my back, several feet wider than Evren's. I didn't do a partial shift very often. My wings were heavy on my shoulders. I shifted my muscles to get comfortable with them. I pumped my wings and spread them wide, letting the wind catch them and reveling in the feeling.

"Who better to teach you than another shifter."

"Hold them open and let the wind catch them," I directed Evren.

The breeze was crisp against my wings as it swept from the north. I got a whiff of something burning. I turned quickly and noticed one of the ratlines had caught fire from Evren's smoldering wings.

"Oops. Too much fire."

I tried to hide my laughter but didn't do a great job at it. With a wave of my hand, a water spurt from the sea rose into the air and denounced the flames.

"Katuri doesn't like me."

I was surprised by my own admittance. I wasn't sure where it had come from, but I didn't want to pass up on the opportunity to hear Evren's advice, so I kept going. I knew Katuri was uncertain about the bondmate thing, but I also knew she was beginning to care for me. I could feel it.

"She does like you. She's just scared to let someone in."

I turned thoughtful. "I get that."

"She doesn't want to be controlled."

"But I'm not trying to control her."

She side-eyed me. "Not intentionally and not at your own fault. Think about it, Garren. Look at her life from her eyes." She extended her wings. "She was told from her earliest memories she was to be bound to a male, a stranger, and she had no choice. Then she was shipped to Kanevvluk thinking she would have time before the blood binding, but instead, she was immediately forced into it. So were you, and it wasn't right. It shouldn't have happened, but it did. She's been told where to live, what to eat, what to wear, how to act on top of being surrounded by a wall and the arctic. She was terrified. That trauma leaves scars, Garren."

I looked off to the water, deep in thought.

"Give her time. I don't think she wants to hate you, but she isn't ready to love you."

PART THREE

THIRTY-FOUR
KATURI

City of Proux

The waters of the Boreas Sea gleamed in the morning sun, and a beautiful view of the City of Proux was mirrored off the glassy surface. We hadn't had any more storms the remainder of our trip, other than the one where I'd jumped Garren. I didn't know whether I should be more embarrassed by my actions or declaration of my true feelings. The waters were dark blue and reflected the sky above. Although snow covered the mountains and spread across the horizon, the dock and city itself were snow free. The houses and buildings were all alternating colors of the rainbow. Although I grew up on Quinterre, I'd never gotten a chance to see all the cities in all the High Fae Kingdoms. I wished I had been able to see Proux as a child.

Nazneen suddenly appeared by my side. The biggest smile I'd ever seen lit up her face as she tilted her face to the blue sky. Evren, too, looked to be enjoying the sun. She had her onyx wings out on full display and not a flame in sight. She'd been practicing and growing stronger each day. It was more common to see her wings than not these days, and she was magnificent. Her and Nazneen were arm-in-arm, talking to Captain Lark. The ship docked, and the sounds of chatter filled the air. A lot of the coastal areas had been raided by Hadeon's goons, according to the scouts report. They'd raided and burned villages up and down the eastern coast. The City of Proux, thank the Powers Above, had been spared so far. It actually reminded me a little of Kanevvluk—little ones running, open air markets, and a bustle of noise. There was an air of excitement at the new trade ship entering the harbor. Kanevvluk was well known for their furs.

Garren arranged for our trunks to be stored at a local inn until we visited the Temple of Anruin and decided whether we'd be staying in

Proux for an extended time or if we'd be moving on to another city. What we discovered once we reached the temple would ultimately make that decision for us. There was no reason to get comfortable if the answers we needed weren't here.

Corynne bid farewell to me for the time being. She would be returning to Laeto Selva to visit her family while we visited Proux. She hadn't been home since I'd been shipped to Kanevvluk and was looking forward to seeing her homeland.

The temple itself was up on a hillside overlooking the city. It was much larger than the temple in Kanevvluk. It reached to the heavens, and pristine clouds seemed to brush the highest point. Captain Lark gave us directions and wished us luck on our journey.

We wound our way through the winding streets and up a cobbled pathway toward the Temple of Anruin. It had been more than forty years since I stepped into one of the original temples created for the gods. It was a brilliant circular building made of white marble columns and a decorative dome on top.

An elderly priestess was tending a flower bed outside the temple when we approached. She struggled to stand when we came into view. A gnarled wooden cane clicked on the stone as she approached us.

"Welcome. How can I help you?"

Her pale skin was wrinkled and almost translucent. Blue veins trailed like road maps across her withered hands. Her hair was white and fell well below her waist in a milky, satin sheet. She offered a friendly smile that made the lines around her eyes and mouth crinkle.

"We're looking for someone," Evren said. "Would you be able to help us?"

"They came for me, Salina."

A tall, willowy female drifted as if on air, past the priestess, and came to stand before Evren. "I've been expecting you, Evren. It's been a long time."

Her wide doe eyes were unreadable. And those eyes, they were two different colors—one the lightest of blues and the other a rich chocolate color. She examined us with open eagerness. She was dressed like a typical priestess of the temple; long, flowing robes of light blue, a long chain with the symbol of the Powers Above, and silver bracelets on her wrists. She looked young, but her eyes showed many years of wisdom. Her arms were covered in pale ancient marks resembling runes. It was like the Powers Above had carved the Essence Scrolls into her very skin. They shimmered like diamonds in the bright sunlight. Was she a priestess or the elemental we were looking for? Her gaze stopped on Delrik. She tilted her head in a curious, feline way.

"How did you know we were coming?" Evren asked.

"The wisps whispered of your arrival." Then she just turned and flitted away. "Follow me."

We all just looked at each other in confusion as the female left us behind, her silver bracelets chiming together. Someone had to have told her when we arrived in the city. Maybe Captain Lark had sent word ahead of us.

The elder priestess appeared next to me.

"Shit!" I started. She moved fast for someone so old.

Salina took hold of my arm suddenly. Her withered hand made me cringe. Her grip was almost painful on my forearm. "Be careful with Nyla. The one of the air." She pointed a crooked cane in Nyla's direction. "She's a dangerous one. Don't doubt her power based on her appearance."

What was that about? How could a priestess be dangerous? The priestesses had always creeped me out, and I'd steered clear of the temple in Kanevvluk. According to Nazneen and Adaris, an air elemental lived here. So here we were. I nodded at the old priestess, watching everyone follow Nyla into the temple. I followed behind them into the main chamber. The dome we'd seen outside was covered in stamped copper and cast the light of the day into a golden hue like fire across the ceiling. All of us tilted our heads upward as we made our way to the center of the chamber.

"Wow," Nazneen said. Her eyes grew wide. "The temple at home is nowhere near this intricate."

"That's because this is one of the original temples built by the gods themselves," Nyla said. "They constructed it to be an exact replica of the Sanctum in Aesira."

The marble floor had a pentagram in the center of the floor, the symbol of the Powers Above. Located at the end of each point were the seats of the gods on raised dais. Starting on my left, the seats were arranged exactly as they were in Aesira: goddess of water, god of earth, god of fire, and goddess of air. Only the fifth point of the pentagram was empty. It was said that the fifth point represents the people of the realm. I had always found that odd, but whatever. The priestesses were all batty anyway. It made sense there were holes in their story.

Garren and Delrik were talking to Nyla in low tones I couldn't hear. Evren stood in front of the seat where the god of fire would sit in Aesira. His seat was the top point of the star. She ran her fingers along the ancient stone. The very god whose power she carried within her. She circled the seat and studied the carvings in the ancient language.

"I've never seen anything so beautiful," she whispered.

When Evren stepped into the inner circle of the symbol, the temple shook. The sun was eclipsed by something, and a hush overtook everything. Then, as quick as it had happened, and like nothing out of the ordinary, the sky returned to normal.

"Interesting." Nyla tipped her head again, eyeing each of us. Then she turned away from the circle. "The broken has been renewed."

We all looked around at each other, confused. Again. This priestess was crazier than any other I'd ever met.

"Was that supposed to be a profound statement we're supposed to understand?" Garren asked.

I rolled my eyes.

Nyla guided us from the main temple out to a row of cottages that lined the hillside. As we were walking, a large shadow passed overhead, temporarily blocking out the sunlight. I had to shield my eyes to look up at the approaching figure. A winged creature circled on outstretched wings in a sweeping arc. Strands of hair whipped from her braid and snapped back and forth across her face. The winged animal drifted by like a cloud, nudged his nose at the priestess's shoulder, then disappeared into thin air. It was all fur and wings. It moved too quickly for me to get a good look at it. Alright, apparently there were flying creatures at the temples too.

Nazneen jogged up to walk beside Nyla.

"I'm Nazneen Zathrian."

"Zathrian." She recognized Nazneen's family name. "You come from an honorable lineage."

"Thank you," Nazneen said.

Nyla opened the door to her cottage and welcomed us inside. Her home was quaint, and with the three tall males towering over everyone, the space was too small. The window across the room looking out over the city opened suddenly on a rush of air, allowing the breeze coming off the sea into the room.

"It was your scouts that discovered where I was," Nyla said.

"So, you're an elemental and a priestess?" Nazneen asked.

"Yes. Air elemental. I told your scouts to have you come to Proux. We have much to discuss."

"Yes. We'd heard rumors of another elemental on the Western Continent and were hoping you could help us," Nazneen answered.

"I know. And I will. I foresaw the fire, earth, and water elementals coming to me, but my visions aren't always clear. I didn't know exactly when, and I didn't know what you all would look like. I could only sense your magic. That's how I recognized the fire elemental. The fates were funny about what they shared with seers."

"How long have you lived here?" Arik asked.

He kept his hands clasped behind his back as he bent down to look out a low window near the couch. When she didn't answer right away, he looked up at her.

"I have always belonged to the temple," she answered. "My High Fae mother gave birth in the temple. She was a seer as well and knew I'd be one too. Her and my father believed my best education would come from the priestesses. We lived at the temple for my entire childhood, and I was trained in the ways of the Powers Above. Then I began to develop powers—air elemental powers. That had been a shock."

"I'm sure, seeing as both you and your mom missed that one," Garren said. "And an elemental? Whoa, someone got a massive power dump from the Powers Above."

She ignored him and continued. "When my parents decided to move to a new city, I chose to stay behind."

"You've devoted your life to the temple?" I asked.

Nyla looked at me. "I sense boldness and curiosity in you."

"I was born here, but I have always belonged to the temple. From my very first breath, I knew I would never have another life besides this one."

"You were aware of that before your first breath?" Garren asked sarcastically—the exact attitude I'd expect from a sea dragon.

Nazneen pinched him. "Don't be rude, Garren."

"The gods must have seen her truly worthy to offer so much to her," Nyla said to Evren.

Nyla gave him a blank stare, then shifted the subject. "You're searching for the relics."

"We are?" Nazneen asked.

"We weren't actually sure what we were looking for; we were just pointed in the direction of an air elemental," Evren explained. "What are the relics?"

"That's what Hadeon's after and why you've come all this way," Nyla said. "I saw you in my dreams."

Garren smothered down a laugh.

Nyla shot him a sardonic look. "I don't usually receive visions through dreams. Typically, they come to me when I am awake and meditating. This dream had been so vivid. At first, I thought I'd somehow been summoned to Aesira. I was overlooking the gods in the Sanctum. The gods held each of their elemental powers in their hands, outstretched toward the center of a pentagram. But it wasn't the pentagram in the darkstone of the Sanctum, but rather a pentagram deep within the ground. They were beneath the Sanctum itself. When their powers combined, portals opened in the universe. This was how they created our realm, the Mortal Realm of Naśbar. I'd read all this before in the Essence Scrolls, so I was confused as to why I was seeing this specific vision. The only thing that stood out to me was a shadowy darkness in my periphery. No matter how hard I looked, or at what angle, the darkness was there. It was hiding something, but I never saw what."

The petite priestess paced calmly like a cat back and forth as she continued speaking. "The next night, I had another dream. This one was slightly different. This time when the gods came together, they stepped through the veils into the Mortal Realm. I witnessed each of them gifting the High Fae leaders of the kingdoms a kernel of their elemental magic. After each king was given a relic, the gods explained that each relic was a key to open the veils beneath their temples to call upon the gods if they were needed. Four ancient, powerful objects that we kept secret deep within the High Fae kingdoms. Again, the dark shadow hovered in my peripheral, and again, I couldn't see what was hidden."

"So the relics open the veils to Aesira?" Nazneen asked. She'd made herself comfortable on the couch next to me. Garren stood behind me.

"All knew that the gods had the ability to visit Naśbar and walk among us. Many within the High Fae courts had seen them, but the knowledge of how exactly they crossed between planes was a well-guarded secret. Four items imbued with magic from the Powers Above. Individually, they are raw, unfiltered magic. One relic to open one veil. However, together they can align all the forces in our realm and open a portal to another. According to the Essence Scrolls, the gods used the veils to move from their realm to ours."

"I remember reading about the relics. They were lost around the time of the rebellion," Evren said.

"That's correct," Nyla said. "After the Uprising, the relics were brought together by the gods and used to banish the Great Chaos. Then the gods closed the veils to our realm forever."

"But there weren't only four kingdoms." Evren turned to her bondmate in thought. "Remember when I said there were five original High Fae kingdoms?"

"So what happened to the fifth kingdom?" Garren chimed in.

"That's what's interesting. There is no mention of a fifth relic or the fifth kingdom receiving any elemental magic in the Essence Scrolls. But I've had visions of a fifth relic. A vision separate from the other two dreams. It was a vision shrouded in haze and deep pain and betrayal. I've studied all of the ancient texts for decades. The only thing I found strange was a small gap misaligned in the parchment itself as if someone had cut it and pieced it back together with a spell. Which isn't impossible. The scrolls were written by the gods themselves. If they were misaligned, imperfect in any way, that means that they were altered by someone after they were originally created. There are five original Temples of Anruin. Or were. The one in the Raven Fae Kingdom was destroyed during the war. This temple is one of them. The veil is still under the temple, even though it's been closed for thousands of years. I have visited all the original temples. None of the teachers or the other priestesses know why the Essence Scrolls are all misaligned."

"And none of the other priestesses find the misaligned scrolls interesting? No one has questioned it?" Nazneen asked.

She shook her head. "Salina is the one I've studied under for many years. She thinks I'm trying to see things that aren't there."

"The City of Proux was one of the kingdoms," Evren said.

"The goddess of air gifted her power to the High Fae king that lived here," Nyla responded.

I shifted to rest my elbows on my knees. "All earth elementals have come from my family's bloodline. The god of earth blessed the High Fae king in Laeto Selva."

She nodded in confirmation.

"But Evren and I aren't from any of the High Fae kingdoms. We were born on Illoterra. I don't know about Evren, but my family has no connection to any of the original royal bloodlines except through marriage," Garren said.

"Elemental powers aren't always passed within bloodlines. Most of the time, the powers skip many generations or are given to another who has been found worthy by the gods," Nyla explained.

"But the relics are gone? Do we even know what they look like or if they are even in this realm? For all we know, the gods could have taken them back to Aesira."

"I don't believe they did. I believe I have felt their presence before."

"So you're just going to hunt them down?" Garren asked.

"I believe that each of us will be able to sense the relic that coordinates with our elemental power."

"That's a pretty big assumption," Arik said.

"It's the only thing we have to go with right now," Evren said.

"Is that why Hadeon wants an elemental? So he can track the relics?" Nazneen asked.

"It's possible," Nyla answered.

"That still leaves the question of the fifth kingdom. In the reference book I found in the Kanevvluk library, it was located on the southern part of this continent," Evren said. "Why would the book refer to five High Fae bloodlines and five kingdoms if the gods only gifted four?"

"I don't know. I've heard rumors and read old maps in search of the fifth kingdom, and only one place fits the description of the kingdom. I've gone to the area, but there are only villages and abandoned cities left over from the war. The land is blackened and nothing grows there. The temple was a crumbled pile of rubble."

"How long ago was that?" Evren asked.

"Ten, maybe fifteen years. When the visions started. When I first started having visions of you"—Nyla pointed to Evren—"I wasn't sure why my visions showed me a fire elemental when I already knew where the kingdom was located for that bloodline. But I think I know now." Nyla turned to Delrik.

"Know what?" Garren asked.

Nyla nodded her head toward Delrik. "I think *he* has something to do with all the questions I've been asking all these years."

"Me?" Delrik asked, pointing at himself.

Nyla simply nodded. Tension formed like a barrier between Delrik and Nyla.

Nazneen shifted closer. "Do you have a map?"

She pulled out a rolled map and smoothed it over the table. She showed us where in the southern part of the continent she'd visited. The closest city still in existence was Menrath.

"That's where the Raven Fae were during the war," Garren said. "We were stationed along their borders."

"And that's where Noirdan is now." Nazneen pulled another map from her pocket and laid it atop mine.

Garren leaned over me and asked, "Does anyone else see it?"

He traced his finger in a circle around the cities. Nyla was leaning over with her hands flat on the table. Her necklace swayed softly back and forth. Suddenly, Garren reached out and took the pendant in his hand. He stroked his thumb over the Powers Above symbol. A circle surrounded a pentagram with a smaller circle in the center.

"May I?" he asked Nyla.

She lifted my necklace over her head and handed it to him. He placed the pendant in the middle of the map. Each of the points of the pentagram pointed to the five High Fae kingdoms. He looked back down at the map and traced the cities again, but this time, in the shape of a five pointed star.

Nyla smiled to herself. "Maybe you aren't as dumb as you appear."

"What? Who said I was dumb?" Garren asked.

"If there were five kingdoms and five High Fae bloodlines, and you've seen a fifth relic, does that mean there were five, not four, gifts given to the High Fae?"

"Exactly."

"Okay. Hadeon is looking for the relics. We know that one opens a veil to Aesira. What about all four? Or five, if we are correct. The gods used all of the relics at the same time the first time they created our realm. The second time the relics were used in unison, they opened a door to another plane to banish..." Arik said.

"Fuck!" Garren raked his hands through his hair. Shock reached through the bond to me. And then fear. "He's going to release the Great Chaos."

THIRTY-FIVE
DELRIK

Nyla shifted slightly, her long robes rustled on the floor. She unnerved me. I knew she could sense the otherness. Did she know about the voice?

Without warning, she went rigid. Her eyes went blank, then turned almost white, as a vision swept over her. The ancient runes all over her arms seemed to glow, and her eyes turned milky as if she were blind. Her face was beautifully passive.

"Is she having a vision?" Evren asked me.

"I think so," Nazneen answered for me. I was too entranced.

Garren waved his hand back and forth in front of her face.

"Stop that. You are such a child." Nazneen grabbed Garren's hand from the air.

"You're telling me you're not the least bit curious if she can still see us or not..." he said to my sister.

I didn't know how long visions usually lasted. I'd never actually witnessed a seer in action. We all stood in silence and waited. And waited. And waited. Just then, there was a knock on the cottage door and the same priestess from the temple let herself in. Salina saw Nyla and shook her head. She hobbled with a tap, tap, tap of her cane into the cottage.

"Nyla had her first vision when she was three. She's been plagued by visions and dreams since then. She even sleepwalks. We are all used to it now."

"Are all the visions the same? I would think not," Evren said.

"There has only been one recurring vision. Promised victory and vengeance from the Powers Above against a dark force."

Evren watched Nyla with curiosity. "How long has she been here?"

"Close to 600 years. I've lost track of the exact amount of time," Salina said.

"She's older than Father!" Nazneen said to me in shock.

Nyla shifted and came out of her vision, blinking away the discoloration in her eyes. "You all will be here for a while. There's no need to stay at the inn. You're more than welcome to stay here."

And just like that, our decision about what was next was answered.

Salina sighed, but said, "There is an extra cottage where you would be comfortable. I'll show you, and we will send for your things."

As we were getting ready to leave, Nyla touched my arm, stopping me before I left. Her hand was warm and soft and light as a feather. She studied me curiously. "Darkness doesn't necessarily mean wicked. It is simply the opposite of light. We cannot have one without the other."

"Okay. Well ... thank you?" I said.

What was with her cryptic words?

She nodded and then closed the door behind me.

Garren was waiting for me in the garden. Evren and the rest of the females had followed after Salina. "What was that about?"

"I'm not sure."

"She's an odd one."

"I don't know if I'd say that too loudly. Didn't you hear her? The wisps told her we were coming. She can probably hear everything we're saying." Garren looked around like Nyla would jump from the bushes. "What are wisps anyways?"

Dark hells if I knew. I just shrugged and followed after my bondmate. I needed her presence right now. It was only when she was near that I felt any form of control over my mind. We were quiet as we walked.

"I owe her an apology," Garren said out of the blue.

"Okay, changing subjects. Who are you apologizing to?"

"Katuri."

"Is this about the bondmate thing again? You can't control that. Why are you apologizing for following the fates?" We winded down the path toward the spare cottage where we'd be staying until Nyla told us otherwise. I was not going to lie; it was kind of nice that we didn't have to travel right away.

"Not about that. About the fact that I'd been blind to her for the last forty years."

"Have you been blind?" I asked him. "I know you've gone out of your way to make her more comfortable here. You've let her make decisions for herself, haven't forced her in any way. That doesn't sound blind to me."

"But I could've done more."

I stopped walking and Garren followed suit. "There are always things in our past that we wish we could change. But we can't. What matters is where you go from here."

Garren nodded but seemed still deep in thought. "How am I supposed to get her alone? I can't peel your sister away from her with all the powers the gods possess."

"I'll handle it."

THIRTY-SIX
GARREN

I was standing in the kitchen, leaning against a stone island. This was more of a house than a cottage. It was large enough to fit our entire group. With Nazneen sharing a room with Katuri (not really happy about that one), Arik and I each got our own bedroom. And we pushed Delrik and Evren to the furthest room. No one wanted to hear what those two were getting up to behind closed doors.

Katuri came into the living room. She didn't notice me in the kitchen. She walked down the hallway to the room her and Nazneen were sharing. She was rummaging through Evren's trunk for something. She stood and planted her hands on her hips in a huff.

"Why did she bother sending me to look for her book if it isn't even in here," she said to the empty room.

I smiled to myself. Delrik must have enlisted Evren's help in getting Katuri alone with me. At least I had them on my side. I leaned against the door jamb and watched her. She turned to leave and jumped when she saw me.

"Shit, Garren!"

I couldn't help but admire her. Her skin was glowing from the sun and she looked ... happy.

"Are you standing there so I can't escape?"

Her tone was lighthearted, but when I pushed off the door frame, she braced herself. I raised my hands in supplication. I wouldn't jump her, not like she had me the other night. I smiled at the memory.

"Yes, but not for the reasons you're thinking."

Her brows pinched together. "How do you know what I'm thinking?"

I didn't know her exact thoughts, but standing this close, her emotions were as loud as if she were screaming down the bond. Uncertainty and desire and curiosity. I raised a brow at her.

"We both know I know what's on your mind ... but *that's* not why I'm here. Although, I'm open to all that too." I winked at her, and she rolled her eyes. "I just wanted to apologize. I was an ass. A blind ass."

She didn't say anything, but she wasn't walking away. Her fingers twisted in front of her, and she dropped her eyes to the floor. I took that as permission to continue.

"You were right. I didn't see your pain all these years. Fuck! It wasn't until you pointed it out that I realized how right you were. All this time, you'd been trying to be strong and brave. I missed the sadness. I was the main reason you weren't happy. If it weren't for me, you wouldn't have been dragged to Kanevvluk." I scrubbed my hands down my face. "I'm sorry I ignored you. I truly thought you'd be happier if I left you alone. I had ... I have nothing to offer you."

She looked up from the floor. Her face had softened. She'd been so closed off, but now my Little Flower was opening for me. I could see the female she'd become—confident, intelligent, independent—despite being caged. She challenged me and kept me on my toes. And I loved her for it all.

"I tried to make your life better. I really did. Corynne. Your greenhouse. That disgustingly sweet guava jam you love so much. Fuck, that stuff is disgusting." She let out a soft laugh, but quickly brought the back of her hand to cover her mouth. "I did it all for you."

She furrowed her brows in thought. Then her features shifted with realization. "I didn't know. You never said anything."

I looked down at the floor. "I wasn't sure how much of a difference it would make. So I stayed quiet. You were still stuck with me. I asked too much of you too fast. I never wanted anything from you. Never your power. I only wanted you to be content. And now I want to give you everything you've ever wanted, even if that's your freedom. If you truly don't want to be with me, despite being bondmates, I'll let you leave. But I'm hoping that maybe one day you'll feel the same way as I do."

I pushed all the adoration I had for her down the bond, hoping she'd accept it. Before, I had wanted it all from Katuri. When I realized we were bondmates, I had thought it would be easy transition into spending the rest of our lives together. I'd been wrong. She'd been hurt too many times. I needed to be patient if I wanted to be with her. I'd be happy with just her friendship until she was ready for me. I needed to prove the words I was saying were the truth.

"Thank you Garren. For everything. Even if I didn't see it. Even if I was still lonely and hurting. I couldn't imagine what it would've been like if you hadn't been there. So, thank you."

When I looked up, she was smiling at me. For the first time ever. Then, to my surprise, she walked to me and placed her palm to my cheek. I closed my eyes and leaned into the warmth of her hand.

"This doesn't mean I'm yours. I need to think. I need some space. But thank you."

And then she was gone.

THIRTY-SEVEN
GARREN

Nyla and the other priestesses were doing their evening prayers and dedications at the temple. I was sitting outside, my mind reeling from pouring my heart out to Katuri. They must have just finished because I saw Nyla appear at the temple entrance. She began walking my way when, suddenly, she dropped to her knees, clutching her head. I stood and started to run to her. Just then, two dark figures flew across the sky, circling the temple like vultures. They were so close that their massive wings knocked into the building, sending chunks of stone raining down like hail stones.

Then the screaming began.

I ran toward the temple, toward Nyla. Katuri was right on my heels. The cottages burst into flames. So much fire. The winged creatures were swooping up and down, dropping flaming balls onto the cottages. Priestesses were running in every direction. I ran up to Nyla, and water erupted from my hands, putting out fires, cottage after cottage. Nyla stood on shaky legs and swung her arms. Gusts of wind whipped through the air and around the wings of the dark creatures. They couldn't control their wings, and they began to fall to the earth. One of the creatures hit the earth hard with a thunk and died on impact. The other one's legs were broken and sticking out at odd angles. Katuri reached into the ground and summoned branches that grew up and wrapped around the creature, securing him. I rushed, continuing to put out the fires.

In a blur of movement, Delrik and Evren were there. Delrik had Evren in his arms. He deposited her beside Katuri and sprinted into the burning cottages. He was a blur as he ran back and forth, bringing out priestesses that had been trapped in the still burning fires. When he'd retrieved the last priestess, he returned to his bondmates side. He wasn't even out of breath.

"We saw the creatures coming from the city. Then I saw smoke. We ran here as fast as we could. What happened?" Evren said.

"We were attacked," I said.

Nyla was kneeling on the path again, too unsteady to stand. Evren offered a hand to help.

In my many, many years of existence, I'd only seen creatures such as these in war.

Delrik stepped up next to me. "Fiends."

The creature before me had once been Fae. I could see the telltale arced ears now, but it had been twisted into a new form. Its eyes were red with slits for pupils, and its hands ended in long claws. The wings that erupted from its back were black leather, stretched over elongated bones. And its skin looked almost charred. A beast straight from the circle of dark hells.

Two priestesses had died. Several more had been injured, and at least four cottages were beyond repair. Two healers made their way around, healing injuries and comforting those that needed it.

"How did they even know we were here?" Evren was talking to Delrik. She was clearly upset by the mangled, broken beast that was bleeding all over the grounds of the temple.

"I don't know," Delrik answered.

Delrik lifted the sword Nazneen had sheathed at her back and swung it. The fallen beast's head separated from its body and rolled across the ground from the force of the strike.

The second fiend laughed. Foul-smelling blood gargled from his maw. "Someone in your ranks shouldn't be trusted," it singsonged.

It turned its red slitted eyes toward Arik, but before it could say anymore, Delrik turned to look at me with such incredible speed that the fiend's blood from the sword splattered across my face. He raised the sword between him and Arik. Blood dripped from the tip of the deadly blade.

Delrik took a step toward him. "You."

"I didn't do anything," Arik said, taking a step back.

"Delrik, stop." Nazneen tried to come to my side, but I held her back with a gentle hand.

"What have you done?"

"Nothing."

"I don't believe you."

"I didn't tell them anything," Arik claimed.

"Tell who? Where did you go yesterday when we were all eating at the pub? You came to the city with us and then disappeared." Delrik was not happy.

When he didn't answer, Delrik pressed the tip of the lilura steel into the base of Arik's throat. A bead of blood welled under the pressure.

"I just met with someone."

"One of Hadeon's goons?"

"Just a random guy. He doesn't work for Hadeon. I met someone in the pub yesterday. A male who I'd been in contact with the last several months. He was a partner of someone I was looking for. He doesn't work for Hadeon."

"But news travels fast," the fiend hissed with delight.

"It's not a secret we are here in Proux," Arik defended. "Everyone knows we are here. Anyone could have spread that information."

He had a point. It wasn't a secret we were here and visiting the temple. We weren't hiding. We were out in public. The whole city knew who we were. I guessed it was hard to be inconspicuous when you were traveling with such a large group of High Fae.

"Why were you meeting with someone?" Delrik asked. Shadows swirled around the hand that held the hilt of the famed sword.

"Delrik, that's enough." Nazneen's voice was rough with concern.

Delrik's eyes didn't leave Arik's face. "No, Naz. He needs to answer. Why were you meeting with someone?"

"I'm looking for someone. A smuggler. The male I met yesterday wanted to know why we were here in Proux. I told him we had questions about the growing restlessness in the south in exchange for the smuggler's location. That's all. I swear."

Delrik growled and bared his teeth. I knew it would take less than a second for him to end Arik with that sword. I saw a ripple in the air as Arik slipped a shield between him and Delirk. The indention where the sword had pressed his skin disappeared, his shield firmly protecting him.

"You gave away our location to a fucking smuggler?" Delrik bellowed.

Arik turned to Nazneen, hoping she would help.

"She sees you for the traitor you are," Delrik said. He was shaking now.

Nazneen stopped fighting against my hold. She just stood there, a dejected look on her beautiful face. Nazneen knew my truth.

"Arik?" She whispered.

"Did you tell them about the relics?" Delrik questioned.

He kept my eyes on Nazneen.

"Did you?" Delrik bellowed.

"The smuggler was the one that kidnapped my mother, and he is the reason she and my brother are dead. I have to find him..." Arik said.

I'd never heard him mention his mother. And he had a brother?

"Fuck!" I released Nazneen and raked my hands through my hair.

Delrik shook his head. "For what? To even a score from 100 years ago? No one gives a shit about that. You put our entire mission in jeopardy to see to your own agenda. What happened to your family was horrible, but you should've known better."

"Nazneen," Arik started, but the fiend interrupted him.

"But that's not all, is it, Arik Hanover?" It enunciated each syllable in his name. "You've been leaking information for years, haven't you?"

"What?" Delrik and I said in unison.

Delrik's shadows appeared, floating across his shoulders. His eyes flashed solid black, and the sword moved an inch closer to Arik's throat, but it was held off with the shield.

"Hadeon knew when you arrived in Kanevvluk, firebird. Hadeon knew High Ruler Adaris Byrnes visited to discuss alliances with Snowhaven Fae. Ha!" It let out a hideous cackle. "He even knew that the lesser son, the disposable son, was leading the charge to the City of Proux. Hadeon knew you were on your way here to find another elemental. All we had to do was wait and you'd walk right into our hands. The confirmation from your contact that you'd arrived was perfect timing."

The fiend's eyes bounced back and forth between Delrik and Arik, thoroughly enjoying the chaos it had caused. Nyla stepped up to the fiend from behind and sucked in a breath of air. She unleashed the full strength of her power with a scream so high-pitched that it shook the ground. The scream ripped the breath from the creature's lungs. Its chest caved in with a crunch. As its body began to fall, Delrik, in a flash, swung the sword away from Arik and decapitated the fiend just like he had the other one. He moved so fast my body barely had time to react before its head rolled to a stop at my feet.

We hadn't seen Nyla use her elemental powers except for minor things. Everyone's eyes were wide with shock and maybe a touch of fear. Salina had said she was dangerous despite her gentle nature. And there was the proof.

"Get out," Delrik said to Arik.

Shadows leached from his hands. Tendrils twisted around his fingertips. Evren took hold of Delrik's arm, and he allowed her to turn him away from Arik. When he lowered the sword, Arik's body relaxed. The immediate threat was gone at least. Arik was safe from Delrik. For now. Even though Delrik had this darkness around him, he wasn't the murderer he'd been forced into during the war. We all turned and walked away back toward our cottage. Everyone except Nazneen. I paused and turned back to watch over her.

Arik turned to her. Her body was heavy with heartbreak.

"How could you? I can't even look at you right now," she started.

She tried to walk away, but Arik reached out and grabbed her arm. She spun around, kicking her leg out to swipe my legs from beneath me, but he caught her leg. She must not have been in her right mind if he was able to stop her attack. Or her heart wasn't in it.

"Let me go, Arik."

She wasn't alarmed or scared. Her voice was dripping with rage, and tears streamed down her cheeks. I knew Nazneen could handle herself, but I refused to leave her alone with him. I was there just in case.

"You have to listen to me," he said.

"I don't have to do anything. I don't owe you anything," she snapped.

He just stared at her.

"Arik, you're hurting me," she said, but she wasn't pulling away from him.

Arik's knuckles had turned white with his firm grip on her leg. He immediately dropped her leg and stepped back.

"Please—"

"No. You can't see beyond your own vengeance, whatever it is." She shook her head, her voice wobbly. "I should've seen this coming. Delrik tried to warn me." She shook her head with disgust. "I can't."

Then she walked away from him, past me, and followed after her brother. Arik didn't stop her. I left him standing in the courtyard outside the temple. All alone.

THIRTY-EIGHT
DELRIK

I knew we shouldn't have trusted Arik. Not that I ever truly trusted him, but he shouldn't have been allowed to come with us to the Western Continent. I swore after Glissden, after I'd watched him slaughter and dismember all that stood against him, if I ever crossed paths with him again I'd rip his limbs off and watch him bleed to death. What he'd done was inexcusable. But Garren had seemed to forgive him somehow. And I trusted Garren. Even Nazneen had taken a liking to him, despite my distaste. Clearly we were all blinded by his charm. Arik's lucky I hadn't seen him since the fiends attacked us. He'd slithered off to some hole somewhere to hide. I'd been tempted in the moment to unleash my shadows on him.

"Yes. You should have."

The voice was back. This was the first time I'd heard it since we landed in Proux. I was hopelessly wishing I'd left the voice out at sea.

"I shouldn't have let him come with us. I should've known he had other motivations. I'd let the last several years cloud my judgment." Garren was more beat up about the whole Arik situation than I was.

"It's not your fault," I told him. "Whatever he's been doing, it's been under the radar. We all missed it."

"Now what?" Garren asked as he paced back and forth. "We no longer have the surprise. Hadeon knows where we are and that we are watching his every move. He knows there are now four elementals in one place."

"We have to find a different approach."

"Do you think he knows we are looking for the relics, too?"

"Maybe. We just have to beat him in the search. It's possible Arik told his contact yesterday, but the fiend's loose tongue didn't mention them. If we could get our hands on at least one, then we are a step closer."

I turned to the air elemental. She was sitting on the counter in the kitchen with her legs crossed in front of her. Her robes were piled in her lap, exposing her legs up to the middle of her thighs. They were covered in runes, just like her arms. All the runes were glowing with waves of light as the visions came and went. Her hands rested on top of the pile of robes, and she had that eerie blank stare. Her eyes flickered between white and blue as visions came and went. She'd been meditating and searching her mind for hours. I was exhausted just watching her.

"We won't be able to kill Hadeon," she said. Her face was still unfocused, her eyes white as she spoke to us even though she was having a vision.

Garren threw his hands in the air. "See! Even the seer says we will fail."

"I didn't say we would fail in finding the relics," Nyla said as she shook out her head and unfurled herself from her perch. Her skirts dropped in delicate waves of fabric to her feet. "I said we will never be able to *kill* Hadeon. We don't need his demise. We simply need to ... contain him. If we stop the spread of his evil, then we stop him without actually ending him. We will go to Noirdan and we will leave in a week's time."

"Bossy much?" Garren said under his breath.

Nyla glared at him, and a gust of air swept his legs out from underneath him, toppling him to the ground.

"What do you think you are doing back here?" My voice boomed through the cottage. The walls shook.

It was night out now and we'd all been preparing for bed. Nyla and Nazneen were in the kitchen tidying up from dinner. Evren and Katuri were murmuring quietly in hushed conversation.

Katuri ran into the living room with Evren. I didn't turn from my fighting stance, facing off Arik, and ready to attack. He was standing in the doorway, and I was blocking his entrance.

"He wouldn't stand a chance against you. Against us."

I twisted my neck, trying to decide if I wanted to listen to the voice or not. The voice, a female voice, I'd noticed now that she was speaking to me more frequently, it was bewitching. I was enraptured by her.

"You think you can sell information about us and then just return like nothing is wrong?" My voice was not my own. It was deep and ancient.

"Delrik," Nazneen said.

I whipped around in an unnaturally quick way. "Stay out of this, Naz. You don't know what he's truly like." I jabbed a finger in Arik's direction, but he didn't take his eyes off my sister. "I watched him slaughter people, Nazneen. In cold blood. And then dismember them!"

"She knows everything. I told her all of it," he said.

"And you think that makes all this go away?" Shadowy tendrils spread out into the air from me. Silver ether was shining around me. My vision blacked out before clearing again. I knew from watching them in the mirror before now that they were solid black; dark and ominous. "You put my Ashlyra in danger. You risked my sister's life."

I spiraled down into my rage, and it fed my shadows.

"Yes. There you go, Master of Death and Darkness. Show him what he deserves for endangering your Ashlyra."

The shadows crept across the ground and wrapped around Arik's body. Like it was an extension of my hand, one tendril snaked up and gripped Arik's neck and squeezed.

"Delrik. Don't do this," Evren said. She stepped toward me. Nazneen tried to hold her back, but she wriggled out of her grip.

"I will end you," the shadows spoke through me.

Evren stepped between Arik and me, directly in the path of my deadly shadows. The blackness curled around her like it recognized her. As if she commanded the darkness rather than me, it released Arik and gathered around her. All my fury refocused on Evren. Molten rage. I turned all of it on my bondmate. Why were my shadows attacking Evren? Or were they? It was almost like there were two sides: one that recognized Evren and wanted to protect her; the other that wanted to snuff out her life. Arik took the advantage and slowly backed away from me. I saw him slink away into the evening.

"Evren, get out of the way," I thundered, my voice unworldly.

I'd never raised my voice to her before, but she didn't back down.

"No." The power she exuded rivaled the death that poured from me. "I'm not afraid of you." Evren was eerily serene. "I'm not afraid of you, Delrik, or your darkness."

I took several steps away from her, but she calmly pursued me and gripped my face with immovable firmness. My eyes were unfocused depths of the umbra. More shadows poured from my hands and encircled my bondmate. They wound around her body, twisting in and out of the spaces between our bodies. Soon we were both consumed by the darkness. My breaths were heavy and short with anger. Evren's voice was calming and unperturbed by the ancient magic surrounding her. The ground began to quake. The windows rattled in their panes, and the lights began to flicker on and off. The shadows churned around them both like thick smoke.

"Evren, back away," I said.

"Never," was her reply. "Never."

"I don't want to hurt you."

"You won't hurt me."

Evren released her fire, and it entwined itself with the shadows. They were two opposing forces. Dark and light. Death and life.

We all stood there together, cloaked in the fire and shadows that danced around us for what seemed like hours, in actuality only twenty minutes, before they started to slowly dissipate. How Evren managed to talk me down from destroying Arik, the temple, and cottages even more than the fiends had was a miracle in itself. The priestesses had already seen enough destruction for the week. When the shadows cleared, I dropped to my knees and pressed my face into Evren's stomach. Sticky blood was crusted down my face and ears, but my Ashlyra held me.

THIRTY-NINE
DELRIK

"You received your shadows from Alux, correct?"

She already knew the answer. I didn't know why she had bothered asking. I wondered if it bothered people when she knew about their lives without actually knowing them. She'd already told us she'd foreseen Evren retrieving the Ring of Teris. So she knew we had gotten them from Alux.

Nyla stood with me in the garden on a bright afternoon. After witnessing me almost lose control, I knew if there was any way to help me from murdering anyone else, I would try. So when Nyla offered to help, I didn't say no. I didn't know if she had experience with shadow magic. I doubted it since Evren had found nothing about the darkness anywhere in the Kanevvluk or Arcelia libraries.

"I know what it is like having power inside you that seems out of your control. It took me many decades to master the two gifts given to me," she said.

"Yes. This is magic from Alux." I eyed her suspiciously.

"I've never seen magic like this before. Can you summon the shadows on command outside your body?"

I held my hand in front of me and the shadows effortlessly came to me. Serpentine ropes curled around my fingers. Right now, the shadows didn't feel dangerous. Not like this. They felt gentle and inquisitive. They explored the surface of my hand and then slowly started to reach out toward Nyla. She didn't shy away, just observed them.

"Can you project them away from your body while remaining in control?"

"I've never tried. I've done it by accident though."

"Let's start there." She lifted a rock into the air and placed it a few feet from us with her air magic. "Cast your shadows out and surround the rock."

It took me several tries to separate shadows from myself physically. Each time I succeeded, Nyla moved the rock further away. I grew more confident as our time went on.

Suddenly, Nyla went distant. I felt a shift in the air around us, like a lightness sweeping around us. And then it was gone as quick as it had come on. Nyla leaned a hip against a retaining wall and refocused on me.

"Sorry. Let's continue," she said.

"Was that a vision?" I asked.

She nodded. "Over the centuries, I've learned to anticipate them coming. Sometimes they can be overwhelming, but most of the time it's the softness of the universe guiding me. That one was like a gentle embrace . . ."

"But?" I urged.

"It had a sinister undertone. Not in its message, but just in the overall feeling of it."

"Was that vision about me?"

She shrugged. "Sometimes it's a mystery who the vision is meant for. Other times I know exactly who they are directed at."

I wanted to know what the vision contained, no matter how sinister it may be.

"I don't know if you are ready to hear what it said."

I let out a disheartened laugh. "If it was something about me, I want to know."

Nyla smoothed her hands down the front of her robes and closed her eyes. "It's easier to give in than to fight against."

That made no sense. Did she want to give in to the darkness?

She spoke again. "It may be easier to give in, but are you willing to sacrifice everything for the surrender? Are you willing to take that risk to understand why you were given this path in life?"

Evren appeared by the garden gate, interrupting my confusing conversation with Nyla. She came to me and kissed me on the cheek.

"How are you?" she asked me.

"Better now." I smiled down at her.

I looked over to Nyla. "I think I'm done for today."

It was almost lunchtime and I'd begun to get hungry anyway.

"Keep practicing when you can," she said. "I need to do some meditation this afternoon. We can pick up where we left off tomorrow."

Nyla nodded her goodbye to us and started to leave, but her robes snagged on a branch. She stumbled and I reached out to steady her before she fell. When my hand touched her arm, another vision struck her, and like a bolt of lightning, it threw me backward. I crashed into the retaining wall and the air punched from my lungs.

I sucked in a breath at the pain, and flashes of light and color covered my vision. Blinding shock of despair and pain crashed into me. My heart was being wrenched from my chest. I tried to take a breath, but my body was still stunned from having the wind knocked out of me. What the hell? What was that?

Evren rushed to me.

"What happened?" Evren's voice was full of concern.

Nyla had caved in on herself. She was crying out, like the despair I was feeling, she was too.

"Is she having a vision?"

"I don't know. The other ones didn't look like this."

I pushed myself back up to stand beside my bondmate.

"Go find Salina," Evren said, not taking her eyes off Nyla. She started to go to her, but I pulled her back.

I shook my head from side to side. "I'm not leaving you here with her."

"She isn't a danger to me, Delrik."

The air whipped around us like we were in the middle of a storm, but there were no clouds or rain.

"You don't know that," Delrik said.

Suddenly, Nyla's body seized, and my body seized too. Had our brief contact connected me to her vision? A swarm of glowing spirits transformed into darkness, and a flash of a female sobbing over the death of her lover came into view. She looked like Nyla but not at the same time. I could see Evren, but she was so, so far away. I was bound by unseen restraints and pain lanced through me. I was experiencing the sharp hurt of this female, whoever she was. All the pain and sorrow she'd felt.

"I'm sorry Alux." It was a voice I'd never heard before. It repeated over and over inside my head. *"I'm sorry. I'm sorry. I'm sorry."*

Then I dropped to the ground on my hands and knees, panting heavily. The voice hadn't been the one haunting me all this time. It had been different but so familiar. I'd heard it before, but I couldn't place where.

Then Nyla screamed, clawing at her face and hair.

"What the fuck was that, Nyla?" I rushed to her and pulled her hands from her face. Her eyes were blank white. Tears stained her face, and the runes all over her body were glowing so brightly it looked as if she were surrounded by an orb of light. I held her like that until she finally calmed and her eyes shifted back to normal. Her breathing slowed and she was back.

"Did you..." she asked.

"Yes. I saw it all."

"But how?" She shook her head in confusion. "I've never shared my visions with anyone."

I had no idea how, but Nyla had shared the nightmare she'd called a vision with me. The garden where we'd been practicing was a disaster. The grasses around me were flattened down, and pots were knocked over, their contents scattered on the ground.

Evren knelt beside me and brushed Nyla's hair away from my face. "Are you all right?"

When I thought Nyla was safe from clawing her eyes out, I released her hands. Angry red lines marred her porcelain skin. Her vision swam before me. Again and again.

It took Nyla a moment to find her voice. "I knew there was something powerful about you. That was the first time I touched you." She lifted her head and found my eyes. I was still kneeling in front of her, Evren beside me. Katuri and Salina had joined us now, too.

"The shadows." She swallowed hard against what I assumed was the searing pain in her throat from screaming. "The shadows. I recognize them now. From my dreams. They are a cover for the terrible tragedy."

"A terrible tragedy?" Evren looked worried.

I didn't blame her. The vision made me uneasy too.

Nyla nodded. "Alux. I've never met her, but I know what she looks like from my visions. At least what she looks like now. But she hasn't always looked like that. She was once..."

"Beautiful," I finished for her. The female I'd seen in Nyla's vision was indeed Alux.

Nyla continued. "Whoever she was, whoever she'd been before, a terrible wrong was done to her that made her what she is today."

It took her several attempts, but Nyla finally managed to stand and make it back to her cottage with help from Salina and Evren. I hung back, too afraid to come close to her again. I was completely drained. Did her visions always drain her like that? It wasn't often that I reached the bottom of my well of power by using the power of my speed. But a tiny vision had knocked me on my ass.

I guess there is a first time for everything.

I pressed my hand to my forehead. I was still off balance.

"What happened to Alux?" I asked once Nyla had settled herself on her couch.

I know I'd seen the same vision as she had.

Evren nudged me. "Give her a moment. She needs to recover."

Salina brought her a glass of water. Nyla thanked her before taking a sip.

"No. It's all right. I don't know exactly what happened. I only saw flashes and felt her pain. It was like I was inside her body, seeing out of her eyes. I was reliving the moment. I didn't see the events that led up to it. There was a male with her, but only for an instant." She pressed a hand to her chest.

A headache began to build behind my eyes as Nyla recounted what she'd seen to everyone else. I didn't need to hear it. I had witnessed it firsthand.

"You said you recognized my shadows. What did you mean?" I asked.

"Your shadows are like the ones I saw in my visions and the ones I dreamed about when I saw the gods create the Mortal Realm. They must be connected somehow."

"Do you think that is why Delrik was able to see the vision when he touched you? The shadows linked you two somehow?" Evren asked.

I jumped up and started pacing. The sudden movement made my head throb harder, but I didn't care. I needed to move my body. "There is no way Alux is connected with the gods. She is evil. Pure evil."

"I agree that Alux is evil now, but she wasn't the same in my vision. I sensed the good in her. I know you felt it too," Nyla said.

I had to concede; the female in the vision had no evil inside her. In fact, it was the exact opposite. She was the definition of light and goodness and peace. If that was truly Alux... No. I couldn't wrap my mind around it.

"We need to go to the chamber of the veils," Nyla said to herself.

Salina, who was still standing behind Nyla, pinched her mouth in disapproval. "The veil has been sealed since the Uprising. You won't find any answers down there. You are looking for things that aren't there," she chided.

I whirled around at the frail female. I was over her negativity. I hadn't known Nyla long, but she was right. There were things that even the oldest priestesses didn't know about. At least Nyla was trying to find answers before Hadeon could tear the realm apart. "How do you know? You have no answers for me. All you do is ignore the things that Nyla clearly sees and tell her she is crazy. Maybe *you* are the crazy one for not paying attention to what's right in front of you."

My sharp tone made Salina step back. She was quiet for a moment. Then she gave a shallow bow. "Do as you wish." And then she was gone.

I turned to Nyla. I was sure I looked mad. I felt like I was going mad. "Take me to the chamber of the veils."

FORTY
DELRIK

Katuri went to find Nazneen and Garren and have them meet us at the temple. The whole time we waited, I paced back and forth with my head low. Alux's grief kept playing in my mind. Nyla had recovered enough to make it to the temple with Evren's help.

"I haven't been down in the chambers since I first began my training as a priestess centuries before. I only went to see the room that correlated with the Essence Scrolls. After that, there was no need to be there. The veils that connected the Mortal Realm of Naśbar to Aesira had been sealed long before I walked this earth."

The stairway was full of dust and cobwebs. The candles that had once lit the spiraling descent had been burned to their quicks. Wax had dripped down the walls and pooled in hardened heaps on the stone stairs. We followed the stairs downward. Evren held a flame in her hand to illuminate the way, but it didn't push away all the darkness.

I had been here, walked this dark spiral before, but in a different time, a different body. I remembered this like a memory from someone else. I let the memory guide me. Our feet left prints in the dust covered stone as we spiraled down, down, down into the heart of the temple. When we reached the bottom and stepped into the pitch black chamber, Evren's firelight danced off the walls.

The chamber of the veils.

I shivered in the cold. Something was off, almost like we weren't supposed to be there, like what we were searching for wasn't meant to be found.

Evren spotted several candles in a tall stand that hadn't been completely burned and lit each one. A soft, glowing golden light filled the space. The floor was solid stone, and the same pentagram carved into the temple above was crudely chiseled into it. A circle surrounded the star. At each point of the star sat an empty dais, all except one. The point where the goddess of air would sit was an arch of darkstone. Its glossy surface reflected the firelight like a mirror.

Nyla walked to the polished arch, reached forward, and brushed her fingers along the edge. Runes similar to the ones on her skin were inscribed into the entirety of the dias around the arch.

"This is where the veil once was," she said in a reverent tone.

Garren stepped forward. "If the symbol of the Powers Above is a pentagram, and it aligns with the kingdoms and capital cities on the map, then that means the City of Kosmima would be here." He stepped to the bottom left point of the star.

"And the City of Agni would be here." Evren stood at the top point. "The City of Proux is where you are standing, Nyla."

Katuri was the last one. She took her place between Garren and Evren. "The City of Laeto Selva."

I observed each of my friends carefully. "Nyla, when you had the dream, the one of the creation of our realm, where was the darkness you saw?"

She closed her eyes to visualize it. "In my dream, I had been hovering above the gods, looking down upon the circle. The darkness was next to the goddess of air. To the left."

"The last remaining point of the star," I said. "Do you remember the first time we were all in the temple together? There was that eclipse. I wonder if that would happen again?"

I stepped up to the final point of the star. "If the maps are correct, then this is where the ruins are located and where Noirdan is today."

A burst of light as blinding as the sun flared behind Nyla. The air buzzed with immeasurable power.

"The City of Lumir." The ethereal voice was the most heavenly I'd ever heard.

I didn't need her to tell me who she was. I knew deep in my bones that the being that stood before me was the goddess of air. Her gown was flowing layers of silk in shades of blue and white. Her hair was white as snow and her eyes a deep navy.

"I've been watching you all. I knew you'd all come together."

We all stood, shocked, at the goddess before us.

"I am Haizea, the goddess of air." She dipped her head in greeting.

We all knelt before her, still stunned into silence.

It was Evren who spoke first. "Did we somehow open the veil?"

Before the goddess was able to reply, with my supernatural speed, I had moved to Evren's side. I was no match against a goddess, but

I wouldn't leave my bondmate to stand alone if something were to happen.

"Gosh no, dear. That was me. For a mortal to open the veil to Aesira, you'd need to have a relic. I, on the other hand, can come and go as I please. I felt the five of you here together and knew it was time to come to you."

"The five of us?" I asked.

"Each of you contains an elemental power gifted by the gods. Including you, Delrik Valhar."

Shadows hovered over Evren and me, shielding my bondmate from potential danger.

"Your shadows, though, are no mere kernel of a god's power. No. They are much stronger than that. They belong to someone else. You took what wasn't meant for the Mortal Realm."

I curled a protective arm around Evren's middle and drew her behind me. I hadn't stolen a god's power. The only thing I'd taken was the horrors that Alux had subjected the realm to.

"The magic you possess belonged to the goddess of spirits. Aluxyeras. Or as you know her, Alux."

"Hold on." Garren strolled over to the goddess with nonchalance. "You're telling us that the evil shadow witch that eats humans and Fae as a snack and bathes in their blood, the one that almost annihilated Delrik from the inside out, is the goddess of spirits?"

The goddess held his gaze without speaking. I wasn't sure what she was waiting for. I wanted to know the answer too. Because it couldn't be true. There was no way in the circle of dark hells or in Aesira that Alux was a goddess.

"And what are spirits anyway? I thought that our souls went to Evermere in the afterlife. Are souls and spirits different?" Garren asked.

Nyla answered this question for him. "Here in Quinterre, we call the intellectual and emotional energy inside us our spirit. In Illoterra, you call it a soul. They are the same thing. Our continent has stuck closer to the old ways, while your home is newer."

"So the shadow witch used to control the afterlife. Damn. I think I'd risk being stuck in the Cessan Void than deal with her for eternity," Garren joked.

Haizea's face was solemn. "When I knew Aluxyeras, she wasn't full of such darkness. Aluxyeras was the goddess who looked over all the spirits that passed into Evermere. She cared for the eternal resting place for both mortals and gods. She was beauty, compassion, and love."

"I felt her pain," Nyla said, barely above a whisper. She gripped the pendant at her chest. I had felt it too, and my heart ached at the still vivid memory.

"I know. I sent you the visions. Not many would've been strong enough to bear even a fraction of what Aluxyeras felt." The goddess turned to me. "I hadn't expected it to jump to you as well. Aluxyeras's power must have drawn it to you."

"What happened to make her turn against the gods?" I asked.

"She fell in love," Haizea said. "Aluxyeras fell in love with a High Fae male. Eryx, the god of fire, was against it. Even though she was willing to give up her seat as goddess of spirits, Eryx refused. When Thane came to Aesira in search of Aluxyeras, Eryx murdered him. It was too much for her to take. She crumbled. She gave into all the darkness she felt, and all the spirits she commanded were transformed into shadows. She retaliated against Eryx and almost destroyed Aesira. I tried to reason with her, but she was beyond saving. There was nothing I could do for her. It took the remaining four of us to get her under control long enough to banish her to the Wasted Shallows and trap her there. A god can't be killed, even by another god. It was our only choice. We created the Ring of Teris with all our powers to contain her. Then we gave the ring to the leaders of the kingdoms. It was only right that they had possession of the one thing that could control her if she ever escaped."

Haizea lowered her head.

"Is that why the ring recognizes the elemental powers?" Evren asked as she stepped around me.

Haizea nodded in reply. "She was my best friend. I couldn't save my best friend. I tried many times over the centuries to bring her back from the darkness. I went to the Wasted Shallows, but there was no good left in her. Every life she took brought her further away from her holiness. Only unending darkness remained."

"The shadow magic then, is it Alux's full power?" Garren asked.

"I don't know for sure." The goddess shook her head.

Nyla spoke up. "Why are there no records of a goddess of spirit? I've read every text, every version of the Essence Scrolls in the temples. Aluxyeras is not mentioned anywhere."

"After she was banished, Eryx used his power to wipe the existence of the spirit from knowledge."

"Is that why the seats of the gods are off-center?" Garren asked. "The fifth point isn't a representation of our realm. One seat has been missing this whole time. The goddess of spirits."

"And the Essence Scrolls are misaligned," Nyla added.

Haizea nodded again.

"Why did you come here? Why are you telling us this now?" I asked the goddess.

"Ever since Aluxyeras was banished, the balance of power in Aesira has been thrown off. Another war is coming. One here in the Mortal Realm and one in Aesira."

FORTY-ONE
GARREN

Delrik and Evren were off exploring ... somewhere. I wasn't paying attention when they slipped from the cottage. Or at least that's what Evren had used as an excuse to get Delrik away from civilization. I knew my friend didn't have full control over the shadow magic yet, even with the help of Nyla, and needed to release some of its pent up energy before it consumed him. Especially after we learned from Haizea that the spirit's elemental power had been transformed into the exact opposite of what it was intended to be. All of us were still reeling from Haizea's information.

Nazneen wanted to hunt, which meant she was wandering in the woods, licking her wounds from Arik. And Arik, the lying bastard, I'd seen him helping the priestesses remove the wreckage from the fire. At least he was doing something helpful and staying out of the way. He'd moved to the inn in the city rather than returning to the cottage. He was smart to stay away. I didn't think he'd survive another run in with Delrik.

I truly thought he'd changed after the war. Once he'd let out his anger and destroyed that village, I thought he would finally begin to allow himself to heal from whatever plagued his past. I'd never asked him about his life before he came to Kanevvluk. It wasn't my business. I didn't really care as long as he stayed in line and didn't have another outburst like Glissden. But I guessed people didn't really change. Now I had to figure out where this mission was going next.

I scrubbed my hands down my face. That was the last thing I wanted to think about right now. I had been left alone in our cottage with Katuri all day. We'd come to an understanding, a truce I guess. And now she was willingly here with me, alone in the cottage. A month ago she would rather have walked on hot coals than be near me. I'd kept to my room most of the day, but I'd grown hungry, so I went in search of a late lunch. Kat was sitting in a chair near the window, twirling her fingers in the air with one of her romance novels open in her lap. A few days had passed since I'd apologized to her. She still ignored the bond, but she wasn't running from me anymore. She was wary, but dare I say friendly. A vine crept up the windowsill and small flowers bloomed along its length, and a slight smile was on her lips at the words on the page before her. The light from the afternoon sun peaking through the pretty clouds made the red highlights in her dark brown hair glow. She was really fucking beautiful. She was definitely made for the sun, not for being trapped in the snowy climate of Snowhaven.

"Why are you staring at me?" she asked without turning back to look at me.

"I'm not staring."

I was totally staring. I studied her profile. The upturn of her nose with that deliciously sexy septum ring. The silver hoop glinted in the light coming in from the window. The curve of her lips. The tribal mark was a contrast to her golden skin. Her shoulders went tense when she noticed I was still watching her. But her hackles weren't completely raised. Progress.

"Seriously," she said, slapping her palm down on the wooden sill, the intricate flowers withering into dust in an instant. Her hair spilled over her shoulder when she whipped her head my way. "What do you want?"

"Little Flower, you know exactly what I want."

What was wrong with me? Why was I pushing her buttons again? We were finally in a good place. I must have had a death wish.

"How did you know where I was?"

Was she kidding? She hadn't moved from that spot since breakfast.

"Even if I were blind, I'd know exactly where to find you."

"Smug ass."

She huffed and stood, then began pacing back and forth in front of the fireplace. Her book was still grasped in one hand, her finger tucked between the pages holding her spot.

"Can we not do this now?"

She was still pacing. It was cute how flustered she got. I had to hold back the smile that wanted to escape me.

"So we'll do *this* eventually?" I asked while motioning between us.

She stopped walking long enough to shoot me a death stare before she resumed wearing a path on the floor.

"Why didn't you go hunting with Nazneen?" I asked.

"She didn't want my help."

Her cheeks had turned dark with a blush as her blood pressure rose. Remembering the taste of her skin on my tongue made my cock stiffen painfully.

"You are the most stubborn female in the entire realm," I said. I leaned against the kitchen counter and crossed one ankle over the other. I braced my hands on the cold granite. "You know you want me. I can feel your affection for me like it's my own." I raised an eyebrow at her. "It's grown since the bond snapped into place. It's more than lust, and you know it. The yearning. The passion. It's deeply rooted in you."

"We can't be together, Garren!" she yelled, waving her book in the air. "We would literally tear each other to pieces."

"That sounds like something I can work with," I said with a shrug.

She shook her head. "No, Garren."

I stalked across the room to her. She didn't back away from me this time. She stood her ground, squared her shoulders, and planted her hands firmly on her hips—hand and book. I reached for her book and she surrendered it without a fight. I flipped it upside down on the chair, making sure to not lose her page.

"Don't! You'll break the spine," she fussed.

"Shh." I trailed my fingers along the delicate tribal mark, down her forehead and along the bridge of her nose, stopping at her plump bottom lip. Her lips parted the barest amount when she pulled in a shallow breath. Her blush deepened with my touch. I traced her cheekbone with the tip of my finger. Being this close was torture. Her scent overwhelmed my every sense. This close, the bond was pulled painfully tight in anticipation.

"You're shaking." I furrowed my brow. "Are you afraid of me?" I asked her. Her dark green eyes held mine.

"I ... I don't know," she whispered.

I smiled at her honesty. She was so brave. She'd always been so brave.

"I'd like to touch you again. Kiss you. I think you want that too."

She leaned into my touch, just the slightest. I swore her breath caught too. My body ached to hold her.

She cast her eyes down and weariness crossed her features. "Can't we be together without swapping powers?" She motioned between the two of us. "Like physically."

"I mean technically we can. I can touch you without using your power." I gripped her chin tightly and tipped it back up so I could look at her face. "But I don't just want pieces of you, Katuri. I want *all* of you. All your sass and attitude. All your gentleness and fierceness. I want it all. I want you to trust me enough to let me see every part of you, including your power." I studied her carefully. I was waiting for her to pull away. I may want her with every ounce of my being, but I refused to force anything on her. "Let me show you how much I want you, how good I can make you feel. Let me show you that I know you, know what you need."

"I won't submit to you. Or the bond."

I felt a pull on our bond; I felt her curl around her earth power guardedly. I let her. I let her pull away and I didn't pursue her. I just waited. I'd wait an eternity for her if that's what she needed. Her brows pinched together. I loved that wrinkled white mark. A question of why flowed back toward me. I projected patience back to her. She softened her grip on herself and I felt her relax a little. I wanted her to know she was safe with me. I'd always keep her safe.

"You submitted to me when I kissed you back in Kanevvluk. You even seemed to like me being a little rough with you."

I waited a second to see if she'd react. Would she pull away from me again? When she didn't, I twirled her thick, dark hair around my fist and gave a firm tug. Her chin snapped up, and a flash of hot eagerness swept down the tether, linking our souls.

"And when you ambushed me in my cabin during the crossing..."

"I didn't ambush you."

"You literally pounced on me, Kat, not that I'm complaining." I chuckled. "When you ambushed me in my cabin, you liked it when I bit into your soft skin."

I traced the spot where I'd sunk my teeth into her shoulder. She shivered under my touch. I brought my hand to her throat and wrapped my fingers around the elegant column. I gave her a gentle squeeze. Her lips parted, and her pulse spiked beneath my palm. I quirked an eyebrow at her.

"You seem to like this right now." My eyes dropped to my hand and then back up to her bold, emerald eyes. "There is no point in lying to me. Your body is giving you away. I bet you're soaked for me right now."

A beat of silence hung between us.

I smirked. "You know I'm right."

She rolled her eyes but didn't deny it. She couldn't deny it. Her eyes bounced back and forth between mine. So much was going through her mind—desire, uncertainty, fear.

"You're overthinking, aren't you?"

I felt her swallow beneath my grip. "It's impossible to think when I'm around you."

I applied pressure with my fingers, just the smallest amount, encouraging her to take a step backward. I guided her backward to my bedroom until the back of her knees hit the side of my bed.

I brought my face so close to hers. "Do you want me to show you?"

She sank her teeth into her full bottom lip and nodded. I wanted to trace the bow of her lips with my tongue. I knew what she was feeling—the desire, the longing, the heat between us. But the thing I loved the most in the moment was the trust, the smallest amount, she gave me.

"I need you to say it, Little Flower."

Green eyes gazed up at me. The flecks of sage and silver shown in the afternoon light.

"Yes." It was barely a puff of air.

"Yes, what?"

"Yes, please. Show me."

With her consent, the bond went from a single thread to millions of strings connecting every part of me to her. Powers Above, I'd never forget this moment—the moment Katuri gave herself over to me, and I'd only just begun.

I released her and grabbed the bottom of her shirt, untucking it from her pants and pulling it off over her head. A demure corset that laced up the back contained her full breasts. The swirls of her tribal marks started just above the edge of the lacey fabric and disappeared down between her breasts, only to peek out from the bottom of the garment above her navel. I gave her breasts a teasing squeeze. They heaved up and down with each breath. I couldn't tear my eyes off her. I loved how she looked. A lot. The elegant slope of her hips and her flat stomach. Strong muscles were hidden under all her clothes. I wished she hadn't hidden herself from me all these years. I grazed my hands down her waist. I wanted to imprint her into my mind.

"You're so soft, so beautiful." Her hips were full under my hands.

I hooked my fingers into her pants, and her breath hitched. With a gentle tug, I shimmied her pants down her legs, squatting down as I went so that I was kneeling on the floor at her feet, kneeling in front of my bondmate. She stepped out of her pants, and I tossed them to the side. A small scrap of fabric matching her corset covered her femininity.

"Open your legs, Little Flower," I commanded, tapping the inside of her knee.

She did as I asked, so obedient and willing. I bent and placed a soft kiss on the inside of the same knee. I trailed my nose up the inside of her thigh, placing small kisses as I went, before repeating the same gesture on the other side. I couldn't wait to bury my head between these gorgeous thighs. She arched her hips forward while I traced my fingers up her legs as I stood. A bead of sweat formed on my brow. I was aching to be inside her already. It took everything I had to hold back, but I wanted her to enjoy every moment. I'd take my time with her. After everything she'd been through, I wanted the absolute best for her.

"Don't worry. I'll start slow," I said.

I quickly pecked her lips before turning her around so her back was flush with my front. I saw the wondrous shock on her face when we were met by our reflection in the full-length mirror across the room.

I pressed my aching erection against her lower back. "Do you feel that? That's what you do to me." I brought my hand back to her throat. "You seemed to like this, so we will start here."

She nodded again. The curve of her body melded to me perfectly.

My other hand snaked around her waist and moved down the front of her body and between her legs, cupping her. She held impossibly still. I nuzzled into the side of her neck. I swirled my fingers over the thin fabric before pushing it to the side and dipping the tip of my finger into her slick, wet heat. She sucked in a sharp breath as I pushed further into her.

"Relax for me, Little Flower." And she did. "You behave so well when you have a hand wrapped around your pretty throat, don't you? That smart mouth of yours doesn't talk back when you're like this."

Her inner walls rippled around my fingers. A small whimper came from her as I alternated moving the tip of my finger in and out and swirling her dampness around her little bud.

"That's it, Little Flower," I whispered into her ear.

I curled my finger into her, and her hips involuntarily bucked against my hand, seeking friction, urging me deeper. I eased a second finger into her, and she let out a rasping gasp. I growled in response and tightened my grip on her throat. She was so responsive, so ready. Her reflection in the mirror was breathtaking. Her lush mouth parted when I pushed in further and hit that spot deep inside her. I smirked at the pleasure-filled shock on her face. Yes. *That's* what I wanted.

I pushed my fingers deeper until I met the resistance of her innocence. The fact that no one had ever been inside her made my desire to take her that much stronger. I wanted her to be mine. Needed her to be mine in every way.

"We need to take care of something," I said to her. "Is that okay?" I was already pushing her boundaries. I didn't want to take advantage of her.

"Yes." The word was a plea.

I withdrew my fingers from her, and she moaned in protest and shifted her hips, trying to find the contact I deprived her of. I moved my hand from her throat to the back of her head. I twisted her hair around my fist again. It was like silk running through my fingers. I tugged her head back against my chest. "After I take away this last barrier, I'm going to claim you as a bondmate should. I am going to make you mine."

"Please, Garren."

With my hand tight in her hair, I guided her down, folding her at the hips. "Elbows on the bed, Katuri."

She did as I asked, and as a reward, I circled my thumb against her clit from behind and dipped my fingers back inside her. Her back bowed in pleasure.

"Take a deep breath." I plunged my fingers deep, breaking past the final barrier and opening her up for me to take, to savor. She sucked in a sharp breath, and I felt her body go stiff. There was a sharp bite of pain through our bond, but I sensed no fear or regret.

"Shh," I cooed to her. I trailed kisses down her spine. "Are you okay?"

She nodded. "Yes. I think so. I think..."

Her groan of pleasure cut off her words as I twisted my wrist to hit her front wall. My thumb circled her clit again, and I slid my fingers from her and slipped back in. I moved slowly at first, setting a steady pace to allow her body to adjust to the newness. It didn't take long before her sex clenched around my fingers. I slowed my movements, and Katuri whined with impatience. I wanted her begging for release. I wanted her begging for my cock. I teased her, bringing her to the edge of pleasure and back. Over and over and over until she was a whimpering mess beneath me.

"Garren."

She was so stunning.

"Yes?"

"Please."

I pressed hard on her clit and thrust one final time. She came undone all over my hand. Shivers of pleasure coursed through her as she rode out the waves of her orgasm against my hand and I soaked it all in. She buried her face in the mattress between her arms to smother the sounds she was making.

I tugged her head back by her hair, and our eyes met in the mirror. "Never hide your sounds from me. I want to hear how good I make you feel."

I loved the feel of her, how she sounded. I loved our reflection in the mirror—Katuri bent over for me, her ass in the air, and panting from climax.

I removed my fingers from her and brought them to her lips.

"Open."

She didn't hesitate in obeying and opened her mouth without breaking my gaze. I pushed my fingers into her mouth, and she automatically sucked, tasting her own release and proof of her deflowering.

"Such a good fucking girl."

I lifted and turned her in my arms. She was boneless with pleasure. I gave her ass a light smack, and then a slight shove made her topple back onto the bed. Her corset strained to keep her breasts contained with her heavy breaths. Her hair splayed around her like a crown of ebony and scarlet. I pulled the scrap of fabric she called underwear down her legs and dropped them on the bed beside her head.

I pulled my shirt over my head and stripped off my pants. Her eyes went wide at the sight of my cock standing proud.

"Garren." Her voice was breathy.

She didn't take her eyes off my hardness. I loved watching her squirm under my watchful gaze. I gripped my cock and gave it a firm pump.

"I'm going to bury myself so deep inside you and make you beg me for more. And when I'm done, I promise you, Princess Katuri Harland of Leato Selva and the Forest Fae, you'll never second guess my intentions again."

FORTY-TWO
KATURI

"I'm going to bury myself so deep inside you and make you beg me for more. And when I'm done, I promise you, Princess Katuri Harland of Leato Selva and the Forest Fae, you'll never second guess my intentions again."

"Garren." My voice was breathy.

I was desperate to touch him. His chest was strong and smooth, showing off the sea dragon inked into his skin. His thighs were as thick as tree trunks and dusted with fine, blond hair. And Powers! He was thick and hard and all male. This was going to be interesting. I wasn't sure how he'd get his cock inside me, but I wanted him. Badly.

His voice was rougher than before. "Lace your fingers together. Hands above your head, Little Flower."

Garren guided my wrists up above my head and pinned them to the mattress. Then I felt something binding my wrists. I looked up to see Garren using my underwear to tie my hands to the headboard. I couldn't move. He had taken away my control. And fuck, I loved it. His power whispered to mine, like the gentleness of waves caressing my entire body. It promised gentleness and peace. I was safe with Garren. Always safe. But it also promised lust and trust and a thorough fucking.

"Is this okay?" he asked me.

I loved that even with him exerting his control over me, he was still checking in to make sure I felt safe.

My throat bobbed when I swallowed. "Yes."

"Good."

Garren knelt on the bed between my legs and pushed my knees apart. He ran his hard length through my wetness, and my breath hitched. Garren leaned back onto his heels and looked down at me. Then he reached forward, gripped the front of my corset, and ripped it clean in two. I was fully exposed to him now and completely at his mercy. He gripped my ankles, spreading my legs even wider. He looked ravenous. His pupils were blown wide, making the icy blue color disappear. He took a deep breath, his nostrils flaring. His gaze moved lower and lower and lower. A deep growl came from him as he moved closer. I could see the monstrous sea dragon stirring to life inside him. Sculpted, corded muscles shifted as he adjusted himself between my legs. My hips were restless, seeking his touch. His strong hands pressed my thighs open. My heart tripped as he bent and ran his tongue through my sensitive folds. A pleased sound escaped his mouth. My power climbed through my veins, reaching for him through the bond.

He paused when he sensed my earth magic lingering just outside his reach. I'd never let him this close to my power. And while I was offering it to him, the magic thrummed and swayed with the pleasure he was giving me.

He sucked and twirled his tongue. I writhed as Garren feasted on me. My back arched, and I pulled against the restraints which only made me more heated. I wanted my hands on him.

"You're Mine, Katuri."

"Yes," I panted.

"You'll never run from me again."

"Never."

Between Garren's commanding voice and the haze I still hadn't fully come down from after the first orgasm, I lit up like dry kindling. I was done. I toppled over the edge of the cliff in a glorious freefall, trusting Garren would catch me. I convulsed and shivered, my toes curling into the sheets. He pinned me down with a strong hand on my stomach while he drank every last drop of my release.

He lifted his head, and the sight of my wetness on his lips was so erotic. He licked his lips clean and then crawled up, blanketing my body with his. He reached up and untied my hands, and I instantly wrapped my arms around his neck. Finally, I was able to touch him, hold him.

I knew what would come next. There were no nerves. I only wanted him. Garren had made me orgasm twice in less than thirty minutes. I'd never been able to do that on my own. My self pleasure came nowhere close to how Garren had made me feel. Powers Above, if he made me feel like this every time, I'd obey every command he gave me for the rest of our lives.

"I know you've never done this before. I'll be gentle, Little Flower."

He placed a feather light kiss on my mouth. The tip of his erection pressed at my sensitive opening.

"What if I don't want gentle?"

His face turned wicked. Without warning, he steadily sunk into me, inch by glorious inch. I opened my thighs wide, welcoming him inside me.

"Fuck," I cried out when he'd fully seated himself inside me. His hips were flush to mine. "So. Full." I sunk my nails into the smooth skin of his back.

I'd never felt so right, so full. Garren looked down at me and pulled his bottom lip between his teeth.

"Fuck, Kat," he said as he buried his face against my shoulder.

I tilted my chin down so I could look at his face pressed to my skin. This beast of a male was panting like he'd just finished sparring with a mountain cat. *I* was doing that to him. *I* made him breathless. "I thought that's what we were doing."

I clenched around him, and I felt a rumble deep in his chest. He began to move. Thrust after thrust, pinning me to the bed with his body. Just before I reached the peak, he pulled out of me. I suddenly felt so empty.

"Garren!" I begged shamelessly.

He grabbed hold of each of my ankles and effortlessly flipped me to my stomach. He pulled my hips and ass into the air.

"I want to watch this ass while I claim you from behind."

A sharp smack of his palm landed on my ass. Then his mouth covered the sting with a soft kiss. I was surprised by the fire that ignited within me. Garren entered me again. He was so deep in this new position. He gripped my hips hard and slammed into me. Again and again. I slid up the bed with each delicious thrust. I pushed up onto my hands to watch him in the mirror. His powerful body towered over mine. Then he reached around and pinched my clit. I came all over again. I didn't think that was possible. Three times—and this one more intense than the last. He followed right behind me. The dominant part disappeared, and his pleasure ripped through him. Watching him, I realized he may be the one in control, but I had the power to make him fall apart. He shivered as he came down from his high. Garren, my bondmate, was perfect in every way.

I was drunk on that power. He rolled off me and onto his side, pulling me with him so we were facing each other. He draped my leg over his hips and wedged his thigh between mine. His hands roamed all over my body, every inch he could touch to maintain contact. And where he touched, my power followed to greet him, just below the surface of my skin. I wasn't quite ready to give up that last part of me. Not yet. But maybe, one day soon.

I closed my eyes and relaxed into the comfortable pillows, tracing the scales of his sea dragon.

Garren leaned forward and whispered against my lips, "How are you, Little Flower?"

"Hmm," I hummed with contentment.

Then I bit down on his bottom lip.

He hissed and pulled back. I cracked open one eye and grinned a wicked grin. I squealed when he swatted my ass in return.

"Vicious creature."

I snapped my teeth at him again. A strand of wild hair fell across my face, and so gently, he lifted it and combed it back.

I'd read about sex. Nazneen had even given me quite detailed descriptions of her encounters as well. But this, what Garren and I had just done, this was more than sex. This was more than physical pleasure. It was a trust. It was the most vulnerable I'd ever been.

Fuck.

Doubt slammed back into me with a force so staggering, if I'd been standing, it would have knocked me over. Had I given in to Garren just because of his sweet words and soft caresses? My grin dropped, and I started to pull away from him.

"Kat..."

I sat up and pulled the sheet over my nakedness. I was a little girl again, standing in the blood binding circle, and suffocating darkness was swallowing me up.

Garren propped himself up on an elbow and tugged gently on a strand of my hair. "Do you want me to say it again? I want you. I need you."

"I can't have someone else controlling my life *or* my future." I couldn't look at him. I couldn't see anything. I couldn't breathe. I couldn't swallow.

"Powers, Kat." He sat up quickly and was kneeling in front of me, his hands gently touching my thighs. He pressed his forehead to mine. "I don't want to control you. I want to see you grow and thrive. The only place I want you to submit to me is here in this bed, and that's only when you want to." He cupped his palms to my cheeks and looked deep into my eyes. "You think you can keep yourself detached from this bond, keep me at an arm's distance, but you can't."

I'd let Garren take me today. And Powers, did he. He held me down. He was rough. He turned pain into eye rolling pleasure. I allowed him to dominate me. And I'd never felt so free. I wasn't afraid of Garren; I was afraid of how willing I was to give him everything. He'd ravished me, and I was helpless to him, but I was also safe. So safe. I trusted Garren, and that trust was the ultimate control of myself and my future. I was empowered.

"You assume I just want you as a bondmate, something to claim and to follow the rules suit me. But what I really want is a queen, someone I can bow down to." He dragged the tip of his nose across my jaw. "This bond isn't a leash or a cage. The choice of a blood binding was stolen from you, and I wish I could change that, but I can't. But, this, who we are, what we become, is a choice we get to make together. Little Flower, I want nothing more than to praise the ground you walk on."

I could hear my heart thumping heavily inside my chest. I knew he could hear it too. I was about to start crying. Was it really this easy? Just say yes, and the bond I'd been rejecting, my life with Garren, would fall into place? Garren closed the short distance between us and kissed me. It wasn't rough like before. It was passion and gentleness combined. When he pulled back, he dragged my lower lip with him. I wanted this. I wanted him. My body relaxed into him. He gave me one more soft kiss and then pulled me down onto the bed into his embrace.

I finally relaxed and settled into him. I hadn't realized the sun had slipped away. Time didn't matter when I was in Garren's arms. Post-sex languish and the sound of Garren's heartbeat lulled me to sleep.

Soft light filtered in the window, and I could hear voices in the kitchen. I was sore. Sore from Garren. Sore from him filling and stretching me in the most glorious ways. Flashes of the previous night came to mind. My hands tangled in Garren's hair. His fingers biting into my skin. His teeth on my neck. His mouth on my...

Okay! I needed to stop this train of thought, or I wouldn't be leaving this bed. My stomach grumbled with hunger.

Garren was still asleep next to me. His scent clung to my skin. For the first time in my life, I had woken up with someone who wasn't Nazneen beside me in bed. I eased out from under the heavy weight of his arm and found my discarded clothes. I held them to my chest as I turned around and watched Garren's deep, steady breathing. I tiptoed to the washroom to wash my face and dress. Then I slipped quietly from the room.

I kept my eyes on my sleeping bondmate as I cracked the door open, slipped through the opening, and pulled the door closed as quietly as possible.

"So it wasn't good?"

I froze. Shit, I'd been caught. I gradually turned to face my accuser. Guilt was written all over me. Nazneen was scrambling eggs at the stove while Evren sat on a stool at the bar, sipping tea. Delrik was nowhere to be seen. Thank the Powers Above. At least he wasn't witnessing my shame.

"What?"

Nazneen swirled a spoon in the air in my general direction. "Well, you're able to walk this morning. That means it either wasn't good sex or he took it easy on you."

"It didn't sound like it *wasn't* good," Evren said.

My head snapped in her direction, eyes wide.

She shrugged. "What? The walls are thin."

"So tell me"—Nazneen leaned her elbows on the counter and waggled her eyebrows—"is he proportionate?"

Again, I was confused.

"Come on! Spill! I've seen his hands. He *is* quite talented with a sword."

I took an elastic band from my wrist and piled my hair on top of my head in a messy knot. I leaned over the counter and swiped a piece of fruit from Evren's plate.

The door to the bedroom suddenly opened, and a shirtless Garren appeared. Loose pants hung low on his hips, showing the impressive display of his sea dragon tattoo and muscled v of his stomach. When he walked by me, he traced a hand up the nape of my neck and gave my messy bun a tug. He went to the sink to fill a glass with water. I turned to look at Garren. Evren's cup froze halfway to her mouth, and Nazneen had a smile stretched across her face. Garren's bare back was streaked with fingernail marks. My fingernail marks. Starting at his shoulders and running down below the band of his pants. Fuck. I'd never hear the end of this from Nazneen.

"It appears that last night *was* good after all," Nazneen whispered to Evren and me.

Garren turned and propped a hip on the counter. His eyes stayed glued to me as he swallowed down the water. When he was finished, he wiped his mouth with the back of his hand and set the glass on the counter. Then he stalked toward me. My eyes jumped from him to Nazneen and Evren, who were sitting open-mouthed at the bar, watching us.

He stopped inches from me, almost nose to nose. The bond sang in my heart.

He brought his hand to my throat and said, "Tell them, Little Flower. Tell them how good it was." His tongue swept across my lips. "And yes, Nazneen. I am proportionate." He winked at me and then disappeared into the bedroom again.

"Oooookay," Evren said, dragging out the word. "Whatever that was, I'll take a dose of that, please."

FORTY-THREE
DELRIK

"Now that we know your powers are similar to the goddess of spirits, maybe we can tap into something new with the shadows," Nyla said.

I was skeptical. Tapping deeper into the shadows didn't seem like the smartest idea to me.

"The one who guards the eternal resting ground of Evermere has the power to give life and take it away," she explained.

"I already know it can end life," I said. "I almost lost my life to the shadows."

Ever since I'd learned where my power originated from, I'd been in a sour mood. My nightmares had become worse, and I'd been hearing that voice in my head multiple times a day. Both were steadily increasing, as was my bondmate's worry. I was finding it harder to keep my boundaries up from Evren and our bond.

We were sitting in the garden outside the temple again. Nyla set a potted plant in front of me. The sapling was only about a year old, with skinny limbs and sparse leaves.

"I want you to try to use your power to give life to the tree. See if you can make it grow."

"This is more up Katuri's alley."

"Yes. We know Katuri could make this apple tree grow and provide fruit to the whole city without lifting her finger. I want to see *you* try."

I pressed my mouth into a firm line and focused my attention on the tree. The shadows rippled down my arm and toward my fingers. A small node of new growth formed on one of the branches. It grew and grew. A leaf. And then another. When a flower bud began to grow, my shoulders began to relax. The flower opened; inky darkness dripped from its petals like a disease and consumed first the branch and then the sapling entirely.

"See. Master of Death and Darkness at your service." I bowed.

I knew she didn't appreciate my sarcasm, but I couldn't help it.

"You're holding back. Your fear of tapping too deep into the shadows is preventing you from using every aspect of the magic." She smiled at me. "Remember, darkness doesn't necessarily mean wicked. It is simply the opposite of light. We cannot have one without the other."

"How do you know that I'm not sacrificing my sanity? If I go deep, I may never return."

"Aluxyeras's power was inherently good. It's masked by the betrayal. I believe if you get past all that, you'll see the true potential of her magic."

"It's too strong. This is a god's power. It's not meant for a Fae. You saw me almost lose control the other day. You want me to tap into *that*?"

Nyla replaced the pot with another. "Try again."

That time, the blackened disease overflowed the pot and seeped into the ground. Katuri had to come and revive the garden.

I stepped back and laced my fingers behind my head. "I can't do this."

I can't do this. I can't just give in to the power.

"Yes. Yes, you can. Let me help you."

As if someone had pulled a hood over me, darkness shrouded my vision and I felt my face go slack. It was like my nightmares were coming to life right before my eyes. Had I been dreaming?

Wake up. Wake up. Wake up.

"No. No." I shook my head. "No, I'm not." My voice was full of terror, and my face had drained of all color. The voice had never been this clear before.

I heard Nyla tell Katuri. "Go get Evren. Hurry."

Katuri didn't question her as she ran for the cottage.

"Delrik?" Nyla asked timidly.

I didn't respond to her. Nyla reached a hand out to touch me, but I yanked back like she had burned me. I didn't know what would happen if she touched me. I didn't trust that I wouldn't lash out at her. I focused hard on remaining in control. I couldn't let the voice lull me into submission.

"No. Stay away. I won't come to you."

Evren appeared at Nyla's side along with Garren and Katuri. Even Arik appeared from the temple. He must've heard the commotion. I could barely see them through the dense fog of my mind.

"You aren't wanted here," Evren snarled at Arik.

She literally snapped her teeth at him, and fire sparked at her fingertips. Arik stopped mid-stride at the protectiveness.

"I just want to help," he replied, but Evren had already turned back her focus on me.

"I think he's hearing the voices again," Nyla explained to Evren. "We were working with his powers and then he just went blank."

"Delrik." Evren didn't hesitate to approach me. She placed her hands on my chest, but I flinched away from her. "Delrik, the voice isn't real. Don't listen to it."

"Evren," I said through gritted teeth.

I felt like I was splitting in two. Half of me was fighting against the bond and protecting Evren. The other half was losing the battle to give in to the haunting voice.

"You will never be strong enough to control the shadows." The voice was sharp talons scraping across my mind. "Not without my guidance."

The next time I heard the voice, it was no longer inside my head. It echoed all around us. I squatted and curled over my legs, gripping my head tight. My fingers dug deep into my hair.

"Come to me, and I will show you the way. Come to me, and I will take the darkness away."

"No, no. I won't. You aren't real."

Evren was crouched near me. Her arms were wrapped around me.

"Give in, Delrik. Give in to the darkness."

Evren gripped my wrists, and I screamed, shoving her away.

"Come to me now, Delrik Valhar, Master of Death and Darkness."

The voice turned commanding. Angry. Then, coming out of thin air, a shape appeared, but it was shapeless at the same time. A split in the world that opened wider and wider. The shape wasn't one of my shadows. I'd grown to recognize my shadows. This was something different. This was something not of this realm.

The otherness. This was what Nyla had seen around me. It formed the shape of a hand and drew my face from my hands.

"Come to me."

Nyla tried to use her air power to push the shapeless form back, to split it, but it whipped around and hissed at her, unaffected. Garren formed a sword of ice and slashed through the shape, but it only regenerated before our very eyes. Except this time, the otherness lashed out at them. Arik threw up a shield just in time, separating me and the shape from the rest of them. The shape crashed against the shield with another hiss. I hadn't seen Arik in days, but I was thankful for his presence now. He was the only thing protecting Evren from this darkness, from me. Evren tried to send fire at the shape, but it bounced back at us thanks to Arik's shield.

"Take down your shield. I have to get to him!" Evren screamed at Arik. I could barely hear her over the roaring of my blood in my ears and the maniacal laughter from the otherness.

"Are you crazy? It will kill us," Arik said as he strained against the otherness.

"Arik! Take your shield down."

"Don't, Arik," I strained. I clenched my eyes closed against the otherness. It was invading every part of me now. "Keep her safe."

"I will," Arik said, ignoring Evren. She was clawing at his arms, leaving streaks of blood in her wake.

Evren pressed her hands against the invisible shield and released her fire into it. Arik screamed as she burned away the only thing between the shapeless form and them. A wall of sparks and ash burst through the air with a loud crack. Arik flew to the ground, holding his stomach as if the fire had burned him from the inside.

Suddenly, everything went quiet. The only things I could hear were the ragged breaths coming from us all. The air cleared, and the sun streaked through the ash that was slowly floating to the ground. Then, the split pulled and stretched, parting the realm and creating an opening.

"What in the circle of dark hells?" Garren said. He pulled Katuri away from the opening.

"Come to me."

The voice spoke again, but this time I knew who it belonged to. A High Fae female with a slight frame stepped up to the threshold of the opening. She had a cruel tilt to her lips, and her eyes—they were ice blue, surrounded by a black circle. A circlet of steel rested on her head with a stone centered on her forehead. I'd seen her before. Briefly during my time during the war. She was Hadeon's bondmate, the seer, Elenora Allerick. Three dark shapes flanked her lithe frame. They all stepped through the tear and encircled me. The longer I looked at the shadowy figures, the clearer they became. They had pointed ears similar to a Fae, but they were elongated so much that they drooped. Their forked tongues darted out from their snouts.

"Come to me now, Delrik." She spoke, and I obeyed the command.

I wasn't in control of my body or my mind. I was stuck within a deep trance. I stood, then went to Elenora. Elenora gave me a deceptive smile and offered her hand to me. I took it and followed her through the tear. Evren tried to come for me, but Arik grabbed her around the waist.

"Delrik!" she screamed.

Evren rammed her knee into Arik's groin and leapt for me, but Nazneen was able to grab her before she could walk through the opening after me. My gaze was transfixed on the seer, unaware of Evren's panicked cries behind me.

"Thank you for your assistance, Arik Hanover," Elenora said over her shoulder.

Then the opening closed behind us, and they were gone. Evren was gone.

KATURI

We all stood frozen in the garden, not sure if what we'd seen had really happened. Nazneen released Evren from her grip. What had just happened? Had I really just watched the shadows come to life and beckon Delrik into the unknown? Garren still had a firm grip on me from behind. I could tell he wasn't holding on to me for my own protection anymore. He was using me to steady himself. His best friend had just disappeared.

Evren turned with a deathly slowness. Her primal fury made the earth tremble beneath our feet. Evren's eyes blazed molten, and fire spit from her hands. Flames of the god of fire. Blood dripped from her nose. I could feel the heat coming off of her like an inferno ready to explode at any moment. For a moment, I doubted whether Arik would live to see the next morning.

"I didn't do anything," Arik said, stumbling backward, his arms raised in front of him. I saw Arik's shield ripple into place between them.

"You did this! You told them where we were. You told them we were looking for Hadeon. You told them Garren was expendable. Find a way to get him back." Her voice echoed off the walls of the surrounding cottages shaking the ground.

"I..."

"Get. Him. Back." She released a feral scream, enunciating each word. Then her voice dropped to almost a whisper. "Or you will regret ever stepping back into Illoterra." Embers danced in her eyes.

Then she swung. Evren's fist burst through Arik's shield as if it were nothing more than a piece of paper. Arik's jaw made a loud crack when Evren's fist made contact. His lip split on the Ring of Teris that was glowing as bright on her fist. Small burn marks marred his flawless skin from the embers Evren was putting off.

"Fuck!" Arik cursed as he clutched his chin in his hands, blood seeping through his fingers.

Evren didn't seem to care that her knuckles had busted open and were dripping blood too. As the ethereal power rushed through her bloodstream, I watched the wounds heal within seconds. "You have ten seconds to leave, or I will hit you again, and this time, I won't hold back." Her fist became a ball of deep red and white flame. I had to shield my eyes against the almost blinding light emanating from her. The scent of ash and smoke filled the garden.

"You need to go," Garren said.

Evren reared back her fist for a second blow, but Arik ran from the garden before she could swing. Evren sagged against the wall and sucked in a shaky breath. Anticipation hung in the air. With each breath, the light from the ring lessened and the flames receded.

"He deserved that," Garren stated. He was trying to de-escalate the situation with his usual humor.

"He deserves much worse," Nazneen said. Her voice dripped with disdain.

"What if we never find him?" She gasped, struggling to get in air. The weight of Delrik's disappearance crashed into her. Her body caved in, and she began to convulse with sobs.

PART FOUR

FORTY-FOUR
DELRIK

Noirdan

I awoke with a start, squinting into the murky gloom surrounding me. I blinked a few times, but the darkness didn't fade. The floor beneath me was cold and it smelled like death and sulfur. The air was thick and stagnant. My head pulsed with pain, and I tried to bring my hands to my head to rub away the ache, but my wrists were shackled. Iron shackles. They were siphoning my power. A drip, drip, drop echoed off the walls. The repetition grated on my nerves.

All of a sudden, something moved nearby, a shuffling and a low hiss. Although I couldn't see what was lurking in the darkness, I could sense its presence. The back of my neck prickled like someone was watching me. I flinched as the light from a bright torch suddenly lit the dank space.

"Welcome, Lord Valhar. It's good to see you're awake."

A male stepped into the circle of pallid, yellow light. The shallow light cast shadows on the harsh planes of his face. I'd never seen this male before. Or had I? He seemed familiar. And he knew my name. His broad shoulders blocked the doorway. But his eyes—they drew my attention. Black circles surrounded his irises. I'd seen it before but couldn't remember where. If I had to guess, Hadeon Allerick was standing before me. Hadeon's voice dripped like overly sweet honey. I'd been lucky enough to have stayed far from him during the war.

"Ashewood, why don't you make our guest more comfortable," Hadeon said.

Renwick Ashewood stepped around Hadeon, and a sly smile painted his disgusting face. Bastard. I had watched Evren stab him in the back, and yet, somehow, the prick managed to stay alive and create even more havoc than before. Renwick moved toward me and unlocked the iron from around my wrists. I wanted to smash his face into the ground, but I remained seated, knowing I was outnumbered with my powers so depleted. My whole body felt drained.

"I'm sorry my companion left you down here. That was quite rude, Ashewood. Come, Lord Valhar."

Hadeon withdrew a piece of cloth from his pocket and wiped his hands clean as if just being in the dungeon was making him dirty. Hadeon turned on his heels and left the holding cell. Renwick shot me a wink before trailing after his new master, like an obedient dog. The problem with a dog like Renwick was he'd bite as soon as you stopped feeding him.

I stood on trembling legs and followed after them. We walked through a maze of dungeons and torture chambers. I would've never found my way out of this labyrinth if I managed to escape. Fiends, prisoners, and more filled the numerous cells. Some hung on the walls, iron nails driven through their arms or wings. Others were just heaps of flesh on the floor, barely breathing, but being kept alive by healers garbed in blood red robes. I covered my nose and mouth with the crook of my elbow to stop the stench from overwhelming me. It did little to abate the rot. Even during the war, I hadn't witnessed such atrocities.

One winged Fae was splayed against the wall. Iron nails pierced each joint of his wings. Blood dripped in that repetitive drip. Infection veined out from the wounds. The putrid smell assaulted my senses. He groaned when Renwick twisted one of the nails as we walked by him.

I was led from the darkness to a sprawling home built above the prison below. Guards opened a set of doors to a dining room.

When I entered the room, the doors were firmly closed behind me. I was trapped in here with two of the most vile males that walked this realm. The dining hall was ostentatiously decorated with things more rare and expensive than anything I'd seen in Rivamir. Even the house was enormous. Noirdan, from what I could see out the floor-to-ceiling windows that spanned the entire back wall, was a wasteland, just like Menrath had been after the war. The ground was black and cracked. It looked like an explosion had gone off and destroyed everything in its radius. Nothing survived. No trees or plants, no homes or wells. Only the skeletal remains of a long-lost city, and in the middle of it all stood Hadeon's home.

Hadeon Allerick seated himself at the head of an enormous table. His muddy boots made a thud when he propped them on the corner. He swirled a goblet of what was most likely Fae wine.

I moved further into the room, bypassing the guards without making eye contact, and sat at Hadeon's right. A young girl rushed to fill a goblet with wine while another brought a fresh, steaming plate of food to place on the table. A slave brand was imprinted on each of their wrists. I eyed each female with empathy. I had no inclination of Hadeon treating the slaves as anything more than things to be used and tossed when through. However, the smell of the food before me pulled my attention away from them. My stomach growled. I was basically drooling at the sight of steam. I wasn't sure how long I'd been unconscious, but I was famished.

Renwick took the seat at the opposite end of the table from Hadeon. Beside Hadeon sat a female High Fae.

Hadeon introduced the female. "Lord Valhar, this is my bondmate, Elenora."

Elenora sat still as a statue, her delicate hands resting on the table, staring blankly ahead. Goosebumps covered my skin at the sight of her. I'd only been in her presence for a few moments, and I already knew she was not someone I'd want to cross paths with. A golden band was embedded into her skin. It wrapped around her left wrist and up her forearm, matching exactly with the one on Hadeon's right arm. A binding mark. I knew for a fact Hadeon would never offer his magic to anyone, so I found it interesting that he'd go through with the blood binding ritual.

Her mystic eyes snapped to my face as if she could hear every thought in my head, and the corner of her mouth twitched. I was still standing, leaning heavily on the chair.

"Lord Delrik Valhar." A voice so sinister and yet, disturbingly sweet. "It's lovely to finally meet you."

Why did I recognize her? She was so familiar. Her skin was pale like she never spent time outdoors. Soft blond hair moved on an invisible breeze at her shoulders, and her pointed ears peeked through the almost translucent strands.

Everything was still a fog in my brain. "Do I know you?" I asked

"No, but I know you."

That voice. I knew that voice. It was the voice that had been whispering to me. The voice that had plagued my nightmares. Elenora stiffened, and her icy eyes went lifeless, the same paleness as Nyla. The scouts had mentioned she was a seer. Great. Escaping just became a lot more difficult.

A circlet of steel rested on her head, an amplifying stone centered on her forehead. Amplifying stones were common among healers and seers, but I'd never seen one like the glimmering stone Elenora possessed. Elenora's eyes were the lightest shade of powder blue, almost white. A black ring encircled her irises. The same as Hadeon and Renwick, the same as Cadoc Byrnes. I couldn't tear my eyes away from those hypnotizing azul depths.

"I know it's strange, but you get used to it." I looked to Hadeon in question. He circled his face with his finger. "The black rings. A side effect of being exposed to and using dark magic. So, how did it happen?" Hadeon's face was lit with enthusiasm.

"How did what happen?" I asked him.

"How did my sweet bondmate convince you to come visit me?"

"I'll show you." Elenora flipped her hand palm up.

Hadeon reached over and laced his gilded fingers with hers. Their binding mark glowed softly when their hands linked. The willowy creature jerked when his fingers made contact with her skin. Then his eyes went white and blank, just like Elenora's. She was showing him her vision, feeding it directly into his mind. Her provocative lips danced with a smile. His face was thoughtful, watching the scene of my kidnapping play out.

I knew exactly what he was seeing. Me submitting to her voice in my head. Evren screaming after me. A smile twisted Hadeon's mouth and then he barked out a harsh laugh, releasing Elenora. In an instant, his eyes returned to normal.

"I love how the fire bitch begged for you." He laughed, clapping his hands together loudly. He took a swig of wine and wiped his mouth with the back of his hand.

"Why am I here?" I asked.

Hadeon gestured to the table and heaps of food before us. "Let's eat and then we can chat."

A fiend crept from the shadows and shoved me down into a chair. The beast made a clicking noise deep in its throat. Another fiend across the room responded in kind. They were communicating. My eyes darted around the spacious room to assess how many fiends were there.

"I heard a funny rumor," Hadeon stated as he sat down in his seat.

"Oh?" I had a feeling there was nothing he could say that would make me laugh.

Hadeon dropped his feet to the floor with a loud stomp. "I went to visit an old friend a little while ago. And she told me that someone had stolen her powers."

He couldn't be talking about Alux? An old friend? He was insane.

Hadeon had been the one to give Cadoc the Ring of Teris all those years ago when they believed they could harness the fire curse and use it to their advantage. Little did Cadoc know what he thought was a cursed bloodline was actually a gift given by the gods. The ring of ruby that had the ability to steal the power of an attacker and contain it to be wielded by the wearer. And now, Evren had run off with it. She'd taken it right off Cadoc's finger. "Not only is the Ring of Teris now missing, the fire elemental slipped through my fingers. I want them back. *Both* of them," he hissed. "After Ashewood saw you in Rivamir and saw your new powers, I grew ... curious."

"Why are you doing this?"

"I need an elemental power. Your bondmate was the closest one to obtain. But it seems you've brought my attention to three more. So many powers to choose from."

Somehow he didn't know that Alux's powers were actually that of the goddess of spirits. She must have kept that little detail from her dear "friend."

Hadeon stood from his chair and went to stand behind his bondmate. He traced the circlet on her forehead. He watched me carefully. "My love has impressive magic, doesn't she? She is a seer and so much more." Elenora tipped her chin up to gaze at him. "See, I stumbled upon this stone while I was mining iron out of the Lendorr mines. At first, I didn't realize its true power. I believed it was simply an amplifying stone. It looks lovely on her, doesn't it, Delrik? Her power has grown strong, and her visions have been more accurate. She was actually the one to figure out that the amulet is actually one of the four relics." He eyed his bondmate fondly.

So he also didn't know about the fifth relic.

"Even without her magnified gifts, it was like she could see the very essence of your soul. The amplifying stone allowed her to not only receive visions, but share them with others and, with a simple touch of her hand, delve into someone's mind to see thoughts and memories. She has developed a talent with dark magic, specifically curses."

He picked up a small iron knife that had been sitting beside Elenora's plate. He spun it on its point. I could smell the iron burning into his fingertips, but he didn't drop it. Then he reached down and withdrew a pendant from beneath her bodice. "With a single drop of blood, she can cast a curse that is worse than death. Unfortunately, when Ashewood brought me a dagger with your fire bondmate's blood, it wasn't actually her blood. It was yours. At first, I was upset, but I quickly realized the best way to draw Evren to me was to use you."

His hand darted out and grabbed hold of my wrist. With the iron knife, he pricked my finger. Blood welled at the tip. I watched as Elenora used a dark spell to call to the blood on the blade. It liquified and levitated in the air. She lifted the chain of the necklace over her head and placed it on the table beside the knife. A glass cylinder no larger than a quail's egg was surrounded by delicate gold and black gemstones. Metal was twisted like chains around it. Creatures from the circle of dark hells held the orb in their claws. Elenora twisted the top, and the cylinder opened. The blood drifted into the reliquary, and she snapped it closed again. She continued her incantations. The more she spoke, the darker the ring around her irises got, swallowing up the pale blue. The reliquary began to glow green. Elenora began making sweeping gestures with her hands around the reliquary and manifestations. Transparent manifestations of the demonic creatures appeared and grew. The creatures shifted and took on more form: pointed ears, long snouts, and forked tongues. They were no bigger than my hand. They hissed and spat, but their eyes were focused on their master—on Elenora. They swam through the air. An apparition appeared between them. As if a mirror was floating in the air, my face came into view. Elenora shook with exhilaration from the wicked magic.

I turned to Elenora. "You. It's been your voice taunting me."

"What can I say? I just wanted to have a little bit of fun."

"The manifestations brought you right to me. And you will bring Evren into my waiting hands." Hadeon's lips twisted into a wicked smile.

With a clap of Elenora's hands, the apparition and shadow creatures disappeared, and all that remained was the necklace, glowing faintly with green light. She placed the necklace back around her neck and tucked it safely against her chest.

He walked around the table and took a seat next to me. When Hadeon leaned in closer to speak again, my fist flew out, faster than average, but still slow for me, landing a punch to his mouth. Hadeon's head snapped back. Elenora jumped to her feet in a rage, but Hadeon rose a hand.

"It's alright, my love." He licked the blood from his teeth. "We only get power by taking it, Delrik," Hadeon said. The smile on his face would forever haunt my memories. "And I will take the power from your firebird, and I will use it to end this world."

Elenora began to laugh with glee. "I can feel his pain. I can taste it."

She was psychotic. And so was he.

Hadeon poured some Fae wine into two glasses for himself and me. "How can I sway you to our side? It would make it easier for your bondmate."

"You have nothing to offer me," I said with disgust.

"Alux's power would be useful to me," he said more to himself than me.

"*My* power. The shadows belong to me now."

"Let me try to persuade him," Elenora purred. She wiggled her fingers in my direction.

"Do not touch me," I sneered.

"She'll be gentle," Hadeon said to me. "She just wants to take a look inside that head of yours. Maybe you're hiding something that would benefit our cause."

Elenora glided on air, her silk skirts whispering across the polished marble floors, to come to my side. The glass pendant swung around her neck with each step. The fiend that had been standing over me the whole time gripped my shoulders forcefully, holding me in place.

"Don't you touch me, you bitch," I spat.

I didn't see Hadeon's fist coming. He hit me in the jaw. Then he punched me again. My teeth rattled inside my skull. Hadeon wiped his bloody knuckles on his dinner napkin. Blood filled my mouth. I spit a clot of mucus and blood onto the floor at Elenora's feet. Droplets splattered the bottom of the fine fabric.

"You will help me. You have no choice." Hadeon's expression hardened.

From the shadows, tucked in the corner, a low keening sound scraped across my senses. Hadeon's monstrous creations. Fiends. The sound the monsters made to communicate with each other was a warning to me of the horror that Hadeon had control of. I turned from my chair to make my escape, but I was struck by Hadeon's power. Like a hood was pulled over my head, everything went dark and my body froze. Hadeon had taken away my sight. Not only blinded me, but removed the sense completely. It was like being suspended in space. My body and mind were disoriented with the loss. My entire equilibrium was thrown off, and my heart rate spiked with fear. My hands flung out to catch myself even though I wasn't falling. Claws gripped my shoulder from behind and pushed me back into my seat. The rasping breath was so close along with a light clicking sound. Too close.

I tried to pull away, but the fiend's claws pierced my skin, through my jacket, into my shoulder. I could feel the warm blood leaking from its hold.

With a cold, cruel smile that twisted his too handsome face, he struck out with his power. I was suddenly swallowed by emptiness. No sound. No sight. No smell. Nothing. I was surrounded by absolutely nothing. Only Hadeon's voice. The darkness shifted, and soon all I could see was him before me. His unnerving timbre echoed off the wall he was forming around me. His ability to block all senses of his victims made them completely incapacitated.

"I will keep you here until you give in. I can be patient. We have plenty of time. I'll break you eventually." I felt a delicate finger trace my bottom lip, and I jerked my head away. "My bondmate is more powerful than you know," he said.

With a snap of his fingers, the wall cutting me off from the world was gone. I gasped as all my senses rushed back at me in a flood.

Hadeon spun a ring on his pointer finger. The stone matched the one on Elenora's head exactly—another amplifying stone? Two fiends grabbed my arms and dragged me back to the depths of the dungeons. I couldn't keep my eyes open. They were so heavy. My limbs were leaden. I drifted away into nothingness. But I knew I wasn't lucky enough to be dead.

FORTY-FIVE
DELRIK

A cry of agony pierced the air, jolting me awake. Except the cry wasn't coming from the dank dungeon—it was from within me. Deep inside my soul, I could hear her. My Evren, my Ashlyra. She was reaching out for me. My brave bondmate was searching for me.

With what little strength I had, I attempted to slide a shield between us. Each time I failed and let the shield slip, Evren's agony sliced me sharper than any whip. I couldn't bear her suffering alongside me. The fiends guarding the dungeon had snapped a pair of iron anklets on me while I'd been unconscious. My face was battered, unhealed because of the iron. I fisted my hands to bring the feeling back to them. My whole body was sore and numb. I knew it was only a matter of time before Hadeon would return. I rubbed my swollen jaw, probably bruised purple from the strikes Hadeon had so generously gifted me already. I knew it was just the beginning. A dull ache pinched behind my eyes, and the stagnant air that reeked of decay only made it worsen.

The sound of metal on metal signaled someone joining me in my cell.

"I will not help you." My frail voice whispered into the emptiness.

Hadeon's face, full of mockery, came into view. "Well, your current situation and weakened powers mean your threats are ... well, they are comical."

I did my best to match the grin on his face, but my face was too swollen. The movement split my lip open again, and blood trickled from the corner of my mouth.

"You know, I prefer to do the torturing myself. It's more fun than just watching." He spoke to someone over his shoulder. "Bring him to my room."

Two guards unlocked my chains and dragged my exhausted body from my cell to an open room. The guards threw me into the middle of the room. My head cracked off the stone floor, and I let out a groan of pain. This was not going to be fun. They linked my shackles to short chains that were embedded in the stone floor. I couldn't fight off a butterfly right now even if I tried. Windows sat high along the wall, and stale light seeped in. Even the sun didn't want to shine in this hell hole.

"You know, I can be reasonable, despite what people say about me." Hadeon stepped into the room as the guards left.

Hadeon was almost as theatrical with his bloodlust as Cadoc had been. Sudden pain lanced through my right thigh. A serrated blade hit bone before Hadeon dragged it out and shredded flesh with it. Dark hells. If I had managed to eat anything at the meal earlier, it would have made a reappearance.

"I offered you a chance, but you seemed uninterested." Hadeon twisted the blade, and a scream was ripped from my throat.

Perspiration dripped from my face as I gasped for air. My blood poured from the wound and coated the stone floor.

From the corner, a brazier roared to life. Renwick stood beside it, heating something in its fires. An iron poker. He handed it to Hadeon with a smirk. Before I could comprehend what was happening, pain exploded in my stomach, searing me from the inside out. Unimaginable pain made thinking impossible. Again, the heated iron lanced through my hands and then my foot. My vision went black when I lost consciousness. Unfortunately, I came to sputtering on the pungent smell of something being wafted in front of my nose.

"I can't have you passing out. You're taking away all my fun," Hadeon cooed at me.

My vision returned. Hadeon was inches from my face, holding the serrated blade. He sliced my skin. Hadeon's power removed my vision. I only sensed what he wanted me to, and he was skilled in using it to torture. I smelled my burnt flesh before I felt the pain. The heated iron against my chest burned more than acid. Was this what Evren's fire felt like to others? Renwick withdrew the poker; my charred skin stuck to the surface, peeling away from my body.

Hadeon bent down close to my face. "Don't fret, Delrik. My healer, Jae, will prevent you from dying on me. That would really ruin all my fun."

The healer stepped up beside me. His healing magic was warm against my injury, but the pain lingered behind the healed skin. He was only healing me enough to prevent me from getting an infection. I could feel my wounds closing, but they were messy and painful. No relief came from this. As soon as I was healed enough to not be on the brink of death, he moved away. The scar left behind by the burn and poor healing would forever remain with me, just like the one on my face.

I was focused on the healer. I didn't see Hadeon withdraw another knife. He sliced into my forearm—right through my Ashlyra.

"No!" I screamed.

I heard Evren scream as if she were right next to me. I slammed my mental shield hard against the bond with all my strength.

Hadeon stood over me with a mallet. He slammed it down on my arm. I howled in pain, then turned my head just in time to hurl onto the ground. Nothing was in my stomach except the blood I had swallowed. The heaving sent sharp pains into my chest. I must have cracked a rib at some point, too. The room smelled of blood and my own waste; it reminded me of a battlefield.

When the heaving finally stopped, I did my best to ground myself again, but it was useless.

Over and over.

Burn.

Heal.

Slice.

Heal.

Break.

Heal.

I didn't know how long it lasted. Hours. Days. Sometimes it felt like a dream, but other times I knew it was real. Each time I gained consciousness, I reinforced my mental shield between myself and my bondmate. I could feel when it slipped. Feeling Evren's agony return to me was ten times worse than anything Hadeon was putting me through.

I had just woken from the latest round of healing. Every part of me ached. I saw something move out of the corner of my eye. Something hidden in the darkness. The thing moved, just a twitch. I squinted hard and saw a fiend was chained to the wall. A soft noise, almost a keening whine, came from it. The fiend was alive. Barely, but alive. It had been there the entire time, but asleep.

"It's been deprived of food for weeks. It's amazing how long these things can live without food."

A guard walked over to the beast with the same poker Hadeon had been using on me. The tip of it glowed red with heat. He jabbed the beast in the side, and it jerked awake. It swiveled its head in my direction, drawn by the death hovering over me. Its claws scraped across the stone floor as it raised its quivering, feeble body. The thing stood over seven feet tall. It looked like death.

Its black tongue darted out like it could taste the air. The beast was frothing at the mouth at the smell of my bleeding and ragged flesh. It roared and then dropped down on all fours like some sort of animal and raced at me. The chain around its throat made it stop only a foot from where I was bound. I could see the drool pouring from its jowls. Its cheeks were sunken in, its ribs showing, so thin. It swiped its claws out in my direction, but I was just out of its reach.

"They tend to go a bit feral when they are starved."

I couldn't find the energy to do anything more than scramble away on my knees as far as my own chains would let me. Renwick cackled at my fear.

"Maybe I can go back to Proux and drag your fire bitch down here," Hadeon said. "I'm sure my fowlest of beasts would love to devour her once I'm through with her. They'd probably fight over her carcass."

Pure terror took over as I thrashed and pulled against my bindings. They cut deep into my skin, but I didn't feel them. I only felt the bond and the need to protect my bondmate.

"*My* Ashlyra," I said through gritted teeth. I was seething. That bastard would never put his hands on Evren.

"What was that?" Hadeon taunted.

He had heard me. I knew he had.

"That's my bondmate. You will not touch her."

"For now." And then something heavy hit me from behind, and everything went black.

A new face came into view. A different person than before. Then I felt the warmth of healing. This time the healer removed all the pain and aches and healed every abrasion. Even the tiniest of scratches were gone. Only the disfigurement from the repetitive cuts and burns remained. Those could no longer be healed. They'd be a permanent part of me. I groaned with relief when the pain lessened, but I knew it wouldn't last for long. Hadeon was nowhere to be seen, thank the Powers.

"Why do you work for this monster?" I asked the healer. This was the first time I'd been left alone with anyone besides Hadeon himself. "You know he is the bad guy, right? Nothing good comes from him."

His eyes flicked up to me before focusing back on his work. He soothed a salve over an area of burned skin that was pulled taunt. He moved on, focusing his effort and concentration on my left arm. Hadeon had crushed the bones in my hand and forearm to powder with a mallet. I almost preferred it when he had let me bleed out from the deep knife wounds. At least then I had passed out from blood loss.

"What is he holding over you?" I tried again.

"He can't speak. I removed his tongue when he pledged his life to me," Hadeon said as he walked into the room. His shining boots clicked off the stone.

Of course he had.

Hadeon wasn't alone. Elenora was by his side. If I didn't know her true nature, I'd say her beauty and delicate features didn't belong in a place like this.

The healer finished his ministrations and bowed to Hadeon before leaving.

"I knew the physical torture wouldn't break you," Hadeon continued as the healer took his leave.

I chuckled at him. "Seems like a waste of your time and energy."

"Don't interrupt me. You know I hate to be interrupted." He crossed his arms across his bulky chest. He gave me a swift kick to my still healing ribs. "Do you really think I'd waste my time? You should ask your Ashlyra if it was a waste of my energy. I know she could feel everything. That is, if you ever see her again."

I snarled at him. How dare he speak of her. I'd done my best to shelter Evren through the bond, but I knew I hadn't kept everything from her.

Hadeon chuckled to himself. "You know, when you were dancing the line of consciousness, you were calling out for her." He tucked his hands beneath his chin and fluttered his eyelashes. "Evren. Evren," he said, mimicking my pleading voice.

My empty stomach rolled. The mute healer rolled me to my side so I wouldn't choke on my vomit. When I was done heaving, he pushed me into a seated position and leaned me against the wall.

Elenora floated on slippered feet to my side. She barely came up to Hadeon's shoulders. So much power in such a small creature. As she grew closer, I could clearly see the black ring around her crystal blue irises thickening again. She reached a hand toward me. I'd seen what she'd done with those hands. I'd felt it, but I was too weak to pull away. My weakness held me in place as the seer approached me at the steady stalk of a predator. Elenora crept closer to me. She held her hands behind her back so I knew she wasn't going to dig into my mind. She needed her hands for that, but I didn't trust her. Hadeon's power blinded me. The whispering shuffle of her slippers sounded as heavy as booted footfalls to my straining ears as she paced back and forth in front of me.

Then they stopped.

Elenora's fingers were cold against my clammy forehead, deceptively soft. I sucked in a sharp breath at her touch, and my vision suddenly returned. The light was sharp and painful. I blinked in rapid succession to adjust my eyes to the glaring light. Elenora's face appeared before me. Those baby blue eyes swallowed by ebony. A sly grin tipped the side of her mouth up. Pain split my head in two as if her fingers were reaching through my skull. She sifted through my thoughts before I felt her vision sweep into my mind. Flashes of light and shadows. I couldn't make out anything.

"He's fighting against me, my love," Elenora whined. Her singsong voice sounded distant.

"Stop fighting it, Valhar. You know it only makes it more painful," Hadeon said flippantly. "Push harder, my love."

His voice was muffled through a haze of Elenora's invasion. He got off on watching me suffer. It's what he thrived on. She sent visions of Evren's torture and death into my mind. Horrendous things I'd never wish upon my greatest enemy. With her magnified power, she forced my eyes open. She was so close. She leaned forward and ran her tongue across my cheek. Then she brought forth the dark shapes that had haunted me for months. They circled me like a predator would its prey. Then she spoke. The same voice that had penetrated my mind for the last weeks. I couldn't remain sitting any longer. I slumped down onto the makeshift pallet. Elenora followed me as I went down.

"It was so easy to sway you to make you think the shadows were the cause of all your negative thoughts. Almost too easy."

I was so weak. Even after the extensive healing, my body was failing me. I was curled on my side and drenched in sweat. I couldn't hold my mental shields any longer. They flickered out like a snuffed candle. The thread linking Evren and me snapped. I was expecting Evren on the other end, but she wasn't there. I reached through the bond for her and came up empty. A black, endless pit greeted me. Had Elenora somehow broken the bond? Was that possible? I peered into the bottomless chasm and then felt myself falling. I'd toppled right into its depths. Coldness and shadows poured out of me, covering everything in mist. Even with the iron shackles touching my skin, the shadows were overwhelming. It was like I was at the bottom of a well, looking up at the world, but unable to climb to the surface. I fell into that darkness. My body had been invaded by the dark manifestations. They were controlling me, and there was nothing I could do.

"Aw. There you are."

It was like nails digging into my brain. Her grip was unrelenting. My heart rate slowed, and everything turned cold.

"See. Isn't it so much easier when you stop fighting? You cannot resist me."

I lifted my head and met Hadeon's eyes. "There you are, Master of Death and Darkness. We've been waiting for you."

I walked on my own accord beside Hadeon as we left the dungeons. I was in a haze controlled by the will of Elenora and her dark manifestations, though from the outside, it appeared I was a willing participant in Hadeon's shenanigans. I followed Hadeon to the pits where he had been breeding and training fiends. It was a deep crack in the earth with molten lava flowing beneath the surface. I could feel the heat radiating from the depths. A narrow metal bridge connected the two sides. We crossed over the bridge and came into a circular arena surrounded by a stadium full of monsters. Hadeon spun in a circle, arms held high, showing off his creation. A chorus of roars and keening howls filled the air. Fiends of all shapes and sizes encircled us. Their teeth gnashed at us, pushing us further to the center of the pits.

We arrived just as a fiend tore into the stomach of a prisoner. Its sharp talons ripped open the flesh. Innards spilled onto the ground with a wet, sickening slap. The carnage caused a crowd of fiends to swarm the carcass. They were a frenzy of madness and bloodlust. I wanted to sprint forward and save the prisoner, but I was trapped inside myself. A snap of Hadeon's power had the fiends cowering away and back to the edges of the arena. Only bones with deep gauges remained of the prisoner. I spotted one fiend picking its teeth with what looked to be a rib.

When Hadeon stepped to the center of the arena, a hush fell over the beasts.

"Ashewood, bring out the next prisoner."

Renwick signaled a guard, who dragged a Fae dressed in scraps and covered in bruises. The guard kicked the prisoner in the back of the knee, and he collapsed at Hadeon's feet. I thrashed and screamed against the chasm holding me, but my body held still, watching and waiting. I was disgusted with myself that I was too weak to save the male cowering before me.

"What are his crimes?" Hadeon asked the guard. The arena buzzed with excitement, as did the manifestations holding me.

"Giving away extra rations," answered the guard.

"What is the penalty for wasting those extra rations?"

"Death."

Hadeon looked at me. I struggled to fight my way up from my inner depths, but the manifestations held me down. They wanted me to draw this out. Draw out the prisoner's agony as long as I could. The prisoner's eyes went wide. I had no control over myself. I was trapped within my own mind, and Elenora was in control. I would be the one to end this male's life. I wasn't strong enough to fight against Elenora, but I could at least try. Nyla and Evren both believed that the shadows weren't evil. Maybe I could somehow communicate with them. The shadows poured from my extended hand. The male cowered and pleaded for his life. The manifestations wrapped around my shadows, battling them into submission. I pushed my will into the shadows; I begged them to respond. Alux had once been the goddess of spirits. The shadows recognized the goodness in my bondmate. They knew the difference between light and dark.

As the shadow tendrils wrapped around the prisoner, I whispered a final plea to the gods above, if they were even listening. "Give this male a swift painless death and welcome him into Evermere for eternity. Please."

And for the first time, the shadows, my shadows, obeyed. I snuffed out the life in an instant. He twitched once and then hit the ground.

I let out a breath of relief. The manifestations surged back into me with fury. Elenora was livid at my resistance, but in the moment, I'd succeeded.

Hadeon laughed. "That was a bit ... anticlimactic. Maybe next time you can draw it out a bit?"

I couldn't deny the rush that I felt through the manifestations as they celebrated the death. Maybe it was Elenora's elation I was feeling. I knew from experience that taking a life had lasting consequences. Even if I wasn't the one in control of my body, I'd killed that male. Add it to the endless tallies. First from the war. Then all the bounties. Now innocent lives. I may not have been in complete control, but I was the one who would ultimately pay the price.

FORTY-SIX
KATURI

City of Proux

I followed Nyla into the garden behind her cottage the day after Delrik was taken. We wandered down the path in pressing bleakness. Garren's worry flowed in irregular waves down our bond. I knew it was tenfold for Evren. I brushed my hand against the medicinal herbs and flowers as I moved by them. Plants always brought me comfort, even before my elemental powers developed. The rainforest was a place of calmness and tranquility. Where the leaves met my touch, they grew and bloomed. Eleni, oblivious to what was going on around her, pounced on bugs crawling across the stone pavers and up the flowers.

"Your garden reminds me of my greenhouse at home," I said with a smile.

Shit! I just called Kanevvluk my home.

I quickly pulled my hand back from the greenery and clasped my hands together in front of me. Nyla pretended to ignore my slip up. I had a sneaking suspense she knew more about what was in my head than I did.

Morning mist hung close to the ground, and the air had a slight chill to it. Summer had come to a quick end, which meant brisk mornings and evenings. I wasn't looking forward to cooler weather. It was still nowhere close to the cold in Kanevvluk.

I ceased my movement down the path when I noticed bright eyes staring at me from the trees lining the garden. An enormous creature lingered in the trees behind the cottages. I couldn't tell how long it had been there, but I had a feeling he'd been tracking us for a while. I wasn't sure if I should be concerned or not. It took Nyla a few steps before she realized I'd come to a halt. She followed my sight line to look in the direction of the woods.

"Knox," she said.

The luminous eyes blinked and then lifted. Higher and higher. Even from this distance, I had to lift my chin to follow the glowing orbs.

"Wh- what?" I stammered.

A silver paw broke through the brush, and a lynx easily the size of my wolf form stepped into full view. He was gorgeous. The feline was covered in thick fur in shades of silver, white, and black. Its large ears ended in tufts, tipped black. It prowled forward several steps. Eleni came bounding out of the garden and came to a skidding stop so quickly that she flopped over in an ungraceful roll. She tumbled down the sloped incline and landed at the feet of the lynx. The great beast looked down at my wolf with utter annoyance. A breeze gently blew through the garden, and I spotted wings on the back of the lynx.

"Knox, meet Eleni and Katuri. Katuri, this is Knox, my familiar."

Knox sauntered forward. He dipped his head low and pressed his forehead to Nyla's. A low purr rumbled in his chest. She stroked under his chin and then continued walking. Knox joined us but kept his distance. Eleni bounced around his feet trying her best to get his attention. The giant feline swatted out a paw and brushed Eleni to the side with minimal effort. And, of course, she went right back to him. She was going to get herself smashed.

We'd almost made it back to the cottage when we came upon Arik sitting on a low stone wall, using a knife to pick at his nails. Eleni growled under her breath in his direction and raised her hackles. I frowned at him and turned to go to the front door. I was having a hard time feeling sorry for him. He'd made his choices, and they'd had dire consequences that he ultimately didn't have to pay. So my understanding was limited. I wasn't sure why he was still hanging around. Nyla didn't question the change in direction, just kept pace alongside me.

Nazneen had stepped from the cottage and looked up to the blue sky. She started down the path toward Nyla and me. It was good to see her outside. She'd hulled herself up in her room since yesterday, refusing to speak to anyone. She'd almost made it to us when she spied Arik. She stopped, pivoted, and headed back to the cottage. The look of pain written on her face broke my heart. Not only had she befriended Arik, she'd trusted him. I was sure she partly blamed herself for her brother's abduction.

"I have to go," I said quickly, starting off after Nazneen.

Nyla reached for my arm. "Wait. They have to talk to each other eventually."

Arik stood and, with two strides, had Nazneen's hand within his. She spun around and ripped her hand from his grasp. "Don't touch me," she snapped.

"Nazneen, wait."

She didn't listen. Her feet were quick on the cobblestones. "You shouldn't be here."

"Nazneen."

"I have nothing to say to you," she said. "And there is nothing *you* have to say that will interest *me*."

"Please," I begged.

The Powers Above were on Arik's side for some reason because Nazneen actually stopped walking. He almost collided with her with how suddenly she halted. She kept her back to him and her arms crossed over her chest.

"Nazneen, you were the first person to see me for who I was deep down, bypassing all the bullshit I'd been hiding behind. If I'm honest with myself, you've been saving me, day by day."

I suddenly felt like I was intruding on a very personal moment. Nazneen's eyes darted to mine in a plea to not leave her alone with Arik.

"I wanted to be worthy of you. I wanted to *be* yours. Be yours. I know I lost your trust by getting Delrik kidnapped. I'm under no illusion that forgiving me will be easy, but I will do everything in my power to earn back your trust."

Nazneen didn't move an inch. She just stood as still as a statue. Her eyes were fixed on me, seeking strength.

"I didn't know the information I was giving away would in any way harm you or your brother. And while I knew it wasn't right, it all started before I knew you. Before you changed me." His voice broke, and Nazneen swallowed thickly. "I'm sorry."

Nazneen's body tensed, and she sucked in shaky breaths.

"You were right. You are more important than seeking revenge for my family. I see that now."

She didn't turn around to face him, but she also wasn't walking away. I saw Arik take a step closer to her, craving her nearness, but I shot him a warning glare. I had no problem ending him if I needed to. Even Eleni left my side and placed herself between Nazneen and Arik. Arik ignored my familiar and carried on with his speech.

"I can't change my past actions. I can't change the fact that Delrik is gone. But I will get him back. And when I do, I will do everything in my power to never let harm come to you ever again. I will destroy any that stand in your way. I will be by your side, at your command, for the rest of my existence." He took another step closer. Now he was close enough to reach out and touch her, but he didn't dare. "And if needed, I will gladly and willingly give my life to save yours."

Hesitation hung in the air.

I watched a single tear trickle down her cheek. She didn't look back to Arik. She took tentative steps toward me. I took her by the hand and led her to the cottage. Nazneen didn't look back.

The air around us grew still when we stepped into the shelter of the cottage. Nazneen released my hand and walked to the kitchen. She turned on the faucet and splashed cold water onto her face. Evren was curled up on the couch, clutching a throw pillow to her chest and staring absently at the wall. She didn't speak or move when we came in. She hadn't moved from the spot in hours.

"Are you all right?" I asked her.

From the corner of my eye, I noticed Nyla stiffen and her eyes shifted to white for a brief moment before they switched back to normal.

"Nyla? Are you having another vision?"

"No. Not right now." She stared off into the distance out the window, looking past the temple and out over the city. "He will be the savior."

Nazneen and I both turned to her.

"Excuse me?" I asked.

I was a little baffled. In the short time I'd known Nyla, I learned she made profound statements that seemed outlandish. Being a seer gave her a glimpse into the future in a way I would never understand. But saying that Arik would be a savior had me thinking twice about her skills. She didn't falter as we both stared at her in confusion.

"He will be the savior," she repeated.

"Arik? Bullshit," Garren said.

Garren strode from the bedroom. He was barefoot and tousled looking. It was hard to focus on my friend's dilemma when he was distracting me by looking like that.

Nyla tipped her head in that feline way so similar to how Knox had and raised her brow at Garren. "You know I can see the future, right?"

"And?" he questioned,

"Nazneen will forgive him eventually." Nyla turned from Garren to face Nazneen. Compassion and conviction were written on her face. "I saw it last night." She walked to Nazneen and gave her arm a reassuring squeeze. "We might as well, too."

That night, I held Nazneen and Evren as they fell asleep. Garren had lifted Evren from the couch and carried her to her bed. She didn't give him any protest, nor did she thank him. The three of us were all piled in Nazneen's bed. Nazneen had cried silent tears, even after she fell asleep. Evren just stared at the ceiling in stunned disbelief until her eyes grew too heavy to keep open. She spent the afternoon switching from hysterical panic and numbing absence. She sat and searched for Delrik through the bond, but she said it was gone. There was nothing, but empty space. Even Aura seemed to need comfort, nuzzling under Eleni's head to sleep.

Once I knew both of my friends were as comfortable as they could be, I eased my way out from between them. Nazneen immediately rolled toward Evren. I'd learned over the last weeks that she was a snuggler.

I, on the other hand, couldn't sleep. I had the urge to shift and go for a run, but I couldn't leave my friends behind. So I slipped from their bed and wandered around the cottage. Before I knew it, my feet took me to Garren's room. I hesitated briefly at his door. We had slept together each night after I accepted the bond between us, but he hadn't kept to himself after everything that happened. Every now and then, he'd reach out to me through the bond for comfort or wrap his fingers around mine. I wasn't sure what he needed.

I decided not to knock and just pushed open the door instead.

I poked my head around the door. "Garren?"

He was sitting on the edge of the bed and looking down at his hands. His body was rigid. He was as still as the icy cliffs in Kanevvluk. A small part of me wanted to walk away and leave him be, but a stronger part wanted to wrap him in my arms. I wanted to go to him and make him forget everything. His stormy blue eyes were glassy when he looked up at me.

"Can I come in?" I whispered.

I half expected him to turn me away, but he nodded and shifted over on the bed. It was a silent offer to join him. So I closed the door quietly behind me. My bare feet padded softly on the wood floor before I sat next to him on the bed. I left a gap of space between us. I didn't know how to act or what to do. I'd never gone through anything like this. The only thing similar was when I had been sent to Kanevvluk and Corynne had been my only comfort. She hadn't tried to tell me everything would be okay or tell me how to feel. She was simply just with me. So that's what I'd do for Garren.

After a long while, Garren took a deep breath. "This is my fault. All of it."

"No, Garren." I closed the gap between us and took his hand in mine. I squeezed it tight.

"My father was right. He knew I would fail, and I have. I let everyone down when I allowed Arik to come with us. I let my bravado cloud my judgment. I've let my family and all of you down; and now Delrik is gone and everything is pure chaos... And a war is coming?"

A single tear fell and landed on our joined hands. I knew nothing I said to him would convince him he was wrong. Not right now at least. This was something that he had to work through on his own, but I'd be here for him. I could stand by him and be the support that he had never had. Even in my loneliest times, I had never truly been alone. Garren had been there watching over me in his own way. I rested my chin on his shoulder and leaned my forehead against his cheek.

"I am here."

We sat that way for a long time, letting the time pass by.

"We should sleep." Garren's words warmed me from the inside.

We. It would always be the two of us from now on.

I cleared my throat, bashful of the words I was about to say. "Will you ... um, just ... hold me?"

He looked down at me. He was the one who had lost his best friend. I should be comforting him, but I was so tired, and I wanted nothing more than to be wrapped in his arms. "I don't want to be alone tonight."

He stood and released my hand. He lifted his shirt over his head and dropped it on the floor. Then he climbed to the middle of the bed and opened his arms wide to me. I smiled at my bondmate. I shucked off my pants and shirt, leaving me in just my underwear and soft corset. Then I buried myself in his chest. There was nothing sexual about the way he held me. Only pure connection. My soft body against his hard one. His water power soothing my earth power and vice versa. As I settled into the solace of my bondmate, I closed my eyes. I didn't hold back my tears. He held me tight, and as my breaths deepened and eyes softened, the last thing that went through my mind was how happy I was to be bound to this male forever.

FORTY-SEVEN
KATURI

It had been just over a week, and we were finally prepared to depart for Noirdan and Delrik. Waiting that long was torment, but it wasn't smart to just go after him without a plan. Nazneen had stressed it to us over and over. We had gathered in a clearing in the forest behind the cottages. We weren't hiding from anyone. Hadeon knew we'd come after Delrik and the relics. We just needed the space for our shifted forms. We'd decided the fastest way to the ruined city was to fly most of the way and then walk the last day.

Arik was nowhere to be found. No one had seen him since the night of his apology. Nazneen was still furious at him. As she should have been. I'd debated telling him that we were leaving to fly south. I'd looked everywhere, including the inns in the city. No one had seen him. So we'd left without saying goodbye. It was probably for the best. We needed to stay focused, and Arik would have only been a distraction.

We broke through the treeline and into the clearing. Each of us carried an overfilled pack for our journey. I dropped my pack on the ground at my feet. Garren came up beside me and put down his pack next to mine. He pressed his hand to my lower back.

"This is as good a spot as any," he said.

He walked the perimeter of the clearing. I wasn't sure what he was looking for. Then he came to a stop in front of me. Garren stripped off his boots and shirt and stowed them inside his pack. He stood and faced me with a smirk. He rubbed his hands together against the bitterly cold morning. Winter came fast in the northern reaches of the western continent. He leaned in and pressed a kiss to my lips, then stepped several paces away.

The zing of magic pierced the air, and my earth power stretched out to Garren. He gave me a wink and shifted before my very eyes. Garren shook his head from side to side and scales appeared in a ripple down his face, neck, and shoulders as if someone were pouring translucent liquid over him. His pupils turned to slits, and his hands grew into deadly talons. Muscled fore and hindlimbs lengthened with what sounded like the snap of bones breaking and reforming. A sea dragon grew before our eyes—all sleek scales and sharp teeth. I'd seen him on the journey over, but being this close to him in his shifted form was intimidating. He stretched his leathery wings wide and pumped them up and down. His wingspan almost stretched the entire width of the clearing. He was striking.

When he'd finished shifting, his serpentine head weaved back over his shoulder in search of me. The earth shook as his taloned feet turned his hulking body to face me. He lowered his head so that his snout was inches from my face. I pressed my hand against the side of his head. I could've sworn he smiled a toothy grin. A purr rumbled up from the back of his throat, making my insides melt. How was he turning me on with a simple noise? Powers.

Garren knelt low and I climbed onto his back as he'd instructed me earlier this morning. At first, I was worried about riding on his back, but the moment the words came into my mind, reassurance wrapped around the bond and my soul. The amount of trust the two of us had formed over the last several days was quite apparent. Before, it had been easy to believe our blood binding wasn't bond-mate related. Now, it was clear we were made for each other. Eleni had shrunk down to the size of a wolf pup and easily fit inside the top compartment of my pack. Her head poked out from the top, her tongue lolling out the side of her mouth.

Garren had offered to carry Nazneen as well, but she'd said she didn't want to be stuck with a newly bonded pair the whole trip. "Gross," I believe was her exact words. So she'd decided to ride with Nyla. Evren shifted next. She shifted in that powerful explosive way only a firebird could. The snow at her taloned feet instantly melted. She soothed her fire to just flowing embers and feathers. Her violet eyes found mine, and she nodded her ready. Aura perched herself on Nazneen's shoulder for now. Knox stood tall beside Nyla and Nazneen. He could easily carry both of them. We'd fly as far as we could today and make camp at nightfall.

As soon as Nazneen settled onto Knox's back, the winged lynx pushed off the earth with tremendous strength and grace. Evren followed.

Garren's powerful body shifted beneath my hips as he prepared for takeoff. That massive head of his checked in with me one last time before, with a thunderous downbeat, we were airborne. The wind stung my eyes and cut into my exposed skin like shards of ice. He pushed, higher and higher, until we erupted from the treetops and I had to squint against the sunlight.

The Temple of Anruin and the City of Proux quickly shrunk to a point on the side of the mountain. The exhilaration of being so high and weightless gave me a reprieve from the sadness that had been hanging over me. Garren's amusement and elation at me enjoying the flight so far was crystal clear in the bond between us. Our emotions bounced back and forth the entire day. I'd grown to love not having to speak for Garren to understand how I felt.

The sun was high in the sky when we rested for lunch. We ate quickly, then we were back in the air after a few more hours and miles of travel. The sun began to set, painting the sky in brilliant shades of golds and reds. Garren's sea dragon drifted on a current. He dropped a wing and turned into the setting sun to touch down in a spot he saw that was clear enough for our landing.

Knox and Evren followed behind. Evren immediately shifted back to her High Fae form and sagged to the ground in a naked heap. Garren, still in his sea dragon form, quickly turned away and took off back into the sky again to give her privacy. I rushed over and draped a warm cloak over Evren. She had to be exhausted. I'd never seen her stay shifted for so long before.

"Thank you," she said weakly and smiled up at me. Aura floated down and whistled and cooed at her master. "I feel like I'm running on empty."

"You did well," I encouraged with a smile. "Let's get you some food so you can rest and refuel."

After about an hour, Garren returned, walking through the trees in his High Fae form, bare chested and with pants that hung loose off his waist. Drake flew beside him. He had several fish in hand, and Drake carried one in his mouth. "I found a river and thought we could do with some fresh meat."

Starting a fire was effortless. Evren had insisted on doing it, but I knew she was exhausted. So instead, Nazneen relied on her wilderness training to cook our dinner.

We all sat around the fire, leaning on our packs, and eating in silence. Garren sat right next to me so that our thighs were touching. That small amount of contact brought so much comfort.

I'd finished my portion of dinner and placed my container of water off to the side. Just then, Nazneen giggled to herself.

"What's so funny over there?" Garren asked.

"Nothing. I was thinking about the first time I tried to start a fire. Delrik sat back and let me try all night long. By the time the sun rose, I was shivering so badly I couldn't even hold the flint. The cocky bastard was a year behind me in Legion training but had mastered survival skills like he was born with them. And he had no problem rubbing it in my face."

"That sounds exactly like something he'd do." Garren laughed.

"I didn't let it bother me too much since I could kick his ass with a sword."

Evren, who'd barely touched her food, smiled at Nazneen's story. I saw her brush her lips with the tips of her fingers. We spent the rest of the evening swapping fond stories and memories of Delrik. Soon, we settled in for the night, all cuddled up against each other near the fire—me on one side and Evren on the other, sandwiching Nazneen between us. Garren was against my back. Even with Evren not using her elemental power, she kept us warm and toasty, just by being so close. Eleni curled up at Garren's feet, and Drake at his head. Nyla snuggled into Knox, and he wrapped himself around her.

I woke up with a sudden start when a cold wind whipped around me. I looked around in the pitch dark. The fire was glowing embers. I blinked and summoned my earth powers to give me my wolf's sight. Everything came into stark clarity. Nazneen had moved to sleep next to Nyla, and Evren was nowhere to be seen. I sat up and looked all around. She had to be somewhere. I lifted Garren's arm off my waist. He woke with the movement, grumbling at me for waking him, and tried to pull me back to him. I swatted him away.

"What's wrong, Kat?" he said groggily.

"Evren's gone," I said.

I'd never seen him move so quickly. In an instant, he was on his feet calling out Evren's name. Aura swooped down from somewhere and pecked me gently on the ear. She barked at me and flew into the trees. It didn't take me long to find Evren. She was only maybe ten feet from our campsite. The sound of her whimpers were drowned out by the natural sounds of the forest.

"Evren?"

She had her hand clamped over her mouth to muffle her sobbing.

"Evren, what is it?" I asked, trying to pry her hands from her face. Garren was right behind me. When she saw the condition Evren was in, he ran back to the camp for Nazneen.

She peered up at me, and pure grief looked back at me.

"Delrik. I … I feel him." Her breathing was rapid and strained. "He's … Hadeon's torturing him. I can feel it. All of it."

I swallowed hard. Okay then. Delrik was being tortured. Shit.

"Not physically. I can't feel the actual pain, but I can sense the torment and fear."

"Can you put up a mental shield?" I asked her.

"I've tried, but I'm so drained. I can't do it. I can't focus." Tears streamed down her cheeks.

Nyla came through the darkness to Evren's other side. She pressed her fingertips to Evren's temples.

"I can't cancel out the bond, but maybe I can ease its intensity," she said.

Nyla closed her eyes and gently massaged circles into Evren's skin.

"How does that work?" I asked her.

"It's something I've learned from my meditation practice. Calming my mind makes my visions not come on in a rush. It allows me to not only sense when one is coming, but to open my mind to accept it rather than fighting against it like many with my gift do."

Evren's face relaxed the smallest amount the moment Nyla's fingers touched her.

"I am channeling my calm into her."

Nazneen leaned over and offered a bundle of purple flowers. "It's lavender."

I rubbed the flowers brisky between her palms. A sweet aroma blossomed from the crushed flowers. I held her hands in front of Evren's face. She breathed deeply. There was nothing else I could do. Nazneen just held her while she felt all of Delrik's agony through the bond. Eventually, Evren settled, her body relaxing into Nazneen's arms—either she'd fallen asleep from exhaustion or Delrik had managed to shield the bond on his end. Either way, I was thankful she wasn't suffering anymore. We knew he was using the mind shielding to protect her from the brunt of it, but it must've been impossible to keep it in place all the time.

Delrik had been gone for a week. So why was Evren just now feeling the effects of Hadeon's torture? Had it just taken this long to break down Delrik's will? Powers, I hoped he could stay strong just a little longer.

The following week went the same way: wake early, fly until Evren couldn't anymore, and then rest for the night. Quinterre was easily twice the size of Illoterra, if not larger. We followed the ridge of the Baxmar Peaks, then along the Milla River that flowed south until it hit the sea. Then we followed the coast all the way south to Noirdan.

On day eight, Evren had spent almost every last drop of her magic and could no longer shift at all. So we switched to hiking the remaining distance to Noirdan. She'd done so well thus far. When I was only a year into my powers, there would've been no way I could have used my magic at such a level.

We decided to stop at a small village of Ozryn to gather a few supplies that would last the rest of our journey. We were all exhausted and filthy. The lower floor of the inn and pub was crowded. We pushed our way through the throng of people.

"I'll go see if they have a room available for us," Garren said.

Nazneen and Nyla split off to find a table while Evren and I made our way to the bar to order some food. My stomach rolled with hunger. We hadn't had much luck fishing yesterday. I couldn't blame the lack of food entirely, if I was honest with myself. The closer we got to Noirdan, the more nervous I became. We were only a day's trek to Noirdan, but we needed to rest and bathe. We couldn't be at our strongest if we were too tired to stand. And we all needed our full strength to face whatever Hadeon put us against.

I scanned my surroundings on instinct. I peered out of the corner of my eye at the other end of the bar where Garren was talking to a male. I assumed he was speaking with the innkeeper.

"I need two rooms, preferably with a washroom," Garren said. He slid a few coins across the counter.

"Traveling with four females, eh?" I heard his gruff voice. The male wasn't doing anything to keep his voice down or to conceal his innuendo.

Garren glared at him with disdain. The question wasn't worth answering, and the innkeeper knew it when he saw Garren's stone cold face. At least he had enough smarts to not say anything else about it.

The bartender appeared and placed two glasses on the bar before Evren and me. "Hello there, ladies. You must be a long way from home."

I internally rolled my eyes at his flirtatious smirk. We weren't the only females in the pub, but we stood out in comparison. The other females wore tight corsets that pushed their breasts up, and several were even perched on the knee of a male or two. I could smell their overly sweet perfume through the putrid cigar smoke and body odor of other travelers.

"We need to order some food for us and our friends."

"Of course," he replied. "Are you staying here at the inn?" He didn't hide his perusal of my body, stopping on my chest before he met my gaze again. I wanted to vomit. At the flash of my disgust, Garren's head snapped to me. I reached down the bond as reassuringly as possible. I could handle myself. Between Master Farreen and Nazneen, I was in fighting shape. He turned back to the innkeeper. My sharp hearing was honed in on Garren's conversation while keeping a close eye on Nazneen and Nyla. From the corner of my eye, I saw the innkeeper nod his head toward me. "Do you need to do something about that? My bartender can get a bit handsy at times."

Garren turned to look at me again, and I smiled down at the bar. He replied without taking his eyes off me. "Nah. She'll cut his hand off if he touches her."

That's an accurate assumption.

"Plus, if I went in all big male protecting the meek female, I'd piss her off enough that she'd probably cut something off of me."

That time I didn't hide my laugh.

Also accurate.

My legs were like jelly as I climbed the stairs. The only thing that kept me going was knowing a bed was on the other side of that door. And a bath. Garren had rented two adjoining rooms that shared a private bathroom as well. Thankfully, even the smaller villages on Quinterre had electricity and running water. Villages like this one in Illoterra still relied on wells to supply water. We would've been better off bathing in the river if we were on Illoterra.

Garren let us all shower and change first while he went back downstairs to wait for the food I'd ordered. I was sitting cross legged on one of the smaller beds braiding my hair when he entered. He had a tray of covered dishes precariously balanced in one hand. He kicked the door closed behind him.

"Nazneen just finished. She's changing clothes. Evren is showering now. Nyla, well, I don't know where Nyla ran off to. But she's fine with Knox. She can take care of herself. It looks like the bartender gave us everything I ordered. I didn't bother asking what was in the kitchen. I didn't think it mattered after eating fish for a week straight. Oh, and a maid offered to launder all our clothes for us, which I thought was a good idea. No one wants to show up to a fancy meeting with an evil guy smelling like the wrong side of a..."

"Katuri."

I looked up, and Garren was softly smiling at me. "You're rambling."

I snapped my mouth shut. Garren knew me too well. I had a bad habit of talking nonstop whenever I was nervous or stressed. That or shutting down completely. I was both right now. Nervous about what we'd find when we reached Noirdan tomorrow. Nervous about how we'd get the relics before Hadeon. Stressed about how we'd left things with Arik and then he'd just disappeared. Now I was babbling in my own head. Nazneen exited the bathroom wrapped in a fluffy towel. As she walked by us to get fresh clothes from her pack, Garren's eyes never left me. He reached out and squeezed my hand.

"We will find him," Garren said. "And Evren would know if ... something ... if somehow..."

I finished for him. "If Delrik was dead?"

FORTY-EIGHT
GARREN

Noirdan

"We need to go this way," Nyla said, nodding her head toward the house.

"How do you know?" I asked.

"Wisps."

"What in the circle of dark hells are wisps? You keep mentioning them, but I still have no idea what you are talking about."

I could tell it took everything in her not to turn and punch me in the face. She raised her hands, and a wisp of air power in the shape of a tiny winged lynx flowed freely between us, bouncing back and forth. Then she pushed her hands out in front of her, and the wisps left in the direction she guided them.

"There are wisps all around us, connecting everything in our realm together like a giant web. I can use the wisps, ask them to do my bidding. They bring me information, guide my path. They speak to me."

I waved my hand through the air like I could reach out and touch the wisps. "They are tiny kittens?"

She rolled her eyes at me before sending a blast of air to smack me in the face. Though my playful banter wasn't appreciated at the moment, I knew I was growing on her.

When we arrived in Noirdan, I could smell the sulfur and iron in the air. It burned my nose with each breath. Nothing good came from Menrath. The city had been destroyed during the war and had never recovered. The land had been practically uninhabitable, even before the war, and the Raven Fae had burned what little remained to the ground. Now the "city" consisted of mostly single level buildings made of mud and chunks of rocks. The people unlucky enough to call this hellhole home lived in lean-tos made of broken boards and scraps of tent material so worn from the sun they were almost transparent. Its only saving grace was its port. Port Kainarr still functioned as a major hub for traders coming from Illoterra and was the closest you could get to Noirdan by ship. We'd have to walk or ride the rest of the way to Hadeon Allerick's stronghold. Thankfully, I'd been able to find a few horses. It was only a day's journey on horseback.

Noirdan had once been the capital city of the Raven Fae Kingdom. Now it was nothing more than ruins at the base of Baxmar Peak. I sat astride my horse, not far from the gates Hadeon had erected around his house. The ground beneath our feet was as black as I remembered; though last time I'd visited, this house wasn't here. The only thing I had seen was the smoking remains of the city after the war. The moment we entered the gates, Aura began screeching wildly and flew ahead of us. She flew several feet ahead and then back to Evren.

"You should follow your Aura." Nyla nodded in the direction of the fire beast. "She will bring us to Delrik."

We walked through the gates. On the outside, everything almost looked normal. We kept our heads covered with our hoods even though it was too warm. Aura brought us to an old, crumbling home nestled close to the mountain. As we approached, the light from the sun seemed to be sucked away.

"It looks deserted," I whispered.

"Then why are you whispering?" Katuri said at a normal volume. I tugged on the end of her ponytail. Nyla rolled her eyes at us. She was just jealous. If I ever pulled her hair, I'd come back with a stub for a hand.

"Delrik is here. We will find him," Nyla confirmed.

As the scouts had told us, the grounds were barren. Not a single guard stood at the main gates or doors leading into the house. Nazneen led our group despite the grumbling from me. I'd been more watchful over her since my best friend was taken. I also knew better than to go against the Arcelia warrior's commands. We pushed open the door and walked inside. All the torches were burned out except the ones in the hall to the left. No guards. No one in sight. I knew we wouldn't come up against anyone. I also knew that Elenora was expecting us. Nyla had told us that much.

"My guess is you need to go that way," Arik said. His words made everyone jump. He was sitting on the floor, his back against the exterior wall, partially disguised by the shadow of the house. He'd disappeared after he'd apologized to Nazneen. Nyla had seen in a vision that he wouldn't be with us when we went after Delrik, but she'd said we'd see him again.

"How in the dark hells did you get here?" I cursed.

"Did you even bother to hide your tracks on the way here?" Arik said.

"Elenora knew we would be here. Why would we lurk around?" Nyla asked.

Arik just shrugged and picked himself up off the floor.

Evren eyed him up and down with a hard glare. "Figures we'd find you here. You've been working with Hadeon this whole time."

Fire formed at her fingertips. She'd been on edge all day. I'd recommended that she didn't use her power the last few days so that she could store up her strength. She was bursting at the seams.

"I only arrived a few days ago," he answered.

"Mh hm."

Evren didn't believe him. Of course, she didn't.

"The dining hall is that way." Arik pointed down the hall. "I've used the last few days to scout out the house's layout and find the fastest routes of escape."

"And I'm just supposed to trust you all of the sudden?" Evren said.

He let out a long sigh. "Ask Nyla."

Evren's head turned toward me without taking her eyes off Arik.

My eyes bounced between the two. "How would she know you're telling the truth?"

Neither Arik nor Nyla answered my question.

Evren's mouth formed a tight line, and she narrowed her eyes. "Fine. But the only reason you're coming along is so I can offer you in exchange for my bondmate," she snapped.

Flames flared from her fingertips. She didn't seem to be joking. The only plan we had was to get Delrik and get out. And if we happened to stumble upon a relic or managed to behead Hadeon in the process, then we got a bonus win. I could totally see Evren exchanging Arik for all of that.

"We won't get to that point," Nyla reassured her.

We continued down the hall, keeping to the shadows where the torch light didn't shine.

Nazneen suddenly stopped. "Something doesn't feel right."

"I feel it too, but I don't know what it is," Garren agreed.

A single guard was standing at the double doors at the end of the hall. Without a word, he bowed as we approached, then opened the door. The smell of food wafted toward us, and muffled voices came from what appeared to be a dining room and spilled into the corridor.

"They know we are coming, right?" Evren asked me.

"Yes. They are expecting us," Nyla responded.

I didn't like this one bit.

"Good," Evren said with determination in her voice.

Evren stepped out of the shadows. With flames dancing in her hands, she strode through the door into the dining hall. Scorched marks smoked where her hands touched the wood of the doors and embers singed the floor where her feet walked.

Evren stopped short. We were behind her in a matter of seconds. My heart stopped in my chest, and Katuri gripped my hand tight. Delrik was sitting next to the seer, unharmed, dressed in fine clothing, and completely at ease with his captors. He turned to Evren when she entered. The dark smudges under his eyes were the only evidence of the suffering he'd endured over the last few weeks.

Delrik's mouth tipped into an awkward smile. "Hello, Ashlyra."

FORTY-NINE
DELRIK

My power and the bond pulled me like a million threads. I lifted my head from my plate of food and looked to the door. Directly to my bondmate. Evren. She was here. I was frozen in place. I just sat there. Not a care in the world. And eating a meal with Renwick Ashewood of all people. My stomach twisted at the sight Evren was seeing. I fought against the manifestations holding me down. I clawed and screamed, and nothing came out of my mouth except a greeting.

"Hello, Ashlyra."

My words were acid in my throat. I was gripping my fork so hard I could feel the cold metal biting into my fingers.

"My pet, you've come at last." Renwick's slimy voice clung to me like an odor.

Evren reached out with the bond and I couldn't respond. There was a solid wall where my mind usually was open to Evren. The manifestations fortified it against her. I knew she had felt every single horrid act that I'd gone through. She couldn't feel the exact pain, but my anguish and fear cut as sharp as a knife. And then it suddenly stopped. Once Elenora had gotten her claws in my mind, I'd been given a reprieve from the torture. But now, being this close to Evren, she could tell that there was something blocking our connection. I was aware of everything happening around me, but I was silenced by Elenora's control.

Evren pressed against the invisible wall, her magic searching it for a crack or crevice. But there was nothing but cold silence.

The look on my Ashlyra's face was pure anguish. It almost killed me to not let her know I was alright. I'd been in the dark for so long. I'd given in to Elenora's dark magic. I was at the bottom of a chasm, looking up to the unreachable sky above. But when I hit the rock bottom, the shadow magic was there with me. I realized there was nothing dark about this power. The goddess of air had told us about the spirits, and now I could see them. They weren't cast in the dark shadow of Thane's murder and the betrayal Alux endured. They were heartbreak. Evren had said she never felt in danger from the shadows and this is why. The spirit elemental power was dwelling in me. It had always been there; I was just too afraid to see it.

Evren spoke with ferocity. "I will burn them all."

She lifted her hands before her, and the Ring of Teris flowed red hot.

"The Ring of Teris! It—" Hadeon said with greed.

She turned to look directly at him, interrupting him. "Is mine."

Like a blaze of a thousand suns, Evren threw her fire at me. Renwick and Elenora dove out of the way of the flames just as it struck me. The bondmates' elemental magic surrounded me, but I wasn't afraid. My Ashlyra was saving me. She knew exactly how to free me from Elenora's mental chains. The fire burned through the otherness and manifestations, just like it had during the nightmares. The shock on the faces of our friends behind her at seeing Evren burn her bondmate alive was hard to watch. They knew her flames had never hurt me before, but I was sure it was startling to see her surround me in an inferno. I trusted her, and they needed to trust her too.

Elenora began to scream. It rang in my ears. Evren's fire reached all the way into the deep chasm to me. The manifestations in my mind ran in terror from her fire as it followed the seer's hooks in my mind all the way back to her. She could either release me or burn from the inside out. When Elenora released her hold on me, the flood of the fire and spirits swept in with a strength I'd never known. My mental shield snapped back up, guarding me from Elenora and Hadeon. After so long, it was stronger than I'd intended. I couldn't sense anyone's movements. I could only feel the spirit inside me. This power of life and death. Evren appeared next to me through the smoke. Just seeing her so close was a wave of emotions, our bond reaching out stronger than ever for each other.

My Ashlyra.

Then all hell broke loose.

"Evren. Run." My voice was hoarse.

But she didn't move. Not even a single muscle balked at the fiend coming at her. The beast ran on all fours directly at her. My muscles coiled, readying to jump in front of her, but Aura swooped in. She flew to Evren, growing larger and larger until her wings merged with

Evren herself and she shifted into her firebird. Her luminous wings swept forward. The explosion of light and fire burned the fiend on contact, and the whole house shook on its foundation. My bond-mate, my Ashlyra, roared. Fire rained down on everything.

Arik appeared through the door and shielded me from the embers and ash falling from above. The house was burning. The walls of the dining hall exploded upward, and the firestorm raged out of control. Evren's strong wings beat up and down as she breathed fire at any fiend or guard running from the blaze. She shredded fiends with her talons as they tried to run. She didn't let anyone escape. No matter where they ran, she burned their paths with her scream of fire. Evren's radiant wings were the only things I could see against the smoke and debris. Evren locked her wild, violet eyes with mine as she shifted back to her High Fae form, but her ebony wings remained. They dripped with the blood of her enemies. She touched down beside me and took hold of my hand. Her clothes were singed scraps clinging to her body. She walked on bare feet the short distance to me. I was worried about the glass and shards of stone beneath her feet, but they turned to ash with each step. Her fire was protecting her from much more than the fiends.

"You didn't run when I told you to."

I wanted to scold her, but I couldn't. She'd come for me. She'd saved me. She pulled me close, burying her face into my chest.

"Why would I?"

When our bodies met, our bond flared and our binding mark ignited. Combined, they came to life and our powers—light and dark—joined in a force I'd never felt. Like it was a living entity, her elemental power flowed through the binding mark and into my veins. Power like I'd never felt before. It was ancient and limitless. The unending depths made my vision streak with silver light. It flowed white hot through me; the intensity of it almost knocked me off my feet. It twisted and tangled through every fiber of my being until it was embedded in my soul. And my shadows flowed into Evren like they were at home inside her. I'd never felt more connected to my Ashlyra than now. The spirit and fire elemental power flowed freely between our souls now, even after we broke apart from our embrace and prepared for the attack we knew was coming.

Suddenly, Evren was ripped from my grip and tossed against the table. Her body made a crack as it crashed into a nearby chair and fell to the floor in a pile of shards of wood. Invisible hands gripped me. I swept my eyes across what remained of the burned dining room until my gaze landed on Renwick. His hand was outstretched to me and his lips were curled up into a sneer. My body lifted from the ground and then came down hard across the room. Debris fell from above, half burying me. What was with him and throwing me into things?

Pain shot through my head and my vision drifted in and out. Blinking rapidly, I scrubbed at my face. No. This couldn't be happening again. I lifted a piece of plaster from my chest and looked down at my legs. One of my legs was trapped beneath a heavy beam. A whisper of magic danced in my veins.

I saw Renwick's focus entirely on my bondmate. The bastard had his hand outstretched in her direction, and she was hovering above the ground, her hands grasping at his hold around her neck. I struggled to stand, pushing debris off my legs. By the time I got to my feet, Evren was being carried across the room with Renwick's magic, straight toward his waiting hand. Her toes and tips of her blood-drenched wings dragged across the ground, across broken glass and splintered wood. The moment his hand made contact with Evren's skin, our bond screamed in fury. How dare he put his hands on her!

Renwick spun and slammed Evren up against the wall. Her hands were clawing at his forearms. The breath punched from her lungs when Renwick crushed her body between his and the wall. Her head whipped backward from the force and rebounded off the wall. The plaster split and veined outward. My leg screamed in pain as I limped toward her, throwing chunks of wall, snapped chairs, and pieces of the table out of my way. Flames were still coming down around me, but they couldn't harm me. Not with my bondmates fire rolling through my blood.

Renwick was towering over Evren. Her face was covered in splotches of blood and soot. Seeing Renwick with his hands on her sent the dual powers into a frenzy. He leaned in close to her, his mouth practically against hers. He spoke words against my Ashlyra's mouth. Sour acid filled my mouth. Renwick's hand landed possessively on her hip, then traveled up her side to her breast. Everything was moving in slow motion, and I was running through mud. His fingers dug into her throat and he trailed his nose across her jawline. When he pulled back to look at her, Evren did something that I wasn't expecting.

Evren smiled. A smile of victory.

She wedged her hand between their bodies and extended her arm, pushing his body away from hers. He squeezed her neck tighter but was forced to release her physically, but his power still held her in place, trapped against the wall. Evren was still smiling. Her eyes darted to me when she saw me running at her, and she winked. Evren lifted her hand, rotating it back and forth. The fire burning all around us glinted off the ruby on Evren's finger. She wiggled her fingers at Renwick in a wave. His face dropped when he realized what he'd done. Powers Above. My bondmate was brilliant. Pride surged in my chest and I pushed it down our bond to her.

I could see when Renwick's power draining from him and flowing into Evren, the ring its conduit. Evren's body relaxed when his mental grip released her and her feet touched back down to the floor. She took a step forward, and Renwick began to retreat. He opened his mouth to say something, but Evren interrupted him, holding a single finger out to quiet him.

"If you didn't resist me, I wouldn't have to be so rough." Through the bond, I could feel the disgust dripping off the words as she spoke them. "You bring this on yourself."

I'd never known Evren to be revengeful. She had to have a reason behind her actions, behind her precise words. Then a flash of a memory appeared in my mind. One of Evren's memories. She looked over Renwick's shoulder and made eye contact with me. Evren's memory formed clearly in my mind as if I were looking back on my own past. Renwick breathed the same exact words into her ear back when she was still living in Rivamir. Instead of fear and shame though, confidence and strength were in the forefront of her mind. Then, through the bond, she tugged at our powers. Asking permission to take the full extent of both our powers.

I didn't hesitate as I opened myself up completely to my perfect bondmate. I gave her everything I had in me. I sent both the fire and shadow spirits to my Ashlyra.

Evren's eyes flashed with fire and then blackness before turning violet again. She took quick strides to Renwick and grasped him by the front of his shirt. He shoved her away. Evren tipped her head back and laughed. She lifted both arms straight in front of her and opened her palms. Fire and shadows floated there, waiting for her to command. Flames and tendrils of shadows poured from Evren's body, coming from her eyes, mouth, and hands. A swirling mass of divine destruction. It enveloped Renwick, wrapping around him tight and squeezing. He thrashed and screamed. The magic took its time in devouring him until he was nothing but ash on the wind.

I hadn't thought there was anything better than watching Evren kill her father. But this? This was better. My Ashlyra was so beautiful as she was surrounded by her darkness and glowing light. One couldn't exist without the other. We were that darkness and light. My existence wasn't possible without her. I rushed to her side and wrapped her in my arms. The shadows and flame opened up to me like a warm embrace.

"Um, guys. I could use a little help over here," Garren grunted as he lifted a large chunk of debris. "The fire may not eat you, but it's getting a little warm for my liking."

Evren lifted up on her tiptoes and gave me a quick peck on the cheek. Then she twisted her hand in the air, and all the fire smothered out in an instant.

Garren came up beside Arik and doused a pathway through the flames that was still smoldering. This building wouldn't hold out for much longer. We needed to move and move fast. Katuri and Nazneen followed behind me as we sprinted for our lives out into the open air.

Somehow, Hadeon and Elenora had survived the fire and were standing in the courtyard with a group of fiends at their command. Their jaws snapped at the air, and their keening sounds made me cringe.

Time seemed to stand still for a moment. Then the fiends attacked. Fire spewed from my hands, obeying my every whim. Being this connected with our magic through the binding mark brought down any and all barriers between our minds. I could hear all my bondmate's thoughts as if they were my own. My body responded to her before she even moved. We moved like two halves of a whole.

I was a blur across the battlefield. Blood and ash and death were the only things left in my wake. Evren stood stationary, letting the fiends come to her. The moment they touched her, they burst into ash. Katuri appeared and slammed her fist into the blackened earth. The ground split with an ear-piercing crack. The courtyard was split in two, Katuri, Evren, and me on one side. Garren, Nyla, and Arik on the other. I pushed twisted flames and dark shadows into the fault lines. They raced forward and consumed everything in their path. The wildfire released a tortuous heat, but it didn't touch us. With

Evren's expert control and Arik's shields, we all remained safe from the blaze.

Nyla and Garren fought side by side across from us on the other side of the ravine. The priestess looked like she wasn't bothered in the least by the carnage surrounding her. Her blond hair floated on her invisible winds, gleaming like spun gold in the fire light. With one hand, Garren sprayed water to smother the fires approaching us while the other shot ice spears with precision at the enemy.

Then, Hadeon and Elenora, flanked by the largest fiend I'd ever seen, stepped through the smoke and into our circle. I recognized the fiend as the one who had ripped out the innards of the prisoner when I first went to the pits. Anger burned hot inside me. My flame encircled him, slowly closing in. It licked up his leathery legs before engulfing him completely. His skin melted, contorting his already deformed face. His miserable screams echoed through the air. I plunged my hand into his skeletal chest—where a heart would've been if the creature wasn't from the circle of dark hells. This wasn't a kill I added to my list though. This was retribution.

FIFTY
KATURI

Before I knew it, fiends and guards were on us. I dodged one coming straight for me only to be caught around the waist by another. My earth power surged forward and struck the guard—a thick, twisting vine straight through his chest. I whipped around, and my hair stuck in the thick blood that coated my cheek. I swiped the back of my hand across my face and withdrew my sword. A fiend stepped into my field of view. The gangly body towered over me. A smile spread across his too thin lips and it's eyes were feverish in the chaos. It opened its mouth, and the putrid smell of its hot breath hit my face. A forked tongue darted out. Right as it was about to pounce, I thrust my sword into its gut. Thick, hot blood coated my hands. The beast dropped to its knees. It swayed back and forth before it toppled over. Using my foot as an anchor, I pulled the weapon from the fiend.

Suddenly, my back hit the ground, punching the air from my lungs. I was only quick enough to bring my sword up, right as the fiend's jaws came toward my face. The flat edge of the sword was the only thing separating the fiend's teeth from tearing into my chest. It snapped around the blade. My arms shook with the effort of holding the beast back. The sharp edges of my blade dug into my hands, mixing my blood with that of the fiend's. Just before my arms gave out, the fiend's eyes went wide and it let out a gargled yelp. Blood spurt from its mouth. A blade of ice poked through its chest. Garren stood above the beast with a look of pure rage on his face. His sea dragon scales covered a portion of his face and his eyes were dark slits. With little effort, he flipped the fiend off me. He stood over me, panting heavily. Sweet relief flooded my mind. Then he extended a hand to me and lifted me from the ground. He planted a swift kiss on my forehead before returning to the fight. My heart thundered in my chest at his soft kiss.

I shouldn't be turned on right now.

We were in the middle of trying not to die. Garren flashed me a knowing grin as he decapitated another guard.

I spun in a circle, looking at the carnage that surrounded me. Guards and fiends littered the ground, but still, more were coming. They were pouring from a pit in the ground. A breeding pit. I'd never used the extent of my powers like this before. The ground below my feet answered my demands as they came to me. Vines and branches erupted from the earth. They latched onto the fiends' feet, trapping them where they stood and slicing them to pieces. Animals made of earth and mud sprung from the ground and attacked anything they could get their jaws on. I crouched down and punched my fist into the blackened earth. I was drunk on the feel of the power pulsing through me.

When I slammed a fist to the dead earth, the ravine I'd created opened into a gaping hole. Debris and fiends alike were swallowed up into the depths. Evren released a ball of fire and shadow into the opening and then I slammed it closed, trapping the fiends in a fiery death.

I slashed my blade through another fiend and looked around. No more were coming at me. I took advantage of the break and sucked in deep lungfuls of air. Elenora appeared several feet ahead of me. She started for me, but stopped all of a sudden. She was looking past me with a wicked glint in her eye. I looked back and saw Garren, his back to me and in an evenly matched sword fight with a guard. I whipped around to face her again. Over my dead body was she going to touch my bondmate. She winked then ran—straight for Garren. Fuck, she was fast for being so small.

"Garren!" My voice rang out like a howl, but it wasn't fast enough.

Elenora sprang on him. She slammed into him, knocking him to his knees with the force. The guard he'd been fighting stumbled backward and impaled himself on a fallen conrad's sword. Elenora dug her fingers deep into Garren's mind, and he crumbled forward to the ground. Nyla, who'd been fighting next to him, whipped around to pull Elenora off him, but Hadeon struck out with his power. He smothered her senses so quickly she had no time to respond. Where the fuck had he come from? Nyla was sent flying, but was caught by Knox sweeping into the fray before she collided with the ground. Evren sent a horde of shadows at Hadeon, and his grip on Nyla faltered with the distraction. Nyla shook off the effects of the strange magic, and Knox dropped her back down into the fray.

Garren yelped at whatever pain Elenora was inflicting on him. His eyes were squeezed shut, and blood ran from where her fingers were buried in his skull. The sight ripped my heart from my chest. The heart that belonged to him. That wasn't the bond; it was my love for him. Fury built and then erupted from me.

"He is MINE!" I bellowed.

I took two steps before I shifted into my wolf form and bound toward the seer. Hadeon tried to stop me, but Arik threw a shield around me for protection. Elenora tried to scurry away, dropping Garren to the ground, but it was useless. I was on her in a flash. I clamped my jaws around her throat and snapped her neck with a satisfying crunch. Then I ripped her head from her body for a bit of added flair. I turned to Hadeon with his bondmate's head clamped in my jaws.

Hadeon screamed, but it didn't matter. Elenora was gone. Hadeon lashed out at the closest person he could get his power to. Arik was caught in the line of fire and stood frozen in place. A fiend appeared in the sky, then swooped down and snatched him from the ground. He flew higher and higher. Then the monster threw him. His limp body went flying to the demolished ruins of Hadeon's home, then crashed to the ground. Knox and Aura had both sped toward him, but they weren't fast enough. Shards of splintered rock protruded from his back, and one of his arms was bent backward, the bone poking through the skin. Hadeon stalked closer to Arik's lifeless form. He wasn't moving, but his chest still rose and fell in shallow breaths. Hadeon raised his hand to land his final blow when Nazneen, quiet as the night, attacked him from behind. She swept her legs out and sent him crashing to the ground. He was fast, though, and righted himself with ease.

"The famous spy of Arcelia, Nazneen Zathrian," Hadeon sneered as he turned to face the warrior. "It's an honor to face off with you."

Nazneen withdrew the Warblade of Silverlight from her back. She readied herself for Hadeon's attack. Nazneen was a skilled fighter. I'd seen her train with Garren and Delrik. She was quick on her feet and patient. She'd let Hadeon stumble over his own feet. Hadeon did not disappoint. He lunged, but Nazneen was faster. She dodged each blow that Hadeon attempted. She swung the blade to counter each attack. Hadeon backed up with each strike, away from the ruined house and closer to his fallen bondmate. Closer to me. I didn't dare interfere. I would wait until Nazneen was ready for me.

"Don't let him near the seer! She has a relic," Delrik called to Nazneen.

A relic? I stayed in my wolf form and placed myself between Hadeon and Elenora's body, her decapitated head between my front paws. Delrik and Evren began to close in while Nyla rushed to Arik's side. The sound of the blow reverberated across the arena.

Hadeon struck Nazneen with the hilt of his sword under her chin. Her teeth made an awful noise. He was so much larger than her in height and strength. I took a step toward her, but two fiends were closing in, drawn in by the pool of blood at my paws. I growled low in warning. No one was going to touch this relic. Nazneen lunged forward, but Hadeon parried out of the way. His sword swung through the air and nicked her arm. Her shirt and skin split open, and blood dripped from the wound.

Hadeon circled Nazneen, but she kept her back away from him. She took a deep breath, waiting for his next strike.

Hadoen's eyes went dark with fury. The fury made him careless. His sword came for Nazneen, but she brought Silverlight up. Hadeon's sword shattered to a thousand pieces when it made contact with the legendary weapon. Hadeon held the hilt of his sword in shock.

Nazneen slammed her hilt into Hadeon's groin. He doubled over with a grunt, and the hilt caught him in the face too. Blood spurted from his mouth and nose. He dropped down to one knee.

Maniacal laughter came from the male as he looked up to Nazneen's face.

"This isn't over. Once I release the Great Chaos, it will devour the world."

Hadeon looked around to see he was completely surrounded. His fiends had fled from the fire and chaos and crawled back into their hole. Nazneen lifted her sword one more time, high above her head, and thrust it downward. The blade was about to meet Hadeon's chest when there was a "pop" and he was gone.

FIFTY-ONE
GARREN

"Did anyone else know the bastard could blink?" I said. I was still sitting on the ground. I was too dizzy from Elenora's mind invasion to stand. Eleni was curled up at my feet, nudging my boot with her nose, whining softly. Katuri was still in her wolf form with her hackles raised. She'd dispatched the fiends that had been drooling over Elenora's mangled body. Katuri paced in front of me like a sentry on patrol, not letting anyone near me. Delrik had tried to come to me, but Katuri had almost taken off his head too. I reached for her through our bond, but all I found was wildness. She was consumed by her wolf and it would take some time for her to come back to me.

Arik had regained consciousness, but barely. He needed a healer and fast. Nyla had lifted him on a current of air. He had a nasty gash across his forehead that was oozing. His arm hung at a disturbing angle. She'd tied a tourniquet near his shoulder to stop the bleeding from the protruding bone. He was a mess. I was glad Nyla had been able to move him without touching him. It would've been nearly impossible to move him otherwise.

Arik had saved Katuri. He'd thrown himself in the line of Hadeon's fire with his shield. Dark hells, he'd saved us all when the house caved in. I'd be forever grateful.

Delrik and Evren were standing over Elenora's body with their foreheads pressed together. Delrik bent down and removed a circlet covered in blood from the seer's head. He held it at arm's length.

"How did you know she had a relic?" I asked him. I tried to stand, but Katuri put her body over me and a sharp *"no"* sliced down the bond.

"Hadeon mentioned it when I first arrived. He was bragging about how strong she had grown since she started using it. It's how she was able to send the manifestations and voices to me in my nightmares."

"That was her? Not the shadows?" Garren looked as shocked as I was when I'd found out.

"Yeah. She used my fear of the shadows against me to get to Evren."

"Fuck, man," I said.

I went to rake my hands through my hair, but winced at my still healing wounds. At my hiss of pain, Katuri rounded on me. Her teeth were bared at the unseen threat. Fuck, she was hot when she was so protective.

"Kat, it's okay. They're all gone," I said in as soothing a tone as possible.

Her eyes darted around frantically. I moved to my knees and edged closer to her, kneeling in front of her massive wolf form. My bondmate. My queen.

"Kat. I'm fine. You're safe," I tried again.

Her emerald green eyes finally found mine. Her full pupils were wide and frightened. I reached my hand to her, but she pulled away from me and curled into herself. There was a flash of light and then Katuri was in front of me in her High Fae form. She was sitting in a crumbled mess on the ground, covered in jagged cuts and the oily blood from the fiends. There wasn't a clean part of flesh anywhere on her. Her clothes were torn to shreds. Dirt and blood and soot were smeared across her face. Her head was pressed to the ground, leaning down on her elbows. Her face was turned to the side with her cheek pressed to the ground so I could see her face. Her hair was caked with Power's knew what and plastered to her shoulders and back. She looked worse than all of us combined. Even Arik wasn't as filthy.

"Katuri."

She didn't move.

"Kat?"

I slowly crawled toward her. I kept low to the ground. Brown lines radiated from Katuri's chest where her shirt had been torn open. They lined up with her tribal marks. Shards of splintered wood stuck out from her skin, but they weren't debris. They were from her elemental power. Thin, green vines were wrapped around her fingers and streaked through her hair. Every inch of her was covered in the evidence of the fight. I knelt beside her, my knees crunching as they made contact with the gravel. I brushed a strand of hair off her face. I could feel her heart thundering in her chest. She pushed herself upright and rested back on her heels. Her emerald eyes shone bright—green streaked with sage and silver. The wood and vines reabsorbed into her flesh and the veining faded.

"You've never looked more beautiful," I whispered. I ran my finger down the center of her forehead, the way I always did.

"You're a terrible liar," she joked. Her voice was hoarse, but she was alive and unharmed. Thank the Powers Above.

I brought my hand to her cheek. She turned her head and pressed her cheek into my hand, even with the sticky blood coating it. I felt the dampness of tears on my palm. With my other hand, I brushed away the wetness. I leaned into her, closing the distance between us so that our faces were inches apart. She closed the remaining gap and pressed her lips to mine. When she pulled back and her eyes roamed my face, an overwhelming sensation of fullness and possession took over.

"You are my bondmate. My queen. Ashlyra. And I will give you the world."

"Shut up so I can kiss you." And then she crashed her mouth into mine.

After we'd picked ourselves up from the bloodied battlefield, we'd made our way back to Menrath to find a ship and a way home. We'd released what few prisoners were left in the pits. The fiends had finished off a majority of them. And even more carcasses of half fiends or partially changed fae littered the dungeon. Delrik hadn't gone into the depths of the prison with us. I didn't blame him. Only twelve males had survived the dungeons and fiends. But we brought those twelve survivors out of Menrath. Nyla had flown Arik with Knox to Menrath in search of a healer. All of us had been too tired to make the trek by foot or sky all the way back to Proux. We'd been lucky that one of the contacts Arik knew of had a ship heading north.

We'd gone straight to the docks in hopes of finding a ship we could purchase passage on. Evren, Nazneen, and Katuri had hung back and handled returning the horses we had borrowed and would meet us at the docks when they were through.

A finely dressed male came swaggering up to Delrik and me. The brass buttons shone with the sunlight on his velvet overcoat. The hat he had perched on his head sat off-center.

"Delrik Valhar?" the male asked. He wasn't High Fae, maybe half human. Sometimes it was hard to tell.

"Yes?"

"Rishley Boldnaire at your service." He gave a deep bow. The extravagantly beaded braids brushed the boards of the dock before he stood again. "Arik said to be ready for your arrival. He and Nyla are already aboard. This way." Then he turned with a flourish and waved his hat in the air for us to follow. His polished boots clicked as he walked.

At first, Delrik was cautious about sailing on a ship of smugglers, but after extensive conversation with the male, we'd discovered that, although Arik had indeed been sending him information about our whereabouts and plans for years, he'd also been providing money to help get former slaves and refugees away from Menrath and to safety on other parts of the continent. Some even made it all the way to Illoterra.

"You may see Arik as a spy, but the information he's given me has helped me free slaves and allowed refugees to escape."

There was also a healer on the ship that the smuggler kept on hand for injured refugees. She worked hard to make sure all of them had restored health before starting their new lives. I was shocked when the smuggler told us everything. I'd never known Arik to have a soft bone in his body. I guessed I didn't know him well at all. Between saving Katuri and now helping those in need, I hoped he'd wake soon.

I'd come to check on Arik each afternoon. We only had a day left at sea before we'd arrive at the City of Proux. I wasn't sure what Arik's plan was after this. He was in rough shape. The healer had to keep him sedated. Heavy doses of dolor were administered at regular intervals to make sure no pain broke through. His wounds were deep and took multiple rounds of treatment. High Fae healing was too fast sometimes. Infection had set before he'd even made it to Menrath. The healer had to keep cutting the wounds back open to make sure all the debris was gone and they were healing correctly. Nazneen hadn't left his side the entire time since he was unconscious. She silently cried each time the healer had to slice into his skin.

"He's doing well," the healer said to Nazneen. She didn't turn around when the healer spoke to her. She brushed her fingers across Arik's forehead. "Despite the long process, he should make a full recovery and not have any lasting issues."

I waited for Nazneen to respond to her. I didn't think I'd heard her speak since we boarded.

"He hasn't had a dose of dolor in several hours. He should be waking soon."

"He's not ready," Nazneen snapped.

I put my hand on her shoulder, but she pulled away. She took Arik's hand in hers and rested it in her lap. She'd grown close to Arik since she arrived in Kanevvluk. I'd known they had spent a lot of time together. I think his betrayal had hit her the hardest.

"He is through the worst of it. I won't have to do any more procedures. He needs to get up and get walking. He's already been out for too long, in my opinion." Her voice was kind but firm.

Just then, Arik's finger twitched in Nazneen's hand. Her chin snapped up and she studied his face. The healer leaned in and pressed her fingers to his temple.

"It won't be long now," she said with a smile.

Nazneen stood abruptly and smoothed her hands down her pants. She seemed to hesitate before turning and walking out. I was confused. Did she not want to be here when he woke?

"She has some healing to do of her own," the healer said absentmindedly.

Arik let out a ragged cough and took a gasping breath. His eyes sprung open.

"You're alright. We're almost back to Proux," I said to him, patting his foot. I quickly pulled my hand away, not remembering if that part of him was injured or not.

His eyes searched the room frantically. "Nazneen?" It was barely a sound, but I saw his mouth form her name.

"I'll let her know you're awake."

I had a suspicion that Nazneen wouldn't be back anytime today.

I nodded my thanks to the healer and left the room. "Thank you."

When we arrived at the temple near the City of Proux, the priestesses greeted us. After they'd fed us until we were about to explode and gave everyone fresh clothes, the priestesses offered the twelve males safe refuge in the city. A few of them took up their offer, but others went their own ways.

Hadeon was gone, and he knew we were looking for the rest of the relics. Although Nyla had said we only needed one to prevent Hadeon from being successful, Hadeon wasn't stupid. He'd figure out a way to open whatever doorway he was planning to open. We needed to find the other relics and be sure they were protected.

"Once I release the Chaos, they will devour the world."

I shivered at the thought. I wasn't around the first time the Great Chaos and the Uprising almost ripped our realm apart, but I'd seen enough of war to know it would be disastrous.

FIFTY-TWO
GARREN

The moment we walked into our cottage near the temple, I knew I needed Katuri in my arms. I hadn't been able to hold her the way I wanted for too many hours, too many days. We'd been granted a free ride with the smuggler, but we'd also had to share a room. And Delrik snored. I didn't know how Evren hadn't smothered him in his sleep yet. I didn't remember it being that bad back when we had shared tents during the war.

Katuri and I ripped each other's shirts off in a frenzy of mouths and tongues. We broke apart, panting. I kissed her gently, then stepped back to lean against the kitchen island. If I didn't put some space between us, I'd take her on this floor right now. Her eyes dropped to the sea dragon tattooed on my chest, and she licked her lips.

"Take off your pants," I commanded.

Her pants hit the floor so fast.

"And your bra."

She reached behind her and unclasped her lace bra and dropped it on top of her discarded pants.

When she went for her lace underwear, I put up a hand to stop her. "Not those. Not yet."

I wasn't even sure what the purpose of them was. They barely covered anything. I stood there, taking in my bondmate in all her beautiful glory.

"Get down on your knees," I commanded.

Katuri lifted a single brow at me, crinkling her tribal mark, but obeyed and dropped to her knees before me.

I traced my eyes along her jaw. "You look so beautiful on your knees for me. You may be Princess of Laeto Selva and my queen, but you will bow to me."

Her gorgeous face broke out into a dazzling smile. Then she did something completely unexpected. I had to pick my jaw up off the floor because my bondmate, my defiant, powerful, stunning bondmate, crawled across the room to me. Her hips swayed as she prowled to me. Those vivid emerald green depths I'd grown to know and love looked up to me through lush lashes.

Fuck. I almost lost it right there.

She stopped at my feet and glanced up at me. Then she ran her hands up the sides of my legs until she reached my waistband. She tugged my pants down to the floor and grasped my cock firmly. Powers, I felt like a teenager again, ready to lose it before I'd even taken her. Katuri circled her tongue against my tip.

My head fell back at the glorious sensation. "Fuck."

I wanted to feel her wet mouth around me right now. She drew me between her lips, testing my size. She slid my cock as deep as she could and then pulled back again.

I stroked my thumb across her cheek and then down the tribal mark. "My beautiful Ashlyra."

She opened her mouth and stuck out her tongue, an invitation for me to take control. I tangled my fingers into her hair and sunk back into her luscious mouth. When I hit the back of her throat she gagged and tears sprang to her eyes. I tried to withdraw but she gripped the base of my cock in her hand, refusing to let me go. I raised a brow at her in question, and my sweet bondmate nodded her head. A smile tipped the corner of her full mouth. Katuri reached up her hand, the one with the gilded binding mark, and splayed it across my stomach. I didn't think the sight of her could ever be better.

I couldn't resist anymore. I pumped into her mouth, building higher, teetering on a wild edge of pleasure. And then the most wonderful thing happened. Right as I was about to climax, Katuri opened herself to me. Her mind shield slowly fell, inch by inch. The threads of our bond ignited with new vigor. Our binding mark flared even brighter, connecting our powers. I felt the earth elemental timidly reach out for me.

My eyes shot to her face. "Kat?"

She slipped me from her lips. "Garren," she whispered and quirked a brow at me.

"Are you sure? We don't have to. I know you..."

"I want this, Garren. I want to give every part of myself to you, including my magic. I want you to have all of me."

Katuri turned her head and kissed the binding mark that wound around my hand and fingers before taking my cock back into her mouth. Her hand returned to my stomach, and I laced my fingers with hers pressed across my abdomen. Our binding marks joined and they flared to life. The golden light made the red streaks in her hair stand out. With each thrust of my hips, our powers grew higher and higher. I pulled out of her mouth, and right as I released my seed across her chest, the full extent of her power flowed into me like a rush of a mighty river. I cried out her name.

My elemental water poured into her. Together we shared the magic the gods had gifted us. She sucked in a shocked breath when my ice and water mixed with her orchids and earth.

She gasped. "It's so strong. How..."

I dropped to my knees and stopped her words with a kiss. "One thing at a time, Little Flower. We can test our powers later. Right now, I want to be deep inside you."

"You have me."

"Stay here," I said and went into the bathroom to get a wet cloth.

I cleaned my seed from her golden skin, admiring the tribal marks between her breasts with my mouth.

"Come on, Ashlyra. I'm not done with you yet."

I wrapped my hand around her throat and lifted her from the floor. Her hands came to my forearm, but she didn't fight against me. I turned her around and bent her over so she was leaning over the end of our bed, just like the first time we'd made love. I slipped her lace underwear down her hips, and she stepped out of them. My hands kneaded the globes of her tight ass. So soft.

"Little Flower."

She let out a shaky breath of anticipation.

Her ass shook as I brought my hand down with a crack. My palm hummed with the delicious contact. Excitement shot down the bond. I was dancing that line between pleasure and pain. My Ashlyra loved it.

"Garren," she whined.

She wanted more. Another smack, on the other side this time. I smoothed my palm across the reddening skin.

"You defied me." My words were not gentle. They were rough and dominant.

She peered over her shoulder at me and angled her hips up into my touch.

"I don't know what you're talking about?" she said with a sassy wave of her hips.

I gave her another smack.

"I'll never stop defying you."

I gripped her hips and flipped her, pulling her to my chest. She let out a squeal of surprise that I silenced with a ravenous kiss. Her hands were eager as she ran them over every inch of my body. We lowered to the floor, too impatient for the bed. She straddled me and slowly sank herself onto my straining cock. Her mouth parted with a moan of awe as she went lower and lower. Her fingers dug into my shoulders, and she bit into her bottom lip. Her tightness was pure bliss. Her head tipped back, and her long, silken locks fell down her back. The long column of her neck was tantalizing. I sunk my teeth into her neck, above her pulse point. She whimpered and arched her neck more. She loved it when I did that. She rolled her hips while I thrust up into her with forceful strokes. I was lost in her exquisite beauty and grace. She was lost in me. The weight of her body on mine, her hands all over me, it was euphoric.

"Don't stop." It was a plea. Her hands curled around my neck and burrowed into the hair at my nape.

And I didn't, as wave after wave after wave crashed over us.

FIFTY-THREE
GARREN

I was standing in the garden with Katuri, who was tossing tiny spheres of water to Eleni, who was jumping up and chomping on them.

"What?!" Nazneen screeched. "You finally swap powers."

It wasn't a question. Katuri flushed crimson, but the broad smile on her face confirmed everything. Her blush made me think of what else we'd done last night after Katuri had opened herself to me completely and gifted me the most beautiful gift. She had given me everything, every piece of her power, and she'd opened her mind to me too. She held so much power. I was surprised I hadn't seen it before last night. But the fact that she willingly submitted to me was more of a gift than her earth elemental. Her trust would forever be an honor. I hadn't tested the earth elemental power yet. I wasn't going to lie; I was intimidated by it. We were practicing opening our minds to each other. My water power was floating on the tips of my fingers, reaching out for Kat as I showed her how to bring it to the surface.

"Last night," Katuri confirmed.

"Well, you'll have to stop being adorable because Nyla wants to start planning. You know how she gets," Nazneen said.

She took my bondmate's hand and pulled her away. Kat looked over her shoulder and gave me a shrug.

Delrik and Arik were standing in Nyla's kitchen when I walked in. The circlet and amulet sat on the counter. We stood, staring at it. It looked harmless. Like a simple steel and gem headpiece.

"Where are the girls?" I asked Delrik, but he ignored me. He was focused on the relic.

Evren and Nyla came inside right after I'd asked my question. They had gone with Nyla to inform Salina about the relic and determine the best plan on what to do with it. Nazneen came to stand next to me—until she saw Arik.

He'd arrived late last night. I was surprised he'd been able to make the trek from the city. He was still super weak. He insisted on coming back to the temple.

"Nazneen," he started, but Nazneen raised a hand in front of him. She managed to stay away from him after he woke on the ship. It was impressive since the ship wasn't all that big. The moment we docked, she literally jumped the rail and ran straight to the temple. The healer had done a fabulous job. I could barely see the scars that were left behind by the constant reopening of the wounds. Arik had given Nazneen space up to this point.

"Don't." She left the kitchen and went to stand by the window in the living room. She leaned against the windowsill and crossed her arms over her chest. Delrik's gaze bounced back and forth, but he knew better than to get in the middle of the two. I didn't blame Nazneen for distrusting Arik. I'd refused to even look at him for years after the war, and he'd told Nazneen everything about his past. I didn't even know his whole story. But he'd saved my life, and he'd saved Katuri. And helping the smuggler. I'd give him another chance. I didn't believe he was bad. Deep down, I thought he was in pain and doing the best he could.

The amulet thrummed and began to emit a pale light. Nyla approached the amulet, but she didn't touch the stone.

"It's an amplifying stone." Nyla's hand hovered over the stone, and it began to vibrate. The power emanating from the amulet was strong. "Elenora was using it to amplify her own powers."

"I thought this was supposed to be good magic," I said.

Nyla's head tipped in thought the way it always did. "It isn't good or bad. It's just rare magic. Once you open yourself up to the power, it can be used in any way. It's why amplifying stones are so dangerous and many seers and priestesses no longer use them. The relics were meant to open the veils to Aesira, not to be used by High Fae to gain power."

"We should destroy it," Arik said.

I shook my head. "Is that even possible? It was made by the gods."

Delrik stood up straight and snatched the circlet from the table. "I have an idea. I'm not sure if it will work."

Evren gasped. "Delrik!"

Was he insane? We didn't know how it worked. He was an idiot for touching the damned thing. Delrik didn't say where he was going.

He pushed through the door, made his way to the temple, and down into the chamber of the veils.

"How does a relic work?" he asked Nyla.

"I'm not sure." She studied the runs on the dias.

I took the amplifying stone from Delrik and waved it around in the air near the archway. I looked at the relic, then tried tapping it on the platform. "Um ... hello? Goddess of air?"

"I don't think that's how it works." I heard Evren speak from behind me. "Plus, that stone was found deep in the Lendorr mines. It probably only works for the veil of the spirits. Each veil has a specific relic."

"Didn't Haizea say that god's blood opens the portal?" Evren asked. She flipped the blade from the hidden holster on her leg and pricked Delrik's finger. Her movements were so fast Delrik hadn't seen the poke coming.

"Ow!"

Evren squeezed his finger, and scarlet blood pooled on the tip. She lifted his hand to the firelight. Silver swirled and shimmered in the drop. "It's worth a try. If you have the goddess of spirit's power, maybe you have the ability to open the veils."

Delrik brought his finger to the cool stone and smeared his blood on its surface. Suddenly, a translucent sheen appeared like an ever-moving curtain.

"I see you discovered your blood would open the veil." Haizea's voice came through the portal before she stepped through. "And you've seen that your blood has features of the gods now that you've accepted the full strength of Aluxyeras's spirit power."

"Hey, Haizea," I said. "Good to see you again."

She pursed her lips at my casual greeting, but I saw a twitch at the corner of her mouth.

"We found one of the relics," Evren told her.

I spun the circlet once around my finger and then tried to hand it to Haizea, but the goddess refused to take it.

"You should keep it. Although it won't open this particular veil since it was given to the old City of Lumir, it does magnify powers."

"I don't think the circlet is quite my style," I said. Katuri swatted me in the chest.

"Use it wisely," Haisea warned. "Don't become drunk on the power. You need to search for the other relics. Maybe it can help you.

Hadeon can't open the portal to release the Great Chaos, but if he finds a relic, he will be able to access Aesira."

Night had finally come, and we were all exhausted from the day. My mind whirled from the events of the day, but it kept going back to my bondmate. She was sitting across from me at the kitchen table.

"Where are we going to keep the relic? Should we hide it somewhere?" Katuri asked no one in particular.

"I guess it depends on what our next plans are. Are we going to find the other relics?" Delrik asked. He was currently holding the circlet and turning it in the light. It seemed to respond to him more than us. Maybe that was the spirit power in him. Even the shadows on his skin stayed close to his fingertips, where the cool metal of the circlet met his skin.

Searching for the other four relics wouldn't be easy, but keeping them out of Hadeon's hands was necessary. "If we do go looking for the other relics, I don't think we should leave this one behind. We don't know who we can trust. No offense, Nyla. I'm sure the priestesses are trustworthy, but I don't like the idea of the relic being so far from us."

"I agree," Nyla said.

Evren took the relic from Delrik's hands to get a closer look at it.

"Well, whatever we are going to do, we need to decide quickly," I said.

"What? Why?" Katuri turned to ask me.

I pointed at Nyla, who'd gone all seer with her blank eyes and still-scary face. The runes danced with light across her body. Except it wasn't just Nyla that was seeing a vision. It was Evren too. Nyla was grasping Evren's hand in a vice-like grip. Both their knuckles were white with the hold.

Delrik reached for his bondmate but Katuri stopped him. "Don't. You don't know what will happen if you sever their connection before the vision is done."

Delrik stood and began pacing.

We all held our breaths as we waited for Nyla's visions to cease. It couldn't be a good vision. She was holding her breath, and a single drop of wetness tracked down her rosy cheek. I'd never seen her like this during a vision.

"How did this even happen? I didn't think Nyla could share her visions?" I asked.

"It must be the ring," Delrik pointed out. "Or the relic?"

"Maybe a combination of the two?" Nazneen offered.

Evren and Nyla blinked rapidly, coming back to the present, coming back to us. Evren clutched her chest, and Nyla looked up at us, her face twisted in horror.

"I need a pen and paper," Evren said, frantically looking around her.

Nyla ran to a drawer and started throwing things from it until she found a pen and a scrap of paper. Evren put pen to paper and began to draw.

"Are these..." Katuri started.

Nyla answered, "Yes."

Evren stepped back into Delrik's waiting arms. She was trembling and her hand covered her mouth in dread. We all looked at the four objects she'd hurriedly sketched.

The relics.

"What did you see?" Nazneen asked quietly.

"Hadeon retrieving them," Nyla said.

"Hadeon. Releasing the Great Chaos," Evren finished.

Then Nyla spoke in a tone so soft I barely heard her over the pounding in my chest. "Destruction. Blackness. And fiends tearing through the veils into Aesira."

FAMILY TREES

River Fae Bloodlines of Illoterra

The River Kingdom consisted of all the land below the Qana Mountains and Scared Forest, including the Arden Valley, and stretching across Illoterra to the Magnoch Sea. Rivamir is set as its capital.

CADOC BYRNES, High Ruler of the River Kingdom, Rivamir, and the River Fae. Power of Mind Manipulation. Now deceased at the hand of the fire elemental.

— his consort, ARABELLE HALLORAN BYRNES, from Kilnard of Quinterre/Western Continent. Power of Shielding. Now deceased at the hand of the High Ruler Cadoc Byrnes.

— their children:

— ADARIS BYRNES, eldest son and current High Ruler of the River Kingdom, Rivamir, and the River Fae. Power of conjuring.

— EVREN BYRNES, youngest daughter. Fire elemental

RENWICK ASHEWOOD, Head of the Black Guard. Power of Telekinesis. Unknown family descent.

GARRETT SORRELL - Black Guardsman. Power of blinking.

VIDARR FANENOS, Leader of the Centaur Clan of Arden Valley in the River Kingdom

— mate, WREN FANENOS

— their children:

— SON

Mountain Fae Bloodlines of Illoterra

The Mountain Fae Territory consisted of all the land covered by the Qana Mountains, spanning the northern border of the Sacred Forest. Arcelia is the largest city and the capital.

ARAMIS ZATHRIAN, High Ruler of Arcelia and the Mountain Fae

— his consort and bondmate, CALIA ZATHRIAN

— their children:

— NAZNEEN ZATHRIAN, eldest daughter and heir to Arcelia and the Mountain Fae, Areclai Legion Commander, Power of aberration.

— DELRIK VALHAR, adopted son, Arcelia Legion Commander. Power of speed.

ELLIOT VALHAR, High Fae-Human, deceased at the hand of the High Ruler Cadoc Byrnes. No known powers.

— his consort and bondmate, MORGAN VALHAR. Power of speed. Kidnapped at the command of the High Ruler Cadoc Byrnes, believed to be deceased

— their children:

— DELRIK VALHAR, eldest son, adopted by Aramis and Calia Zathrian. Power of speed.

LIAM WINFIELD, Arcelia Legion member. Power of blinking.

Snowhaven Fae Bloodlines of Illoterra

The Snowhaven Territory consists of all the land north of the Qana Mountains and the Thawvale, stretching from the Boreas Sea to the Magnoch Sea. Kanevvluk is the largest city in the Snowhaven Territory.

HOLDEN ECKHARDT, High Ruler of Kanevvluk and the Snowhaven Fae. Power of mind projection.

— his consort, GENEVIEVE HANOVER ECKHARDT

— their children:

— JACE ECKHARDT, eldest son and heir to Kanevvluk and the Snowhaven Fae. Power of mind projection.

— GAREEN ECKHARDT, youngest son and water elemental. Consort and bondmate to Katuri Harland

LILLIANA HANOVER, sister to GENEVIEVE HANOVER

— children:

— ARIK HANOVER, sired by CARPUS MUSMAR, tribal leader of the Tuskan Clan of Quinterre/Western Continent, nephew to High Ruler Holden Eckhardt. Power of shielding.

— OLIVER HANOVER, sired by CARPUS MUSMAR, tribal leader of the Tuskan Clan of Quinterre/Western Continent

ENDRI SALCIDO, Weapons master for the Snowhaven Fae and Legion. Born in the City of Kosmima in Quinterre.

RIKARD FARREN, weapons teacher for the Snowhaven Fae and Legion, under Master Endri Salcido

TAGE LARK, Captain for the Snowhaven Legion, no known powers

ZJI'NDAR ABRIL, First Mate to Captain Tage Lark. Born in Laeto Selva then moved to Kanevvluk with his father before the war, no known powers

Forest Fae Bloodlines of Quinterre

KAIROS HARLAND, King of Laeto Selva and the Forest Fae. Power of Compulsion.

— consort, NEFALI HARLAND

— their children:

— KATURI HARLAND, eldest daughter and heir to Laeto Selva and the Forest Fae. Earth elemental. Consort and bondmate to Garren Eckhardt.

— LOGAN KATHMOR HARLAND, youngest son

— household:

— CORYNNE, boto encantado shifter, head servant for Katuri Harland.

ZJI'NDAR ABRIL, First Mate to Captain Tage Lark. Born in Laeto Selva then moved to Kanevvluk with his father before the war, no known powers

Air Fae Bloodlines of Quinterre

NYLA, priestess at the Temple of Anruin in the City of Proux, Power of seer and air elemental

SALINA, priestess at the Temple of Anruin in the City of Proux

Raven Fae Bloodlines of Quinterre

GRANDFATHER ALLERICK, Guild member and contributor to the Uprising

— children:

— FATHER ALLERICK

— children:

— HADEON ALLERICK, OCCUPATION and TITLE. Power of Sensory Deprivation

— consort, ELENORA, Power of Seer and Mind Walking

— conrads

— CADOC BYRNES, High Ruler of the River Kingdom, Rivamir, and the River Fae. Power of Mind Manipulation. Now deceased at the hand of the fire elemental.

— RENWICK ASHWOOD, Head of the Black Guard. Power of Telekinesis. Unknown family descent.

— JAE, healer

Taskun Clan of Quinterre

CARPUS MUSMAR, tribal leader of the Tuskan Clan or Quinterre/Western Continent.

— LILLIANA HANOVER, concubine to Carpus Musmar, sister to GENEVIEVE HANOVER, consort of HOLDEN ECKHARDT. Deceased at the hands of clan raiders.

— children:

— ARIK HANOVER, sired by CARPUS MUSMAR, tribal leader of the Tuskan Clan of Quinterre/Western Continent, nephew to High Ruler Holden Eckhardt. Power of shielding.

— OLIVER HANOVER, sired by CARPUS MUSMAR, tribal leader of the Tuskan Clan of Quinterre/Western Continent. Deceased.

Water Fae Bloodlines of Quinterre

ENDRI SALCIDO, Weapons master for the Snowhaven Fae and Legion. Born in the City of Kosmima on Quinterre.

The Gods Realm of Aesira - The Powers Above
ANDER, god of spirit
— Succeed by his daughter, ALUXYERAS, goddess of spirit
DUSAN, god of earth
ERYX, god of fire
HAIZEA, goddess of air
ONDINE, goddess of water

GLOSSARY

ABERRATION - the ability to distort sound

AFFINITY CELEBRATION - a weeklong celebration marking the day the War Across the Sea ended and the legion returned home.

ALUX - older than any creature in the realm. An ancient one that seduces her victims by conjuring visions and luring them to her with her voice. Then once she had them in her grasp, she'd rip the flesh off their bones and bathe in their blood.

AMPLIFYING STONE - a rare stone that helps concentrate one's magic and magnify it, typically used among healers and seers.

ASHLYRA (ash-lie-ra) - the physical, mental, and emotional tie between bondmates made even more powerful through the blood binding ritual. Also used as an endearment.

BLINK- the ability to move from one location to another instantly

CESSAN VOID - the space between realms

COMPULSION - the power to force someone to act or behave in a certain way, especially against one's conscious wishes through touch

BLOOD BINDING - a ritual performed between two magical beings to combine their lives, souls, and magic.

BLOODTHORN - a poisonous herb that can be used to suppress magical powers.

BONDMATES - two halves of one soul or spirit

BOTO ENCANTADO - also referred to as encantado; a mythical creature native to the rivers of the Forest Fae Territory. They shift between a river dolphin and a humanoid form. They prefer warm waters. They are known for protecting those they cared about and drowning those who double-crossed them by luring them to the water with their mesmerizing songs.

DARKSTONE - one of the rarest materials in the realm, given to the mortals by the gods. The Sanctum in Aesira is built entirely of darkstone.

DOLOR (doe-lor) - an herb that grows in the wild across Illoterra and in parts of Qiunterre. Used to make doloryum.

DOLORYUM (doe-lor-ee-um) - a powerful drug made from the dolor herb. If ingested, it has a deadly effect. If crushed and added to a carrier oil, the aroma temporarily paralyzes and sedates. It is commonly used among healers to treat patients with painful injuries.

DI-GARA (die-gar-a) NEVE (nee-v) ROTH (raw-th) var (var). CONSORS (con-sore-s) PAR (par) RIKNI (rik-nye). KAJ-FAR (ka-j-far) ATO (ah-tow) UN ISLA (oon-is-la) - the ancient chant done by the priestess to finalize the blood binding ritual. Your souls are bound as one. Bound to each other and bound to the gods. A bond not even broken by death.

ESSENCE SCROLLS - written by the gods and given to the mortals of Nasbar, Explains how the gods created the realm and all the creatures within it

EVERMERE - the final resting place of the mortals and gods, watched over by the god/goddess of spirits.

FAMILIAR - can be used as messengers

THE FATES - the Powers Above

FIEND - a hellish creature created using dark magic. Originally created from Fae being transformed, but over time the beasts gained the ability to breed. They come in many shapes and sizes, including wings.

GLAMOR - the ability to alter one's appearance to hide specific features. For example, pointed ears or an Ashlyra mark.

THE GREAT CHAOS - released by the guild during the Uprising and then banished by the gods.

THE GUILD

LILURA STEEL (lil-er-a) - a metal found in the mines under Mount Lendorr, lighter than any other metal

MIND MANIPULATION - the ability to cause pain to another with one's mind.

MIND PROJECTION - the ability to change or influence one's thoughts

MIND SHIELDING - protecting one's mind from intrusion. A skill anyone with any level of magic can learn.

MIND WALKING - the ability to see into something memories and thoughts.

POWERS ABOVE - the five elemental gods: the god of fire, the god of earth, the goddess of water, the goddess of spirits, and the goddess of air.

QUINTERRE - another name for the Western Continent used by the native High Fae kingdoms.

THE RELICS - five magical objects created by the gods as keys to the veils that connect the Mortal Realm of Naśbar to Aesira. The relics were hidden after the Uprising and the release of the Great Chaos

RING OF TERIS - magical ring created by the gods to contain Aluxyeras by stripping her powers. It has the ability to steal any powers used against its wearer and can be wielded as desired. Teardrop shaped ruby on a lilura steel band

SANCTUM - the center-most part of Aesira where the thrones of the gods sit

SATYR - a creature with the upper body of a human, lower body of a horse, and curled horns coming from their head.

SEER - the ability to receive visions of the past, present, and future

SENSORY DEPRIVATION - the ability to remove the senses of someone.

SHIELD WIELDER - the ability to create a shield of protection from physical attacks

SUPREME ELEMENTALS - Elemental powers aren't always passed within bloodlines. Most of the time, the powers skip many generations or are given to another who has been found worthy by the gods

TELEPATHY - one that can see thoughts

TELEKINESIS - the ability to move things with one's mind.

THE UPRISING – a group of Fae who went against the gods.

THE VEILS - portals from Aesira into the Mortal Realm of Naśbar used by the gods to cross back and forth between realms. Accessed either with the blood of a god or a relic. They were closed after the Uprising and the release of the Great Chaos.

WARBLADE OF SILVERLIGHT - made of Lilura steel and impregnated with the wisdom of the Powers Above. Mountain Fae believed it brought guidance to the one that wielded it.

WISPS - threads throughout the realm connected like a spiderweb.

ACKNOWLEDGMENTS

This year has been a wild ride, with my debut novel coming out only a few short months ago. Bound by Earth and Ice, the second volume of the Volumes of Elementum series, came to me quickly and was such a joy to write.

I've dedicated this book to my husband, Paul. He has showered me with love and support from day one. Words can't express how much I love this man. Thank you babe for encouraging me each step of the way and helping me reach all the goals I've set for myself.

Emily, aka Pigeon—As always, we are a badass. You never fail to stretch my imagination and provide feedback for all my insane ideas.

Rio—It's a shame we didn't become friends until after we both left college and became mamas while living in different parts of the country. It has been so fun getting to know you over the last year. You have been the best sounding board and friend. Thank you for always being there and willing to help when I got stuck. I truly appriecate you.

Beta Readers—Simona Demez, Ashleigh Carter, Samantha Knight, Constança Baptista, Emily Bergman, Katie Friend, Susie Bergman, Vicki Woodard, Amber Wright, Rio Thompson, and Sadie Nickles. Thank you for all your patience and encouragement throughout the writing process.

The character and location naming committee, Grey and Carly, Rob and Katie, and Randy and Emily—Thank you for all your imagination when it came to names places and characters in my fantasy world.

Aaron Torres—Thank you for the inspiration behind the character Master Endri Salcido.

My friend, Jen Russell—Thank you for all the love and support over the few months we've known each other. You have quickly become an amazing friend and I'm thankful to have you in my life.

My Artists, May Harte and Emily Bergman—Thank you for taking my written words and bringing them to life.

The Members of the Court of Dreams Book Club, Miranda, Laura, Amber, Ruveanna, and Amy—Thank you for being the first book club to read *Shadows Within the Fire*. It was so much fun chatting with you all and hearing all your kind words. I hope to meet you all in person one day.

My ARC readers and street team—Thank you for all you have done to help share my novels.

My editor, Kate Washington—Thank you for all the time you dedicated to *Bound by Earth and Ice*. This project wouldn't have happened without your expertise and patience.

And lastly, thank you to all the readers out there across the world for making a dream come true.

ABOUT THE AUTHOR

Megan L. Adams is a stay-at-home mom and military wife from Washington DC. She earned a Bachelor's degree in Biology from North Georgia College and State University but has found a passion in writing over the last few years. She is a new indie author focusing on fantasy romance. Her books have been sold in the United States, Canada, and across the world. When she isn't writing, she's exploring local bookstores and historic libraries while sipping on a latte. She loves to take care of her many orchids and house plants, as well as spend time outside. Her best writing buddy, Toma, is a two-year-old golden retriever-husky mix. She also enjoys a good glass of wine and reading to her heart's content.

You can keep up with Megan on her social media and website.

Instagram @author_meganladams
www.meganladams.com